MW00978300

THE ALTERRAN LEGACY SERIES
Book 2: Khamlok

By
Regina M. Joseph

Copyright © 2012 Regina M. Joseph
All rights reserved.
ISBN: 1479377473
ISBN 13: 9781479377473
Library of Congress Control Number: 2012917942
CreateSpace Independent Publishing Platform,
North Charleston, SC

The Alterran Legacy Series

Khamlok

CHAPTER 1

LIL

"I'll be back. Something *wonderful* is happening." At dawn's first hint two days after the Rite of Summer, Alana brushed Lil's sleeping lips with a kiss and slipped from his intertwined arms and legs. If she hadn't been so excited, she wouldn't have been able to detach herself from his perfect body. Still warm from Lil's tight embrace, she stretched, lingering a sweet moment to relish his tantalizing scent. *Is this real?* She sighed contentedly, remembering his intense lovemaking. Were all men like that? Although she didn't have a comparison, she knew the women's circle wouldn't have complained so much if their men had made love anything like Lil. He'd been as competent at exploring her body as he was at everything else he did. *If only he'd say I love you.* Hearing him stir, she quickly donned her brown traveling robe. It would take only one of his half-lidded, smoldering looks to make her disappoint Zedah.

At late morning, while still awaiting her return, Lil paced, continually scanning nearby campsites from under the full hood of his traveling cloak. His mood darkened as each moment passed, moments that were so much more precious now that he lived under the threat of mortality. Mate or not,

Alana had to respect his position. No one made him wait. He huffed impatiently. *Where did she go?* His mind strayed to the privacy cocoon where he'd spent the entire day following the Rite of Summer. For centuries Nersis had entertained him, honing his skills with her unusual talents, but she hadn't prepared him for the euphoria of knowing Alana. He'd planned another delicious tryst before leaving, and he'd been angered to awaken to an empty pallet. Alana was *his* now, and he hadn't given her permission to leave. Sensing his simmering temper about to explode, Yamin cautiously packed their belongings, his eyes cast down. Lil admonished himself for being distracted by her. The unexpected insatiability of his desire instinctively alarmed him. *Control yourself—attend to your duty!* They must be on their way. Before the ever-shorter warm season ended, his people must plant Ki's special seeds and construct dwellings, even if initially crude. If he didn't swiftly provide suitable living conditions and food, people would despair. Despairing, they'd grow indolent, or violent, or worse. His men weren't accustomed to primitive living. *Why is she keeping me waiting?* Emotional disruptions were cropping up already, since Enuzial and others had consumed nourishment bars until leaving Hawan. Yamin treated their withdrawal with Alana's calming teas. With monumental tasks to be accomplished before winter, no precious time could be lost to dawdling. *Where is she?* He shouldn't yearn for her body when his duty was to manage their departure. Few were packing. If he had the Net, he'd sting his men with a punishment ray. It was annoying to be forced to motivate them. Their purpose was to create the next Alterran civilization, not drown in carnal desire. He'd awarded his men ample time to indulge. The time for work was at hand. He despised signs of sluggish habits; unchecked laziness would be their downfall. His duty was to keep them too busy to dwell on their precarious circumstances. *She'd better return soon; we're leaving.* Lil sent scouts to check the terrain and ordered Jared and Azazel to have the men break camp. After watching with revulsion the filthy, unkempt people in nearby camps, he swiftly ordered via *mencomm* that all his men must clip their shaggy hair and shave their beards.

Azazel and Rameel were attaching packed travois to their horses when they were jolted by Lil's *mencomm* order, which was infused with his irritation. "Aah," gasped Azazel. His chest heaving, he pulled off his work gloves and threw them to the ground, being incensed at Lil's mind invasion.

"What is it?" Morgana exclaimed, alarmed by his seizure. "Have you been stung?" She felt his hands for a puncture wound. Nasty spiders and wasps had bothered nearby campers.

He spat with disgust, "Our captain ordered us to shave and clip our hair."

Yanni worried at the startled face of her new mate, Rameel, and shared a puzzled glance with Morgana. "You too? How?"

"Don't be concerned," Rameel said gently, dutifully adhering to the captain's orders to reveal little about themselves. "Azazel, calm down. We *are* looking rather scruffy, and it itches. I agree with our captain." He good naturedly rubbed his stubbly chin and searched for his grooming kit.

Yanni wrinkled her brow, not comprehending how the message had been delivered. *Like Earthkeepers, do they have special powers?* On her mating night, she'd been overwhelmed by the energy she felt from Rameel, increasing his usual luminosity so much that she could see as if the moon were full. Feeling so much energy invade her body from his, she'd barely noticed the pain. He'd been so gentle for a big man, and so much more skillful than Maliki.

"Still," Azazel grumbled, as he pulled his shaving gear from his pack, "I don't like him trying to control my mind."

"Control your mind?" gasped Morgana, her eyes wide with empathy. She liked the captain, or at least the image created by Alana's glowing compliments. People weren't always what they seemed on the surface. At times, even Shylfing had been charming. She'd had enough subservience in her life. Never again. She couldn't imagine why her mighty Azazel endured this insult. "Why do you let him?"

Rameel arched his eyebrows to silence Azazel. Open criticism would cause their group to lose cohesion. "Azazel, it's critical that we all work together if we're going to succeed in building a new life in this wilderness. Even he must have doubts. Try to understand him. As with any endeavor, we *must* have a leader. The captain is doing his duty. How else could he communicate efficiently at this moment? Give him time. The better we in turn perform our roles, the better it will turn out for us all."

Azazel rolled his eyes, remaining edgily silent as Morgana fussed and insisted that his hair be properly styled. Her question haunted him. Why *do* I let him? After he slid to the ground, she clipped his wavy hair, refusing to cut it as short as his guardsman's cut. Azazel hadn't questioned the Ens' control on Alterra, but Lil's invasion through *mencomm* was a far worse intrusion. *Where will it end? Could Lil make me do something against my will? Could he probe my mind while I'm making love to Morgana? If he can, will he?* Azazel believed that he could detect the foreign iciness of Lil's probe and closed his mind, as he'd done during the first hunt. Since *mencomm* was such an efficient means of control, why hadn't the Ens used it back home?

* * *

At midday, Alana danced into camp wearing a floor-length white robe and her silver headband. Maya and her friends rushed around her. Jumping with joy, she squealed, "I completed the last test! Zedah blessed me. I'm a full Earthkeeper!" Zedah, having foreseen her imminent death, had visited Alana's dreams during the night, summoning her chosen one at first dawn. Zedah had prayed to the Mother that Alana's new love of Semjaza wouldn't prevent her from heeding her call.

"That's your dream!" cried Maya, joining Alana's excited leaping. "The Mother has truly blessed you."

"She's blessed us all," exclaimed Yanni, beaming with admiration. With Alana as Earthkeeper, their village would be the most prominent in the entire land.

Alana slid away from her friends. "I can't wait to tell Lil!" *I'm special too, like him.* While skipping to tell him the good news, she pondered Zedah's departing message—*You bridge two worlds. You will be remembered for millennia, although by a different name.* She knew that Lil and his men were from a far-different, mysterious land of which she had merely a hazy understanding. Her own name, she clearly understood. Why would she change it? *I have my wonderful Lil, and I'm an Earthkeeper—my dreams have come true.*

Lil, standing hands on hips at their traveling packs, could barely suppress his fury at being kept waiting. He was an Alterran ruler, whose merest whims were sacrosanct matters of state. Alana had to be publicly punished so that his subjects wouldn't disrespect him. However, seeing the ecstatic glow on her lovely face and feeling her bubbling energy when she jumped so trustingly into his arms, he couldn't help but to soften. Her innocent beauty once again inexplicably captivated him. She rushed her good news with so much happy excitement, that he didn't catch everything. His anger dissipated, he said in a gentle voice that he barely recognized, "I'm happy for you." *Why is being an Earthkeeper so important?*

Alana grinned happily, unable to keep still. Lil wiped the tears running down her face, perplexed at the tenderness he felt. She rested her head on his chest, her hips still swaying with excitement. He closed his eyes, enjoying the flowery scent of her soft hair, losing himself in her. He felt a new emotion for this woman—was it the ancient emotion called love? Like being kicked in the head, a strange sensation overpowered his mind. He felt as if Jahkbar were standing before him, his dark, steely eyes bursting with disdain and his voice dripping venom. *You let a woman captivate you? Do your duty.* The apparition stung like a *mencomm* intrusion, gripping him with pangs of intense guilt. *Am I, too, programmed?* Reflexively, he drew away from Alana. *It's not the sex my family thwarts, it's the emotion.*

"What?" she asked, dismayed by his abrupt mood change. As she watched, his eyes hardened, as she'd seen them at the horse barn. *No!* She clutched at his hand, relieved that he didn't shake her away.

Nearby, a black-haired woman screeched, "I chose you. You follow!" Since Akia's family was breaking camp, she'd come to fetch Tamiel, expecting him to observe the custom for the male to move to his new mate's village. Prepared for traveling, Akia had tied her thick, dark ringlets into a swinging ponytail. Other non-village women stood defiantly, some with arms folded across their chests and others tapping their feet impatiently. Little Akia tugged with all her strength at Tamiel's arm. Unsuccessful at getting flustered Tamiel to budge, she kicked his shin and screamed in frustration, "The man goes with the woman!"

"What now?" Lil spat furiously, striding to confront Akia. *Will we never get underway?*

Alana caught his arm, not intimidated by the burning intensity of his blue eyes. "Lil, please, I'm the Earthkeeper. I can handle this." He fumed but nodded to let her try; it provided him an escape from an odious personal confrontation with primitives. Taking a piece of finely cured hide and a fox pelt, she grasped Akia's small hand and marched to her family's campsite over her loud protests. "May the Mother bless you," Alana greeted Akia's parents with a bow. She nearly choked from their repulsive odor and was thankful that Akia, despite all her loudness, was far better groomed than her elders. Alana smiled, not betraying her contempt. With hostile glances, Akia's parents evaluated this newcomer in her white robe—a color worn only by a shaman. After eyeing Alana's ivory Earthkeeper ring and silver headband, they squatted near their doused campfire and signaled for her to join them. "I brought gifts," she began with a smile practiced to win disagreements with Ewan. "We'd like Akia to live with our people."

Akia's black-haired mother, adorned with a fishbone necklace around her fleshy neck, fingered the pelt, eyed Alana's fine clothing, and conferred noisily with her mate in their guttural dialect. The woman shook her head no and shoved the pelt at Alana, but Akia, crying and stamping her feet, pleaded for her parents to relent. "We're undecided," the gray-haired, leathery male smirked in the common tongue.

With exasperation, Alana asked, "Did you hear about Azazel's new knife?" They nodded that they had. Everyone had. "Then you know that the strangers have magical things. Your daughter will grow wealthy if she lives with us. She'll have fine things, like your beautiful necklace. We are building a new city a long day's horse ride from the white cliffs. There are excellent hunting grounds nearby. We have many plans. Akia and her mate will have a fine new hut. You will, of course, be welcome to visit." Akia's filthy brother spoke crossly in dialect, but Akia pointed eagerly to Alana's fine clothing. Grimacing, her mother finally nodded her consent, and Akia squealed with delight. Alana met similarly with families of brides of others not of her village. With her gentle persuasion, each agreed to break custom.

* * *

Lil rode beside Alana at the head of their procession, which traveled along the southeast trail through grassland, leading to the thick forests of their new home. Despite his initial plan to keep the ranks tight for safety, their line soon became strung out. Akia's poorly tied packs tumbled from her travois and had to be redone with Schwee's help. Women deep in conversation walked slowly, ignoring Lil's sense of urgency. Alert for animal attacks, Lil monitored his people by *mencomm*, wishing that he could have brought the wolves as scouts. He worried about bandit attacks as well, especially after Alana confessed her suspicion that Koko was a Dane spy. The biggest excitement occurred when a wild boar charged, and Azazel beheaded the beast in a blinding-fast thrust of his sword. That evening's dinner now swung from stakes tied to Azazel's and Rameel's horses.

With *mencomm* tiring him, Lil dismounted and strolled beside Alana, who found riding too uncomfortable. She beamed ecstatically at him, and he smiled back. Brushing her hips against his and fluttering her eyelashes, she invited him to respond with the previous day's passion. Part of him wished he could. He still smarted from Jahkbar's rebuke, which had seemed as real as if he stood before him, striking him with a punishment wand. Reflexively, he resisted her charms, not knowing if the apparition would reappear. Alana was his mate, and he couldn't desert her, no matter how much rebuke he faced from his family's implanted controls. She was such a fascinating blend of innocence and competence. He couldn't turn his eyes from her angelic face, which still held the morning's happy glow. "I know that you're proud of being named an Earthkeeper. What does it mean?"

"Zedah blessed me to follow her as our people's spiritual leader. Since I didn't complete my training, I'm not as powerful—at least, not *yet*."

"Spiritual leader?"

"Yes, I will lead our people in honoring the Mother and the ancestors, as we did at the Walk of the Ancestors. Yoachim officiated because Zedah was too infirm."

"Oh," he said with surprise, having assumed that the women would adopt his religious views. This would come in time, he decided; no need to argue now. Anyway, their beliefs held similarities, which he could easily mold. "I've been meaning to tell you how moving I found the ceremony before your Walk of the Ancestors. Your father must have been a great man."

"Yes, he was," she said with reverence. Although Alana's eyes showed her pride, she no longer became teary at his name. "He's been honored as he deserved. His was a good death, like his life."

"What do you mean by a 'good death'?" Without the rejuvenation chamber, the risk of death lingered on Lil's mind of late; he had never given it serious thought during his previous lives. The risk of permanent death from a distempered animal charging from the brush, consumption of impure water or poisonous berries, or innumerable other accidents made him view life anew. His guardsmen didn't speak of their fear, even in their monitored thoughts, but he could sense that they'd grown more cautious. If they had a true choice, most would return to Hawan. Lil, having chosen this path, had to devote every ounce of energy to achieving success and proving the wisdom of his action. He had to make the fearful ones believe in him.

She raised her eyebrows, surprised by so obvious a question. "Our people desire a life that benefits others so that those who come after will remember them with happiness and respect. Is this not the way for you?"

"Yes, of course," Lil agreed, forgetting how little of his past he'd told her. He wondered how much the women suspected. These tribes were isolated, but surely they didn't think that people merely a continent away possessed flying ships. How would they react when they knew?

"How one dies is sometimes most telling about one's character. If one dies while being cowardly, few will want to remember and repeat that tale. Without memory by the living, the cowardly truly die. However, if one dies in the selfless act of protecting others, for example—"

"An act of heroism," Lil interrupted.

"Exactly. A hero's faults are forgotten, and only the good is remembered. So the hero lives forever in the stories that are retold. That's what we call a 'good death.' Maliki and his men had a good death because they died trying to rescue their women and children. A hero is also one whose life produced goodness. My father was honored in death because he created a good life for his people, and of course, he was trying to save Maya and me when he died. It's important that their stories be told to those who come after us. My father used to say that the desire for a good death gave him a boost of courage when all else was lost. One cannot fear death; it's coming no matter what we do."

"Hmm," murmured Lil, absorbed with how he'd be remembered in this new world where death was a certainty. *Will fear of death make me brave or a coward? Will I be reluctant to send my men into harm's way, knowing that their bodies can't be easily repaired?* He'd been well trained—in a different world. His operational plans tested how fast they could reach a rejuvenation chamber, not whether guards would need to be buried. *Until tested, I can't be sure how I'll react. This I do know—I'll always protect my precious Alana.*

* * *

At night, camped along the trail, with people huddled for safety, little groups snuggled by the fires and happily planned their new dwellings. Although the hoots of owls and the howls of distant wolves unsettled the men, the women teased them about fears that Earth people had known since birth. As captain, Lil ordered Enuziel and Jetrel to take the first watch. Being idle, Jared sketched the city's terrain in the dirt, and couples began scoping new huts. Because the Ens planned all details of the Alterran society, an exhausted Lil felt guilty for not fulfilling his duty. Out of necessity, he cautiously experimented with letting others develop the city plans. Through consensus, they agreed where to put huts, fields, and animal pens. With the shell of the Great House already constructed, Jared suggested that Lil and Alana's rooms should be connected by a passageway. When the couples chose locations, Lil grew apprehensive. He left the group to ponder whether he was making a mistake. These initial actions would set the tone for the rest of their lives.

Alana languidly laid her head on his back and put her arms around him, expecting him to feel relaxed after a long day. Instead, she felt his tension. "Is something wrong?"

Lil took her hands and whispered, "In order to promote harmony and stability, my family makes all decisions—where people live, housing, their work, everything. Permitting individuals to choose for themselves is considered dangerous. Curtailing free choice was the way my family eliminated wars and cured the environment. My fear is that violence will inevitably break out if I don't take command and decide these things. I might appear weak." He wasn't sure why he was so frank with her; he hadn't explained himself before to anyone other than Anu or the Elders.

Alana frowned, troubled that he hadn't shared his past. "Your family controlled everyone?" She couldn't envision how they could control so many people. Their population must be tiny or have many slaves. *He'll not control me!* With their magical things, perhaps they had traveled through the spirit world, as Drood did. His world must be similar to her land, since their bodies, including their man parts, were the same. When her women had questioned her about the men's background, she had counseled them to wait, and they'd been too impressed, and needed them too much, to insist on knowing more.

"We were welcomed. Our people *craved* the stability that our rule brought them. We called it the Great Awakening." Lil's eyes glowed with pride. "The people had lived through a time of massive death, and they yearned for order and stability. A perfect world was my family's fantastic gift to our people. In return for our service, we are loved. I want to grant the same gift to people here."

Perfect? It *must* be another world, as if she'd truly had any doubts after their very first meeting. "But here we're making decisions as a group. That's *our* way." She couldn't see how Lil could control everyone. Nor did she like the idea of control. The guardsmen showed him respect, but so did her people respect Maliki and Ewan. His world sounded akin to being the slaves of the Danes. Ewan had made decisions only when necessary. For the most part, people did as they pleased, and she preferred it that way.

"I fear that we're turning back time, abandoning the lessons of our past and embracing something that is unwise." Lil grew distant, remembering Zeya's lectures on a utopian society.

Alana couldn't fathom what he was imagining, but it was imperative that her plan turn out well. Her women hadn't escaped the Danes to end up living as slaves simply for different masters. They weren't hungry and desperate, as they'd been at the cave. She was *not* about to be dominated, and she felt herself getting upset. *He hasn't tried to control me. I should give him a chance.* She gently took his hand and pointed at their friends. "My love, what about *you?* Does worrying about every detail make you happy? No wonder you didn't have time for me." Surely, going forward, he'd find happiness. *Surely he'll love me.*

Reflexively, Lil felt repulsed by plebian emotions. He'd been born into the ruling caste, and his sacred duty was to be the perfect, dispassionate leader. In his training, his own happiness hadn't been relevant; had he complained, Jakhbar's derision for succumbing to vulgar impulses would have known no bounds. Shrugging off discordant feelings had been easy under the friendly influence of adulterated nourishment bars. This life required more self-control.

Alana nudged his face to focus his distant eyes on hers. "Don't be troubled. Look at them. They're happy. No one is fighting. Your friend Jared is merely guiding the discussion."

"For now," he whispered. He hadn't thought of Jared as a friend, but he supposed he was, at that. Happiness and friendship were not words of their hierarchy.

Alana didn't understand his worry. "There's no sign of fighting. Much is being accomplished, and they're going to thank you as the leader when they build this great new place. We women know how to survive." She kissed him, feeling that she would need to gentle him at times.

Lil drew back, remaining tense with inner conflict. Through clenched teeth, he growled, "I've gambled my life on this venture to preserve what I can of Alterra. It was *never* the plan to abandon our philosophy. It's what gives meaning to our lives. I've risked much. I'm troubled by too many things that I haven't foreseen." He sat brooding and took a deep breath. He'd preached to Anu the need for adaptation. He needed the same lesson.

Alana wrapped her arms around his neck and stroked his hair, yearning for him to take her, as he'd done on their mating night. But he was being Lil the ruler, distant and analytic. She liked that he'd let his hair grow a bit longer, with curly, white wisps falling onto his forehead, ending just above those beautiful, blue eyes. "True, people sometimes disagree. If that happens, of course you'll need to take control. For right now, couldn't you wait and see?"

Tensely, Lil gazed at happy faces lit by the flickering campfire. He noticed that those who had initially chosen the same site worked amicably to find another location, once by casting lots, another time by trading. He interlocked his fingers and slid them below his chin, as relaxed as a cornered sabertooth tiger. After a while, he snarled softly, "For now, let the discussions continue." He took her hand to rejoin the group.

Schwee stammered, "I still have nightmares about the Danes attacking our village without warning. Is there something you can build to protect us?" Jared thought for a moment. He hadn't thought to construct a barrier because Alterran cities were peaceful.

"I'd sleep easier," Akia added, eager to participate, "knowing that wild animals couldn't sneak up on us. In our village, an animal, we think it was a jackal, once snuck in at night and dragged away a baby." As if to emphasize her point, a wolf bayed at the moon, knowing that it must be hidden somewhere above the oppressive clouds.

"How was your home city defended, Jared?" asked Morgana, cradling Azazel's sleeping head. Azazel had lifted loaded travois over mud holes and carried many children throughout the day. He wouldn't admit to being tired, even though he'd dozed off soon after sitting down.

"We had things that won't work here," Jared answered deep in thought. "It would take more trees, but we could build a fortified barrier, I suppose. A wooden wall." Schwee smiled happily that the strangers had listened to one who was mateless.

"One thing we have plenty of is trees," smirked Erjat. He had his arms around his new mate, Kranya, a dark-haired widow from a southwestern village. Before leaving for the Summer

Meeting, Erjat and a crew had spent a week felling trees on the little mountain bordering the eastern land they'd plotted.

With Maya perched on a tree stump to peer over his broad shoulder, Jared drew more lines in the dirt. "We could construct one around the perimeter."

"How could we do so much?" scoffed Akia, disdain showing on her dark features. She was attractive, with a round face surrounded by dark, curly locks. In her village, she'd been considered stunning, although demanding. Her mother had groomed her to step into her shoes as her village's leader. Searching the women's eyes for support, she smirked at their gullible enthusiasm. Unless these people had a horde of slaves, they couldn't build all of which they spoke. Fools. Her tribe lived in the south, along the coast, where they'd been content to limit their work to setting their fishing traps each day. She would do no more. Feeling depressingly alone, she slumped sullenly and scowled—did they intend to make *her* a slave? Her brother had warned her that she'd regret her decision to come with these odd strangers. Her mother had given her a sharpened knife and advised her, at the proper time, to fight Alana to become the women's leader. Before calling her out, Akia needed to foment discontent and forge alliances.

Rameel scratched his cheek as he envisioned how he'd manage the work. "Since we did the initial planting before we left, everyone can work building the new huts. When it's time for weeding or harvesting, we'll organize groups of men and women for that, while the others continue building."

"I organize the women's work," said Yanni, not noticing Akia's hostile look. "Who organizes the men?"

"Those with special knowledge will be the leaders," suggested Rameel, eager to be the manager. "They'll teach small groups who'll learn the needed skills. For other jobs, we could ask for volunteers, or draw lots." He saw smiles and heads nodding in approval.

Alana felt Lil's contracting muscles. He interrupted, barely suppressing a glare at Rameel's effrontery. Before leaving,

Lil had designated his chiefs who could absorb the requisite knowledge from the Teacher. "Jared is chief builder, Azazel is chief hunter, Rameel is chief of agriculture, and Tamiel is chief of the orchards and vineyard. I'll make other appointments as needed. The outer perimeter must be a perfect square, and the dwellings must be arranged in perfect, circular formation. We *must* use sacred geometry to preserve harmony with nature. At least wherever possible." Being accustomed to Lil's commands, the guardsmen stared blankly at the ground or slightly nodded their agreement, not wanting to be disciplined through *men-comm*. Azazel, alone among them, dared to show annoyance. He folded his arms over his chest and cleared his throat, but remained silent and didn't meet Lil's glare. This time.

The next day, Alana walked by herself, remembering everything she knew about Lil. The women had to know more, and they had to know it now. Although the men had been kind and thoughtful so far, it puzzled her why they were living as primitives. Why would they give up their flying machines and other magic? Lil had promised to tell, and Alana meant for him to keep his promise. She prayed to the Mother that he wouldn't make her seem a fool. At the campfire that evening, after they'd roasted the day's kill over the spits and couples cuddled comfortably, she said so all could hear, "The time has come for you men to tell us your story. We need to know about your past."

Maya giggled, poking Jared in the ribs. "Where *do* you come from?"

The guardsmen said nothing, although they stiffened with their eyes downward, casting furtive glances, fearful of Lil's reaction. Azazel slid behind Alana, prepared to defend her if Lil erupted with anger. Lil was caught off guard by Alana's demand. He pressed his lips into a grim line and then let out a breath, putting down his drink. He had experienced many new things, which he'd decided to accept. He wasn't happy about public orders from Alana, but he remembered his mother's strength; after all, he'd known that Alana was the head of her village. Despite his annoyance, he decided the time was right to tell the story, especially since some men had leaked tidbits to their mates. He picked up a twig and twirled it while he chose his words. Vesta ran to tell those sitting a distance away to move to their fire. With everyone huddling close together, Lil began slowly, gazing into the fire. "You're right, Alana. You're all part of us now, and you're entitled to know." Alana thought she heard a collective sigh of relief from the men, who visibly relaxed. Azazel slid down and drew Morgana to his chest. "We were born on Alterra, a planet that circles a star in a cluster that we call the Pleiades. From Earth, the star clusters form a sky picture called Taurus, the bull—"

Yanni gasped loudly but didn't release Rameel's arm or object to his hand on her leg. Along with other mumbling women, she looked quizzically at Alana, who seated herself at Lil's side. Alana intertwined her arm firmly with Lil's, and with a regal expression and preaching voice imitating Princess Petrina, dismissed their concerns with a wave of her hand. "These are mere details. We've always known in our hearts the things that matter. Who among you truly thought that people born of this world could fly ships through the skies or have clothing that changes form or light knives that cut mighty oaks as if they were little more than air? You knew even if you did not speak the words aloud. If these things did not disturb you before, they do not matter now. Let us politely listen to all that our captain has to say." She smiled and nodded to encourage him to tell more. Morgana squeezed Azazel's hand and gave him a reassuring smile; long ago he'd said that he was from another world, and she'd assumed that the others had been privately told, as well. Her heart swelled with love that he'd put so much trust in her.

Lil chuckled, relieved at last to know Alana's thoughts. Of course, they'd more or less known, and they had still chosen them. He continued, "Our scribes also call the star pattern in the sky the seven sisters."

Akia quivered when she recognized the name of this picture in the night sky and suddenly understood. She shrieked at Tamiel, "You're not people? You tricked me!" Tamiel ran his fingers through his unruly hair, not knowing what to say.

"Shh," hissed Morgana, narrowing her eyes and putting her finger to her lips. "Let him speak. He saved us." Akia smoldered, but finding no ally, she resorted only to deep, disapproving breaths.

Ignoring the distraction, Lil explained, "Our civilization is very ancient, and we have many things that you might call magical. Our people sought new worlds to explore. Our scientists found that this planet, Earth, was similar to our own, and unlike any other planet we'd discovered, it had people like you, who resemble us. Our leaders sent us to explore the planet. My grandfather is the supreme leader of my planet, my father was to become leader, and I was to be leader far in the future, at a time written in the stars."

Alana's eyes grew wide. Maya, grinning, nudged her.

"My people," Lil continued, "built a stone city inside a remote mountain. We traveled over the land in invisible flying ships, which enabled us to learn about your people." He paused and looked around for their reaction. If they were frightened, he would stop.

Alana said quickly, enlisting others for support, "We're lucky that you did. Without your help, we would have died." Lil heard murmurs of appreciation.

Morgana asked gently, while stroking Azazel's head resting in her lap, his long body outstretched by the fire, "My love, why did you leave all that?"

"During our time on this planet," Lil said slowly, "our sun caused harm to Alterra. When we first came to Earth, we thought our stay would be short, by our measure. That has changed. During our stay here, our planet lost its air, and the few who survived were forced to hide underground. We're not able to return. Since we can't obtain new supplies from our home world, we were running low on food. To make matters worse, our colony was damaged by the comet that you call the dragon. Our people began to die. My men and I grew concerned that we would die and our civilization would disappear unless we attempted to learn to live as Earth people do."

"Is that why you wanted mates?" Maya asked, grinning at Jared.

"Yes," Lil replied. "There are few women with us, and we couldn't take Earth women there. So we men agreed to leave our home to make a new life for ourselves. We were fortunate to find good women." Lil smiled and squeezed Alana's hand.

"Where is your mountain?" Akia probed eagerly, her dark eyes darting with excited thoughts how her kinsmen would pay handsomely for this knowledge. Lil's people must have riches beyond their imagination. They must have trunks of shiny jewels like Alana's beautiful ruby necklace — just what she needed to show her ample cleavage.

"For the safety of our remaining people," Lil said, distrusting her greedy look, "we won't reveal the location. I want all who know to swear that they'll forever remain silent."

After swearing the oath, the camp grew still, and the women gradually gathered at an abandoned campfire to talk quietly. Keeping her distance, Alana heard Kranya remark with incredulity, "I mated with someone from the stars?"

"Why didn't they tell me before?" demanded Akia, growing more shrill, having found an ally. "I wouldn't have come if I'd known that they aren't people." Poking her finger at Morgana, she accused her, "how could you have betrayed us? In our village, the women stick together."

"How dare you!" Morgana huffed, defiantly folding her arms across her chest to avoid slapping this irritating woman. "We shared our good fortune with you. You knew they were different, didn't you. What Earth man's skin looks like that? Sure, they're a little different, but in a wonderful way! The people on the mainland would have shunned me for having a child by Shylfing, but Azazel overlooks my past. He loves me. And he loves Tara." Pointing her finger at Akia, she demanded, "Don't you dare talk bad about these men. They're wonderful!"

Maya, too, was incensed, her dark eyes lit up to match Akia's. With her chin indignantly raised, she pulled her furs tightly around her chest. "I like the difference. We'd have been attacked by Drood if it weren't for them. Alana spoke the truth—we all knew in our hearts that they were from some-place far different, even if we didn't know the details."

"I completely agree," asserted Morgana, stamping her foot with agitation that anyone might jeopardize her good fortune. "And we're *very* lucky to have them." If the others renounced their new mates, she would leave with Azazel, wherever he might go. No question.

Maya gently took Akia's arm, trying to calm her. "Jared will build us the best huts you've ever seen. And the men are *much* nicer than the men who live here." Akia snapped Maya's arm away with a glare. Seeing Yanni listening, Maya winced, expect-ing to be upbraided again. The truth was, though, that Jared was superior to Jonk in countless ways.

"And they take better care of themselves," argued Mor-gana, stooping to make eye contact with Akia, who stubbornly looked into the darkness. "There's no one who will protect us better than Azazel." She crossed her arms again over her chest and firmed her stance, vowing to be more stubborn than Akia. She'd been annoying with her superior airs since Morgana first met her at camp, and she felt sorry for Tamiel.

"Kamean is so skilled with a bow," asserted Vesta, "that we'll never go hungry again!"

Maya, tossing her dark, curly tresses in the wind, pouted, "I love Jared, and that's all that matters. Leave if you want. We won't let you interfere with *our* Mother's blessing!"

Seeking to cool the argument, Yanni, her dark hair laced with silvery gray, slipped her arm through Akia's and patted her hand. "Akia, dear, I was reluctant to accept these men at first, especially because I'd just lost the love of my life. I didn't think that I could ever love again. But Rameel is the most thoughtful man that you'll find on any planet. You didn't experience our captivity and being left in winter without provisions. Believe us when we tell you that we all would have died without them." Maya smiled at Yanni, appreciating her support.

Unrelenting, Akia scowled, searching for a friendly face. Kranya looked away. Erjat had been nice to her, and he had kept her laughing. She'd been amazed, not upset. Maybe the points of light in the sky were close, like when she rolled up two ends of a hide and the sides touched.

Schwee, hovering silently in the shadows, stepped forward to scold Akia, her eyes glaring. "That's right. We and our children would have died. No doubt about it. That man of yours is a hard worker, and any woman should get down on her knees to thank the Mother for sending him!" Schwee had been too self-conscious about her harelip to be in the mating line. Before leaving camp, she'd silently packed her family's belongings and strapped them on her back, as she'd always done, simply grateful that she and her children weren't being abandoned. Seeing her stooped with weight, Tamiel had insisted on loading her packs onto his travois. Schwee didn't understand why the pretty ones were so unappreciative.

Since Schwee had helped Akia repack when her belongings fell, Akia refrained from lashing out at her and instead chose to plop down near the fire. "I'll think about it."

Overhearing, Alana smiled at Lil and led him behind a thicket. Alana slid her arms around his waist and rested her head on his chest. "That was difficult for you, I know. But it's good for us to know how much you've lost."

Yes, we've lost an entire world and a way of life, he thought grimly. Holding her tight, he assured her, "We'll make this work."

CHAPTER 2
DROOD

"Weena, come here." After a night spent thoughtfully staring into the fire, Drood abruptly announced before breakfast, "I go to spirit world." He kissed each of his children and Weena, whose lower lip trembled with worry over his unusual display of affection. "Maku, come." Drood picked up his bony cane and hobbled down the forest path toward the crystal cave, waving impatiently for Maku to catch up. After a lengthy silence, he confided, "I must learn to control my actions in the spirit world. If I don't, I'll die. It's the only way."

"What is the spirit world like?" Maku pestered him, hinting that his father should take him for protection. Ignoring Maku, Drood silently brooded. Near the cave entrance, he ordered, "Maku, stand guard. I can't judge the passage of time in the spirit world. If I don't come back by the end of the third day, you will be chief." Drood placed his hands on Maku's shoulders and looked softly into his eyes, almost worried. "It's always changing. If I master it, I'll take you next time."

* * *

Lying flat on his back, Drood noticed the unnatural quiet. There were no birds chirping, insects humming, or wind rustling the leaves. Although the ground underneath him was flat and grassy, no familiar scents came to his nostrils. Opening first one squinting eye and then another, he saw green foliage; he could have been at home. From the pinkish light, he knew he wasn't. Although the place was dimly illuminated, there were no shadows. He searched the slate-gray sky for the sun to ascertain the time, but no friendly orb was in sight. Leaning on his cane, he struggled to stand but awkwardly fell, sprawling in the slippery grass. He grumbled, "My blasted leg should be straight." His leg tingled. Looking, he saw that his leg *was* straight. After blinking with amazement, he arose unaided and ventured a few cautious steps. "I thought it, and it happened," he gasped aloud and snapped his bony fingers. How far could he alter his appearance? "I am as tall and muscular as Azazel and as handsome as Semjaza, only," he chuckled, "with dark hair. I wear a long hooded cloak, made of fine wool, the color of autumn leaves." He tingled again and felt his body momentarily disappear. He felt faint and wobbled to steady his feet. The ground was farther away, and a golden brown robe covered his long body. Flexing, he reveled in the feel of his sturdy, new muscles. A rare grin lit up his clean-shaven face, and his tongue licked a full complement of teeth. In prior visits to the spirit world, he hadn't realized that he could control his body. Pursued by a winged monster and a vicious two-headed wolf, he'd been unable to limp out of its way. With the red-eyed, winged monster about to devour him, he'd cried out, "I wish I were home!" and when he awoke, he'd lain sweating on his pallet. In the weeks since his last visit, he'd mulled each detail and decided that he was alive because he'd inadvertently ordered that he be brought home.

Thunder shook the ground. He'd erred by fleetingly thinking of that red-eyed, winged creature—a black-plated dragon with a wicked, spiked tail, like the beast that Azazel had killed in Drood's dream. The dragon flapped its dark wings and menacingly circled lower and lower, its evil eyes focused on Drood. The leaves fluttered from the breeze caused by its immense wings. "Hah, not this time, you pathetic demon," he boasted, shaking his fleshy, white fist. He experimented by running on his newly sturdy legs. After only a brief spurt, he'd covered a mile, his feet seeming to skim the ground. He easily hurdled a fallen oak tree blocking his path. The surprised dragon squawked. Even at his distance, the sound boomed like thunder. Spying him, the beast sharpened its flapping to increase speed. Drood again began running, savoring the feeling of properly functioning muscles and flesh. He discovered that the more he concentrated, the faster he sprinted. Fir trees became a smudge of dense green forest leading to boulder-strewn hills, which he effortlessly skipped in giant leaps, laughing joyously like a toddler learning to walk. Images blurred into a collage of colors, and he tingled as he passed through trees and boulders as if he were a ghost. If this were Earth, he would have traversed the entire mainland.

Feeling safe and desiring to see the landscape, he skidded to a stop and found himself on the white, sandy shore of a crystal blue lake. The lake water was still. He tossed a rock, and it plunked into the water with a deep, kettle sound, leaving few ripples in its wake. He scooped his hands and slurped, finding the water tasteless. Gazing upward at the empty sky, he smirked at eluding his nemeses. In celebration, he yelped and cast off his cloak, enjoying the sight of his sweaty, muscled chest. The placid lake waters mirrored the sky. He fell to his knees to gaze in the water to admire his handsome face. The piercing blue eyes were a particularly effective touch; he could have stared down that two-headed wolf. Within a few seconds, the watery image transformed into a leering grin sporting razor sharp teeth. Two snapping heads burst from the water. Startled, Drood lost his balance and fell backward. The monster snarled, saliva dripping from its pointed fangs. It pounced, and Drood spiraled away, narrowly avoiding its bite. He stared into the wolf's eyes, daring it to attack. *Cage*, he thought, and the monster snarled and lashed at him behind strong, metal bars. Breathing heavily, Drood stepped back from the grasping claws and twirled his finger and pointed toward the lake, sending the cage heading end over end. He laughed and leaped in a dance—he'd eluded that nasty dragon. His feet left the ground, and he groaned with the pain of talons piercing his back. The earth's features became flat as he was swiftly carried aloft. Struggling against the talons' grip sent knives of pain through his shoulders. *No pain*, he told himself, to no avail. He turned himself into a mouse that slipped from its grasp. Falling, he transformed into a feather, which floated randomly in the wind, too small for the monster to perceive.

Reaching the ground, he assumed his human form and created a flaming sword like Azazel's. He imagined a black stallion and clothing of boiled leather leggings and a sleeveless vest that partially covered his chest. *Let there be peace*, he thought, envisioning tranquil landscapes. He kicked his steed, sending it trotting down a crushed stone pathway that was evenly bordered with flowering shrubbery. Beyond the borders were fields of multi-colored wildflowers nestled among pockets of evergreen shrubs. Birds twittered in the trees, and flocks flew harmlessly overhead. He licked his lips with thirst, and he encountered a bubbling fountain, from which he drank. No coincidence, he knew. He held out his hand and wished for a tasty, roasted quail, and the succulent meat appeared. Could he live here forever and bring his beloved Weena? No, they couldn't control their thoughts. A child might imagine a precipice—momentarily, he teetered at a crevice's crumbling edge as tumbling rocks found no bottom. *Tranquil landscape*, he calmly commanded, and the fountain and his waiting steed reappeared. Since this place produced his thought, what use could he make of it? *Give me a window to my people.* The air shimmered, and an oblong picture appeared at chest height. Weena sang softly to herself as she stirred stew at his hearth. His small children played at war games under her watchful eye. Try as much as he could, he could not make her feel his touch or hear his voice. She screamed and ran to her children while threatening something out of sight with her cooking utensils. He heard the growl of a lynx. Where was Maku? Guarding the crystal cave entrance, he knew. No warriors protected her. He swung on his horse and galloped toward the vision of his village. *Jump*, he ordered his horse. The horse leaped through the vision. Drood felt an icy tickle and then an endless sensation of falling—it could have lasted a lifetime—until the horse's hooves hit firm, familiar ground between Weena and her stalker. The startled lynx crouched wide-eyed with fear at the stallion's mighty hooves and then slunk away.

"Drood," Weena cried, raising her arms to greet him. "We thought you dead."

Drood slid from the horse, his crippled body collapsing at its side. The horse shimmered and disappeared. Weena and his children fell upon him with shouts of happiness. "Weena, something wonderful happened. Send for Maku at the crystal cave." After he'd rested, he told Maku and Weena how he'd learned to control the spirit world.

"Father, with new power, we conquer all!" exclaimed Maku, leaping to his feet. "I'll prepare the warriors."

"Wait!" said Drood calmly, waving him to sit again. "We conquer *without* fighting. I will train you and warriors I trust to understand the spirit world. You will visit the villages and show them your power. They will worship."

CHAPTER 3
JARED

"Erjat and Kranya are done," reported Jetrel, a member of Jared's work crew, wiping sweat from his stubbly upper lip with his hide sleeve. Guardsmen performed tasks formerly done by Dalits, although Jared had heard few grumbles. Jetrel's boots were muddy, since the skies had poured rain the day before. Within the shelter of an Alterran emergency tent set up outside the new Great House, Jared had been scratching out more plans, working by the light of a stolen glowglobe. "Before the harvest is in, we'll move the last couples from the Great House," said Jetrel.

"Excellent." Jared clapped his hands, beaming with pride. Before him lay the model city, which Lil had named Khamlok, an ancient home to noble warriors in an Alterran legend. Khamlok—a good name; even Azazel had approved because the warriors had shared power with the king. Jared had never known such creativity. Even though on Alterra his destiny certificate made him an architect, architects were in surplus. They'd spent their days endlessly creating building plans for new monuments and dormitories modeled on sacred geometry, all the while knowing that their meticulous creations weren't needed and wouldn't be built. After approving Khamlok's detailed site plan, overworked Lil had delegated responsibility for the city's construction to Jared, admonishing him to devote every ounce of his energy to completing huts. *Winter snow falls early*, the captain frequently reminded them. Following the captain's driven example, Jared and his crew had plunged in, working every waking minute. The fruits of his labor now surrounded him like beloved children. Before abandoning Hawan, he feared losing its safety net. Now he felt as if he had emerged from a fog. Like others except Lil, Jared had put aside his tunic when its energy charge dwindled, and he wore tanned hide clothing made by his wife. Little Maya liked to tinker with the edges, so his had fringe. Like others, he'd let his hair grow shoulder length, although it was greasier than he liked. The days passed so quickly. Running his hands across his lower face and feeling the stubble, he planned to shave—when he got around to it. He wasn't comfortable with the beards of many guardsmen, even the trimmed ones. Grooming in the cold river wasn't popular, and only Lil and Alana had water brought to their rooms for heating.

Yanni, passing by with a crew hauling fishing nets, called to him, "Jared, thank you again. The hut is bigger than I ever imagined. And you've done so many. I can't believe how much progress we're making!" With a happy wave, he shyly acknowledged her compliment, which he still wasn't accustomed to hearing. Having prepared the logs before leaving for the Summer Meeting, the men began construction the minute they'd returned; the captain hadn't tolerated a moment's delay. Posts were laid, sheared logs were stacked around the insulated tents brought from Hawan, and clay mud was baked to seal the logs and to provide a hard floor. Jared had devised a model floor plan and for harmony, had staked locations around the Great House in concentric circles representing the cosmos. The captain painstakingly verified his sacred geometry. Small teams assembled each hut, together with a table and pallets for parents and each child. In the Great House, he had had sufficient crushed stone to build a floor. The logs for the great perimeter wall had been cut last spring, and a portion of it had been completed then, adhering to a square representing terrestrial unison with as much accuracy as he could achieve with their crude implements. Rameel's crew had planted the fields in lined rows within squares, using Ki's cultivated seeds that grew even though dark clouds still hung heavily overhead, blocking direct sunlight and sending showers of stinging, acidic rain. In a special plot, they planted Ki's newly developed medicinal plants, which were little trees genetically enhanced to produce leaves with life-enhancing nutrients; Ki called it the new Tree of Life. Tamiel's crew planted the orchards and vineyards with Ki's cultivated, cloned cuttings.

After stretching with a contented yawn, he arose to inspect his team's continuing site preparations. Although a hut for each original family had been initially planned, more dwellings were becoming necessary. Outsiders had come. They'd heard of Azazel's gleaming sword and his martial prowess at the Summer Meeting, and they wanted to be like him. Also, in the worsening weather, the peninsula's usual food sources were disappointing, while Khamlok enjoyed plenty. Under the captain's skillful leadership, Khamlok was developing far beyond their hopes. The mood was vibrant, and even those who'd been weaned last from the nourishment bars had become well adjusted. The notoriety of Khamlok having an Earth-keeper made peninsula dwellers feel entitled to admission at Khamlok. The newcomers, with their matted hair and beards, lice, and filthy clothing were troublesome; the women didn't welcome them. Maya was actually frightened of their coarse ways. They defecated wherever they stood. Apart from Azazel's training and their expert flora knowledge, they had few usable skills. The captain didn't permit them to stay close, so Azazel had them camp at the horse barn. Even at that distance, they might bring disease, since they refused to deposit their waste in the latrine. Only Azazel found something redeeming and was willing to take responsibility for them.

Jared drew a drink from their aquifer well, relishing in the delicious, pure water. Even with their growing population, drinking water would be plentiful. Looking toward the river, he watched women pulling in their nets full of big, flopping fish, which grew large because of the rich glacial minerals. A smokehouse was planned for fish tumbling off the nets.

He waved to Maya, who was working with Morgana and others by the central hearth, a song continually on her happy lips. What a beautiful and kind person Maya was. Although Maya was a product of this place and time, she'd been tutored with Alana's Atlantean knowledge. Naturally intelligent, she demonstrated the innate promise of her people, if provided the right guidance. Morgana, assisted by Schwee and Midri, had strung up elk and reindeer hides along ropes made of braided vines, which they worked into clothing. The pieces were sewed using the sinew and fish bone, sometimes adding feathers or small bones for decoration. Akia, sat on the ground, happily choosing ornaments she desired for a shift that Morgana was making for her. Morgana was becoming the leading creator of clothing because of her skill and the little artistic details she added.

Maya smiled lovingly as she spied Jared admiring her. She was working a prized bear fur brought in by Azazel, which Maya planned to present to Alana, telling everyone that she deserved it for bringing these wonderful men and their prosperity.

As he came near, he heard Maya exclaim, "What a difference! Less than a full sun ago, our village was destroyed, and we were destitute. Now, we're wealthy!" With her usual joyful, melodic giggle, Maya stood on a log to hug him, being only half his height.

CHAPTER 4
URAS

"Of course! I'll see that your relatives gain access to your memory book," Uras said softly, her voice muffled through a facemask. She hoped her vow wouldn't become a lie—they *must* regain contact with a thriving Alterra. Yet another patient with the coughing disease lay dying, and for comfort Uras had programmed the wall panels to display her patient's cherished memories. Having frantically scoured through dusty storerooms, she'd discovered an old-fashioned medical robot used by their first space travelers, and it now hovered near her, its colored lights blinking as it assessed the patient's vital signs. When Uras had learned from Ki's Library search that ancient Alterrans had treated contagious diseases like this one with isolation, she'd ordered her staff to convert all available storage rooms to quarantine units. Although the drab, cramped cubicle was hardly a befitting place to spend one's last hours, Uras had to protect uninfected colonists.

"What's wrong with me?" the trembling, sweaty patient asked Uras, who held a cloth to catch her spittle between heavy bouts of bloody coughing. She was so pale that her blue veins bulged from her skin.

"We have leads," Uras answered in a professional tone, having learned to distance herself from the question she'd faced many times before. "It's a virus that was most likely caught from a lab animal." It was maddening that Ki's scientists hadn't discovered a cure. The virus was far deadlier to them than to Earth people. Uras bravely shouldered the burden of solving the colony's medical problems. After the colony's only other physician had died, Anu had permitted Kosondra to absorb the Teacher's physician program. Having an assistant didn't help. Although the Teacher gave them information, it related to treatments using equipment and supplies they didn't have, which might not exist anymore on Alterra, nor anywhere in the universe. Curing a disease, though, was easier to face than the other malady that afflicted her patients—the loss of hope.

She felt helpless without the rejuvenation chambers, which diagnosed and cured everything from a minor cut to the most severe injuries, working its magic even after death unless no trace of the patient's aura remained. Since it served as the centerpiece of all her medical learning, she knew no other way to treat patients, and she had no medicines. Through electrical and chemical stimulation, the chamber restored to health the patient's electromagnetic aura. Ki had told her that when the rejuvenation technology was discovered in that ancient time before the old society was destroyed, the politicians kept it secret because the planet was grossly overpopulated. A generation after the Great Awakening, when the population had been reduced to a mere five percent of its level before the terrorist attacks, the ban was lifted. Supreme leader Zeya determined that a long-lived population was easier to manage than successive generations of new people.

Life would never be the same, Uras sighed, as she sought solace that evening on the observation deck. Rather than being comforted, she grew sadder with her view toward Alterra blocked by the omnipresent dark clouds. She couldn't let herself descend into the depression suffered by her patients. Feeling chilled, she shivered, and a scribe, his eyes politely downcast, brought her a wrap, which she acknowledged with a nod and a smile that he couldn't see. Change is not always for the better. Her heart ached that she might never see her daughter again. And she missed Lil. Although she was used to his being away for long periods, in the past she'd understood the reason for his absences. Like a good mother, she'd raised him to perform his duties. Being the named successor, he'd been granted special knowledge and talents. He should be using his abilities, not running away when he was needed most. Where had she gone wrong? He hadn't even said good-bye. He'd sent a message through his Dalit; how insulting. Although Lil's note didn't elaborate, he must have thought that the colonists wouldn't survive. Why else would the named successor leave? Why didn't he love her enough to take her with him? She admired his fortitude. If Lil was right, he'd taken control of his life in a way that defied Alterran tradition, defying destiny in favor of choice, as Zeya had done.

Wiping tears from her eyes, she remembered her happiness at giving birth to her first child, Ki, whose name meant "bringer of light." With the En family subject to birth control the same as the general population, she'd been permitted to give birth to only one other child, Ninhursag, who, through Uras's persistence, had been divined an occupation—a physician, like her; eternal life without a useful occupation made no sense to Uras. Uras had also raised Lil as her own son. In order for the named successor to have a full, untainted bloodline, it had been planned that Antu, Anu's half-sister, would conceive Anu's first born child. The conception had been scheduled to coordinate with the sign of Cancer, at a time when the star charts foretold a favorable horoscope. When Uras unexpectedly announced her pregnancy—Anu's parents accused her of intentional manipulation and had never forgiven her—the House of En panicked, and they had raced to have Antu inseminated and her pregnancy accelerated, so that the purebred child would indisputably be next in line for succession as firstborn. Uras experienced complications and gave birth prematurely, just hours before they could safely induce Antu to deliver Lil. Even though Lil was Anu's second, because of his full-blooded status shown by his cobalt blue eyes, the supreme leader decreed that Lil was named successor. As Anu's official spouse, Uras had treated Lil like her own son. Thank the stars that the rejuvenation chamber had worked when they'd needed it before. Shortly before coming to Earth, Lil had required rejuvenation when his *tri-terran* crashed on Alterra, giving him youthful looks that belied his true age. Under the rules set down by Zeya, her children were all near the age when they'd be assigned a spouse and permitted to have a child. With all the recent deaths, they now needed people. These antiquated rules should be abandoned. The trouble was, there was no one satisfying the genetic requirements for either son at Hawan; to give birth to the next named successor, Lil needed to mate with Ninhursag or Antu. Official spouses needed to be a more distant En relative and were usually divined in order to cure a family rift. Perhaps, in the underground bunkers of Alterra, a suitable match survived. But, she shivered, they were a universe away. At least neither son could be divined into a political marriage with an infidel from the House of Kan.

She heard breathing behind her and realized it was a scribe completing his daily work through a device that penetrated the clouds. It was comforting that, no matter what happened, their work continued. Or was it? They hadn't foretold their disasters, so who really knew the future? If her patients had a virus, she couldn't predict when the contagion would end. She had treated the dying and held their hands. If it spread by personal contact, she could be next. If she neared death, she couldn't even tell Lil good-bye. For all she knew, he'd been injured or worse. It was maddening not knowing. Then she brightened—*she* could search for him. Energized, she hopped on the camouflaged transport tube and materialized outside Ki's suite. She hesitated to enter unannounced because she was uncertain what he might be doing. Unable to curb her excitement, she said, "En.Uras." When the door slid open, a hot breeze and brightness surprised her, and she wished she had the eyewear that the guardsmen wore. The glaring sun baked a humid land whose flatness and low-lying vegetation seemed to extend for a thousand miles, ending in the faint outline of mountains encased in a damp mist. From the position of the sun, she surmised that this vision lay close to the planet's middle. "I didn't know Ki could do this," she wondered aloud, but nothing that Ki did truly surprised her. *Could he recreate Alterra for me this way?* Living in an illusion might be the best alternative. She laughed, remembering an ancient religion preaching that this universe was merely an illusion, a mere creation the mind. "Ki," she called, cupping her mouth, afraid to leave the door's faint outline. "Where are you?" Cautiously stepping in a few yards, she glimpsed him bent over a tripod, with his eye on a surveyor's scope. His hairless chest was bare, and he wore a short, white linen skirt and sandals. Surprised at being interrupted, Ki scowled, and bolts of lightning cracked across the cloudless blue sky. Before she could react, the scene collapsed into his nondescript, beige panels.

Uras didn't visit often, but she'd always wondered at the plainness of his suite and his seemingly solitary life. With the replicators, Alterrans needed few possessions, and the Ens preached that good citizenship mandated the conservation of resources. However, most people had at least a few mementos or self-made art, or they creatively programmed their wall panels. It was as if Ki stubbornly refused to expose any hint into his inner life. Did she truly know this son any more than she knew Lil? She'd always tried to hold her offspring together as a traditional family, but living in a world where, thanks to the rejuvenation chambers, grandparents sometimes appeared younger than children or even grandchildren, relationships became awkward, and memories of original youth were often preserved only in memory books. It was disorienting, she sighed, but better than the alternative.

Ki, whose clothing had transformed into his usual silver uniform with his maroon insignia glowing at his shoulder, ran his fingers through his unruly hair and looked at her crossly. "Mother, what are you doing here?" After the initial shock of being disturbed, he produced a smile that he knew women found irresistible. His mother was special. Being usefully occupied had become a rarity among the cloistered En women, who frequently passed time in the blissful stasis pods. He admired his mother for remaining engaged in life, and her independence had influenced him as well as Ninhursag. Lil's upbringing, to his detriment, had been usurped at a tender young age by special tutors, principally Jahkbar, to ensure that he'd rigidly hew to the principles of harmony and stability.

Uras angrily met Ki's gaze, clenching her fists. "What was that? Is that where Lil is? Are you thinking of leaving me too?" She hadn't known that Lil had been thinking about leaving, and she wasn't going to lose another son.

"No, Lil isn't there. Don't worry about me." By her determined look, he knew that he couldn't avoid the truth, even though he wasn't accustomed to sharing his thoughts. It was the only true way to keep a secret; no eyes and ears lurking deep within the Net to betray a careless moment. Since he wasn't a named successor, Ama and Jahkbar didn't bother to invade his thoughts to guide him, as they did to Lil.

"You can't tell Father. What you saw is a surprise, and I'm only in the earliest of planning stages."

"Of course I won't," she sighed with relief that he wasn't running away too. A surprise would delight Anu, particularly something designed with the perfection that only Ki could create. She hoped that whatever it was, it would bring Anu out of his constant, dark mood and the withdrawal that was causing their growing estrangement. Anu was a contemplative man, and she'd always admired the deep thought that he gave to the slightest decision, striving for perfection. Their present circumstances, however, required decisive action.

"Since the Leo constellation, Anu's zodiac, is now predominant, I'm planning a memorial to honor his ascension. If the Darian tower is functioning, the beacon has no doubt been triggered by the first stars of the Leo constellation entering the meridian. I don't want him not to be honored simply because Earth has become our home."

"You sound as if you've made peace with living out our lives here," she sighed, wishing that she could accept her fate so calmly. "Will it resemble Ama's monument?"

"In part. Father would no doubt want the classical lines of the sacred triangle, with the point reaching into the sky to become one with Leo."

"As above, so below," she murmured reverently, eyes downcast and placing her hand over her heart. "There's more?"

"Yes." His eyes beamed with pride and unusual excitement. "The monument nearby will be unique. His face will gaze toward Leo on the body of a lion—a resting, peaceful lion, of course."

"Putting him at one with the universe," she said haltingly, the reverent project moving her to tears. Ki handed her a cloth so that she could wipe tears from her eyes. When she could speak, she muttered, "Anu will truly love this gift." Whatever rift that Anu or the Council had felt for Ki would surely be cured.

"Exactly, Mother," he stroked her arm and smiled, pleased at her reaction. "Recreating the best of Alterra is the best we can do at present."

"Ki, you're so thoughtful!" She stood on tiptoe and kissed him on the cheek. "It's what I love about you." Changing to a demanding tone, she said, "Right now, though, I need you to do something for *me*."

"Yes," he said hesitantly, annoyed that his nanobots hadn't alerted him to what had brought her here so unexpectedly. He didn't like being caught off guard, even for her.

Putting her hand on his chest, she gazed up into his eyes, pleading, "I need for you to help me search for Lil. I need to know that he's not hurt. You'll do this for me, won't you?"

"You don't need to search for him." He drew away, plopped down at his workstation, and began reviewing research reports, seeking to end the matter. After the Guard's departure, Ki had easily deflected Anu's commands for an aerial search since Anu didn't truly want to be distracted from his meditations or to have the Ministry diverted from their attempts to reach Alterra. Few of those who remained had flight knowledge, and Ki's nanobots would alert him if anyone absorbed a flight program. Before tonight, it hadn't occurred to him that Uras might attempt a search. After exploratory flights when Uras had initially arrived on Earth, she'd rarely left Hawan. She needed a Teacher session to operate a *tri-terran*, which Ki didn't volunteer to facilitate. In truth, he didn't want Lil found, which worked well since Lil didn't want to be found; at least, not yet. She waited patiently, hovering by his side. She took out her recorder to check on patients, intermittently smiling to let him know that she wasn't leaving. "Trust me, Mother, Lil is fine. Like me, he's trying to preserve our civilization."

"How do you know that he's fine?" she exclaimed, narrowing her eyes with suspicion and sliding into the chair next to him. "I thought that the Net didn't extend beyond our walls. Anu said that no ships or soundguns were taken."

Ki drummed his fingers on the table, deciding how to craft his reply. *Why does Lil continually leave me to explain his actions?* When he'd crashed his *tri-terran* on Alterra, Ki had had to break it to her that he'd been rejuvenated to puberty again. She deserved to know. "His goal is to recreate a viable city on Earth, so that the rest of us can join him when Hawan isn't habitable."

Giving him a long, suspicious look, she probed, "He wouldn't need to sneak out in the middle of the night to do that. There's more to this story." Uras had spent many a sleepless night trying to imagine the possibilities. Since Lil was so conscientious of his duty, he had to have a good reason. Had Ama given him secret orders before they'd left?

Ki avoided her eyes and decided to get it out as dryly as possible. "They've just taken part in an ancient Earth ritual. The guardsmen have married Earth women, who either are maidens or newly widowed. Lil's bride is the tribe's medicine woman, Alana," he said, rocking back, trying to be casual. "He says that she's stunningly beautiful and extraordinarily intelligent."

Uras's eyes widened with surprise and a bit of hurt. "She must be. I've heard him say a million times that Earth people are disgustingly dirty and stupid."

"She's exceptional." He nodded, avoiding her gaze. One of his deepest secrets was that he'd retained the master code for eavesdropping through the *mencomm* implants whether the recipient sought privacy or not. He'd experienced Alana through Lil's eyes, feeling his passion. If Lil hadn't pursued her, Ki would have, although his methods wouldn't have been as straightforward; he'd found many Earth women to be appealing, and he'd appeared to them under many disguises. "They're building a new city because her village was destroyed by marauders."

"Ancient ritual? Marauders?" Uras asked in dismay; she was open minded, but this was too much. If they made it home, Lil couldn't be burdened by an alien wife. She again narrowed her tired eyes with suspicion and put her fists on her hips. "How do you know? You've been here working the entire time. I've seen you."

"Mother," he said, pretending to squirm so that she'd relent, "it's a secret that you don't really want to know." He yawned and rubbed his eyes. "It's late. I'd like to get some sleep."

"Of course I want to know," she said crossly, slapping his arm. "Stop treating me like one of those insipid En women. You've created something. I want to speak to Lil."

"Mother, trust me. Let this go." Ki yawned and stretched, trying to avoid her alternating hurt and angry look. "The only way I'll tell you is if you swear that you won't tell Father. This isn't exactly permitted."

"What are you talking about?" When Ki raised his eyebrows and waited, she raised her eyebrows and huffed impatiently, "Oh, I swear, now tell me."

"Well," he paused and looked at her askance. "Have you heard of *mencomm*?"

"*Mencomm*?" Uras wrinkled her brow in thought and tapped her finger against her lips. "It was used to commit genocide. It was banned, wasn't it?"

"Yes, in the old days, it was used by terrorists. It's not innately bad. Fundamentally, it's simply telepathy achieved through implants. Lil had a link installed in his brain, as did I. It's similar to interfacing with the Teacher. When both parties are receptive, it permits you to focus deeply and communicate as if you were speaking over a device. Only in short bursts, though; it saps your energy."

"Install a link in me!"

Ki raised his hand to reject the idea. "Mother, as the wife of Hawan's leader, no. The use of *mencomm* is banned, beneficial or not. Even a user with good intentions might not control it."

"What does any of that matter now?" she pouted, folding her arms across her chest. "We could all be dead soon, and we can't communicate at all with the supreme leader. I don't need to think about it. I've made up my mind."

"You're absolutely sure?" Ki raised a single eyebrow to demonstrate his reluctance.

"Yes!" she said with exasperation, throwing up her hands. "You said it's similar to the Teacher, which didn't hurt me. Who knows? Maybe I'll need it for my own safety. It may be the only way to find me if this place continues to fall apart. Don't argue."

"All right." Ki let out a loud sigh and turned to his computer to transfer the requisite knowledge from the Library onto a disk, which he added to the Teacher's program. Going to the rooms housing the Teacher, he had his mother insert the Teacher's electrode net over her head.

When it was finished, she eagerly closed her eyes and leaned back comfortably. After several minutes, she frowned and opened her eyes. "Why isn't it working?"

"Patience. If you heard everyone's thoughts at once, the noise would be unbearable. You can close your mind if you don't want to be disturbed. Concentrate on Lil, mentally calling him until he responds. It gets easier with practice, especially if the other person expects the contact. Just relax." He gently massaged her shoulders.

Uras again scrunched her eyes and focused all her mental energy on Lil, bracing the chair arms with tension. Not working at first, she tried again, digging deeper into her consciousness. "Lil, Lil," she thought, "This is your mother."

A thought floated back. "Mother? Father won't be happy that you're using *mencomm*."

"I'll handle your father," she cut him off. "Are you all right?"

"I'm fine, Mother," he replied, and she could actually *feel* his amusement.

"Don't be flippant. You're not in danger of being attacked by marauders? Ki said that the Earth woman's village had been torched. Did you take weapons with you?"

"Mother, I'm sorry to make you worry, but I've been in danger before. Yes, we have weapons," Lil replied patiently. "I won't be gone forever. There's something I must do. I'll tell you everything when I can. Trust me."

"Ki told me that you and the Guard have taken Earth brides. Something about an ancient Earth ritual. Is this true?"

"Yes," he said, feeling her disappointment at being excluded.

"I should have been invited to the ceremony," she said, on the verge of tears. Both her sons were apparently resigned to living out the rest of their lives on Earth. If that was their fate, she wanted to be included, not have them run off, leaving her alone to perish.

"Mother, I can feel your pain. I'm sorry, but there was no other way. You know Father wouldn't approve, nor would he permit you to attend."

"He doesn't control me. Anyway, Ki says that her name is Alana and that she's a medicine woman. I'd like to meet her; it sounds as if we're kindred spirits. I'm afraid that I can't talk more. This *mencomm* is making me too tired. I'm relieved you're all right. We'll talk again soon. If anything happens, let me know. Do you promise?"

"I promise. Good night, Mother. I love you."

"I love you, too."

Uras opened her eyes, deep with worry. She'd overheard Anu reporting to the Council that no ships were missing and only a few lasers were unaccounted for, and even those could have simply been mislaid. Lil must have felt so guilty about leaving that he didn't want to put them at risk. He'd always been noble and self-confident. "Ki, does Lil have access to the Net?"

"No."

"Couldn't you create something, like a miniature Net just for him? Let him access a special weapon, so that he could better protect himself. He was no doubt too proud to ask you to create it for him."

"Or, he didn't want Father to trace him," Ki replied, shaking his head. "If he wanted something, he wouldn't have been shy about asking."

"But you could prevent a trace, couldn't you?" She gave him a knowing look.

Ki sighed, uncomfortable at revealing a secret power. "I probably can. If Lil's ego will let him accept it."

Uras smiled and yawned, her eyelids drooping. "You make it. I'll assuage his ego."

CHAPTER 5
KI

Ki tasked Laurina, Mikhale, and Rafael with finding an alternative to the broken rejuvenation chambers. He'd had a few ideas, but they required immense power. After another frustrating day spent delving through dusty tomes in the Library, Ki set his entry code to refuse everyone, even Laurina, who frequently spent the night. He'd told Lil that too much time in the Library was a bad idea, and he was right. It was deeply upsetting that the old society had been deliberately destroyed. For diversion, he turned his suite into an island beach, with the sound of ocean waves to soothe him. He produced a wine bottle, made his tunic transparent, and relaxed to enjoy the sun. Unable to quiet his mind, his old resentment flared up. He was the first-born! He'd been robbed. He hid it, although occasionally he dared to sabotage Council directives as payback, laughing at their ignorance. In his frustration, he'd researched how the leadership of a technologically advanced society had evolved into a hereditary game. He'd heard his mother threaten Lil in his true youth that he should act properly so that the Council didn't reinterpret the stars to avoid his successorship. That had been his first clue that their society wasn't as it seemed on the surface.

Just that afternoon, he'd read about an isolated individual conceiving an idea and converting it into a worldwide manufacturing enterprise. Except for the ruling inner circle, individualism was impossible after the Great Awakening; everyone was essentially a scribe, a blank mind awaiting orders from the omnipotent supreme leader. The system of peace and harmony under the command economy was deeply entrenched, and people had forever lost their sense of personal responsibility. The complacent Alterrans couldn't function independently. Neither did the government. Without the need for economic accountability, the Ens were unconcerned whether positions were grossly overstaffed or the work useful. Having eliminated the option of firing a lazy worker, people had no incentive to work. A manager's only recourse was to institute a series of punishment protocols. Fear proved useful, and they began to apply the punishment protocols in other ways.

Agitated, he paced the shoreline, watching the sun glistening in the restless waves. Usually the sea's constancy comforted him, but tonight it reminded him that Alterrans had become a single sea of undifferentiated droplets. He picked up a rock and hurled it into the water. "How could you have done it?" he demanded of those who'd given up their freedom for the illusion of security. He decided a storm sequence better fit his mood. A thunderclap rang out, followed by the sound of wind and pounding rain. He stood alone on the bow of an ancient sailing ship, blown by typhoon winds and with waves splashing over the deck. A faceless crew scurried to unfurl the sails. Why didn't they value their human rights? The Party of Harmony and Stability had started them down the path toward dictatorship by preaching that a benevolent, monolithic government was their only hope for equalizing society and supplying lifetime jobs for all. Drastic depopulation and complete industrial ownership were essential to elevating society to that level. Pointing to geologic cycles, they blamed industry, ignoring

that both the universe and the planet were always uncontrollably evolving. It had been hubris to claim that controlling a few
emissions here and there would control evolution; even the
Party of Harmony and Stability abandoned that conceit after
they'd consolidated control. Herding the population into
densely concentrated cities, purportedly for environmentally
friendly reasons, was useful for spying and control. Eliminating money to prevent destructive economic cycles made it possible to control all production and consumption. The Teacher
hadn't been completely wrong saying the people had accepted
the principles of the Great Awakening; the vast majority had
accepted the social safety net as if sleepwalking. A fool's dream.
If he could master time travel, he'd pull them by the scruff of
the neck and shout in their faces, "Wake up!"

Reigniting the spirit of independence in Lil's guardsmen
had been only a start. Lil wanted to recreate Alterra on Earth,
and Ki agreed to an extent. Certain strains of the Earth people
could learn quickly; he and Ninhursag had seen to that. Civilization would ignite like wildfire, and he needed to mold it.
He couldn't act openly, though. His assistants revered him and
would do anything he asked. Would clandestine followers serve
his purposes? Would Mikhale and Rafael do his secret bidding?
He laughed, thinking it absurd. So what would an absurd name
be? Remembering how he'd once become a snake to slither
among the mute hominids in search of promising specimens
for Ninhursag, he chuckled at the idea of naming his secret
sect the Brotherhood of the Snake.

Enough idle thoughts, he chided himself; he needed high
voltage for the rejuvenation chambers. An impossible task with
only naturally occurring resources available on this primitive
planet. Yet, nature was a potent force, and one that he had harnessed already for the wave energy system that serviced Hawan.
He simply needed more of it. During his *mencomm* connection
with Lil, he'd felt a surge of electromagnetism during the solstice ceremony. He'd been focused on the human behavior
at the time, but the sun must have distorted a ribbon of the

magnetosphere, causing an electromagnetic wave to temporarily touch the Earth. If collected through superconducting material, could he capture sufficient power? He'd need a strong structure. Without Alterran alloys, he needed something available on Earth. When the Dalits operated the mines, they had primarily mined for gold to send back to Alterra, but there were other metals. Since the last mining shipments could not be sent to Alterra, Ki had an ample supply of gold and copper. It was much too little to create a power generation device, and he didn't have a fabricating facility. The colony's crystalline façade over the granite stonework, containing over a million nanobots, had permitted him to efficiently capture wave energy, but only enough for Hawan's needs.

A small fleck of energy came from the access pad outside his suite doorway. The fleck grew into a small hologram of Laurina dressed in a low-cut, clinging red gown that he'd specially replicated for her by subverting the replicator controls. She'd curled her white hair so that it hung below her shoulders in soft waves, and she wore the makeup that he'd made for her. "Don't turn me away again," she pouted, giving him her most seductive smile from plump red lips. He chuckled at her ingenuity before transforming his clothing into a floor-length dark robe, revealing his muscular bare chest. He transformed his room into a white marbled portico lit by basins of burning oil, centered with a large pillowed bed surrounded by sheers. Soft chimes blew melodically in the breeze below their view of the Milky Way. He opened his door and pulled her into her arms.

CHAPTER 6
AZAZEL

Azazel's black stallion galloped through a break in the dense forest undergrowth. "Veer right, Kamean," he ordered by *mencomm*. He motioned Augue to follow Kamean. Augue, a scrawny, black-haired admirer who'd followed Azazel from the Summer Meeting, knew every poisonous plant and venomous thing that moved. Through the eyes of the hawk soaring among the treetops, he tracked a pair of escaping wild hogs, which had been chased within a mile of Khamlok by the wolf pack. Through his own eyes, he watched the escaping sows scurry into the thick brambles. Astride a spotted mare, Kamean bore right and waited in the nearest clearing, fixing an arrow on his bowstring and pulling back. With rustle and crackle, the sows raced from the thicket. Kamean rapidly shot two arrows, killing them both cleanly through the head. Smirking, he slung the bow over his back. No one was a better shot than he was.

Erjat and Mika followed close behind, bringing along a wood wagon that bounced and was frequently stuck in the uneven terrain. Kamean ignored Erjat's perpetual grumbles about doing Dalit work as he gloated, "How's that for clean! Am I good?" Erjat made a face at his ego. Picking up a large, shiny knife, he jumped from the wagon and headed toward the sow. Augue waved his hand and pointed to the leaves into which the sow had fallen, scratching his skin with exaggeration.

"More bad leaves?" asked Erjat. "These nasty things are everywhere." He'd been caught before and once had to lie in bed for over a week with his swollen, painful skin wrapped in Alana's ointments.

Prepared, the men donned gloves and covered their arms before pulling the carcass out of the poisonous leaves. They then set to work deftly slitting open the bellies to perform the field dressing. With Mika's help, Erjat loaded the carcasses into the wagon and covered them with a guardsmen's tunic that retained a bit of nanobot power. Quickly, they guided the hitched horses in the direction that Azazel and Kamean had cantered in pursuit of deer that were trapped by their wolves.

Azazel and Kamean rode up a small incline, slowing their pace to pick their way through overhanging branches. They waded across one of the many small streams that interlaced this marshy area of the peninsula and made the hunting so rich. "Watch for snakes," Azazel cautioned. "Augue, go first," he motioned. On an early hunting trip, Enuziel had been bitten on the face from a viper camouflaged by just such an innocently appearing branch. Enuziel's skin began turning black before they'd made it back to Khamlok, and he had been too far gone for Yamin's healing wand or Alana's herbs to stop the poison's progression. He died in contortions of agony, with his blackened skin peeling away. It had been a stark reminder how precarious their life had become. To minimize their risk of stumbling into poisonous plants and animals, Azazel now included one of his Earth followers on all hunts.

Augue grunted and grinned broadly at being called to guide the mighty Azazel. He pointed to vines twining around a tree and made a face. "Bad," he uttered, one of the few common words he knew. Azazel waited for Erjat and Mika to catch up with the wagon before proceeding at a walk through the dense foliage. Augue stopped them and put a finger to his lips for silence. He held out a long rod that he'd brought and poked overhead leaves. *Hsss.* Augue's horse reared, and Augue hugged its back and gripped his mane, barely holding on. Azazel withdrew his shining sword from the scabbard on his back and hacked at the branch, slicing it in two as he rode quickly a few paces away. Augue slid from his horse and gingerly stepped toward the branches, testing with his rod. The snake, which had been coiled on the tree branch, lay in multiple pieces. "Augue, gather the venom pouch and give it to Erjat," Azazel ordered, intending to present it to Alana for her medicines. Augue picked up the snake pieces as well, considering them a delicacy.

"I'm sure glad that the wolves bring prey close," said Kamean, wiping the sweat from his face. "Too many directions for danger." The day before, Augue had found a tree toad as small as his thumb, saying, "*Very* bad," aided by a look of horror.

"The wolves have six deer trapped," said Azazel, starry-eyed as he focused through the distant wolf eyes. "One has a nice rack. I've ordered them to chase the victims down this trail to us. That will be enough for today."

"You've got to love those wolves," said Kamean with a grin that annoyed Azazel.

* * *

Azazel loved his new life. He was proud to have been chosen by statuesque Morgana. Her lovely face exactly matched his old daydreams. She was intelligent and self-sufficient, traits that suited him. Unlike men with shorter wives, Azazel had had no difficulty mating. Since leaving Hawan, he felt like a new man, independent and assertive. Even Lil had recognized Azazel's special skills. Although Lil had initially admonished Azazel for what Lil called his "theatrics" at the Summer Meeting, Lil had nevertheless appointed him as chief hunter. Using *mencomm* and the animals, his hunting success had been prolific. His growing team cared for the wolves, the horses, and the hawks, housing them in a barn and pens at Khamlok's edge.

With Khamlok's population growing, Azazel and his hunters maintained the city's supply of fresh meat despite the increasingly hostile environment. His hunting also brought valuable hides and furs, which the women skillfully worked into clothing. Koko promised trade with distant mainland trade centers, or at least the few surviving ones that struggled to recover from the flood's decimation.

All the young ones—even more than the original village youngsters—eagerly pestered him for training. Azazel had won admirers from other villages for his athleticism at the Summer Meeting, some of whom pleaded for admittance, especially with food outside the wall becoming sparse. Seeking to instill a sense of camaraderie among the diverse group, he had created a strenuous training regimen. When they mastered hunting techniques, Azazel devised athletic games to occupy them. Worried that the wall was inadequate, he began sword training. Since Lil hadn't designated a chief defender, Azazel assumed that role. He'd been deeply affected by Morgana's harrowing tale of her capture by the Danes. The stories of the other women, for whom he now deeply cared, had moved him. He solemnly vowed that as long as he lived, he'd protect them.

Even more than he enjoyed hunting, he loved demonstrating the ancient forms with his gleaming sword. Each set of movements flowed smoothly into the next as he gracefully dipped, pivoted, charged, and twirled through a fantasy battle, calling out the patterns' names and slicing the air with his magical sword. He executed the difficult forms with poetic grace. Watching, youngsters admired Azazel with open-mouthed awe. At his request, Jared had created small wooden swords that the youths used in mock battles. Azazel required his apprentices to practice at dawn, followed by chores. He rewarded his most promising students with the title of field commander. Each week Morgana and her friends prepared a special meal for his men, giving them the opportunity to joke and tell stories.

Whenever Azazel entered the room, they stood and respectfully greeted him. After Morgana was finished serving the meal, she'd hold Tara's hand and watch. She was proud of the special bond that grew between Azazel and his men, and she adored the reverent way that they spoke his name. Azazel was fulfilling his promise to protect them, she thought proudly.

Unlike Hawan's other guardsmen, Azazel had a pure military background. All the men in his family, going back all the generations to the Great Awakening, had served in the Guard. Even the women had served. Azazel had been conceived during a time when Alterran leaders had determined that they needed additional population for off-planet exploration, and he'd been permitted to grow larger than most. From the moment of his birth, his destiny certificate had set forth "Guard." With his father as his special teacher, he'd learned unique martial skills not taught by the Teacher. In the Alterran way, his parents had accepted their assignments, as well as his conception, without question. From birth, he'd been given the "Guard" nourishment bar in preparation for an active and physical life. When of age, he'd received notice to report for work. With this position came steady, predictable wages and everything he needed for life, and he'd never questioned his assignment.

On a pre-dawn morning, he strolled about the practice area, enjoying the clean scent carried by the blustery wind. Remembering the eager faces seeking to join his band, it struck him that he'd had no career choice, and he marveled that the thought hadn't occurred to him before. His parents hadn't fathomed a choice, since his destiny card at birth was marked "Guard." If asked, he would have chosen the Guard because it suited him. He'd always loved the Alterran heroes of ages ago and was delighted to now live the old legends with his trusty sword. He wore the hide clothing skillfully made by Morgana. She'd embroidered an eagle signet on the collar of his favorite boiled hide vest, which left his powerful arms bare. By growing his hair long, he emulated his favorite hero, a warrior of valor who fought for goodness. The heroes in those legends hadn't sat back and complied with a destiny certificate from the House of En. Somewhere along the way, he thought, Alterrans had lost individual initiative. Maybe he could restore it.

At Khamlok, the idea of choice over one's life was new and strange, yet wonderful. Some eagerly embraced choice, while others were adrift and needed to be led. Lil stepped in at such times, issuing orders. Many who struggled without the old safety net had been assigned to Jared's team to construct huts or to Rameel's team to maintain the fields. Although grumbling about performing Dalit work, such men accepted Lil's direction. Azazel had requested the right to handpick his hunters, but Lil had agreed only after Alana pointed out that it was wise for hunters to work well together to obtain their prey.

Curiously, when out hunting he sometimes glimpsed shadows following him through the trees. Mystified by this eerie sensation, he'd see them moving in his peripheral vision; snapping his head, they'd disappear. If it weren't for Maya, who told him that they were Drood's shadowmen, he'd have dismissed the odd occurrences as imagination. They were cannibals, she'd said, who traveled in the spirit world; only Alana and little Tara could see them. He scoffed that they were a curiosity, not a worry. But he had no inkling that Drood had become attuned to Azazel's *mencomm* communications.

CHAPTER 7
FRIEND-SISTERS

"Where should we look, Alana?" As she had done in their pleasant childhood days, Maya trudged behind Alana through the twisting forest path, hunting for mushrooms and medicinal herbs. With the old favorite spots more than a month away, Alana sought nearby sources. Lil hadn't wanted her to go, but Alana had slipped away when he was busy with Rameel. Together with Morgana and Tara, these friends had donned their old, stained hide work shifts and boots and ridden by horseback along the low mountain path bordering Khamlok. When the foliage became dense, they hobbled the horses and walked. The mountain facing Khamlok had been deforested, but its sloping rear preserved pristine evergreens and giant oaks, with dense undergrowth leading down to marshland and meadow.

Since the pounding rain had relented after three dismal days, Alana was hopeful of finding her special mushrooms. Although Zedah had promised that with her talent she could penetrate the spirit world, she hadn't succeeded. Mud splashed on their boots as they slipped and slid through the ferns and slopped through rain-swollen gullies. They tied hide scraps to mark their trail in the unfamiliar forest. "Look under low evergreen branches and fallen logs," she instructed. "Lift with your spears to avoid poison leaves and snakes. Keep an eye out for bushes with the small red berries and plants with purple leaves."

"And those pretty little yellow flowers," Maya remembered. "Maybe they'll be in the meadow."

"Yes," Alana said. "Get roots or stems if you can. Rameel might be able to grow them. Lil says the stinging rain is killing the delicate flowers." She sniffed, and the forest didn't smell as fresh; it was acrid.

"That's so sad," said Maya. *We're so lucky.* "How do you suppose others are faring?"

"Oh, I suppose they'll do whatever they must to survive, just as we did." Alana grimaced and shrugged her shoulders. At night, she oftentimes lay awake fearing the tragedy that must befall the less fortunate. Lil said heavy clouds blanketed most of Earth. If she could command nature, she'd gladly dissolve those evil clouds. She couldn't, nor could Lil, and so she stifled her nightmares; the dragon wasn't her fault. Lil had comforted her that their role was to survive so that life could begin anew. "I especially need white willow bark." *Mother, please let those trees survive.*

Not wanting to dwell on tragedy, Morgana sighed. "It's nice to get out. Everyone works so hard here!" Living with Azazel, she couldn't be happier. Across her back, Morgana carried Azazel's sword in its scabbard. He'd given her lessons and promised to make her a gleaming sword of her own. Even little blonde Tara proudly carried a small wooden practice sword. When Azazel instructed the hunters, she earnestly copied his gentle grace as the flowing arm movements and shifting stances formed a dance. She delighted in calling out the patterns' ageless names, drawing upon the animal totem's power in her thrusts. Tara posed with her sword, her blue eyes focused, forming Azazel's signature sign, a horizontal eight. "Mother, I'll protect you from any mean bears. Watch me! I'll lure it with Embrace the Moon. When it lunges, I'll pretend to draw back like this," she said, leaping in tight whirls, "using Wild Horse Leaps the Ravine. When it's confused, I'll draw it off balance with Heavenly Steed Soars Across the Sky, landing where it can't see me. To finish, I'll thrust my sword down into its back with Compass Needle to the South."

"Clever," applauded Morgana. She called out the names in imitation of Tara's fluid movements, thrusting her sword into the imaginary bear and victoriously celebrating with upraised arms. "No mercy for mean old bears!"

Doubled over with laughter, Maya said, "I feel *so* safe with you both. Maybe we should all learn to use a sword."

"Or a bow and arrow," suggested Morgana, doubting that little Maya had the strength to wield a regular sword made of heavy metal. Morgana needed both hands to swing one. Although Azazel's glowing sword was lightweight, she wouldn't part with her treasure, even for Maya. "Kamean is teaching Vesta and Kranya to shoot."

"I think I'd be good at it," said Maya, aiming an imaginary shot.

"I prefer my spear and knives," said Alana. "Nothing fancy, just point and thrust, pure and simple." Using a spear reminded her of Ewan. And she had more than enough tasks. She lifted low-lying evergreen branches. "Thank the Mother. Perfect mushrooms." She produced one of Lil's bags and stooped to scoop up the gems.

"There must be more; let's spread out," Maya suggested. As she searched, Maya danced, twirling in tight circles and humming a melody that Yanni frequently played on her flute.

After a strong breeze, Morgana sniffed and eyed a downward path. "Thank the Mother, I smell lavender. We need to make soap. Come with me, Tara."

When Morgana was out of sight, Maya asked, "Alana, do you feel any different now that you're an Earthkeeper?"

"Not really."

"What happened at the initiation?" Maya discovered some wild thyme and parsley, which she cut and put into a pouch slung around her waist. "Did Zedah transfer her powers to you?"

"No, I don't think so. This must be our secret, Maya. Do you give me your oath?" Alana felt distressed—Zedah had told her not to tell. *Telling Maya isn't any more wrong than if I told my hand or my foot.*

"On my mother's grave, I swear not to tell," Maya assured her, swearing her most solemn oath without a hint of her usual mirth. Earthkeeper matters demanded reverence.

Continuing to gather mushrooms and whatever herbs she found, Alana began her story. "Zedah took me to a sweat tent. She gave me a menthol tea and chanted soothingly. I was deeply relaxed, almost in a trance. She told me to close my eyes and reach out with all my heart to the spirit world and to be absolutely confident about touching it, as confident as I am now of touching this tree. Guided by her voice, I felt as if I were traveling, floating really. It seemed as if I glided without effort, as if my body had no weight. I sensed that I climbed, although I'm not sure that I actually moved. I slid along two pieces of wood connected with wooden steps. Around me, the most incredible living colors filled the air, swirling and changing patterns. Within the colors, I glimpsed images that melded into new ones—sometimes a face or an animal, or simply a design. I felt welcome. As I moved on, I became surrounded by little pools of brilliant light. The light felt warm and happy, almost like liquid love, if that makes any sense. I saw figures that I didn't recognize, but they seemed to know me, and they greeted me as a cherished friend coming home from a long journey, although they didn't speak with a mouth. I felt like a pure spirit connected with other spirits floating effortlessly among the light."

"Sounds incredible," gushed Maya, her eyes wide with admiration.

"Zedah said that I was blessed with buds of spirit talent, which must be nurtured until they blossom. Blossoming, though, will happen only if I fully believe in my powers and I open myself so that the spirit world may enter."

"What powers?"

Alana shrugged her shoulders. "That's a mystery; everyone is different. Yoachim bragged that Zedah caused lightning to strike the Danes when they attacked a fishing village she was visiting. I once saw her walk through fire without being touched."

"*You* have those powers?"

"I have no idea. She told me that if I'm calm and confident, I can command nature." Feeling the weight of her responsibility, Alana didn't smile. "In my sleep, the night when Lil told his story about Alterra, she said good-bye and kissed my cheek. 'You're the Earthkeeper now,' she said." They worked for a long time without speaking. "Maya, I'm afraid that I won't live up to expectations."

"Give it time, Alana," advised Maya, glad to be the advisor for once. "There's only so much one person can do."

"That's just it," she worried, pursing her lips. "I can't achieve the calming state with so much activity around me."

"Zedah lived alone in the forest."

"Yes, in isolation to achieve mindfulness and feel union with the forest spirits. Elaine lived alone as well. But Maya," she said, her voice trembling and her lip quivering, "I can't leave you or Lil or the others, although I *do* want to be an Earthkeeper. Priestess Petrina served in a temple filled with life and purpose, and I want to be like her. That's a small price to pay for not having Zedah's powers."

Maya hugged her. "I'm so glad we're together. We're *so* much more than friends. Even more than sisters."

"Friend-sister, then," Alana said, sniffling and wiping her eyes. She could see Morgana hiking up the trail with lavender peeping from her bags. "Morgana's our friend-sister, too."

"She is!"

Opening a bag as she drew near, Morgana revealed her treasure of yellow and pink flower tops. "The meadow is rich.

I found a nut grove and—" Noticing their tears, she halted. "What's wrong?"

Alana drew her close and slid her arm around Morgana's waist. "We're celebrating our good fortune. We're so close, that we should call ourselves friend-sisters."

Morgana blushed and stammered, "Friend-sister. I like the sound of it."

Little Maya, dwarfed between her two tall friends, raised their hands and tilted her chin skyward. "May we always be together, friend-sisters!"

"Absolutely forever," Morgana yelled skyward, smiling happily.

"Forever!" cried Alana. She impishly tugged and they toppled to the ground, giggling.

Righting herself, Maya asked, "Alana, did Princess Petrina have friend-sisters?" She took apples from her bag and passed them around. Morgana shared her freshly picked nuts, which she opened with a flick of Azazel's sword.

"Not that I remember. She had attendants, like my mother. We're equal, of course. Anyway, I have no temple."

"Lil might build one someday," said Morgana. "It sounds like something he'd do."

"It does at that," Alana mused, intrigued by her childhood memory of finely chiseled, marble archways. Out of necessity, Lil had temporarily built wooden huts. She knew that he dreamed of magnificent buildings. "For now, we have nature's throne for our sisterhood—the sisterhood of wise women."

"We *are* wise for our years," agreed Maya, stretching her legs. Without the constant running that she used to do, her calves had a cramp from their hike. Lately, her stomach had been feeling queasy, especially in the morning.

"Do you think the men will grow old when we do?" worried Morgana.

"I don't think even they know how life here will affect them," said Alana. "What worries me most, though, is whether they'll return to their people and leave us." They became silent at such an unhappy thought.

"Oh, look!" Morgana pointed to a reddish-brown hawk that majestically folded its wings, settling itself on one of the oak's lower branches. It intelligently cocked its head, its beady eyes transfixed on them through the still leaves. "My darling Azazel must be watching."

"Or Jared," added Maya, giggling and blowing kisses.

"Or Lil," said Alana, waving, but vexed. *You'd think we are helpless children the way that Lil the ruler acts.* "I hope they didn't overhear."

"Mommy," Tara yelled. Her voice was calm, yet stern. "Be gone, you demon!" She backed against an oak tree.

Morgana's heart skipped a beat and she ran, calling, "Tara, what—"

In her fighting stance with sword pointed, Tara slid around the trunk and stared into the brambles, not moving as she put her finger to her lips to hush her mother. She pointed and then slowly removed her sword from its scabbard. Tara assumed a ready stance, prepared to strike. "Mother, I could use a bigger sword," she whispered.

Morgana peered over her shoulder. Seeing nothing, she assumed it was a game. Playing along, Morgana whipped out her sword, mimicked her daughter's stance, and perused the thick bushes. Nothing moved. She whispered, "What did you see? A great, hairy beast with fangs? Are there one or two heads?"

"Mother, seriously, can't you see? It's the false shadow."

Morgana tensed. Even her mighty Azazel grew cautious at unnatural shadows. "Where? I can't see it."

"It brushed me, and it felt ice cold," Tara said, guarding her stance. "It floated over these bushes."

After carefully securing the bags with their treasures on their backs—Alana had lost too many in the past when emergencies arose—Maya and Alana drew close with their spears.

Morgana whispered, "She sees a shadow." The agitated hawk darted in tight circles, searching for the cause of their concern.

Spotting the stocky warrior, Alana warned, "Straight ahead. His spear is pointed." The warrior's scalp was shaved except for a thick, dark topknot. On his chest was painted three descending, flaring lines, each topped by a closed circle. On his left cheek was painted a crescent moon. Alana gripped her spear with its metal tip, ready to charge. Startled at being observed, the spherical shadow withdrew into the copse of bushes. "What do you want?" She inched forward and jabbed her spear into the bush, finding nothing but brambles. The hawk hovered above. It fluttered its wings and settled overhead.

"I don't see anything," confessed Maya.

"I don't either," said Morgana.

"It's one of Drood's warriors," said Alana, cautiously turning, her eyes searching the foliage. "He's found the spirit world. I never guessed that puny man had such talent."

The bushes rattled. The hawk swooped again. Finding nothing, it alighted on the same branch.

"Drood must have heard me," smirked Alana.

"That must be how that horrid Maku disappeared," said Maya, peering intently into the bushes. Her shiny knife was drawn. The women put their backs to one another, and Morgana shoved Tara into the middle despite her pouting protests.

The bushes shook more violently.

"What else can they do?" Morgana shivered. No degree of practice had prepared her to fight a shadow.

The shadowed warrior jumped into their path, poised to strike with his sharply chiseled, stone spear. Alana gasped, "Straight ahead."

"What's he doing?" asked Morgana, straining for a telltale sign of the invisible creature. She noticed bent leaves and held her sword high. "Tell me when, and I'll strike." She made circle eights with her sword, shifting her weight to extend her reach. Her rapid strokes blurred into a pulsating white light.

"He's baring his teeth and pulling back," warned Alana. The squawking hawk tried to nip the hazy shadow with its talons. The warrior's spear slapped it, sending the bird spinning, although it quickly righted itself and soared back. Morgana propelled her spinning light as Alana drew back her spear and sent it hurtling toward the warrior's chest. In the instant before the weapons struck, the shadow shimmered and shrank to a small dot, which disappeared. Alana's spear struck a tree, and Morgana's sword ignited the copse of bushes. "It shrank and disappeared," gasped Alana. Watching the fire die, she added, "It's good that the forest is too wet to burn."

Protecting little Tara in their tight circle and with knives drawn, the three women stepped in unison to retrieve their weapons. Although Azazel's sword still pulsed with undulating energy, its handle was cool. As if receiving comfort from Morgana's touch that the danger had passed, its light dimmed. They scoured their surroundings with their eyes, maintaining their ready stance. The hawk flew circles around them, offering its protection.

"Witches!" a woman accused in a common tongue dialect. She and two black-haired companions, their spears drawn, watched the friend-sisters from the high oak branches. Their clothing was woven of coarse wool. Their dirty cheeks were hollow with starvation.

"They must come from the mainland," said Alana. "Koko once traded that material."

"I didn't finish telling you," said Morgana in a low tone. "I discovered a campfire in the nut grove. More must be near." Through the leaves, she glimpsed an abandoned beehive high in the trees, the honeybees having been early casualties of the dismal weather. "They were searching for honeycombs."

"Mainlanders aren't friendly." Maya frowned, remembering past skirmishes. Before the flood, the mainland population had grown too large for gatherers to find food, and small, warlike groups occasionally followed the migration herds. It was rumored that they were killed in the north by the fierce highlanders. A spear landed at her feet. The hawk fluttered with alarm and soared into the branches to claw Maya's attacker.

"Helum," the black-haired woman shrieked. Panicked, she raised her arms in a futile attempt to protect her face from the furious birds' claws. She lost her balance. Screaming, she tumbled through the branches and landed with a plop in a mud hole. Groaning, she called out to Helum in an unknown language.

Hearing heavy, running footsteps, Morgana warned, "Her kinsmen come." She again prepared her sword, glad that Azazel had insisted that she take it when he couldn't dissuade her from accompanying Alana and Maya.

"I guess it's too late to make friends," Alana sighed, resolving to learn to use a bow and arrow, maybe even a sword. Lil had been right; life on her beloved Albion was rapidly deteriorating. With their backs again to one another and Tara in the middle, they moved away.

Three skinny, wool-clad men of Maya's height scampered among the trees. One went to the fallen woman, whose two companions soundlessly dropped from the tree. Crouching, they followed behind the men stalking the friend-sisters. Morgana sliced through a narrow tree trunk to demonstrate her sword's power. The startled intruders ducked behind trees. "Witches!" a woman screamed. The friend-sisters ran, casting furtive glances behind. Trailing close behind, the hawk guarded their backs. Tara slipped on the muddy trail. Barely slowing, Alana and Morgana each grabbed an arm and carried her until she regained her balance.

Glancing back, Maya huffed between strained breaths, "They're chasing." *I wish I could run like I used to.* She stopped for a moment, holding her side.

"Run, Maya," Alana urged, her eyes scanning the trail. Twigs snapped nearby and she jumped. *It's only squirrels.* Running with Tara, Morgana hadn't seen them stop, and she was out of sight.

"Are we lost?" Maya asked, gasping for breath. *Why is my stomach cramping?*

Nodding at the bird waiting patiently, Alana said, "Follow the hawk." They trotted slower, allowing Maya's shorter legs to keep up through the twists and turns of the forest path. They heard hooting owls to the right and then the left. *They come closer.* Sensing from Maya's heavy breathing that she was exhausted, Alana urged, "Sweetie, you must find a way to keep running." An arrow grazed Alana, causing warm blood to trickle down her left arm. She sprinted, dragging the panting Maya. Maya tripped over a tree root. Alana helped her regain her balance. An arrow bored into the tree trunk a few inches from Alana's head. Alana jumped in surprise. Alana held Maya by the shoulders. "Look, our marker. You can make it." Instead, Maya collapsed to her knees and vomited.

A female armed with a sharp stone knife snuck from the bushes just paces ahead of them. Defiantly, she spat, "This land is ours now." Blocking the path, she pointed her knife at Alana's stomach. The males emerged from the brush, pointing their chiseled, stone spears. One jabbed the puking Maya in the leg, drawing blood. Maya screamed and choked, holding her stomach.

Fury consumed Alana. Her mind focused, she glared at their attackers. Outstretching her arms, she commanded, "Creatures of the forest help us!" Twigs in the brush snapped with an army of scurrying feet. Attacking squirrels scaled up the males' bodies, tunneling under woolen shirts to sink their incisors into tender flesh. Cursing, the man grabbed the little beasts and felt clenched jaws ripping his skin. Each man tossed his assailants, only to be forced to fend off bites of the swarm. The circling hawk nipped the men's ears.

The woman advanced with her stone knife, dancing around the squirrels nipping at her mud-caked, naked legs. "Witch," she sneered. Pointing her spear, Alana kept her at bay. They circled each other. The woman drew her arm back to throw. Abruptly, she jerked, and her eyes grew dazed. Blood dripped from her mouth, and she fell forward, revealing Morgana's knife protruding from the middle of her back. Morgana crouched in a fighting stance, her sword drawn.

Unwilling to leave Maya's side, Alana drew a knife from her boot and readied her spear. Morgana circled, waiting for the squirrels to finish. A wolf howled, joined by another, and then another, each time their growls growing closer. Alana commanded the frightened attackers, "Be gone! Do not return!" Bewildered, they scrambled into the forest. "Animals, rest," she ordered. Fading into the distance, Alana heard the men shout, "Witches!"

Morgana helped Maya to her feet. She ripped fringe from Maya's shift to bind her bleeding leg. The squirrels gently mingled at her feet, and Alana laughed. "Thank you, little ones." She threw nuts from Morgana's bag. They grabbed them and scurried away.

Led by the hawk, gray wolves appeared and stood at guard positions. Kamean ran close behind. "There you are. The captain sent me; I was closest. The captain, Azazel, Jared—everyone's worried. They watch a hologram through the hawk."

Morgana huffed, "We didn't need your help. You come when the enemy is defeated, and I suppose now you'll take credit for saving us. Men!" She shook her head.

The three women joined hands, smiling broadly. "We did it," Alana said. "Friend-sisters forever!"

"Forever," Morgana cried.

Maya's lips quivered with sickness. With worry, Alana pulled back Maya's hair. "Sweetie, when was your last blood?"

"On the road to the Summer Meeting, when everyone else bled," she groaned, holding her belly. Alana and Morgana exchanged knowing looks. *She's with child, as am I.*

"Well, Kamean, since you're here, carry Maya. We're ready to go home. One thing Lil was right about, our land is changing for the worse."

CHAPTER 8
YOACHIM

Stretching before Yoachim was endless blue ocean, its waves rolling restlessly onto the broken rocks and fractured tree stumps, the logs strewn about as if twigs had been tossed into the blustery wind. Before the giant waves had thunderously crashed ashore, tiny fishing villages containing a hodgepodge of crudely made shacks had dotted the shoreline. All had been washed away, and only remnants of bones or pottery now and then washed ashore as a reminder of the lost lives. Now, lulled by the serenity of the gentle waves, Yoachim had to remind himself of the terror. His people living inland needed to conquer their fears and repopulate the shore. Summer, if that's what those cool few months could be called, had not left behind sufficient food in the interior. Apple and pear trees had blossomed, but the pickings were not nearly as rich as the Mother usually sent. Berries and legumes were meager as well. Animals were lean, and mothers abandoned newborns. The coming hunger would be worse if they had had all those mouths to feed. Then again, the fishermen would still be alive to share the sea's bounty.

He didn't need Zedah's prophetic talent to predict the approaching famine. That was why he was here. Inlanders *must* learn to live from the sea. Being so deep, it wouldn't ice over in the winter that would surely be harsher than any in recent memory after the summer had been so cool and brief. If inlanders didn't relocate, the people of Albion truly had little hope for survival. Tribe would turn against tribe to fight for scraps, and Drood's cannibals would no doubt be the victors. Traveling southwest from the Meeting Place, he'd found scrawny villagers resorting to animal sacrifices, desperately hoping to placate an angry Mother. Such folk were ripe for Drood's dark mysticism. Others frantically gathered whatever they could find and set foot for the mainland, abandoning the old and the weak— if they didn't starve or freeze, they would surely be slaughtered by the hostile mainlanders defending their land. Still others huddled in their huts with whatever they'd been able to gather; they waited, trusting childlike in the Mother to provide. These gentle folk Yoachim took in hand, helped them to pack travois with all their possessions, and traveled to the coast. Along the way he persuaded Khat, a wood carver, to gather his relatives and follow him. Until mated, Khat had lived by fishing in the ocean with his kinsmen. Yoachim needed him to remember how to prepare traps and create netting. Yoachim knew of an old man who might remember how to build boats, and he hoped to find him, if he still lived. Before the leaves turned crimson, he would bring many other starving tribes to the seashore. Yoachim had always been one to take matters into his own hands, a trait that had made him invaluable despite his inability to enter the spirit world.

"Look," Khat shouted, deftly scaling the rocky shoreline. He waved to Yoachim and pointed. A birch dugout canoe bobbed in the rippling waves. "The Mother *does* provide!" he cried joyfully. Sliding into a cove, he waded into crystal waters reaching his hairy chest and steered it to shore. From his youth, Khat knew his nets would overflow if he dropped them in the sea, where the snowy mountaintops only peeked at him over the watery horizon. The old ones had steered by night stars, now hidden by the heavy clouds. He'd cursed the sea gods that he had no idea how to carve a seaworthy vessel. "Only a coincidence," muttered Yoachim with a wry smile, "but certainly a welcome one." *We must make our luck.* Just that morning, he'd lectured people against complacency. They should learn self-reliance by planning ahead. In lengthy times of plenty, people forgot the lessons of the lean years. Zedah had foreseen a time when the people would control their destiny by mastering the art of growing the grains that grew wild in distant meadows. It was only in the lean times that people could be convinced that the difficult planting work was necessary. At this time of year, grains produced seeds, and he told the people to collect as many as they could find. He carried them in little pouches slung around his waist, planning to have them planted here and in the next springtime.

Khat's mate, Kamta, climbed over the slippery, moss-laden rocks and waded into the chilly sea. Together they guided the boat into a small cove, where the waves gently lapped the ancient rocks. Khat ran his fingers over the boat's smooth edges and felt a familiar paste that increased buoyancy. Tasting it, he guessed the paste's ingredients. Testing the small hold for sitting, he found only a splash of water. "Yoachim talks of hard times ahead," said Khat. "This boat is well made. I will be able to paddle to the good fishing grounds." He smiled broadly. "Our family will eat well."

Kamta smiled and brushed aside scraggly, wet hair from her dirt-streaked face. Although she was not yet eighteen, she'd given birth to two children, one only weeks before leaving for the coast. "My sister's mate is strong. He will help you."

"I can build a second boat from this copy," Khat murmured, still examining its carefully crafted contours.

"On our little one's name day, we'll call him Yoachim," Kamta said, her eyes glistening, "for the one who has brought us hope."

CHAPTER 9
ALANA AND LIL

As the crops grew and vines ripened, the people happily gathered their bounty, finding by early autumn that they had a significant surplus. The women hadn't known surplus before. After a satisfying evening meal around the central hearth, Lil and his chiefs sat embracing their mates, feeling content with their accomplishments. Maya asked, "What should we call you men, now that you're no longer the Guard?"

"We shall be called the Anunnaki," Lil responded. "They were mythical visitors from the beginning of time who brought civilization to our ancient ancestors." The men relaxed in silence. It was comforting to think that they were, in turn, sowing the seeds of civilization.

After a while, Alana loosened Lil's embrace. The others contentedly stared into the fire or slept. She stood, put a finger to her smiling lips, and mysteriously motioned for him to follow. He was tired and his mind was busily planning the next day's tasks, but she looked too entrancing to protest. *Why is she wearing the ruby necklace?*

Late in the day, a strong wind had let pockets of sunshine miraculously burst through the clouds. Everyone, even Lil, had danced in Khamlok's pathways. Hoping to have a rare night for viewing stars, Alana had made plans. Taking a torch, she climbed the steep mountain path to her new favorite spot—a rocky crag overlooking the valley below. A parting of the tips of the giant firs revealed an unobstructed view of the rising, full harvest moon. Lil grinned boyishly, feeling as if he were at home on his observation deck. Earlier, Alana had carried her new, luxuriant bear fur up the steep path. After fastening the torch, she drew him down to her fur.

"You've gone to a great deal of trouble. It's nice." He stretched his long legs and leaned back on his elbows, enjoying the view. She loved watching his profile—his long forehead, now cropped by white hair that neatly hung to his shoulders, his straight, noble nose, and his full, sensuous lips. He was, by far, the handsomest man she'd ever seen. Under the stars, he began to relax. *Maybe there's hope,* she thought. Lil the ruler, competent but dispassionate, had been in control since their mating. In the moonlight, Lil's relaxed features reminded her of their dinner at her cave, the night that he'd playfully slipped the necklace around her neck, letting the cold ruby slip down her chest to tickle her breasts. She touched it, remembering how deliciously close they'd felt at the Rite of Summer, and the intensity of their lovemaking. She desperately wanted *that* Lil. He worked to develop Khamlok as if running from demons. She was awed by his vision and ability. She didn't interfere with his working time; he was protecting them. She believed him when he confessed, almost apologetically, that she enthralled him. He *certainly* enthralled her. After the first days, though, something was missing. A veil of anxiety seemed to coat his mind. In his sleep, he uttered the names Ama and Jahkbar, and he frequently argued with his father. *He looks at me with pangs of guilt.*

The bits and pieces that she'd gleaned about Alterran life led her to conclude that his people were emotionally detached. Rumors that she couldn't understand were whispered in the women's circle about imaginary, yet solid, lovers. *Perhaps that's what happens if you live as long they do.* Why did Lil argue with his disapproving ancestors? If he couldn't go home, why did he listen? They seemed to interfere with his emotion for her. Having experienced sublime intimacy after the Rite of Summer, she was tortured by his remoteness, even though he remained fiercely protective. She craved a deeper, everlasting bond, like Ewan had felt for her mother, and like Morgana enjoyed with Azazel. She needed to crack the Alterran shell encasing his heart. If she failed, she'd be crushed, but far less than she'd be crushed if he left her to return to his people. Ewan had warned her about pursuing false hopes. *Atlantis is gone, my little one. Those who persist in fitting their hopeless desires for the past into the far-different present find only heartache. Accept life as it is.* Despite the risk, she took a leap. That afternoon, she'd bared her heart to Morgana and asked how to please a man. After cups of wine and a blood oath of secrecy, Morgana bashfully explained the tricks she'd learned to stay alive as Shylfing's bed slave.

While Lil enjoyed the stars, Alana sprinkled a potion smelling of lavender and poppies on their furry bed. "Tonight, I want you to put away Lil the ruler," she whispered, her soft voice teasing with command. "And no fighting with that Jahkbar or Ama."

Lil raised an eyebrow. *Is it that obvious? If only I could get rid of them.*

"Let me take control," she said, as if reading his mind. "Will you give it a try?" He gazed at her uncertainly, and her heart leaped into her throat that he'd refuse. He smirked as the edges of his lips curled into a wicked smile, and his eyes lit up. *He's so handsome; I can't believe he's mine.* "I'll take that as a yes. Wise choice." Sitting on her buttocks, she lightly blew in his ear, flicking with her tongue and nipping his ear lobe. He sighed and gazed into her eyes, his deep blue eyes sexily narrowing with delight. He smiled—not the everyday one, but the warm, too-long-absent seductive smile of desire that excited every cell her in her body. She kissed him, running her fingers through his silky hair and circling her tongue inside his lips.

"Alana, you're so beautiful," he muttered. After whipping off his hide shirt and breeches, revealing his trim, muscled body softly glowing in the darkness, he greedily nuzzled her breasts and tugged at her skirt lacing, taking control as always.

"Wait!" She teased, eluding his sensuous fingers and sliding to sit cross-legged. Her green eyes sparkled in the torchlight and her hair cascaded, outlining the delicate features of her oval face, leading his eyes to her unblemished cleavage adorned by the deep-red ruby. "I have a surprise." He arched a lone eyebrow in amusement, letting his hands glide downward. She produced two small Alterran cups buried beneath the fur's warmth. After pouring a few drops of cool water from a flask, she stirred the contents with her slender fingers and then slowly sucked each one, teasing him with narrowed eyes. "It's my special mushrooms." She grinned in delight at seeing his body respond, relieved that he was willing to play along. After she stirred the second cup, Lil intercepted her paste-covered fingers and pulled them to his eager mouth, pausing to smell the aroma.

"This is what you use for your visions?"

"Hmm," she hummed. For once as an Earthkeeper, she intended to give herself a present. And Lil. "It enhances our sensations."

He sucked the potion from each soft finger, rolling each one slowly around his warm, sensuous tongue. "It tingles," he murmured with half-closed lids, enjoying the pungent taste.

"You need only a tiny bit more." She impishly smiled and handed him a cup. Scooting forward, she interlocked her arm over his and encouraged him to drink. In the flickering torchlight, she gazed into his huge, blue eyes and saw the potion's power take hold. Quickly, she slid from her furs.

Reclining, he sighed and pressed her soft breasts to his chest, faintly noticing that her breasts seemed larger than before. His body burned with heat. "So this is the spirit world!" He felt calmness settle over his mind, hushing the prickly admonishments of Jahkbar and Ama.

She whispered, her voice a sweet, seductive melody, "Each of our senses, whether hearing, seeing, or touch, is increased tenfold in the spirit world. Lovemaking will be even more intense than at our mating night."

"Impossible," he smirked.

Her smiling lips kissed the back of his hand, while her eyes narrowed with promise, meeting his. She trailed kisses down his lower body as Morgana had taught her.

"Aah," he gasped with sublime pleasure.

* * *

Hours later, they gazed contentedly at the stars, still delighting in the mushroom-enhanced euphoria. Deeply relaxed, Lil marveled that Jahkbar and Ama had been quieted in his mind; he hoped it was permanent. When the moon was overhead, Lil pointed out the Pleiades rising above the horizon. "The Alterrans believe that we're one with the universe, and that the universe speaks to us through the stars. As a means of understanding the star messages, my people long ago used images to divide the night sky, calling it the zodiac. They make twelve pictures." He pointed out to her Orion, the hunter. "The three stars in its belt are sacred to us. The first Anunnaki who seeded our civilization were said to use it as a marker."

"A marker to where?"

He sighed. "We're not certain. Maybe to the axis, if it's not a myth. Or maybe the purpose hasn't yet been revealed. My people have myths that the Anunnaki will return one day."

"My father used similar names for the shapes in the sky. Lil, do you know for sure when your people first came here? We have so much in common. Is it possible that they came much earlier? My father had little hair on his body, like you."

"We've had small outposts for a long time. So maybe my green-eyed beauty is really Alterran?" he joked, stroking her silky hair. Were the rumors about Ninhursag's genetic experiments really true? Or were Alana's people simply proof of creation repeating its best patterns, like the fractal patterns of a tree?

"Who knows?" she said, laughing. It was good for him to guess, in case he found a way to return home.

"It's always amazed me that the zodiac appears much the same on Alterra. It shows the vastness of space. It's not exactly the same, of course, and when we first came here, our scribes made adjustments. When the age of Cancer begins, it is—or was—my destiny to ascend to the Alterran leadership, but now—" he paused, choking back emotions released by her potion. Alana understood more deeply Lil's loss. He had promised her his kingdom. *If he could go back, would he take her? Would his people accept her and their children?* Casting aside her own nagging worry, she tickled him to bring him back from his sorrowful thoughts. "Will I be your Queen of the Universe?" she said, giggling.

"Of Alterra, which is the sum of the intelligent universe," he murmured, taking her question seriously. "Of course, you will, but we don't use that title. As I was saying, the zodiac is a way of measuring time. It takes about thirty-six thousand years for the full precession, which we call a Great Year. The zodiac is also a means of predicting the effects of celestial waves of space-time. The waves vary depending on their source and purpose."

"Oh, tell me about the timewave," she said, running her fingers along his chest. She'd do anything to keep him talking, prolonging their sweet rapport. *He's all mine tonight.*

"They govern change in the universe, and the waves carry the seeds of creation."

"Seeds? Do you mean the tree of life?"

"You know about that?"

"I've heard the source of life called that. Morgana said that even Shylfing referred to it."

"It's a symbol of the universal axis. In the purple insignia, the line dissecting the triangle represents the axis. These are universal points, roughly formed as a line around which our universe rotates. It's an aspect of the Universal, or Quantum,

Consciousness to which we're connected at the quantum, or smallest, level. The axis controls the emission of energy waves through the Universal Consciousness that initiate significant evolutionary jumps. At one time, Alterrans believed their planet was the only one receptive to the waves. Now that we've found that Earth is developing in a similar pattern, the more humble ones accept that the Universal Consciousness connects all life."

She furrowed her brow, plopped on her back, and searched the skies. "I see no waves."

Shifting to his side, he explained, "We can't see them. We couldn't even detect them until our technology became extremely advanced. Nevertheless, they affect the moods of my beautiful Alana, even though she doesn't know it." He tapped the tip of her nose.

She brushed her finger across his lips. "Did they predict our love?"

The scribes had not foreseen the catastrophe or anything else. "Our union transcends the multiverse," he said, playfully tickling her.

Why can't he say that he loves me? With desperation, she asked through her giggles, "So we rule the universe?"

"In time," he replied quietly, stopping the tickling, unsure where his destiny now lay. His eyes glazed over with a distant look. Even if his world recovered, they needed to relocate their population to a newer, suitable planet, perhaps even more than one to better assure their civilization's chances of survival. If none could be found, they needed to perform the terraforming that they'd previously eschewed. Eventually, their settlements might rule the universe. So much work, he sighed.

She arched her brows at his seriousness, remembering how small reminders of Atlantis used to cause her distress. Or he was quarreling with his family again. *Not tonight.* She straddled his hips and with a finger, gently drew his chin upward. "Then why don't those mean clouds and the wind obey me?" she demanded, grandly waving her arm to punish the unruly elements. "Do I need a secret chant? Tell me!" She tickled him again. "Or do I command as the mate of En.Lil, so if they don't obey me they'll face your wrath?"

Thinking her serious, he said, "Controlling nature isn't that simple, silly. We don't pretend to control nature; no one can. In fact, we embrace the chaos. We admire the unfolding creativity of all the universes bubbling through time." Seeing her laugh, he found that she was joking. Aghast at her audacity, he burst out laughing, a great belly laugh, causing her to slip to his side. Her levity infected him. Would marriage have been this sweet back home? The women he'd known there had been properly reserved and in awe of his position, as if he were a museum piece.

"It's good for you to laugh so hard. I love being with you. You inspire me. You're so smart and creative."

"And you're so incredibly alive and beautiful."

He stroked her hair and she smiled, happily feeling the connection that she yearned for so desperately. "I feel so close to you tonight. More than ever before." She ran her lips across his knuckles and kissed his hand. "I love you."

He smiled, and his eyes creased with an emotion she hoped was loved. "Destiny indeed brought us together, my sweet."

"The timewave?" she asked, masking her dejection. *Please, say you love me.*

"Exactly."

"All right, tell me more." *There must be an element of love in this.*

"The waves are cyclical, at times providing long periods of tranquility lasting many Earth centuries, when life is undisturbed by cosmic agitator waves. The Alterran philosophy of harmony and stability loves the long waves."

"Yeah, they love for you to control everything," she said, poking him.

"Alana, I'm serious. You need to understand because you're mine. When the troughs of the timewave shorten, particularly when a timewave is approaching the end of a cycle, the wave speeds with ever-increasing velocity. The vibrations stimulating our worlds are catalysts for upheaval. It could be geological, such as volcanic eruptions and earthquakes."

"Or dragons?"

"Comets—yes, exactly. Or our minds could be stimulated, provoking wars and physical violence. It's not always something bad, though. There might be spurts in scientific knowledge, such as decoding a fundamental secret of the universe, leading to a scientific revolution. Our knowledge of deep space travel came during the short waves. Here, it might be as simple as insights into forging metals or farming. We can't predict what will happen."

"What causes the wave?"

"The timewave is energy propelled by the Universal Consciousness, what you'd call the Creator, who is growing and evolving through its creations. On a clear night like this, when you can almost reach up and touch the starry blanket, you can almost feel the wave coursing through the universe, coursing through our bodies."

He reached up, and she extended her hand to his against the full moon.

"Can you predict the future this way?"

"Not specific events. No one can; the future shifts as choices are made. We simply know, depending on whether the wave is calm or hectic, that life for us will be calm or undergoing rapid change. I don't want to frighten you, but some think that we're now at the end of a timewave."

"That's why so many things are changing?"

"Yes," he said, stroking her hair, noting how quickly Alana picked things up.

"But you're now on Earth. Does that mean that your world and mine are tied together?"

"Hmm." He wasn't sure that Earth people were connected with Alterrans; surely his relatives would abhor this notion. But they didn't know Alana. When they did, surely they'd see his point of view. Maybe he needed to commission more studies of how it worked. His true destiny might be as a bridge between worlds.

"So your troubles caused ours?" Somehow, this made her feel much closer to him, as if they were one people after all.

"I don't know if we brought our timewave here or intercepted Earth's, but we're now firmly joined."

"How do you predict the future?" she demanded with a little laugh, needing more levity. "On Atlantis, we had soothsayers."

"At birth, our scribes fix the stars' alignment to determine the babe's career path." Mentally, he flinched, knowing each newborn's destiny certificate was his family's ruse. It hadn't been intentional; the ingrained explanation had simply slipped past his lips. "I prefer a system using sixty-four hexagrams, a sacred number influenced by cosmic energies. In a reading, those energies lead a person to select yarrow stalks to form the hexagon." He kissed her forehead, holding her tight. "One trained in reading the hexagon finds the true meaning of life's events." Lil grew silent for a while, wondering if he'd have the benefit of a hexagram reading again.

Alana broke the silence, saying brightly, "As Earthkeeper, I have visions, sometimes about the future. I know of special plants."

Lil had seen her administer herbal teas to those not feeling well. "Tell me about a unique one."

"Well, there's a bird that builds its nest in tunnels burrowed into hard rock. It had always puzzled me how it made the tunnels. One day, I happened to see the bird rubbing its beak in a wet plant. Then it flew up, rubbed its wet beak against the rock, and quickly pecked the stone. In a short time, the bird had carved a round hole. Later, the stone appeared as strong as before."

"You must show me where you found this plant." He needed to tell Ki.

"Yes, of course, my love," she said pulling him back, kissing him again. "But please, tell me more about Alterra. I want to know everything about you."

Lil opened up to her about his family, early life, and coming to Hawan. *Finally*, Alana thought joyously. She learned for the first time that he had had previous lives and, despite his appearance, was immensely old by Earth standards. *Will he still love me when I'm wrinkled and gray? Perhaps he has magic to keep me young, too.* She had much to learn about Lil, but she knew nothing about him would be dull.

She'd tried to keep him talking until he said I love you, but she couldn't stay awake. As she was drifting off to sleep with disappointment, Lil lovingly gazed upon her peaceful face in the moonlit shadows. Her persevering spirit had lightened his dark mood. He took a deep breath, drinking in the familiar silvery points of light overhead, feeling a part of the great, ever-changing cosmos. One by one, the lights were extinguished by the greedy, dark clouds unjustly reclaiming their fiefdom. Feeling as contented as he ever had, he closed his eyes. He'd worked furiously, in part to keep at bay his own torturous recriminations about having abandoned Hawan. What choice did he have? His father wouldn't let go of his obsessive faith in a return to Alterra, and Lil needed to be there to pick up the shattered pieces when the colony could no longer support life. He hadn't fought Jahkbar's programmed restraint, letting himself be distanced emotionally from Alana, so that he could prove to himself that he didn't act based on lust. It was time to turn the page. His world was gone, and he told himself to appreciate what he had, starting with the precious jewel to whom destiny had led him. Alana was not the destiny path that would have been chosen for a leader of the House of En, but she was his choice, and he was happier than he ever thought he could be. He kissed her soft hair, smelling its lavender scent. "I *do* love you, my sweet. Deeply. You are forever mine, anywhere, any time."

At last! Her eyelids fluttered, and her lips curled in an ecstatic smile. She murmured, "I love you, too, deeply," and squeezed his hand, falling happily back to sleep.

CHAPTER 10

LIL

For Khamlok's first Council meeting, Lil arranged benches in a circle, similar to the Supreme Council. Zeya had begun this tradition—in place until Ama dismantled the Council—to emphasize the equality of all Council members. Lil strove to emulate Alterra whenever circumstances permitted, even if his egalitarian Council was incomparable to the Alterran Supreme Council dominated by Elders of the House of En. He needed a new mold. When Jared, Azazel, Rameel, Tamiel, and Yamin, entered, Lil and Alana greeted each with the salute of the sacred triangle and said, "Peace and Harmony." After they were settled comfortably, Lil began, "Yamin's recorder is still operational, so he'll make the customary history. We've been so busy in the past four months that it seems like yesterday that we returned from the Summer Meeting. Jared, you've done a fantastic building job. What is left to be done before winter sets in?"

"The last huts were completed a few weeks ago, and the wall is nearly complete. The last posts will be hoisted before snowfall. It's time consuming because we're bracing the trees for sturdiness. It measures a perfect square, I'm proud to say."

"That's fast construction, given the size. Don't you dig a deep hole for each post?" asked Rameel.

Answering, Jared first cast his eyes downward and shifted his feet nervously. "I brought lasers from Hawan, together with extra fuel cells."

"You did?" snapped Li disapprovingly. He hadn't known Jared to disobey an order.

"Captain, I couldn't do all this construction with simple tools. There were plenty of lasers left at Hawan." Jared felt uncomfortable, not having debated Lil before.

Lil paused and decided to move on. "What else?"

"Azazel's horse barn is done. The women asked for a building for smoking fish and preserving meat. With the harvest of wheat and millet, we need a storage building."

"We must have a bathhouse with heated water!" Rameel pleaded. "Bathing in the river was moderately acceptable while it was warm, but I dread an icy bath."

"What a wonderful idea!" exclaimed Alana.

"We have too many tasks before it snows," observed Lil. "We'll come back to this. Rameel, the wheat fields are full. You've done a fantastic job, as well." Rameel grinned, unaccustomed to compliments from an En. In his years at the Ministry of Central Planning, silence had been considered a compliment.

"The cultivated wheat seeds took well to this mineral-rich soil," reported Rameel. "The wheat grew a bushy top and turned golden yellow despite the weather. We're about to harvest it— we'll need all available hands. If Jared can spare a laser, the job will go faster. I didn't know you had them. The guardsmen are grumbling more and more about performing Dalit work."

"Yanni said that you plan to make something from the grain," Alana interrupted. She sensed that the men were speaking too freely for an initial Council meeting. She didn't want Lil to dispense with the Council. It was such a wonderful idea.

"Yes, bread, it's delicious," answered Rameel, squirming uncomfortably. He nervously glanced at Lil, whose face remained inscrutable. On Alterra, his secret vice, despite all the risk, had been to buy bread in the secretive underworld markets, where hackers had created a bubble immune to the Net. No one spoke of the underworld, at least not openly, for fear of the nanobots. Old, secretive habits were hard to break, even now. "It won't be ready immediately. After the wheat is cut, it must be left to cure. Then we'll separate the grain from the chaff, and the chaff can be fed to the horses. Until we devise something better, we can build a stone fireplace and attach a flat stone to a handle. When the grain is pounded into a fine meal, we'll mix a bit with milk, if we can capture a cow. The batter is then baked over the fire when the stone is extremely hot. As we improve, we can add slivers of nuts and herbs for a variety of taste."

"Stop, you're making me hungry!" said Alana, laughing.

"Will we have plenty of grain until the next harvest?" asked Lil.

"Even though this is our first harvest, we will indeed," boasted Rameel.

"Tamiel, even though our fruit trees are newly planted, I've seen them full of fruit," noted Lil.

"Yes. Ki's cultivated clones are bearing apples and pears already," said Tamiel. "There are also some wild sweet apple trees nearby that are delicious. Ki's grape vines will render a harvest. Many women have picked fruit. We need a building to press the grapes, Jared. Also, since you have a laser, I'd like to cut a deep cellar for storage."

"We owe much thanks to Ki," said Lil. "I'm inviting him to a celebration. And last, Azazel. We've had an abundance of meat, and our people wear new clothing. Thanks to you, Kamean, and your group. A job well done."

Always suspicious, Azazel gave a barely perceptible smile. Compliments from the captain were new. "It's becoming more difficult to find game in this area even with the wolves. With the horses, we can travel for several days to get to the herds that the hawks scout for us."

"The game must be diminishing with the flood and the cold," observed Rameel.

"Some species are not doing well at all," said Azazel, nodding his head. "Certain others, better adapted to sparse conditions, are still thriving, especially because of the reduced hominid population. Animals prepared for cold, harsh conditions, like caribou, are moving south and are within range of our animals. At least the herds will thrive so long as their traditional food sources can be found." He paused and cleared his throat. "In addition to hunting, my men practice daily to defend us in case of attack." Because the military training hadn't been ordered by the captain, Azazel said it as casually as possible, but he showed his discomfort by repositioning himself. His discomfort irritated him; old conditioning was difficult to abandon. But he was right. Defense preparations were too important to ignore.

"Those men trickling in are from the most backward tribes, and they aren't capable of living as we do," said Lil, getting around to his real purpose for the meeting. Ruling by persuasion, rather than dictating, required creativity. Azazel needed to understand that Lil wasn't alone in detesting the newcomers. Their task was to create a new Alterran outpost in order to preserve their civilization. They had to provide an established base for the remaining colonists if worsening conditions made it impossible for them to stay at Hawan. Tutoring unruly primitives hadn't been part of his plan.

"I'm working with them," said Azazel uneasily. "True, they're rough, and they don't have the work habits to which we're accustomed. Still, they have their uses. They know the land. Our men complain about being used as Dalits, so we need someone to perform grunt work that no one wants to do. Rameel, your team grumbles, too. Won't they be useful in your fields?"

"They're filthy, and their beards must have lice," spat Rameel with disgust. "And they refuse to use the latrine!"

"Azazel, everyone must follow the latrine rules," scolded Lil. "We can't risk disease."

"They scare the women, Azazel," Alana complained. These uncouth men were the very type that she and Maya had sought to escape.

"Morgana isn't scared," said Azazel defensively, taken aback by her vehemence.

"Morgana would die before she'd criticize you," said Alana, throwing up her arms with exasperation. "Everyone else is afraid."

"They're not so bad," he protested with irritation. "All you women were seen as primitive at one time."

Seeing Alana about to lose her temper, Lil interjected sternly, "Azazel, if you truly believe that they can be trained, keep a closer eye on them and make them abide by the latrine rules. If they don't, you must send them away." Azazel sullenly refused to look at him and sulked with his jaw clenched. To change the subject, Lil turned to Alana and smiled warmly, with a gleam in his eye. "Alana has the best news of all."

"Yes, I do. Some of you may have heard rumors that some women are pregnant. Mother Earth must *truly* love us. *All* the young women are pregnant!"

"I knew that Maya and I were blessed, but I didn't know that *all* the others were pregnant," exclaimed Jared.

"Yanni is positively ecstatic," boasted Rameel, smiling broadly and slapping his knee.

"Akia is happy, too," Tamiel lied, hoping that this birth would improve her attitude.

"As is Morgana," said Azazel, beaming with pride.

Yamin involuntarily sighed, wishing that Kosondra could join them. She, unfortunately, was *not* pregnant.

"Are you keeping track of the due dates?" asked Rameel, his mind reeling with thoughts of organizational details.

"That's what's truly remarkable," said Alana, with her eyebrows raised. "With the Mother's blessing, everyone seems to have conceived at the Summer Meeting! You men are certainly virile," she said, chuckling. The men looked at one another with puzzled looks. On Alterra, they didn't use birth control, and women rarely became pregnant. Lil simply smiled, being the only one who could appreciate Ki's fertility shot.

"On top of everything else we have to do, we must plan for these babies," noted Rameel, excitedly moving to the edge of seat and moving his fingers as if preparing a checklist. "We'll need cribs—"

"And birthing chairs," Alana said happily.

"That, too," Rameel agreed, pointing his finger. "Yanni has started a list, and it's pretty long already. We're going to be *very* busy."

"We *are* indeed blessed," said Lil, smiling broadly. "Our plan is working extraordinarily well, which confirms that we follow our divine destiny!"

Leaving the Great House, Rameel asked in a low voice, "Well, Azazel, I know you had misgivings, what do you think?"

"I'm pleasantly surprised," he said without expression, still chafing at being chastised about the newcomers' toiletry habits. Once again, the captain had passed over their defensive needs. For this, the primitives were useful. Why did only he appreciate the primitives' obsession for warfare? Although their tools were mere stone, such tools were nevertheless sharp and lethal. "We'll see."

CHAPTER 11
NEW LIFE

When the first snow began to fall, Alana supervised the preparation of a feast to celebrate the great good fortune of the harvest and the many wonderful pregnancies. For fresh meat, Azazel's hunters killed caribou that were herded south by the wolves. Rameel baked bread from the new milled wheat, and the delicious smell floated throughout Khamlok. Tamiel set out vats of the first wine produced from the new grapes, although he cautioned that they should let it age.

In the early evening, a *tri-terran* landed, carrying Ki, Laurina, Mikhale, and Kosondra, and they brought with them a few special requests from Hawan. The largest was a floating transport, which Azazel had insisted that Lil request to make it easier to bring back their kills over a greater distance. Jared recharged the lasers.

That evening, everyone gathered in the Great House before a roaring fire and the pleasures of flute music played by Yanni, Rameel, and Tomin. Having received a regeneration of his tunic from the *tri-terran*'s energy, Lil dressed in his Alterran silver tunic, on which he proudly wore his purple insignia. Before the meal, Lil greeted his people formally with the sign of the sacred triangle and "Peace and Harmony." Picking up his cup, he offered a toast: "We've all worked hard, but we couldn't have been so successful doing this without Ki and, of course, Laurina and Mikhale. In the initial year, we've enjoyed new housing, abundant animal products, cultivated grain, and trees and vineyards that bore fruit—this is truly remarkable, even by Alterran standards. And of course," he said with a sly smile, "we're especially thankful for the unprecedented virility of our men. Nothing more wonderful could arise from the ashes of our recent tragedies. Here's to the new generation that will ensure the survival of Alterra!"

* * *

By the coldness of late December, six months after the Summer Meeting, expectant mothers walked around Khamlok happily showing with child. They prepared small clothes, blankets, and other necessities. Jared's carpenters prepared cradles, which they filled with boiled lamb's wool from captured sheep. Grandmother Marita, an experienced midwife, gave the carpenters her requirements for birthing chairs. The elevated chairs were to have a seat with a large hole for the baby to fall into her waiting arms. For good luck, Maya and Vesta carved pictures of healthy babies into the chairs' arms, which ended in a nub to be gripped by the expectant mother during labor. During the autumn, Alana had discovered a large quantity of the root of vervain to be administered during labor.

As time passed, the bellies of many women became much larger than when women bore children to Earth men. Happiness gradually became worry, and then fear. By the eighth month, some women experienced tremendous pain. Alana put Maya and those like her to bed, where they screamed in agony. Alana and Morgana, who didn't suffer, mixed special herbal teas for them. The teas didn't relieve the pain for long, and they became overwhelmed with the number requiring care. To help them, Lil had the men bring all the expectant mothers' pallets to the Great House. After finishing her rounds, an exhausted Alana came to their chambers and put her arms around Lil as he worked.

"What's wrong?"

"I'm afraid. They're in pain, and my herbs aren't working well. Marita has never seen bellies so large."

"How do *you* feel?"

"I feel fine, and so does Morgana." With tears brimming in her eyes, she cried, "Others might die if the child is too large. Maybe there's even more than one baby."

"Darling, don't cry, we'll find a solution," he comforted and hugged her, feeling an extreme anxiety unlike any he'd experienced in his life. He'd confidently assumed that he could manage any complications created by mixing their two worlds. After all, the controversy had arisen on Alterra precisely because their genetics were fundamentally the same. The fact that pregnancy would cause extreme agony was something he hadn't foreseen. Ruling requires making difficult decisions, and he was accustomed to doing so with the detached reflection ingrained in him by his family. This matter was personal, and his stomach clenched in tight knots.

In the ensuing month, Alana frantically raced to prepare for the births. She knew that since the conceptions had occurred around the Rite of Summer and they'd begun showing at the same time, the babies would likely be born about the same time.

Kamean came to the Great House to help Vesta, but delirious with pain, she screamed, "You did this to me, you monster."

Akia, her eyes red and swollen and her dark hair deeply tangled, screamed at Tamiel, "Go away. All you want is the baby, you don't care about me." She picked up a cup filled with water and threw it at him. Distressed, Tamiel backed away.

Although willing to help, but with the women's stares and complaints not the least bit welcoming, men guiltily hovered outside the Great House. Jared silently passed them by, entering the Great House to take dinner to Maya. She tried to sit up and smile, not blaming him, but she was in too much pain to do so. Disturbed after listening to their anguish, Jared led the men to Lil's rooms. The usually impeccable Rameel was disheveled, with dark circles under his eyes. In anguish, he said, "Lil, what's going wrong? Why is my wife in so much pain? Yanni had several children before without any problems."

His face showing his deep worry and lack of sleep, Lil replied quietly, "I don't know."

"Can't we do something?" demanded Jared. "I wish we had better medicine." He paced with agitation, running his hand through his greasy hair. "I feel responsible."

Rameel grimly expressed their unspoken fear. "My wife is in so much pain that I'm afraid she'll die when the baby grows much more. Lil, we must remove the babies. If I have to choose between her and the baby, I choose her. She trusted me. We'll have to find another way to have children."

Tamiel, in anguish, said, "I agree. I can't bear the screaming. I wouldn't have mated if I'd known it might kill her."

"What if the women die but the babies live?" Rameel worried. "How would we feed them all until they can take solid food? We have no wet nurses, and using goat's milk is risky without experimentation. Unless we plan ahead, they all might end up dying no matter what we do."

Lil had no answer. He had no medical equipment. All they had were Alana's herbs, which were not solving the problem. He stared quietly with guilt. Being focused on preserving their civilization with women who seemed so like them, in their haste they hadn't thought through what might happen. They had simply taken the plunge.

"I'll think of something," he numbly assured them.

After the men left, an exhausted Alana waddled in and collapsed on their pallet. Lil spent the night pacing, trying to devise a plan. Toward dawn, he finally drifted off to sleep but found no respite. He dreamed of babies born with deformities, some with single eyes, rendering them uncontrollable beasts, not the proud Alterran lineage he'd anticipated. He shouted "No!" and Alana shook him awake.

"Lil, you're soaking wet, you're having a nightmare," cried Alana, shaking him. Lil had been so unflappable that his fears accelerated her own anxiety. "What's wrong?"

"It's nothing," he assured her as his mind cleared, becoming as calm as possible. Inside, he couldn't forget the horrific images. When Alana arose the next morning to begin her long day caring for the moaning women, he remembered when, at the cave, he'd convinced her to have her survivors meet with his men. He'd sought to remove her stress. His men were rescuers. Overconfident they were. In truth, they saved them from the cold only to die in childbirth. The bitterness of failure stung in his mouth.

He took the only action left. Swallowing his pride, he sought Ki's help. He went deep within his consciousness. After a while, the message floated back that Ki was busy, but he would go to the Library to be alone. Soon, he felt Ki probing his mind. He projected memories of moaning, pregnant women with overly large bellies and Alana describing their pain. He showed Ki his memory of his men's fear of losing their wives.

"They're all in trouble, except for Atlanteans Alana and Morgana. We *must* have the babies removed surgically as soon as possible. I know the medical chambers aren't working. Can you think of *any* way to perform the surgery?"

After a long silence, Ki replied, "I know nothing about delivering babies." The Teacher would be of no help in delivering babies without advanced medical equipment. "I'm here in the Library. I'll see what I can learn."

Ki was dubious that a situation this delicate could be solved by finding an article in an old text, but he had no other idea at the moment. He scanned a few things, grew frustrated not finding what he needed, and decided nevertheless to try the Teacher. But the Teacher simply informed him to position the expectant mother in the medical treatment chamber. He hurried back to the Library with a supply of beverages, prepared to spend the night.

Seeing him scurry down the unused corridor, his mother followed, pushing behind him through the Library door and demanding, "Ki, darling, with all you have to do, why are you losing sleep camped here looking at these old books? Can't your scribes do this? I'm worried about you. You're going to make yourself sick."

"Mother, I'm fine. This is nothing for you to worry about." Ki tried to close the medical books he'd left out, but she swiftly stuck her finger where he'd been reading. "Mother, please, this is none of your business."

"Everything is my business," she said absently while she perused the ancient pages. "Why, this is about surgery to remove babies from the womb!" She looked up and squinted to study his face. "No one here is pregnant," she reasoned, "so why are you burning the midnight oil reading this?"

Suddenly her eyes grew wide, and she collapsed into a chair. "It's Lil's wife, isn't it? They were married around the summer solstice, weren't they?" she said as she began to count the months on her fingers. "My stars, if she conceived right away, she'd be nearly ready to deliver." She put her hand on Ki's arm. "Well, am I right? Is this for Lil?"

Ki blinked with exhaustion. He didn't want to tell her, but he couldn't conceive of any possible way to help Lil without her. "You're right, it's for Lil. But it's not for his wife. I gave each guardsman a fertility shot, and it worked far better than I'd hoped. They impregnated nearly all their brides on their wedding night. The women must ovulate at the same time by living so closely together."

"Why that's wonderful, I think," she said, frowning. Pointing to the book, she asked, "So why are you reading about surgical extractions? Our two peoples aren't blending well?"

Ki repeated Lil's story. "Just a short while ago, they celebrated their good fortune, and now the women call them monsters."

"Sounds terrible," said Uras, drumming her fingers on the table. "There must be something we can do."

Ki pointed to the book and said, "Before the chambers, they removed babies surgically, and everything usually turned out fine. Not surprisingly, the ancient items required aren't available through the replicator."

"Let me see," demanded Uras. She perused the old text, its pages thin with deterioration, while Ki looked for other reference works. "There's an incredible wealth of information here, Ki. Very detailed. I've been getting better at these old practices. We need equipment, though." She pondered what she had that might be repurposed. "I've got some ideas." Uras searched the infirmary storeroom, picking through discarded items from the early outposts. At the rear, she discovered nine bulky bags. "Whatever are these old, dusty things?" she said aloud. Reading the tags, she exclaimed, "I don't believe it. These are from Eridu!" Since the first Earth outpost hadn't had power to energize a medical chamber, the Alterrans had created special medical equipment. She opened the bags and laid the contents on the floor. "I wish I'd found this stuff before," she muttered, thinking that she might have saved some colonists. "This is perfect. Now, I just need Ki to rig up a power device, with batteries or something." With excitement, she raced through the internal transport to the Library where Ki lay napping. She gently patted his shoulder to rouse him. "Ki, sorry, I know you need your sleep, but you'll want to hear this. I think we can put together everything we need. I can do this!"

"Are you sure?"

"No, I'm not sure, but I think so. I'm going to need help, of course."

Ki had to agree, since this was beyond his capabilities. Although creation of a surgical field hospital was new for her, she devoted herself to the task. She told Anu that she was spending nights on the observation deck praying for the colonists, and Anu understood. She thoroughly reread the old texts and swore Kosondra and Schwara to secrecy. They synthesized necessary medications and practiced the surgery on holographs. Ki planned to bring a replicator, just in case there was something in its catalog that was needed. Completing their preparations, they had Dalits secretly move equipment to a hovercraft to await their departure.

One afternoon, Alana returned to Lil's workroom, collapsed in a chair, and sobbed. "Lil, they're being ripped apart!"

He carried her to their bed. "Alana, my sweet, don't cry. You've done everything you can. You're exhausted. Your own time has come. Stay here, and I'll take care of the rest."

"What do you mean?" she murmured groggily. "What can you do? I can't rest now; they need me." She attempted to rise, but fell back.

He assured her, "Rest, my love. Worry only about our child."

"But—"

"Rest! I've arranged for help from my people. My mother is a healer, and she's coming with help. Everything will be fine."

"Everything will be fine?" Alana said, drifting off to sleep.

After controlling his raw emotions, Lil linked with Ki, projecting his thoughts in his usual command style. "The women are critical. How soon can you get here?"

Uras, Schwara, and Kosondra prepared to leave at dusk, and Ki and Laurina came to assist. When the hovercraft door opened, Lil hugged his mother. "Peace and Harmony, Mother! I've missed you."

"I've missed you, too," she said, smiling and hugging him. "Peace and harmony, darling."

The tension showed on his face. "The situation is critical. Yamin and the men will get everything unloaded for you."

"Show me around so that I can find the best location." Taking charge, Uras selected the spot for her surgical center. Schwara put up sterile tents illuminated with glowglobes. Yamin set up the surgical tables. Kosondra produced a supply of soft linens, gauze, and blankets, and ordered the men milling around outside to boil water to sterilize the instruments. The medicines they brought with them were laid out for injection to calm the women and deaden pain during the procedure. Having no experience with Earth patients, they made educated guesses on dosage.

The medical team walked the rows of pallets in the Great House, assigning each patient a number signifying how critical she was. Tamiel and Kamean transported patients on Uras's mini-hover to her surgical tent. Laurina and Ki, wearing surgical garments, prepped each one. Uras rotated among three tables, performing surgery aided by her medical robot, while supervising Kosondra and Schwara performing surgery. Yamin, having donned sterile clothing, handed them instruments and coordinated with Rameel and Jared, who sterilized instruments outside in their boiling water.

As each healthy baby was born, the child was wrapped in linen and handed to the baby's father with great happiness. A few were less developed, and Laurina watched over them in incubators powered by Ki's batteries.

When Alana experienced labor pains, she whispered to Lil, "I want to try it naturally. I didn't have the pain of the others."

"Alana, are you sure?" asked Lil with concern, stroking her hair, which was wet with sweat. "I don't want you to take any chances."

"Grandmother Marita has birthed all the babies in our village. I'll be fine," she assured him.

"I know what to look for," said Marita, her wrinkly, kind face exuding her confidence. "If I need help, I'll call your mother immediately."

Alana lay beside Morgana, who also wanted to give birth naturally. Marita ordered Azazel to bring the birthing chairs. Following Marita's direction, he put them at the edge of the Great House's center platform, removing the chair Lil used for governing. Marita laid a pile of boiled wool nearby.

Examining her patients and timing their contractions, she instructed, "Alana will deliver first, but they're both near time. Help them into the chairs." Marita helped each woman settle into a birthing chair, moving her hips so that her vagina appeared over the hole. Then she gently positioned their arms on each chair's arms. "For good luck, dear, gaze upon the healthy baby carved right here on the arm. When the contractions come strong, grip the nub with all your might and bear down. Now watch me. This is the way you breathe and push."

To Lil and Azazel, Marita directed, "Since there are no free women, I need each of you to help. I don't normally use men, but I have no choice."

Watching their shock, she laughed. "Don't worry, I'll tell you what to do. For now, just comfort your wives and gently rub their backs." The men gave each other worried looks but followed orders.

"My contractions are close," warned Alana between deep breaths. "It won't be long."

"I think I'll be a little bit longer," said Morgana, although she winced with a new contraction. The first time she'd given birth, she had lain on her pallet screaming for over a day since the Danes had no herbs to give her. The midwives had moved her from side to side until the baby slid down the birth canal.

Marita left for a moment and returned with flat bowls and two cups of tea. Jared followed behind her with boiling water. She laid the bowls on the floor. "Pour the water in each bowl," she directed. After Jared did so, she slid a steaming bowl under each chair. "The steam will ease the delivery," she explained. Handing each a cup, she said, "I made a tea using the root of vervain for each of you, just as you instructed, Alana, dear."

Leaving, Jared called, "Good luck to you both." He wished Maya were doing as well as they were.

Alana reached for the hot tea but dropped the hot cup with a scream.

Lil flinched in shock. "What's wrong?"

Marita massaged Alana's shoulders and snapped, "If you jump like that every time she screams, you'll be of no help. You must gently encourage her, make her comfortable, and during a contraction, hold her arms firmly but not too tightly while she's pushing." She demonstrated what Lil should do, breathing rhythmically along with Alana.

"Where will you be?" he asked uncertainly.

"Me? I've got to catch the baby," she said with a chuckle. She felt Alana's swelling. "The baby's got a strong kick. That's a good sign." She felt Morgana and said, "Your baby is strong, too. It's a good thing for me they won't come at the exact same time."

During the next hour, Marita had Jared refresh the bowls of hot water and provide more tea, while Lil and Azazel did their best to comfort their moaning wives.

Alana screamed again. "Coming," she panted, gripping the chair arms and pushing out short breaths.

Marita moved the bowl and stepped down from the platform so that she could reach underneath the chair to grab the baby. "Lil, this is it. You've got to help her bear down and push during the next contraction."

"Alana, my love," he whispered, "push hard the next time."

"I am pushing!" she screamed.

With Marita urging him not to give up, he encouraged her. "It'll be over soon. Just push a little harder." Alana gripped the nub and pushed until her knuckles were white. When the contraction was over, she relaxed, sweat running down her face. Another contraction soon followed, and she pushed even harder.

"Push a little more, dear," Marita soothed her. "The baby's head is crowning."

Alana closed her eyes and directed all her energy to her lower muscles. With the next push, the baby dropped into Marita's outstretched arms. She cut the umbilical cord, cleaned the baby, and gave it a little spank.

Alana groaned and rested her head. "What sex is it?"

"A boy," she said as the newborn cried. "He's got excellent lungs." She tightly wrapped the fourteen-pound baby in the linen lined with boiled wool and handed him to Lil. "Here he is. Hold his head like this." She demonstrated holding the newborn's delicate head. "He looks just like you."

Lil stood speechless, swaying with his baby in his arms. His heart swelling with happiness, he could only grin at his family likely a silly Earthling.

Marita wiped her hands. "Alana, let me help you lie down so that you can nurse him." After helping Alana, she took the fussy baby from Lil. "This little one is hungry." She laid the baby at Alana's breast, and the baby tried to suckle. "Don't worry, he'll learn." Marita moved her finger to help the baby catch his mother's nipple.

Morgana experienced strong contractions but hadn't wanted to interfere with Alana's delivery. Unable to hold back, she let out a little scream and blew puffs of breath, panting, "Soon!"

Feeling her belly, Marita said, "Azazel, quick. You've watched Lil, so you'll be an expert." Marita stood on the floor behind her chair and removed the bowl.

"Oh, my!" she said. "I see the crown already. Push, dear."

Azazel kissed her forehead and put his hands over hers. "I'm here, just relax and push."

Morgana closed her eyes, pushing. She felt the baby slip down the birth canal.

"Caught her," boasted Marita, triumphantly.

Azazel, strangely tongue-tied, stammered, "A girl?"

"That's right, you lucky man," Marita said, giving her a little spank and wiping her. Azazel gingerly lifted exhausted Morgana from the chair and laid her on her pallet. "Here you go," Marita said, gently putting the fifteen-pound baby into Azazel's waiting arms. Azazel, his rugged face beaming, strutted around Morgana's pallet as if he'd been declared the supreme leader. Sharing happy glances with Lil, he exclaimed, "I can't believe it! I'm holding my own child in my arms. And she's so beautiful!"

After Marita adjusted Alana's pillows, Alana sat up, cradling her peacefully sleeping baby in her arms. Lil stood at her side, gently smoothing her hair and gazing at his child. "Isn't he wonderful, Lil? Ten fingers and toes. Everything is just where it should be. Who would have thought people of two planets could come together like this? Since I gave birth naturally, maybe I have Alterran blood?"

"Maybe you do," Lil murmured, not taking his eyes off his remarkable son. He sighed; a ruler always has a duty to attend. "Since everything is all right here, I should check on my mother's progress."

"That's fine. I'm *so* glad she came." She gave him an ecstatic smile.

"Yes, I'm glad too," said Lil softly, beaming with pride.

Uras and her staff were able to save all but a few of the pregnant women, whose deaths caused everyone considerable sorrow in the midst of their joy. Of the five who died, two of their babies could be saved, and Schwara and Kosondra offered to take them back to Hawan. Alana insisted that the women at Khamlok would prefer to raise them.

In examining the babies, Uras observed that a few had abnormalities. Some had extra fingers or toes, and she sensed that a few might have other problems by failing to cry. A couple had misshapen heads, although she thought their cranium might yet develop properly. Only time would tell. When the last of the women had given birth, an exhausted medical team collapsed around the hearth fire, with many of the guardsmen standing near, holding their babies. Jared brought them freshly made stew.

"Ki, how are people faring at Hawan?" Lil asked, fearful of the answer.

"The situation has stabilized," said Ki. "Mother discovered new, or rather old, medical treatments for the contagion, and no one has died since she began treatment. Without the guardsmen, the nourishment bar supply is lasting longer, and everyone fits into the usable living space. So we're doing all right for now."

Rameel presented his sleeping babe, showing him off to everyone. "Uras, I can't thank you enough. Yanni is doing fine, and so is my son. Ki, before you go, could we recharge our recorders from your batteries?"

"We won't need the incubators much longer, so sure," he nodded.

"Fantastic idea, Rameel!" said Jared. He knew all the men would welcome the opportunity to make a record of their babies.

"Ki, I noticed you brought a replicator," said Rameel. "In my recorder, I've stored most of the Alterran legends. Some of them have implements that would be useful. If I were to project a hologram from a story, can you connect with the replicator and create permanent objects?"

He rubbed his chin, thinking it over. "That should work. I don't have the molecules for these items stored in the replicator, but I should be able to synthesize them at Hawan. Rafael could deliver the products."

"Great, I'll be right back," said Rameel, carefully handing his child to Marita.

The eyes of those remaining at the hearth were drawn back to the Great House. "I don't want it!" they heard Akia scream hysterically. "It's not human." Tamiel's baby had been one born with extra toes and fingers and a disfigured head.

Kamean, returning his eyes to Uras, showed her his baby. "Thank you, Uras. Vesta wouldn't have made it without you." The child had an extra toe on each foot, but the happy parents didn't care.

Suddenly, everyone grew silent and parted as Alana and Lil came forward with their baby, and Alana, her silver headband gently tinkling, gingerly put the swaddled babe into Uras's eagerly outstretched arms. Although Alana tried to keep her eyes respectfully low, she longed to learn about this great healer who was now her second mother, of whom Lil had spoken with admiration.

"Mother, here's your first grandson," said Lil softly. During the intensity of the birthing process, Uras hadn't had time think about Lil, although she'd kept looking in surgery for someone named Alana. Now tears streamed down her face as she proudly admired her first grandchild, who struggled to open an eye, giving her a little frown. Ki gave Lil a pat on the back, grinning happily. Ki felt as invested in this plan as Lil was.

"Oh, how beautiful!" Uras gently rocked him while gazing at his peaceful slumber, stirring long-forgotten memories of her first delightful moments with Ki and Ninhursag. "Except that he's got your lovely green eyes, Alana." She kissed his forehead, briefly closing her eyes. Perhaps she should have more children—if Anu would accept that they lived beyond the Ens' dictates now; her people needed more children, and she needed someone to love. "He's *so* very precious. He looks as intelligent as his father and uncle."

"And his mother, of course," said Ki, giving Alana an elegant, brotherly smile.

"What will you name this darling child?" Uras asked, gently stroking the child, and then she reluctantly handed him back into Alana's outstretched arms. Alana has a commanding presence, she thought. I wish I could get to know her.

Alana hesitated, anxiously biting her lower lip, not wanting to hurt the feelings of this kind woman, to whom she owed many lives. "Mother, I beg your forgiveness, but our custom is not to reveal the name until the naming ceremony. I am unclean at the moment." She wasn't sure what would happen if she broke custom.

Looking hurt, Uras demanded, "When will this naming ceremony be? After we rest a bit, I need to pack up and return to Hawan. Lil, I've missed too much of your new life already!" Her eyes pleaded with him to include her.

Alana nodded her head and said thoughtfully, "I understand, these are unusual times. I think our ancestors would understand."

"You're the Earthkeeper, Alana," Maya prodded her softly. "You decide our customs."

With a nod from Lil, Alana said, "All right, I'll improvise. Tomin, quickly, get your flute." The lanky boy flew to his mother's hut and returned a few moments later, breathing deeply but still able to play. Listening to his melody, Alana nodded to Maya to begin the chant. Near the foundation of the Great House, Alana squatted and swept loose dirt into her cupped hand. Returning to the others, she hummed with Maya's ethereal soprano voice. At the song's conclusion, she sprinkled grams of soil over her newborn's pure, white forehead and gently made a double circle, her people's cherished symbol for the continuous bounty of Mother Earth. Although the baby's eyes opened a slit at the disturbance, he didn't whimper. "Great Mother Earth, we pray that you will bless our son, grant him a long, full life with plentiful food, and grant him many children and friends. May he honor the Mother and his ancestors, whether they live on Earth or Alterra. Our baby is loved by Lil, his father, by me, his mother, my dear friend-sisters, Grandmother Uras, Uncle Ki, and by Grandfather Ewan and countless ancestors watching down on us from the spirit world. Mother, with your blessing, we give the baby the great name of Iskur, which ties my world with the world of my precious baby's father." Alana then kissed Iskur on the cheek and held him up to Lil, Uras, and Ki for a welcoming kiss.

Lil took Iskur into his arms and held him up to the sky. "In the name of Alterra and of Anu, my father, and all my forebears of the House of En, I celebrate the birth of my son and his naming as Iskur. May his name be a guide to a new path bridging both our worlds, and may peace and harmony reign in his heart." To Iskur's blanket, he pressed the Ens' sacred triangle and axis line, but in the background was Alana's symbol for Earth, the double circle. He presented his son to his people. "I give you Iskur, true son of the House of En." Uras exchanged a worried glance with Ki.

After the ceremony, Uras drew Lil apart. "Iskur," she mused, narrowing her eyes as she studied his determined face. Lil had changed in more ways that his choice of clothing. He'd always been dutiful, but he'd truly come into his own as a leader. "A vaguely familiar name, but not one used by our House." After a moment, it suddenly came to her, and she snapped her fingers. "He was one of our primeval heroes, right?"

Lil winced. "Iskur was a great explorer and seeker of truth. His time wasn't primeval, Mother. It was simply long ago."

"Interesting," she answered, contemplating the meaning of such an unprecedented choice. Interesting how much he'd changed, or so it seemed. She'd been too busy before to see beyond her patients. She gazed about, studying the uniform huts arranged in circular form around the Great Hut, and the city's eclectic inhabitants adorned in well-made animal hides. If she didn't know better, she'd have thought that a city of this size would have taken decades to construct. Lil had completed it in only a few months. The people looked not only healthy, but happy. They were nothing like the ignorant, filthy primitives she'd always pictured from her son's stories. With admiration, she looked again at Lil. "You've accomplished a miracle here, son. If our colonists must relocate, you've made it very easy. I'm certain that was your plan along."

Lil squeezed her arm for the compliment.

"One other thing." From a bag at her side, she handed him a triangular, coarse crystal that was amethyst in color.

Puzzled, he raised a single eyebrow as a question.

"I had Ki make something for your protection. Naturally, it's far beyond what I'd envisioned. It's attuned to only your brain waves. You can create a small Net about your person, providing a power source and a miniature replicator. It can produce an assortment of weapons."

Lil grunted, looking faintly cross. "I take care of everything."

"Of course, you do, darling. I'm your mother; humor me! I'm too tired to argue. Don't use it if you don't need it."

She looked exhausted, so Lil nodded and handed the crystal to Yamin. "Mother, thank you for everything. You saved us from disaster. With all these healthy babies and our wives recovering—it's the most incredible feeling. The babies..." he was too choked up to continue.

"Will ensure that Alterra lives on," Azazel finished his sentence, stepping by his side.

Uras, in her exhaustion, felt content; medicine was more satisfying when results were produced by her skill. After resting, she and her aides began to pack up.

"Ki, if I could bother you a moment," said Rameel, anxious not to let Ki go without getting things he needed. "Let's see if this works." He projected an image of a primitive village and isolated a wooden butter churn, an apple press, and an ancient device driven by horses used for crushing grain.

Ki paused, dismayed that Rameel showed no sign of obeisance. Wanting Khamlok to turn out well, he nevertheless programmed the replicator to absorb the items' molecular structures. "I have it," he said, the slight upturn of his lips betraying mockery. "Anything else?"

Eager for supplies, Rameel wasn't deflected by Ki's tone. "Actually, we could use as much insulated piping as you could spare." What Rameel wanted most was a decent bathhouse, with plenty of luxurious hot water. Ki snickered. He'd make Rameel pay another time for not displaying the proper deference.

Uras hurried toward him and interrupted, passing floating boxes being levitated into the hovercraft. "Ki, this old medical equipment might help me treat our people. Schwara, where is Kosondra?"

"She's with Yamin," Schwara said, nodding her head toward the shadows with a smirk.

"Oh," said Uras, hoping that she wouldn't lose a valued assistant to the lure of the wild. "We can't wait for long."

Before leaving, Uras cradled her grandson in her arms again. "Mother, if I may call you that," said Alana softly, her eyes downcast when she took back her child. She felt awed by Lil's mother. Not only was she a powerful healer, but she was also the wife of a planetary ruler. She far exceeded even Priestess Petrina's rank.

Uras hesitated, sensing Alana's vulnerability. Lil's arrangement with her was new to both of them. Uras hadn't thought of this young, alien woman as a family member. "Yes, of course, darling," she said, not wanting to hurt her feelings.

Alana brightened and smiled happily. "Then, you'll visit us? In our villages, grandmothers are treasured."

"If I can. My people depend on me, and I might not be able to get away." Uras looked away, avoiding Alana's eyes. Anu firmly believed that they'd return to Alterra. If he was right and Lil was wrong, what would she do?

"Oh, I understand," she said, her enthusiasm deflated. "When Lil made his proposal, he explained that we couldn't come to your home because we wouldn't be accepted."

"Did he?" She arched her eyebrows and crossed her arms over her chest. This was, as she'd long suspected, the reason for Lil's dramatic middle-of-the-night escape. He hadn't included her, and now she was expected to forgive all and ignore the complications?

"If you can find the time, it would be wonderful. Iskur needs to know about the greatness of all his ancestors. If not, I'm sure that Lil will teach him." Alana's grip on Iskur tightened protectively. *I will always be there for you, little one.*

Seeing Ki motion that he was ready to leave, Uras anxiously said her last good-byes, relieved to be getting back. She fretted that she hadn't been gone so long that Anu had come looking for her. Impatiently, she saw that Kosondra still lingered with Yamin, refusing to acknowledge her hand signals to leave. Sharply calling to her, Uras prevailed.

During the following months, the mothers made a full recovery. At first, they kept the babies in the dimness of the Great House, in case their eyes were sensitive to light. As they experimented, they discovered that the eyes of only a few needed to be shielded. None of the babies' skin was luminous, and none had the pure white hair of their space-traveling fathers.

CHAPTER 12
ANU

When Uras entered her suite, she discovered Anu waiting for her, holding a rare drink and looking disheveled for the first time since she'd known him. "Where've you been?" he demanded, glaring with those cobalt blue eyes that his people found so compelling. Uras, exhausted, didn't appreciate his tone and avoided his stare. For one who spent his days meditating, he didn't miss a thing. Her husband was losing his grip, disappointing her. Not wanting to fight, she considered running off to live with Lil and his new family. That wouldn't be so bad, would it? Well, maybe it would. Lil might find living in the wilderness a marvelous adventure, but she preferred indoor plumbing, at least for now. After all, Lil would have faced disaster without her.

Continuing to glare and following her around the room, he raised his voice. "In case you didn't hear me, where have you been?"

She decided he'd find out eventually. "I assisted in birthing the guardsmen's children. Lil's wife, Alana, gave birth without my help. You have your first grandson. His name is Iskur." Ignoring his fury, she continued while unpacking, "Surgical removal was required for almost all. Alana and our grandson are doing fine. Lil is enormously happy, and so am I. They built a very nice city. They've plowed fields, begun a vineyard, and started a new life. Who would have thought them capable of all this in such a short time? It's impressive. It's not as primitive as you might imagine. Rather pastoral, actually." She paused, remembering the city. "They have a little mountain behind them, and nearby is the cutest little stream—"

"Pastoral," he spat. His pulse had quickened as she spoke. Now he trembled. "He actually had a child with an Earth woman?" His upper lip curled with contempt. "That child is an abomination of nature! A freak!" Hawan was crumbling around him, Alterra might be lost to him forever, and now this, the cruelest blow of all. He had personally trained Lil to follow in his footsteps as the noble leader he was destined to be. By abandoning not only his post, but also his destiny as successor—a destiny written in the stars—he'd made a mockery of Anu, his family, Alterra, the Universal Consciousness, everything. His family had molded society to their vision for eons. They'd achieved a level of technology unique in the universe. Had he no faith? Of course, Alterrans would recover. Anu and his family, the Council, and all the colonists would return home. The scribe reports said so. When they recovered, did Lil think they'd let a primitive Earth savage be in line to the Alterran leadership? He was handing the House of Kan a golden opportunity to claim the successorship. There would be war again. He staggered to the wall and slid to the floor in his pain. After all these ages, it would be his unpardonable shame to see the House of En come to the end of its rule. Bitter, he swallowed his drink to dull his senses.

Speechless, Uras tugged at her earlobe, searching for a compromise. She loved Anu and understood his deep devotion to his family's principles. His belief in Alterra's recovery was steadfast. She wanted to comfort her anguished husband, but she believed in Lil as well. Just as firmly, Lil believed that his new city was the sole path to preserve their civilization. "Anu, you should try to understand Lil," she admonished.

His face contorted with rage, Anu pulled himself to his feet. "I understand things perfectly. The named successor denies his cosmic destiny and fathers an abomination, thereby disobeying and bringing disgrace, shame, and disaster on himself and all Alterrans." He pointed his finger menacingly in Uras's face. "And my wife wants me to 'understand Lil,'" he mocked. "So you're abandoning me too?"

She hadn't planned to move out, but she took the hint. "Lil didn't cause the disaster, he just dealt with it." *Which is more than I can say for you.* While Anu poured another drink, she repacked, planning to sleep at the infirmary. She had no regrets. With only tragedy on the horizon, Lil had seized his one chance for life. He hadn't abandoned Alterra; he'd taken what he could from the dying colony and preserved it, to live in this planet's legends.

As the door closed, Anu made up his mind to prepare an edict.

En.Lil and the old Guard are traitors to Alterra. They have committed unspeakable offenses. Their children are abominations. They are subject to the highest penalty of Alterran law. Judgment and retribution is upon them. They may never return to Hawan. No one may speak, assist, or aid them in any manner. They are to be imprisoned upon sight. Henceforth, En.Ki is the named successor – it is written in the stars.

En.Anu, Leader of Hawan
First Named Successor to the Supreme Leader of Alterra

When the message appeared on Uras's monitor, she cried in disbelief, "No!" The House of En was all powerful, she fumed. Didn't the Alterran Code apply to Anu? Was he above the law? That stupid edict wouldn't prevent her from helping her son.

CHAPTER 13
YAMIN

Excerpts from Lil's history, as recorded by Yamin:
I decided to mark time beginning with our first summer solstice at Khamlok. That was, for us, the beginning of a new civilization.

. . . .

In Year 2, we honored the summer solstice with a ceremony at Khamlok, although the day was too cloudy to see the sun. Each baby, now three months old, was presented in the naming ceremony, at which I presided with Alana as our Earthkeeper. Jared gave his son the name Krishna.

. . . .

Despite the coolness of the air and our short growing season, with Ki's help, the fields are once again full of grain, our orchards bear fruit, and our vineyards are bursting with grapes. Our women work the many fine hides and furs that our hunters bring. Some day, we may use our surplus for trade. Perhaps we can find the former Atlanteans that Alana speaks of.

. . . .

Our women, along with our growing infants, greatly enjoy playing in the warm bathhouse, since it has turned cold early again.

. . . .

It is becoming apparent that a few infants are experiencing uncontrollable bouts of crying and flailing of their arms. Alana is working with the mothers to develop a soothing herbal drink. The parents of these infants are greatly distressed. Tamiel's wife is not taking well to the abnormalities of her infant.

. . . .

The women have created pens for the sheep and goats that are plentiful in this area since they are fed with our grain by-products. The goats supply milk that we use to make Rameel's bread, and the children are particularly fond of it. The sheep are dirty, but their fur, when boiled, produces soft wool that the women make into clothing and bedding.

. . . .

In Year 3, to honor the summer solstice, Rameel organized our first athletic competitions and a theater piece to teach the young about our beloved Alterra. There was archery and horseracing. As usual, Azazel won them all, although Kamean actually gave him competition in archery. As part of the theater piece, Maya sang, accompanied by our musicians Yamin, Tomin, Rameel, and Yanni. Koko visited and told us that a new city is growing on the mainland. Perhaps they may have something to trade in the near future.

. . . .

Morgana and Yanni bring the youngsters together every day to learn storytelling, much of it telling their knowledge of history. Other youngsters are taught by their parents.

. . . .

Although the winters grow ever colder and the summers ever shorter, we continue to be blessed once again with full fields, orchards, and vineyards. Rameel continues to seek improvements. He now houses many pigeons in a building near the fields, and he is converting their droppings into fertilizer.

. . . .

The women are fearful of pregnancy when they stop nursing their young, as am I. Except for our Atlanteans. I am hopeful that my lovely Alana will again conceive.

. . . .

Our city has grown in part because Azazel continues to take in people of the peninsula, many of whom are near starvation. They are disruptive.

CHAPTER 14

DROOD

In the fourth year after the dragon, a dry, unnaturally frigid autumn wind swept down from the forbidding highlands of the north, where long ago those who left had followed the herds to the lush land reclaimed from the receding glacier. Or so the storytellers said. Such people hadn't been seen by any of Drood's tribe alive today. Even though the mountains had protected highlanders from the comet's direct mayhem, the growing cold had burned the lush highlands to an ugly brown. Many had died. Seeing no end to their misery, the highlanders straggled down the abandoned migration trails. At midday, a thousand starving men, women, and children gathered their courage to ignore the skeleton warnings and cross Drood's meadow. They were motley Picts, Gaels, a few Celts, and others bearing unknown markings, who had met on the migration trail and forged a desperate alliance. Some men wore their greasy hair long, while others shaved the sides, leaving only a long topknot. A few families wore gray, furry hides dotted with white spots. United by their desperation, males and females alike bellowed war cries, threatening Drood's tribe with their most formidable stone axes and spears. The highlanders had grown much larger than Drood's men, even though most were now skeletal with hunger. Except for a few; the mighty ate first. Three grizzled, scarred men, their faces bearing resolve to take Drood's land at any cost, warily strode across the brown field, crunching the tall weeds. They cast a wary eye for hidden traps.

Unperturbed, Drood sprawled on the elevated wooden throne that he'd received as tribute from a western Celtic tribe, watching the intruders. Without Ewan's interference, Drood had secured loyalty oaths from the struggling tribes, and his influence was expanding south, touching tribes owing long-held allegiance to his nemesis, Yoachim. Beside Drood stood his son, Maku, and his bald priests, their long beards floating in the stiff breeze. His painted, well-fed warriors, who formed uneven lines behind him, stood motionless with their spears. They were unaccustomed to battles on an open meadow, pre-ferring to attack hidden from forests or to jump from secret windows that Drood had learned to open from the spirit world. Shadow warriors stalked the forest surrounding the meadow, where the prickly remnants of hardy flowers and underbrush had been trampled. The great, clawed paws of a white polar bear were draped carefully over Drood's shoulders, and the immense bear's fur hung down his back—impressive that mere men could overcome such a magnificent beast. On his head, he wore jewels embedded in boiled sheep's wool, and by his side on a narrow stone table stood his precious crystal. He'd broken the remnant from the ceiling of the crystal cave, the source of his powers. Seemingly unconcerned, he watched the highlanders approach. He could only decipher an occasional word that they uttered, but he had no trouble understanding their gestures. They jeered at the sight of Drood's distorted body, confident of an easy victory. They pointed to the ground, demanding his submission.

Drood chuckled and shifted in his chair, his voice perpetu-ally raspy, yet chilling even to those who admired him. He was amused by the ravens coming to roost in the trees nearest the meadow. Initially singles came, then pairs and small groups.

The sentinels squawked. It was the harmless sound of only a few gliding in the wind. Soon, however, entire flocks arrived, blackening the trees. The intruders glanced at the birds but paid them no mind, instead tapping the ground with their spears in a demand that Drood and his army submit. A one-eyed warrior, with a red scar that seared the length of his leathery cheek, laughed and thrust his finger sharply across his throat. Drood laughed in return and wagged his finger. Aided by his femur-bone cane, he stood. He picked up the inert crystal and majestically held it out in his palm. Slowly, it began to glow with increasing brightness. Unaccustomed to magic, the intruders eyed the crystal, keeping their confident grins. Drood chuckled again, casting his hand around the crystal, and then opened his fingers to reveal a glowing ball of fire. He held it up to his thin lips and gently blew. The ball shot from his hand and exploded a nearby bush, sending sparks and embers swirling in the brisk wind. Drood raised his eyebrows, signing whether the intruders wished another demonstration. They glanced at one another, but the tall one growled, and they firmed their stance and again tapped their spears in a demand for submission. To live, they had no choice but to settle on Drood's land.

Drood chuckled merrily and shrugged his shoulders, delighted to display his powers. He cast his hand around the crystal again, and then pointed to the sky. Lightning cracked and hit the ground, causing chunks of dirt to spray the intruders, leaving a shallow crater. After the shortest of the three turned to run, the tall one thrust his spear upward in defiance and then trotted behind. Drood stretched his arms toward the trees and signaled an attack through *mencomm* to a raven overlooked by the Alterran guardsmen. The lead raven chased the fleeing men with a fury of flapping wings and squawks. The flock encased their prey in a cape of death. Their screaming people scattered, sprinting as fast as possible from the pursuing ravens.

"Go, capture the docile ones, men and women alike," ordered Drood to his closest warriors. It was time that his dear wife, Weena, had a washwoman and a cook. Slaves would be useful for many reasons. "Fetch the woman who came to us last year, the one who speaks the language of these highlanders."

* * *

A painted warrior brought Sheban to him and threw her down at his feet. She hit her knees and groaned with pain. "You speak the intruders' language?" Drood demanded. After Sheban nodded her gray-haired head, he ordered, "Bring prisoners to me." With Maku's help, he descended from his throne and walked the line of prisoners. He stopped before a man whose markings he didn't recognize. Although large, the man kept his eyes submissively downcast, tightly grasping a woman and child. Less emaciated than their companions, they were warmly dressed in gray, spotted fur. "Ask them where they came from and what animal wore their furs."

With Sheban translating, the man replied, "We come from the most distant northern land, along the icy sea. Orkney we call it. We wear the furs of seals, which swim in the cold waters. The seals used to sun themselves on our shores in summer when the ice broke. Because there is no melting now, the seals swim farther south. We followed them along the coast."

"Where are they now?" Drood demanded.

"Not far."

"Are there many?"

"Yes. They live well in this weather."

"Tomorrow, show us," Drood ordered. Animals that thrive in an ice world would be extremely useful.

CHAPTER 15

AZAZEL

Koko strode through Khamlok, his mouth open with wonder. Each time he came, he was more fascinated by their ability to create wealth. His traveling had few stops these days, mainly to the struggling port cities and to King Azor's redoubt on the mainland. Elsewhere, the flood survivors were too poor for his trade; all their energy, if in fact they had any, was devoted to adapting to the weather, which grew colder and more inhospitable each year. The animals were leaner, and edible plants were more difficult to find. Only those who relied upon fishing were eking out a modest existence. Koko would have ceased the difficult journeys to the peninsula altogether if it weren't that Khamlok was such an enticing jewel. Thus, he visited frequently, bringing news, but creating material for his bard songs, which he retold wherever he traveled. Many a hearth was willing to trade hidden food stores for hearing about the wonder of Khamlok. In his epic stories, he told of Khamlok's magic and abundant food supplies. The unfortunate primitives who were banished by Lil spread the Khamlok tales throughout the impoverished peninsula.

The star of Koko's stories was Azazel, who was painted as the greatest warrior of all time, with unequalled skill and valor, wielding a magical sword called Caledfwilch, which glowed so intensely that enemies went blind at its sight. In Koko's tales, Azazel commanded a mighty, growing army. Believing the stories, starving men and women arrived daily, seeking their fortunes. Azazel, being flattered, thought he could train the new ones to defend the wall. Disturbed by tales of skirmishes by the primitive newcomers, Lil asked Yamin to bring Azazel to him.

"Good, Petus," Azazel roared, slapping him on the back. Petus, practicing with a wooden sword, had bested all the other new men, who lay groaning on the ground. One of the most muscular men to arrive in these lean times, he possessed a natural feel for the footwork and swinging of the metal swords that Azazel had manufactured in the smithy. On a hunting trip, Azazel had discovered a rocky mount containing metals mentioned in the ancient legends, and he'd found a text with sufficient detail that he could recreate the metal weapons. Plenty of starving young men were eager to learn and work over the hot fires. Few had been produced thus far, and the men regularly trained with the crude stone weapons that they brought with them.

"Azazel, Lil wants to see you," interrupted Yamin. "Why are you blocking *mencomm* again? It's such a nuisance." Yamin didn't come to the practice yards often, and he was surprised to see how many Earthmen there were engaging in swordplay, even practicing battle formations.

Although Azazel scowled at the interruption, he'd been supervising the practice throughout the day and needed a rest. Entering the Great House, he made a face when he saw the raised dais with Lil's chair. Lil looked down at a group of former guardsmen, giving orders. *This isn't the way it's supposed to be.* He hesitated, prepared to leave.

Seeing Azazel, Lil stepped down. "My old friend, come. Let's sit over here." He stretched out his arm toward one of the long tables. He poured him a drink. "Our wine remains a far cry from our Alterran wine, but it's pleasant in its own way. These things take time." Azazel noted to himself that Lil no longer gave the greeting of Peace and Harmony, nor the salute of the sacred triangle. Good riddance, he thought.

"Yes, things are indeed going well," nodded Azazel warily, enjoying the wine.

"Actually, that's what I need to speak to you about," said Lil. "I understand that yet again outsiders are coming here, even many more than before. Some say they desire to fight as warriors. I've heard that they actually believe we're developing an army." Showing his displeasure with his penetrating eyes, he said, "I wasn't aware that we were developing an army, were you?"

Azazel looked away uncomfortably. "We don't have an army, merely a defensive force. We don't know where our enemies may be, do we?" He stood and paced around. "That wall isn't impregnable. Morgana told me of the raiding parties of the Danes. Although they haven't been seen since the flood, it's inevitable that raiders will rise again." Putting his foot upon the seat, facing Lil, he challenged, "Wouldn't you agree that we should be prepared to defend ourselves?" Azazel searched Lil's face, seeking to understand his intentions.

Lil returned the intense gaze. He had no desire to adopt the Alterran practice of controlling the population through the food supply, but as the leader, he had to control through persuasion. "I agree with the wisdom of protecting our people. You've done an excellent job of providing sufficient meat for this growing city, and I didn't ask you here to criticize you, my old friend. I just wanted to have a friendly discussion about these new so-called warriors who are arriving." Lil looked out the window where they were congregating and pointed to them. "They have a wild look in their eyes. They're undisciplined. They won't be content if warfare is limited to defending the wall from a foe that might never appear. How do you intend to control them?"

"I won't tolerate troublemakers. I keep them busy with training exercises and hunting."

"More is required. We need to instill in them values of integrity and honor."

"We're working on that," said Azazel defensively.

"That may be," urged Lil, "but we need structure. I'm thinking that the time has come for us to take the next step for a lasting community." Lil came away from the window.

"The next step?" asked Azazel, suddenly realizing that Lil was confiding, rather than chastising him.

"Don't worry. I don't expect you to take on more duties. You're much too burdened as it is. To govern us, we need more formality. The informal Council that met once should commence regular meetings. Planning will be one of its duties. I, of course, want *you* to serve."

"Yes, of course, I would be honored," Azazel replied with pleasure but checked his emotion with a nagging doubt of being manipulated.

"Excellent." Lil clapped his hands with what Azazel perceived as uncharacteristic enthusiasm. "I personally treasure your insights. We need to integrate your natural sense for our defenses into a governing plan. I'll be calling the first meeting very soon. In the meantime, I trust that you'll keep a firm hand on those joining us. If you don't mind, I have many things to attend to." Lil headed back to his private rooms. Scowling, Azazel left.

Taking a long walk to mull things over, Azazel ended up by the river and began skipping stones across the water. What was Lil's plan? Was their success the result of his error or brilliance? If Lil's intention had been to control everything, as his family had done, then he needed to think of everything, didn't he? Azazel thought how he'd devoted long hours for the good of the city, filling a void, a serious void, left by Lil. Maybe it wasn't his fault; maybe it was too much for a single man, but if Lil insisted on personal control of all aspects of their lives, he had miserably failed. On the other hand, when they'd first arrived, Azazel had assumed they were deliberately leaving behind the old control structure, creating a new way of life in which everyone had a say in how things were handled. Hadn't Lil permitted them all to vote whether to leave Hawan? He'd said that each person had to agree to the plan. Azazel had thought this was proof of a new path. If a participatory system was, instead, Lil's plan, then he'd succeeded brilliantly. Which did he intend? Yes, much had been accomplished, and Khamlok was thriving. Azazel had demonstrated his leadership. The hunters, whom he had personally selected, trained, and nurtured, made the city prosperous, giving them a surplus of furs and hides, which were now available for trading with others. After all this, was Lil going to assert control? He threw more stones. Was he overreacting? Creating a council wasn't necessarily a step toward the old command structure. Perhaps it was an alternative, something new. Maybe Lil was brilliant. With their city's growth, it would be difficult to have each person vote on everything. He could influence this new system to preserve individual initiative and what was called, in the ancient legends he so loved, liberty. He threw the last stone. Was it more effective to be in the inner circle subtly influencing action than to be agitating for change from the outside?

CHAPTER 16
THE HARVEST

"Jared, we need more room; this one's full," teased Maya, having slipped her last load from her slender shoulder into the mountain of grain bags stuffing their large storage building. They, along with nearly everyone else at Khamlok, had spent days harvesting, threshing, and winnowing the plentiful grain crop, working feverishly to avoid the ruinous, stinging rain, although Azazel's black-haired people had borne the brunt of the menial labor. Ki's hybrid strains were one of the increasingly rare edible plants able to survive under the showers of acid rain that sometimes poured from the heavy, gray clouds. So delighted were the people at their abundant harvest that even Lil had lent a ceremonial hand. Jetrel, grumbling under his breath about being assigned Dalit work when Earth primitives were idle, was the only Anunnaki still working. He led two draft horses at turning the heavy circular grinder that created flour for bread. Having finished their work, the Anunnaki and their wives milled around enjoying a nip of Tamiel's newly made wine, his grape crop also being plentiful. Their children were given apple juice, fresh from the press. Prodded by Maya, Tomin began to play his flute, which he always wore hanging from his belt.

"Come on!" Maya said, giggling as she playfully tugged Vesta's and Kranya's arms and waved to Morgana to join them in the nearby clearing. A braid down each woman's back swung as they trotted to the clearing, inviting all the women to follow. Morgana had made a crown from discarded stalks, which she was weaving into Tara's braided, golden hair. Tara, though, frowned and complained impatiently for her mother to finish. Wearing her wooden sword sheathed in the toy scabbard across her back, she preferred to participate in the boys' chasing games. At Maya's urging, the women, even Grandmother Marita, soon held hands in a circle, where they danced the bouncy steps of the celebration dance. The dance had been performed at Summer Meetings of days past. When Erjat and Mika tried to break the hand chain to join the dance, Yanni and others scolded them so severely for interfering with a women's dance that they stumbled away as if they'd been burned. Azazel nearly fell over laughing at them. Mika refused to rejoin the laughing men, instead retrieving his drum. Akia was permitted entrance into the dance line, even though she'd stubbornly refused to help with the harvest. The mood was too festive to be wrecked by another tantrum. Schwee shuffled her feet and looked away from Akia, barely masking her disgust for Akia's laziness. Since Akia refused all work, Schwee made clothes for Tamiel and cooked his food, hoping he'd overlook her deformity and love her back, or at least permit her family to live with his; it wasn't unknown in their land for a man to have two mates. A few scraggly women who'd trailed after the black-haired men who'd followed Azazel squatted a distance away, their eyes inscrutably watching from beneath their matted hair. They did not attempt to join the dancers.

Milling around the new wine cask with the other men, Azazel took wagers for an impromptu archery contest. "Come on, Tamiel, what's your wager?" bantered Azazel.

"No more than a hide," argued Tamiel, shaking his head and spilling his overflowing wine cup. "No one can best Kamean."

"Two hides, it is," proclaimed Azazel, slapping him on the back with a big grin. "Your wife doesn't work them, anyway."

Tamiel grimaced. "Funny! Oh, sorry, Azazel, the cask just went dry." Tamiel turned away. Living with Akia was bad, but to have it joked about made life intolerable. If he could be readmitted to Hawan without being severely punished, he'd return instantly. Little Wini, Schwee's daughter, had been watching his toddler, Chigi. She carried his loudly protesting child, dropping the squirming, dirty child at his feet. "I'm sorry, but I can't handle him," she apologized, hurrying away. Tamiel sighed, consumed the remainder of his wine in a single gulp, and picked up the child. He massaged his back and gently bounced him, as it was the only method he'd discovered so far to pacify the child. "Let's go watch the dancing," he said kindly, resigning himself to another evening spent alone with Chigi.

"Alana, come join us," Maya lyrically called, spying her friend-sister coming from the Great House with little Iskur. Alana's flowing tresses covered her shoulders. She wore one of Morgana'a new soft-hide shifts, with the Khamlok crest embroidered on her chest. Her leather boots were laced to her knees. Maya and Vesta loosened their hands to welcome Alana, and she began skipping along to Tomin's merry music, which now included Mika on a drum. When Tomin finished the tune, Rameel joined him. The women's circle broke into two lines for trotting repeatedly through hand bridges.

Little Tara burst through the line, chasing an older boy. She began to overtake him at the clearing's edge, but she stopped, her face captivated by an apparition shimmering high above her head. She shouted, "Demons! Mother, it's the demons!"

The music stopped. Azazel threw down his cup and sprinted toward Tara, drawing his sword. Kamean flew behind with his long bow. Morgana screamed, "Tara, draw back!" Tara, undeterred, stood her ground, pointing to the shimmering air at the height of Azazel's head, with the strange distortion growing into a wagon-sized rectangle. The hazy images gradually became focused, revealing flat land draped by a stark, stony landscape, eerily lit.

A tall, muscular man, resembling Lil and wearing a long tan robe, stared down at them. His smile was crooked. His raspy, cackling laughter resounded throughout the clearing. "It's good to see you all again. Have you missed me? Or perhaps you don't recognize me with my new physique." Four shadows descended from the aperture, positioning themselves like pawns in a *treschet* game. "Demons!" screamed Tara, bravely pointing her little wooden sword.

"Warriors hide within the shadows," said Alana, seeing what others couldn't see.

"That's Drood's voice," Maya gasped, at first softly and then yelling at the top of her lungs, her hands cupped around her lips, "It's Drood!"

"He travels through the spirit world, defiling it," said Alana with disgust. She felt the evil taint of Drood's presence. She muttered, "I must cleanse the spirit world of your taint."

Drood scowled and then cackled again, defiantly throwing off his cloak to reveal molded, silver armor. "The spirit world belongs to me!" Alana narrowed her eyes with hatred. *He has such power. Is he stronger than I?*

Rameel attempted to shepherd the women, who remained in their dance lines, shouting, "Everyone, move back and huddle together! Yanni, take the women and children to the Great House." Being engrossed with the apparition, no one could move. From a sheath under her skirt, Morgana withdrew a knife, which glowed like her sword—a present from Azazel. She moved cautiously forward.

Not slowing his pace, Kamean snapped another arrow from the quiver on his back and smoothly aimed at a shadow. Like pure air, it sailed cleanly. Azazel sprang through the air, swinging his great, gleaming sword above his head and cutting the right corner of the apparition's undulating border. His sword sparked with electricity, excited by a power surge. Azazel cried out in pain and let the electrified sword fall to the ground, still sparking. The aperture's edges rippled and grew smaller as if collapsing. Ignoring his singed hand, Azazel snapped a gleaming knife from his belt and steadied his stance, preparing for an attack from the opaque shadows. Morgana stood at his back, her knife ready to strike. Bringing lasers, Jared tossed one to Azazel. He prepared his stance to fight. Other swordsmen trained by Azazel joined them. Kamean shot another arrow, but it sailed through the translucent images untouched.

Drood cast a disapproving look and pointed his fingers right and left, as easily as if making an imaginary drawing, to expand the border to its original shape. He rounded his lips and sent breath to quell the rippling. Satisfied with his work, he smugly smiled with hands on his hips. Seeing no one move, he beckoned to something out of sight. A two-headed wolf, its deep guttural snarl resonating across the clearing, pounced to the ground below, awaiting attack orders. Women screamed. Gray eyes glowed from each head of the beast. It stretched its swinging necks, taunting with their sharp, pointed teeth. The beast paced below the apparition, readying its attack.

With his sword no longer arcing electricity, Azazel stooped to retrieve it, not taking his eyes from the snarling beast. Azazel, Morgana, and Jared took steps backward. "Where's a replicator net when you need one?" growled Azazel. Preparing for the attack, his arms slashed the air in flowing movements that grew ever faster, so that he'd slice the beast if it attacked.

"This one's solid," shouted Kamean. Following the beast's movement with his bow, he launched his arrow. Drood held out his hand. The arrow stopped in mid-air before the beast's right head. After hovering a moment, it fell to the ground. Morgana threw her knife at the beast's eye. Before the blade pierced the beast's pupil, Drood stopped it.

Alana slipped from Maya's hand and angrily strode forward, ignoring her friends' pleas. Only spirit powers could defeat Drood's dark powers. "In the name of the Mother, why do you disturb us?" she demanded.

Drood stared impassively, sniffing with contempt for the southern tribes' worship of the Mother. The crystal cave from whence he drew his power was an abscess in Mother Earth, revealing a more potent majesty. Nevertheless, being in the mood for toying with his prey, he answered, "Because I want to."

"I know you are Drood. Why do you wear a disguise?"

Offended at being questioned, Drood sneered petulantly. "Because I want to. Enough questions. You'll do as I command. Kneel before me."

"No. I am the Earthkeeper of this land. I demand that you leave."

"No."

Lil, dressed in his spotless Alterran uniform, strode confidently forward with Yamin, who held the amethyst crystal on his palm under a snip of hide. Taking his place beside Alana, Lil haughtily returned Drood's smug look and said with mockery, "I'm flattered that you've copied my visage. It's not a bad likeness, although you didn't capture my eyes." He chuckled. "Your tricks are entertaining, but as you can see, you've interrupted some superb dancing and delayed an archery competition. I doubt that you and your creatures have come to take part. So be on your way, and I might overlook your bad manners." He held out his palm and a wine cup appeared, from which he casually took a sip, although his burning eyes never left Drood's image.

"As pleasant as this conversation is," snipped Drood, his venomous voice resonating more loudly, "what I want is food. My people struggle, but you have plenty."

"*You* look well fed," snarled Azazel, only glancing at Drood's image, warily focused on the snarling wolf.

"My body appears as I wish it to be. I *am* doing well, of course. I've developed a rather large following, you see." He chuckled with the familiar rasp through his crooked smile. "Without Ewan's interference, people discovered that they love me! Even those far away. They adore my tricks, as you call them. Let me show you." Eagerly producing his beige crystal sliver from a crevice within his robe, he caused lightning to arc from the aperture, sending chunks of sod flying at Lil's feet.

Lil didn't flinch, but he whispered to Alana, "Get back!"

The floating figure mocked them. "Yes, indeed, stand back, Alana. You've grown soft. Where is the courageous young girl who confronted crusty old Elaine and made her help you?" Drood narrowed his eyes with cold hate. "You should have chosen my son, you know. He would have treated you as you deserve."

Lil reached for the pyramidal amethyst crystal, much larger than Drood's, and held it uncovered at waist level.

Drood's eyes fleetingly sparked with alarm. "So, Semjaza, you foolishly plan to fight my power. You can't, you know. No one can." He had his snarling two-headed wolf take crouching steps forward.

Alana whispered, "Only I can defend against the spirit world. Kamean's arrows cut them no more than smoke." She withdrew the silver headband from her inside pocket and tied it around her forehead.

Through his enhanced eyes, Lil studied the pattern of electromagnetic ley lines flowing through Khamlok that fed the power of Drood's shimmering image. "Not every battle is yours, my sweet," he muttered. He, as well, could draw upon the pulsating electromagnetic power. He caused the crystal to glow, at first dimly, with its power growing until it sparkled. Matching Drood's armor, he transformed his tunic into golden armor that glinted, catching rays of the sun.

Drood's shadow warriors stealthily spread apart. At his order, they yelped a war cry. Becoming visible, the short, muscled warriors, their faces and bodies painted with ochre, jumped forward. With rapid movements, they slashed with their granite knives, which had been chiseled to fine points. Azazel deftly weaved to dodge their choppy, ill-placed blows. Azazel twirled his body and paced his steps, parrying his sword in the fluid form of an ancient blade master. The giant toyed with his shorter opponent, slashing his arm, and then a leg, while eluding the frustrated man's careless thrusts. The warrior crouched and jabbed at Azazel's ankle. Azazel pinned the man's arm to the ground with his leather-booted foot. The warrior thrust with his other arm to pierce Azazel's leg. Seeing that the man would not yield, Azazel thrust the blade into his heart. Beside him, Jared cast his laser as a circling swirl of light, which zapped a warrior leaping to attack him. Other shadows poured from the aperture, remaining translucent. The shadows surrounded Azazel and Jared, whose slashes cut through the air, having no effect.

A circle of laser arced from Lil's crystal, hitting a shadow about to strike Azazel's back. The shadow sparked and glowed, turning ever more transparent until it darkened and disappeared. Lil disappeared, reappearing beside his fighters. Creating a shimmering net, he tossed it onto the attacking shadows and drew it so tightly that they erupted in a burst of fire. Lil pointed his crystal at Drood and stared with his deadly, cold cobalt eyes.

Drood's eyes widened with fear. "Attack!" he ordered the two-headed wolf near Lil's side. Crouching for a mighty leap, the great wolf pounced high in the air.

"No!" cried Alana. She snapped her arm as if throwing a lasso. A bolt of lightning arced from her fingers, encircling the beast's thick necks. Snapping back her arm, she broke them both. With a thud, the beast, its disjointed heads hanging limply, crashed to the ground behind Lil. Surprised, Lil raised his eyebrows at her.

Drood swirled his finger in the air and then pointed to Lil. From the apparition came the thunderous sound of flapping wings and tweets.

Lil ordered, his voice thunderous, "Everyone, draw back!"

Black, bloodthirsty ravens poured through the aperture, passing over Lil and Azazel. They flew like a torrent of arrows toward the screaming women, who cowered, trying to protect their heads. Lil calmly held up his crystal and summoned a dozen giant, feathered anzus with pointed fangs protruding from their lion-like heads. Squawking, their powerful wings required only a few flaps to reach the ravens. The tight raven armada dispersed in the turbulence caused by the anzus' mighty wings. Each anzu snapped up mouthfuls of ravens as if they were tasty insects. After consuming the last ravens, the eagle-bodied anzus settled near Lil at the aperture. Lil patted one's head. "At ease, my pretty pets. Go home now." The anzus vanished. Lil held up the crystal, his cobalt eyes nearly glowing and his voice full of a command that the Anunnaki recognized as a House of En ruling tone. "Through this, your destiny is written."

Azazel seethed, wanting justice for having been stalked. "Let me finish them!" Without awaiting an approving command, Azazel heaved his sword again and again at the apparition's lower border, grunting with each mighty blow. The aperture's borders quivered. With each blow, the distortion grew. Azazel ignored the nasty pinpricks of the electricity arcing through the blade with each thrust.

Drood's furious face filled the collapsing aperture. "This isn't over!" The picture grew hazier, becoming smaller and smaller until it disappeared, leaving the air calm and undisturbed.

The trembling women clung to one another, unable to speak. Breaking the silence, Maya let go of Vesta and ran to Alana, dancing around her. "Alana, I didn't know you could do that!" she cried with amazement. Vesta ran to Kamean, hugging him.

Alana's eyes fluttered and she slumped, exhausted. Lil caught her, and Maya stroked her hair. Weakly, she whispered, "I didn't know either. I saw Zedah do it once to save Yoachim."

"You always surprise me, my sweet," said Lil, lifting her into his arms.

Tilting his great sword respectfully, Azazel strode forward, flanked by Kamean and Jared. Morgana, her arm wrapped around confident little Tara, joined them. Azazel's sword glowed more brightly than ever, adding a pale blue color at its edge. Azazel paused, looking curiously at the crystal that Lil had handed to Yamin for safekeeping. The crystal had grown dark and appeared to be no more than an ordinary, rough-edged, crystalline rock. "Captain, what weapon is this?" Azazel welcomed a powerful weapon, but he was uneasy why it had been hidden. Even more disturbing was Lil's surprise use of the old powers of the House of En. He hadn't told them he possessed such ability. The Anunnaki had assumed that they were safe from the Net's control. Was Lil reserving its power for use against them if the opportunity arose? Azazel studied Alana, seeing no explanation for her sudden magical powers. Had Lil given his Earth woman access to his god-making power? Azazel cleared his throat. "Captain, it seems that you have a personal Net. You no doubt have wise reasons for not sharing with us, who have so loyally followed you. However, please reconsider the wisdom of giving an Earth woman access. They would be like us. Earth people aren't ready. We Anunnaki will watch and protect."

Lil countered Azazel's determined gaze with calm silence, remembering one of Jakhbar's lectures. *A wise leader must appear unpredictable as well as infallible. Make the power of secrets a fundamental part of your ruling arsenal. A sprinkling of fear and uncertainty is an invaluable tool.* There was no need to explain that the crystal was his mother's gift, created by Ki, and accepted only at his mother's insistence. Today he was glad for it. Azazel was frequently blocking Lil's *mencomm* orders for reasons that could only be no good. He engaged in intrigues as well as any member of the House of En, where Lil had ably learned his lesson to trust no one. Azazel had his secrets; Lil would have his. He said quietly, but in a tone not to be questioned, "Leave me, I must attend to my wife." Alana's head rested on his golden armor. He lovingly carried her through the parting people, whose faces expressed reverence.

Short little Maya tagged along too. To keep up with Lil's powerful strides, she was forced to jog. When Maya passed

Yanni, she asked breathlessly, "Did you see? Alana's become as powerful as Zedah!"

"Yes, dear. Bless the Mother! For them both!" Without reflection, Yanni bent her head in respect, as did Marita and the other women.

* * *

"What's wrong, Drood?" Weena cried when Drood dragged himself, limping much more than usual, into their hut. "Maku," she called, kicking the body sleeping on the ground a few feet away. "Wake up. Help." They eased the exhausted Drood onto his pallet. Weena ran her hand across his limbs, searching for broken bones. Nothing seemed amiss. Drood was usually tired when he returned from the spirit world. She knew his moods, however. Something was seriously wrong.

"Father, did you kill them all?" Maku asked eagerly.

Drood scowled at the question, not wanting to admit his humiliating defeat. He fumbled through the pile of furs on his pallet, found his cane, and whacked Maku on the thigh. Weena brought Drood broth with seal meat. He carelessly slurped, analyzing his mistakes. He'd been overconfident and moved prematurely. Despite all their watching, he hadn't known that Semjaza possessed such power or that Alana had become as powerful as Elaine. He hadn't foreseen that that devil Azazel could destroy his spirit world pathway with merely his sword. Maku waited patiently by Drood's side. "Not yet," he finally admitted, his voice a bare whisper above the crackling fire. "We must learn more about the giants. They have great magic. Life will not always be so kind to them. As in any hunt, we will lie in wait and watch for a weakness." Azazel was his obsession, which the day's unpredicted turn of events had merely reinforced.

* * *

After gingerly settling Alana on their pallet, Lil kissed her forehead and arranged her beautiful, golden hair. Exhausted, her eyes were closed. He kissed each lid. *How did you do it?* He was mystified by the natural powers of Drood, and now, his Alana. They each entered a doorway into another dimension with only their thought. During their night on the cliff, she'd taken him along. It had been fascinating. His experience had purged the Alterran minders, and he was intrigued to know more.

Alana's eyelids fluttered, and she drowsily opened them a slit. Seeing Lil hovering so protectively, she smiled happily. "My love, you're taking care of me."

Lil returned her smile and ran his fingertips down her soft cheek. "Of course, you're mine. I love you." He kissed the back of her hand. Since he forbade her to perform any menial labor, her hands were soft and smelled of her rose lotion.

Responding to his touch, she raised her arms, her fingertips reaching for his neck.

Lil took her hands and held them. "As enticing as you are, my sweet, I know you're too tired for lovemaking."

"Then lie beside me," she prodded dreamily. "Hold me."

Beside her, he stretched out his legs and slid his arm below her breasts, keeping her company while she napped. While she slept, he recalled all the sensations of traveling with her in the spirit world, analyzing how Drood and Alana were able to draw upon this vast, unseen power. His science couldn't physically confirm other dimensions, although their existence had long been theorized. Did Earth alone, with its unusually strong magnetosphere, possess a doorway? Perhaps transcending branes intersected here. If so, Earth had a supreme uniqueness that his people could never abandon. *Our mating is truly destiny,* he thought. The discovery of this dimension would intrigue his father, giving him a way to regain his father's good graces. When Alana awoke, he kissed her cheek and smoothed a strand of hair disturbed by her slumber. "You're back in our world."

"Hmm," she mumbled, shifting closer.

He nuzzled her neck, and she moaned softly. "Alana, my sweet, how did you do it?"

"Do what?"

"Throw the lasso of lightning."

She pensively furrowed her eyebrows. *How did I do it? Can I do it again?* "I don't know exactly. Zedah taught me to open my mind to the spirit world and draw power. Opening the right pathway, the one with power, has eluded me until now. I was angry and frightened. I think the spirits responded to my emotion, my need, and gave me the image I had in my mind."

"So, you envisioned the lasso, and it became real?"

"Yes."

"Had you consumed your mushroom potion?"

"No." She shook her head in awe. Zedah had said that she could do it. Did she only need to trust in herself? "I wish I could tell you more, but I don't understand it. I don't know if I'll ever possess the power again."

"You once called upon the forest creatures to save you."

"I was terrified then, as well. I had to save Maya."

He kissed her, muttering, "We'll examine this later." Feeling his desire rising for this bewitching woman, Lil planted gentle kisses down her neck. His hand slid under her robe and cupped her full breast, pinching her nipple. He was pleased that she stirred invitingly. On their mating night, she'd confessed that he enthralled her, and he knew the same overwhelming feeling, as if a drug controlled his mind. He would do anything for her. And she'd given him an excuse if ever he were called home.

"Don't worry," he said softly, "I'll always protect you."

CHAPTER 17
KOKO

"Oh, Koko, tell us another story!" urged the admiring young girls surrounding him. Koko flashed his alluring smile. In the center of the King's Great Hall, the adults of the wedding party merrily danced in the glow of the hearth fire.

"Tell us a story about a great hero," one of the girls entreated.

"Ah, now that would take all night," he replied coyly. "This is a wedding, and I have better things to do, as do you." He grinned as if selecting his prey.

Queen Hilaba of the northwest mainland, richly dressed in wedding finery, appeared behind Koko and said slyly, "Girls, girls, you can't have Koko all to yourselves. He has many other guests to attend to." Taking his arm, she gently pulled him away. Drawing him close to her, she walked back to the dancing, whispering in his ear, "They'll do anything; they're so entranced with you, you lecherous old fox. The king will be leaving soon. Come with me."

"I would be honored, my lady, as always," he put his hand over hers and returned her smile. Hilaba, queen of the mainland's northwestern territory, was his true objective. He joined her to watch the dancers in the flickering firelight. The queen whispered to him, "That's quite an exquisite fur you're wearing. Most unusual. It must be immensely valuable. A gift from one of your lovers?"

"No, no, my lady. You know there's no one but you!" he whispered into her ear. "I picked this up in a growing settlement on the peninsula. It's new. You probably haven't heard of it before. The people are unique. You'd be much impressed, I'm sure."

"Why is that?"

"They've found a new way of hunting. The furs and hides are so plentiful that they don't even view this trifle as rich. I procured it in an honest trade," he said with a smile, knowing she'd be jealous.

She glanced down, knowing better than to reward his taunt with a jealous look. "A new way of hunting? Sounds interesting. Most of the people around here are desperate for food, although the king is oblivious." When the music ended, she announced with a knowing half smile, "I need air." Nodding away from the hearth, she said, "I want to hear more about the new city."

A loud crash came from the dais, where the drunken king had tipped over his antler-adorned chair. Steadying himself, he glared haughtily at his doting audience. He was taller, and his massive shoulders larger, than any man in the room, although his years of self-indulgence had left him with a protruding belly. With a baritone voice, he announced with a flourish, "I lift my cup to wish good health to the new bride and groom," he paused with a wolfish grin, "but, especially the health of the bride." He lifted his cup and took a long drink of the dark, grainy beer. The crowd parted to provide a path between the king and the bride and groom, both so thin that they were like two embracing sticks. The king threw down his cup. Leering, he staggered toward the newlyweds.

Eyes cast downward, the groom stammered, "Your Grace. We're humbled that—"

"Enough babbling!" roared the king. Leaning close and tickling her pale, soft skin with his beard, he savored her terrified shiver. "My dear, you're looking beautiful. I've noticed you since you were a little one bearing my cup. You've become most desirable!"

"Your Grace is too kind," she replied, her eyes respectfully downcast.

The king shouted, "Another drink." After a pause, he added, "And bring one for the bride, as well." Two sloshing cups were quickly brought by slaves eager to please. The king took both and offered one to the bride. "Drink up, my dear. It should make you less tense. The old women say that you're a virgin. I'm exercising my right of First Night." He laughed throatily, joined by a few sycophants.

The groom protested, "Your Grace, don't. Have mercy." He brazenly looked the king in the eye to deliver his half-hearted plea and fell to his knee.

The king forcefully slapped his face, causing him to stagger. His dark eyes gleaming, the king booted his buttocks and sent the humiliated groom tumbling across the floor, hearing the crowd's nervous laughter. "Shackle him," he ordered his grizzled guards. "You fool. That's what you get for questioning me. She's blessed to get me as her first. And if she's truly blessed by the gods, she'll be pregnant with my child tonight." With that, he dragged the squirming bride, ordering his aides to prepare her in his chamber. The trembling bride furtively glanced at her mate, whose wrists and neck were being bound with leather straps.

The king motioned for the music to resume. Some cheered as the limp bride was dragged to his room. Others jokingly advised the groom, as he was dragged by the burly guards, that he would be lucky to raise a child sired by the king.

The king smugly perused the room until he found his queen's eyes. He defiantly raised his cup to her, knowing she had witnessed the spectacle. She played the game by appearing distraught by his betrayal. An aide motioned, and the musician played a new tune. The king once again threw down his cup and paraded triumphantly, arms lifted in a victory walk. He grandly waved good night, beginning to undress as he dashed down the hall to his chamber, forcefully arching back the tarp, with the crowd in drunken laughter.

Taking Koko's arm, the queen whispered, "As I said, the king was leaving soon. Let's go down to the lake."

"Yes, my lady."

The queen nodded graciously to those she passed, who uncomfortably took pity on the betrayed queen.

Away from onlookers, Koko circled her waist and pulled her into the shadows, kissing and caressing her. She straightened her hair, saying, "You're intense tonight. We haven't even made it to our favorite spot. Come," she said as she hurried toward the lake.

"Forgive me, my queen," said Koko. "I get close to you and my passion ignites."

"I think your passions were ignited by those young girls, but never mind. You're looking particularly fetching tonight yourself. The years have been kind to you. Remember that night when you first took me as a young girl no older than those innocent things you were preparing to pounce on this evening?"

"Oh, you've hurt me. I don't pounce, I only instruct." He again interrupted their progress to fondle her, but she drew back, pulling him toward the lake. "My husband may be a fool, but he is a fool with many spies." In the soft moonlight, they quickened their pace to reach the queen's downy sleeping mat. Koko caressed her as he tugged to unwrap her garments.

After they had made love in the moonlight, the queen said, "Tell me about the new city on the peninsula. What kind of new hunting methods?"

"My queen does like to get down to business. I've always admired that." Among his kisses, he said, "Khamlok is a city like no other, although the women are ordinary people of the peninsula. They were abducted by Danes a few years ago, and their men were murdered when the rescue failed. These women, destitute and near death, were adopted by giants, who are themselves refugees from a distant planet to which it is said they can never return. These giants have vast knowledge and skills, although they hamper themselves with philosophical restrictions. You wouldn't understand these, my queen," he laughed as he kissed her hand. "Even though plants are dying elsewhere, they've been able to grow crops—plentiful, far more than they need. Also, they find herds in places where the weather has become too difficult for others to go. They hunt so successfully because they control hawks, wolves, and horses through messages sent by their minds."

"Through their minds?" She grew angry. "Do you think I'm one of those silly young girls that you seduce?"

Koko drew her back. "I'd never lie to you," he said, kissing her. "All of this, as incredible as it sounds, is absolutely true. These giants are very resourceful. In an amazingly short period of time, they constructed a new city of well over two hundred huts surrounded by a great wooden wall, thinking that would keep out the rest of the world. Not only do they grow grain, but they have orchards and vineyards as well. It's truly remarkable how much food—actual wealth—they've created in so little time. They're virile too. Almost all the women gave birth, although not naturally."

"So not only are there a large number of giants, but they're breeding as well?" asked the queen, becoming more alarmed.

"Yes, that's true," he admitted. "They're perplexing. These giants, who call themselves the Anunnaki, have broken away from their leader for reasons that I don't understand. Because of strange feelings of guilt, they rather stupidly left behind their valuable weapons, and they have only swords and knives, although these are made of a mysterious, sharp, gleaming metal. Rumor has it that they had flying ships and knives of light that cut through trees. Contrary to this strange philosophy of theirs, the hunting leader, Azazel, secretly has his men engage in combat training each day, again on the pretense of training to protect them from the Danes.

"Does my story trouble you?"

"You tell me a story of a great power developing on my borders, and you ask if I'm troubled? Maybe that fool of a husband of mine wouldn't be troubled, but I'm certainly troubled. How large a force do they have?"

"Initially, there were about two hundred giants. The one I mentioned, Azazel, made a great impression at the Summer Meeting a couple of years ago, and since then would-be warriors from all over the peninsula have poured into the city for personal combat training from him."

The queen tightened her furs, disturbed yet intrigued. "Azazel. Tell me more. Can he be turned into our ally? What could I offer him?"

Koko laughed, delighted that he'd caught her. "Can he be turned? You are a crafty one, my lady. He's a man, like any other man."

"Meaning?" she demanded.

"He's a leader of men, the leader of a growing army. Yet he's not his people's leader. Oddly enough, the leader is someone named Lil, also known as Semjaza. He's a privileged snob, a member of his ruling house, which he abandoned out of lust for Ewan's daughter when things didn't go his way. His hold to leadership flows from their traditions. He's brooding and philosophical, not a man of action like Azazel. Azazel is a man capable of unlimited power, but he holds it in check, at least for now."

"If I didn't know better, I'd think that you're trying to steer me to favor this Azazel."

Looking wounded, Koko replied, "I admire Azazel. If he were here, I'm sure that you would share my opinion. He's in the tradition of your people's great leaders."

The queen sensed that she was being led but was intrigued; she was used to suffering fools. She saw through men so easily. "Koko, my wise one, you rightly think that a great power developing on my border is a worry. What would you do? Is an alliance possible with either this Lil-Semjaza or with Azazel?"

"My lady, I don't think that the Anunnaki, as they call themselves, intend any harm to you. They're consumed with developing a thriving city and raising their large brood."

"You said that Azazel trains people for combat," she interjected. "What's the purpose of an army, if not an invasion? When these giants have exhausted their hunting grounds, they'll inevitably expand their borders. That's the way of it."

"You're wise, my queen. Azazel trains in case an enemy attacks. You see, his mate was held captive by Danes and abused. He views it as his sacred honor to defend her if savages attack. I've heard rumors that the Danes' village was destroyed by the great flood. The Anunnaki don't know that, though. So Azazel trains hunters who can readily become warriors. It's a large force, actually. Even Yoachim heard the tales, and he's deeply worried."

"Yoachim, that old fox, is worried?" she marveled. This *was* very serious.

"Yes. It seems that they're not paying him the proper respect, and they aren't following the old traditions," observed Koko.

The queen considered this thoughtfully. "Azazel sounds like a useful man. Can you get a message to him for me?"

"A message, my lady? Perhaps. It would be quite dangerous."

"Oh, I'll pay you, of course," she said with a dismissive wave of her hand.

"My lady misinterprets me," protested Koko. "Yes, of course, I will. What message?"

"Give him my greetings," she pondered, pausing. "Tell him that I've heard great things about him, and that I send tribute to one of such high repute. Tell him that the queen values people of talent and rewards them generously, and I will send an emissary."

"What tribute do you wish to send, my lady? I'm happy to serve." *Would it be my fault if thieves rob me? These days, they lie in wait along all the trails.*

"I'll send Margon. You arrange a meeting far from the city, where no one will see."

"Wise," he said, getting dressed.

Swiftly, she finished dressing. "I've been gone too long. Visit me at noon tomorrow in the garden to confirm Margon's plans." She smoothed her hair and resumed her regal bearing before starting back to entertain guests. She paused with a half-turn of her head and a delighted smile. "You've done well. I'll leave a large gift in the usual spot."

CHAPTER 18

LIL

Piercing Khamlok's midnight tranquility, a young girl screamed for help. Lil, having moments before dozed off, sprang up and roused men sleeping in the Great House to follow the victim's screams. Mingling with the screams was taunting and laughter.

In the moonlight, Lil made out the silhouettes of small, stocky men in a circle, drunkenly encouraging their companion. With disgust, Lil threw men aside and entered the circle of black-headed men. He towered over the men. Petus was raping a motherless girl of age ten. Having been beaten, her red eye was swollen shut, and her bleeding nose was broken. With a single arm, Lil heaved Petus through the air, slamming him against a tree. "You animal," he yelled, his face contorted with rage. Petus's companions widened their circle, encouraging him to fight.

Petus shook off the pain, his uncomprehending eyes in a drunken haze. He sneered with hatred. In his village, sex was an entitlement. When males made a sign, the females knew to bend and make themselves available. Resenting the unmanly restrictions of Khamlok that insulted his people, he and his friends had decided that it was time to say no. Petus regained his balance and lunged at Lil, aiming to ram his head into his stomach. Lil kicked the drunken lout, sending him sprawling. Lil's guardsmen picked up Petus by the arms and held him in the air while Petus thrashed his legs.

Alana, having followed close behind, comforted the terrified girl.

"Take this scum to the Great House and tie him up," Lil ordered his men. Unable to contain his fury, he yelled at Petus, "This is wrong! We don't take women against their will here, no matter what your custom was. This will *not* be tolerated." To the other gaping men, he commanded, "Leave now, or I'll have you all tied to these trees."

Grumbling, the men made lewd, threatening gestures, and one burly one picked up a rock and bounced it in his hand. "Who cares what you say?" Lil's guards stood close and drew their swords. Lil glared, his cobalt eyes glowing. Alana caused a cold, dusty wind to gust into their eyes.

"Curse you!" Rubbing their eyes, the men slowly dispersed.

Incensed by their disrespect, Lil's anger escalated during his walk home. Behind him, the guards led the struggling, spitting Petus. A rag was tied around his mouth to end his cursing. Too troubled to sleep, Lil paced outside the Great House. The cloudy sky above gave no hint of the universe's comforts. He yearned for the comfort of the observation deck. With a lump in his throat, he envisioned his father castigating him for bestowing Alterran sophistication on ungrateful savages. Lil couldn't let his father learn about this humiliating incident. He'd put his heart and soul into Khamlok, and he vowed to make it work. To do so, he had to regain control.

The next morning, Alana found him slumped over, asleep at his worktable. She hadn't missed a night by his side since they'd been mated. With Iskur in her arms, she gently woke him. As he sat up, he rubbed his eyes, which were bloodshot from lack of sleep. He'd never looked so stressed before, even when they'd struggled with the birthing. Worried, Alana kissed his forehead, letting her lips linger. "Last night pained you."

"How is that poor girl?"

"She's badly bruised and frightened." Alana paused. "She told me that she doesn't feel safe here anymore." She knew this news would further upset him. He dedicated his life to protecting those under his care, asking in return only their loyalty and obedience. He was so competent. Obedience was little to ask in exchange for the fine life he brought them.

Lil grimaced, sighing deeply. "Things have grown too rapidly. Too much is happening at once, too many new faces. We were comfortable with your women, and we felt that we shared values. We let Azazel bring in the new people, and we wrongly assumed that they'd eventually share our values. The new ones are too primitive. They're little more than animals, and they're outright dangerous. They're an infection. I won't risk their low standards spreading like a cancer." He thought how many Anunnaki were growing long hair and forgetting to groom. He hadn't objected, but now he viewed it as a sign of moral decay. No one else had investigated the poor girl's screams. "Azazel was supposed to watch them, but he didn't. Petus was his example of finding promise in the new people."

"From Summer Meetings, I know Petus's tribe. They admire animal ways. Many in this area do." Alana rubbed his shoulders to relieve his tension. "You've got to do something."

"Right now, we've no way to handle these ruffians. Every little thing requires my personal attention. This is overwhelming me. It's not what I expected."

"What do you plan to do?" she asked, feeding Iskur a piece of bread.

"We can't have fights breaking out in our streets," he said. Once again, he pictured the disgusted faces of Anu, his grandfather, and his great grandfathers if they were to see last night's brawl and his raging emotion. Alterran leaders deliberated in quiet detachment, usually meditating to seek the divine guidance of the Universal Consciousness before making an important decision.

"Expel them," advised Alana. Her women didn't feel any affinity with the ruffians. They disdained their savage ways just as much as Lil did.

"Yes, especially since not even Azazel is here to champion them. I spent the night mulling this over. There may come a time when we need new people, but only if they accept our values. Until we have the capability to teach them, we shouldn't accept anyone new."

"In our old village, children learned from the adults. If someone argued, Ewan decided. That system works when the village is small. Now, there are too many."

Lil stared out the window, glad for the normalcy of people performing morning chores. He thought a while. "People from different villages need to know the rules of our city so they don't make a mistake. On Alterra, we had laws and rituals that everyone knew. Under Zeya, magistrates adjudicated claims. The Alterran Code was absorbed by each person so that people would know proper conduct. Deviations were punished by guardsmen. I need to duplicate the best of our system here." Under Ama, the magistrates had been dismissed. His father, though, planned to reinstitute the traditional rule of law.

Alana put her arms around him, "All the villages look to the Elders for advice, like the Council you created."

"For day-to-day administration, I'm appointing Yamin. That will give me more time to think."

"About what?" asked Alana, putting Iskur down and sliding a hide shift over her slim shoulders.

"Fundamentals of civilization," he sighed. "I need to draft a Code of Laws and develop a ritual calendar."

"Why ritual?"

"You practiced ritual at the Summer Meeting," he pointed out. "It bonded the peninsula tribes that attended."

"I guess we did," she recalled. "I thought of it as fun, even the Walk of the Ancestors."

"Ritual is important for instilling a sense of community. It emphasizes our special place in the universe's evolution. Now that our paths have crossed, Earth people need to comprehend their uniqueness. The vast universe consists of energy forms, inert rock and microbial life; yet here sit the only two known populations capable of appreciating the wonder of it all."

"Are there no others?"

"Other than the ancient Anunnaki who seeded our civilization and then disappeared, we haven't found other sentient life," he said. "It took the early stars' exhaustion and explosions to create the metals necessary for our kind. Maybe there are others out there in late generation star systems. The multiverse is so vast; I doubt that we'll find them."

Alana was called to attend someone who was ill. As she was leaving, she picked up Iskur and said, "That's fascinating. I want to hear more when I have time."

Lil poured a cup of Alana's simmering tea and took a bite of bread, glad that he no longer needed meat for survival. Recreating civilization was the ultimate challenge of his life. Experience was no guide without a fundamental consensus of good and evil. In Petus's society, it might not have been long since they'd lain with animals, so that acceptable behavior was modeled on animal practices run by the dominant male. The females' failsafe was to be only seasonally in heat, or to accept an offer of monogamy from a lesser male chased away by the dominant one. Petus recognized no natural, moral dimension, and he failed to recognize that people were special and shouldn't use animals as examples. What words would convince a Petus why people have universal principles of moral behavior? By contrast, in Alana's village, her people intuitively knew good from evil. That innate notion had motivated Alana and Maya to altruistically risk their lives to reach his colony and debate him about good and evil in the rescue of her people. How could peoples living so close together evolve such fundamentally different premises to their lives? It seemed the key was Ewan, who had seeded the lost principles of Atlantis.

Lil remembered that before the Teacher had been invented, society had devoted vast resources to schooling the young. Here, they had no educational resources, at least not yet. For the time being, if the parent worked in the fields or the orchards, or as a shepherd or fisherman, then the children would do so as well. Values would be taught at rituals attended by everyone. How would he teach all the future generations about Alterra, when he'd be long gone? Each day, he wrote Alterra's history in his recorder, knowing that he must develop another method to preserve his writing. Not paper, which had been once used; it deteriorated too rapidly. Perhaps he'd develop something using clay, like the symbolic ballots he'd used at Hawan. Those in the far future, though, couldn't decipher Alterran script. He'd need to transcribe it into a pictorial code. A long history in such code would require an army of scribes. Maybe, like Koko, he'd develop stories to be retold by the hearth each night. They would be simple stories, capable of surviving thousands upon thousands of retellings, each having the force to mold the listeners' lives to fundamental moral principles. As Alterrans, his descendants *must* be good and honorable, not guiltless killing machines like many Earth tribes. Feeling the futility of his task, he shoved aside his recorder. How would he shoot an arrow laden with his history into the endless, chaotic future? After they died, it was inevitable that their progeny would regress. How do you send a message through primitive people who have no concept of what you're trying to convey? Yet, eons in the future, they'll have the capacity to understand, if only they don't consider the surviving clues as nothing more than myth. Perhaps if they built stone monuments embodying advanced mathematics that would only be appreciated in the distant future, some would decipher the clues. He sighed. His destiny had been to run a thriving command economy with established laws, an immense professional bureaucracy, and wise relatives on the Supreme Council to offer advice. Sometimes, building this city was exciting, but at the moment, the immensity of the task overwhelmed him. He longed to seek advice from Grandfather Zeya.

He arose, stretched, and gazed out the window. He saw Yanni slowly guiding her struggling toddler as she carried a fishnet on her way to the river. Other women drifted by carrying hides, nets, or children. As the sunshine illuminated the bustling morning activities, he was comforted that everything appeared as it should—everything except that Petus was tied in the corner of the Great House, shouting curses. He wanted to be fair to primitives like Petus, who acted according to the only conduct rules they knew. Conversely, he had to be fair to the Anunnaki and the women of Khamlok. Petus had harmed a young girl, and he showed no sign of understanding the norms of their new city. Permitting exceptions for conduct that was, under any moral lens, degenerate would gradually weaken their society. With a sigh, Lil ordered Petus to be brought to him. On Alterra, there once was a complicated process of a charge, a prosecution, and a trial, although the House of En actually controlled each step. Here, Lil knew he was prosecutor, judge, jury, and enforcer. Although this Petus was Azazel's sworn responsibility, he hadn't defended the girl, nor had he appeared to defend the criminal. Lil tried commanding Azazel to appear by *mencomm*, but Azazel's mind was closed to his probes, increasing his irritation.

Wearing his Alterran tunic programmed to appear as the white, loosely fitting garb worn at Alterran official proceedings, Lil sat in his platform chair. He had laughed when Jared first presented the chair perched on the dais, as if he were a king from Alterran antiquity. He now admitted that for him to maintain control over the amoral population, he would need to display the full trappings of authority to command respect and obedience. He needed to adapt House of En methods to primitive Earth. Black-haired Petus insolently looked up at him, daring him.

He signaled for Yamin to record the proceedings. In his formal, baritone voice, Lil commanded, "What is the prisoner's name?" He calmly observed Petus, the cobalt blue of his eyes deepening.

After being poked by Kamean's sword, he said, "Petus."

"Petus, why did you come to Khamlok?"

"I came to be a warrior. I serve Azazel."

"Azazel is our honored chief hunter, not a warrior. We are peaceful. Those who live here must honor the rules of our city."

"Fighting has no rules," spat Petus with all the contempt he could muster. "Rules get you killed."

"You're mistaken," lectured Lil. "Rules reflect our values of right and wrong conduct, and we expect you to have the same values and to comply with the rules. To break a rule is a crime for which you suffer punishment."

Petus burst out laughing, infuriating Lil, who gripped his chair arms until his knuckles turned white. Justice isn't easy, he told himself, and it's tempting to cast it aside, as his Grandfather Ama had done. Like Anu, he didn't think people should be controlled to that degree.

"Petus, you committed a serious crime," Lil intoned evenly. "A young girl was severely injured."

"That was her fault," Petus sneered. "She shouldn't have struggled against her duty. That's our way. It's *you* who don't belong here." He coughed up phlegm and spit at Lil, hitting his chest.

Kamean kicked Petus to the floor, holding his neck with his booted foot. Petus coughed out a broken tooth, blood running down his chin. "See, you're no better than us."

Lil's cobalt eyes glowed with hatred. "You're not fit to live here. You're banished. If you come back, we'll kill you on sight." He said to Kamean, "Have the guards take him to the gate."

After the guards dragged the cursing Petus away, Lil coldly instructed Kamean, "I banish all the black-headed people. Spread the word and remove them, forcibly if necessary."

Heading a squad of Anunnaki carrying swords, lasers, and bows, Kamean searched Khamlok for all the black-headed people. They were hunted down, rounded up, beaten if necessary, tied, and marched to the gate, or carried if unable to walk. Probing Azazel's mind by *mencomm*, Lil found it blocked, further blackening his mood. When the expulsion was done, he sent Kamean to search for Azazel. Kamean reported that Azazel couldn't be found.

CHAPTER 19
AZAZEL

"Where is he?" growled Azazel as he dismounted from his horse and paced back and forth, squinting as he scanned the opposite side of the muddy riverbank. The ever-shorter days were growing colder, and he was impatient to see this through before the river froze. Azazel was frequently impatient these days. Knowing that he was mortal, his days numbered, gave him a new focus. On Alterra, immortality removed any sense of urgency. That was different now. He paced like a wolf. If he was going to make his mark, it had to be now. He was wasting his time hunting and, even worse, harvesting the fields. Yet, he wasn't sure what it was he wanted. All he knew with certainty was the intense frustration of time slipping away without the taste of achievement—without some victory or heroic deed being accomplished. The legends filled his head, and it gnawed at him that he needed to follow the heroes' example. Would he be remembered if he died today? And be remembered as what—the chief hunter of Khamlok? Memories were the only way to achieve immortality in this cruel world, and he wanted to mold them into a story truly worth telling and retelling.

When Koko last visited the city, he'd whispered to Azazel as if sharing a secret, "on the mainland, they have discovered how to specially shape stone and to make it very sharp. The rock is heated over an extremely hot fire, and before it cools, it's finely shaped, then chiseled to a sharp point. Very strong. The blade is wound in small, powerful circles until thrown with a flick of the wrist, propelling it at the target. For a skilled user, a precise blow is lethal. You would be wise to investigate."

Although Azazel didn't trust Koko and Lil wouldn't let him roam freely, the man was the only source of useful information outside Khamlok's walls. Azazel recognized that this simple device could be deadly. Even though ordinary Earth tribesmen possessed no mysterious powers like the bizarre wizard Drood, they had ferocity for mayhem that Lil underestimated. The guardsmen should have taken powerful weapons from Hawan. Although Lil enjoyed power emanating from the crystal, he left the rest of them vulnerable. Lil wanted to recreate Alterra, limited to the women they'd found who were unusually sophisticated for this planet. Beyond that, Lil wanted to live in isolation; mental isolation was not a practical defense when living in the midst of these people. It was as if Jared's wall was supposed to keep out the world, leaving Lil to resurrect their old tyranny for those within. Why else had he hidden the crystal's power?

Azazel knew to defend against all enemies, from any place and without regard to the level of sophistication. The Earth people could be clever, and they perpetually fought, reducing the peaceful ones to slavery and ashes. It was up to Azazel to protect his people. Koko, for payment of a few furs, had agreed to serve as a messenger to the mainland so that Azazel could learn more about the new marauders taking the Danes' place. He'd directed that the meeting occur far away from Khamlok, along this river at the edge of the lowlands. It required an overnight stay. Since he'd been planning to scout with the hawks for new herds near the lowlands, the meeting met his plans.

Now, Azazel spied a boat in the distance. It would be a while until it came ashore, giving him time to relax. Sitting on a log, he rolled his shoulders and took out a flask. He was working too hard. Each morning at dawn, before the hunting trips that took him farther away from Khamlok as the herds grew too thin to sustain them, he'd been teaching the standard forms of swordplay to Anunnaki and the older youngsters. To the black-headed new people, he taught basic military formations and defenses. They were troublesome, and in truth, he didn't want to bother with them. In a true army, there would be a hierarchy, and he'd delegate training responsibility.

Because of his hunting success, new hides were worked into fine clothing and furs were plentiful. From his efforts, the people of Khamlok had grown wealthy by Earth standards. He didn't feel rewarded. He took another drink. *Primitive life has been a tough adjustment.* He regretted not having soundguns and rechargeable lasers. They could have unlimited power on this primitive planet. Instead, they were trying to isolate themselves or at best, blend in. What sense did that make? Even now, Lil remained infected by too much Alterran nonsense. What good was the harmony-and-stability philosophy in this wilderness? They needed military might to defend their city against enemies who would surely find them. Despite his frustration, Azazel felt more alive when taking action into his own hands. He clenched and unclenched his fists, feeling the energy coursing through his veins. Where would they be now if he hadn't created the fine weaponry on which they now depended for their lives? Or what if he hadn't foreseen that they should use the laser guns to prepare the logs and the water well before they left Hawan? Jared received the credit, but it had taken Azazel's persistence as the only guardsman willing to confront Lil. Without him, these people would be barely able to hunt and to feed themselves, or even to build the fine huts for which Jared received all the accolades. He took a few more drinks from his flask as he watched the boat draw closer. It wasn't fair.

The canoe slid onto shore, and a small, black-haired man in a long cloak comprised of a patchwork of torn furs hopped out and approached. "A man of your stature could only be

Azazel," Margon said in the common tongue, smiling broadly. "Your fame has spread all over our land."

"It has?" asked Azazel with surprise. "How?"

Pulling the canoe on shore, Margon explained, "Through Koko! I've heard many stories about you, repeated endlessly at our hearth fires. I even heard Koko himself tell the story of how you rode into the combat competition at the Summer Meeting, and you threw a knife that blazed like the sun while riding full speed on your horse—a perfect throw that bested everyone else. I've heard that all the young men from these parts dream about coming to your city to join with you. It's truly an honor to meet you in person, sir." Azazel didn't trust this man; his compliments flowed too easily.

"Koko also tells that your mate, Morgana, is the most beautiful of all women," Margon smiled, pleased at Azazel's reaction. "She's a warrior too, is she not?"

Beckoning him to sit beside him on a log, Azazel said in the common tongue, "Rest a moment before we get down to business." He produced a second flask, which he offered to Margon.

"Just what I need, sir." After taking a long drink, he marveled, "What *is* this?"

"We call it wine. It's made from grapes."

"This is the finest drink I've ever had. I've heard that your place is amazing. I'd love to visit."

In the years before the flood, Azazel had flown over the mainland many times. He'd seen the thriving port cities along the middle sea and watched the growth of villages dotting the northern rivers that cut through the dense forests. Unable to fly since leaving Hawan, he'd lost contact. He hadn't given much thought to their plight in the flood and the darkened skies. He remembered that the tribes of the mainland had shown greater organization than most of the planet. But development was consistently destroyed by their perpetual warfare. "I presume that many of your people died in the flood. How do they fare now?"

"Yes, multitudes died in the floods and the diseases afterward. In the north where our king lives, the villages suffered less. Initially, we actually benefited because the Danes were no longer a threat. As the coldness and dark clouds have persisted, our people increasingly struggle to find food. Sometimes even the very rain stings the skin, poisoning the streams and killing the river fish. Berries and wild vegetables that we relied on for food have disappeared."

"Who is your leader?"

"King Azor. His home is that way, across the lowlands." He pointed due east.

"That's not far," said Azazel, picking up a stone and tossing it, feeling uneasy. He didn't expect a large, organized tribe to live this close, leaving them with Drood's savages to the west.

"No, it's not," replied Margon, misunderstanding Azazel's concern. "King Azor was, in his time, a great warrior. Now, though, he's grown fat and likes his mead and women too much. The king has many warriors, whom he keeps busy fighting in other lands, for which he's paid much gold. He pays his warriors well to preserve their allegiance." Margon paused to glance at Azazel, assessing whether this fact interested him. Seeing no reaction, he continued, "The king's queen is Hilaba, although he keeps plenty of young ones around." He smiled knowingly at Azazel, nudged him with his elbow, and began to laugh. Azazel laughed as well, thinking this King Azor to be a petty fool. But a dangerous fool.

Margon took a drink and lowered his voice, as if revealing a secret. "The queen is smart. Some say it's she who truly rules the land."

For a time, they silently watched the swirling river currents. Finding his flask empty, Azazel produced another. "How did this Azor become king?"

"Our prior king mistakenly thought his son could lead. The son was weak, with no interest in fighting. He reigned for almost a month because his father had had all the warriors swear a blood oath that, upon his death, they'd support him.

King Azor sent the warriors secret messages promising great wealth. Each agreed to be absent on a hunting trip when he arrived. Azor won control without a fight. He put the son, shitting himself, to his sword and displayed his head. Upon the warriors' return, they swore allegiance to King Azor."

"Interesting." Not a noble tale like an Alterran ancient legend, he thought. "Do you have the weapon to show me?"

"Oh, yes." Margon hastily set down his flask, spilling it. Scurrying to his boat, he pulled back a dirty hide to produce the promised war hatchet, which he handed to Azazel to examine. "I can't tell you how proud we are. When carving it, the stone is heated. Notice that the stonework is thinner than the clumsy carvings of the Albion tribes. Its edge has been finely shaped. It's narrow and sharp."

Azazel observed that they'd inadvertently discovered rock laced with iron, producing a stronger, far more lethal point than he'd seen from the Albion tribes. The blade had been melded, rather than clumsily tied, to a wooden handle, which bore signs of treatment to a polish as if petrified, making it stronger than regular wood. With superior weaponry, it was no wonder that this Azor's kingdom was growing.

After stacking debris on a distant mound, Margon steadied his stance. "Watch this." He rapidly circled his right arm several times and then released the hatchet, crushing the target.

"Impressive," said Azazel with reserve. The weapon was deadly at short range.

"A line of men can throw the hatchets while running at full speed," Margon boasted. "Properly trained, they're more lethal than archers!"

Not having their Alterran weapons, Azazel needed his men to master this hatchet. "I'll take one hundred, if you train my men. I'll pay in fur and hides. When will they be ready?"

"I'll personally train your men, sir! We can deliver them by the spring equinox," said Margon, beaming proudly.

"Good." Azazel began to leave.

"But, sir," he stopped Azazel.

"Yes?"

"Sir, I've enjoyed this meeting. May I call upon you again?"

"You're coming for the training," he replied.

"Yes, of course. I was hoping that I could facilitate communications," Margon said warily, looking askance.

"What communications?" Azazel demanded. He didn't know whether to be amused or insulted.

Margon had hoped that Azazel wouldn't be this direct. Insinuations suited his style. "You might find it useful to send a message to my queen on occasion. Or she to you."

Azazel studied him. What gave this odious, little man the impression that he might be receptive to this preposterous overture? He mounted his horse and rode away without looking back.

CHAPTER 20
LIL AND AZAZEL

What about Azazel? Lil fumed and held the cool crystal before his eyes. He imagined bringing Azazel to his knees with agonizing waves of energy coursing his entire body, which he'd continue until the wayward Azazel begged forgiveness and pledged his undying loyalty in repentance. The punishment would be easy, quick—and justified. Or he could extinguish his life in a single photon of light. Or he could control Azazel's mind, bend him to his will, like a Dalit or an old-time puppet. Punishing Azazel wouldn't salve the wounds inflicted by that miscreant, Petus. Wounds inflicted by Azazel cut Lil much deeper, if indeed Azazel had betrayed him. From time to time, Lil had had suspicions, most of which he'd dismissed as absurd. But they never went away. Confrontation simmered in Azazel like a summer stew boiling in the sun. He challenged Lil by closing his mind to *mencomm* orders. It was nasty effrontery, but Lil had believed that, over time, Azazel would recognize *mencomm* was merely a convenience. A bad decision. Excessive leniency in a leader is a weakness. He'd refrained from punishing Azazel because he needed him—another weakness on his part. No more.

Where had Azazel been? It gnawed at him that he didn't know and that Azazel could elude him. And why? Lil had proved his benevolence. He took care of his people like his children, treating them with respect and dignity. And still Azazel rebelled—in his heart, certainly, and perhaps even further. Was Petus right, that Azazel was grooming his own force? Azazel was proof that the Ens needed the behavior modification in the nourishment bars. Men were restless no matter how many benefits they were given.

Alana lifted the tarp to his workroom and stuck in her head, hesitant to disturb her mate when he brooded. She knew Lil loved her, yet Lil-the-Ruler was ruthless. "Darling, Azazel is finally here to see you."

Azazel had dithered two full days. He was compelled by duty not to delay more, yet repelled by guilt. When he'd ridden into Khamlok after meeting Margon, he'd instantly known something was amiss. Those he passed stared at him with narrowed eyes and silence, and the camp of the black-haired people was empty, their debris blowing in the wind. When he reached his home, Morgana had greeted him with cascading tears of relief. She thought he'd been captured by the shadowmen. How else to explain his strange absence? He'd feigned rage when told that Lil had banished his black-haired men. In truth, though, he was relieved not to deal with their nasty problems, despite being insulted that Lil had acted alone. If he'd been here, it might have been different.

The preposterous overture from Margon had made him search his feelings. Would leading an army of primitives make the historical mark he so very much craved? No, savagery didn't fit his idealized view of ancient legends. His yearnings were absurd. If only he could trust Lil without reservation, as Rameel and others professed to do. His ages-old guard service had shown him too much of the dark side of En rule for him to confer any level of trust. Yet here he stood, drawn to Lil—to confess? To seek absolution? He waited to be received, watching Alana serve the evening meal to little Iskur, who ate eagerly.

"Not too much, Iskur," she warned, reaching for his bowl.

"But it's good," he protested, stubbornly refusing to put it down.

She tilted her head, unable to refuse her towheaded son. "Then thank Azazel, sweetie. He brings the sweet meat that you love."

Iskur slid from his seat and stood before the giant man. He tugged at his leggings and motioned by a crook of his finger for him to bend over. Azazel, looking amused, did as he asked. Iskur kissed him on the cheek and smiled. "Thank you for the meat, sir. It's my favorite." He waited only to see Azazel's return smile before running to his mother and demanding more stew.

Alana smiled at Azazel. "Thanks to you, he'll never know the starvation that we faced, and I have a second serving to give him." She came closer, put her hands on his face, and stood on tiptoe to give him a kiss on the cheek. "All the women love you for what you've done for us, Azazel. Please believe it. Lil will never say so, but he loves you too, in his way. We're your family." She looked into his dark eyes, wondering why he looked so troubled.

Lil raised the flap, eyes smoldering, and sharply beckoned him to enter. Without speaking, he resumed his seat at his worktable, gazing at the crystal that he cradled in his palm. Lil didn't invite Azazel to sit. Nor did he offer him wine. This was to be a sober meeting. He studied Azazel, his cold anger no less deadly than the heat of the days before.

Azazel's stomach churned, but he kept his face blank, his back straight, and his feet unmoving while meeting Lil's regal gaze. With the pride of a heroic knight, he would meet his fate. Nervously, though, he gripped his sweaty fingers behind his back. Although Lil appeared much younger, Azazel felt cowed like a guilty little boy in disgrace before his father. What was his guilt? He'd indulged in a harmless fantasy of having his own kingdom and had been gone when he shouldn't have been. A daydream. A trifle. He stood awhile, not uttering a word. As unexpected as the first lightning bolt of a summer storm, he was jolted by the frigid jab of Lil's mind probe. Caught unaware, Azazel's defenses were down, and Lil invaded. Azazel threw up the few mental blocks he could muster, but Lil had instantly perceived Azazel's frustration and absorbed his recent memories.

Nothing is a trifle. With deliberation, Lil positioned his amethyst crystal on the worktable. He placed his elbows on the table, crossed his thumbs, and slowly tapped his upraised fingers under this chin. After moments that, to Azazel, felt like hours, he raised his cold eyes. "You took those ruffians under your wing, promised to keep them under control, and then you were absent when they caused trouble. Severe trouble. You've heard what they did?"

He nodded, admitting, "You were right to banish Petus and his group. But they aren't all like that. Some could have been kept. They're useful."

Lil's eyes glowed with fury, and he thumped the table. "You question me?"

Azazel looked down and he shifted his weight. "What Petus did isn't my fault."

"Petus is lucky to be alive," Lil said. Blistering with contempt, he spat, "He said he fought for *you.*"

"Lies," said Azazel, finding that his throat had gone dry. "He only taunted. You can't believe what these savages say."

Lil raised an eyebrow over his piercing blue eyes. He growled, "Where were you?"

How much does he know from his mind probe? Is this a trick? "I needed time to myself."

"Why?"

"To think."

"What worries you?"

"Can't you tell? You probed me."

"Don't be insolent. Answer me."

"I'm mortal, and I want to be remembered. It's no more than the fear we all share." *Or maybe you don't. Will the power of that crystal rejuvenate you?*

"That's no reason to abandon your duty. Why do you block *mencomm?*"

"My mind is my own business," he defended, his eyes growing narrow with anger. *If you mean to harm me, I will fight. If I can.*

Lil paused. What was he to do with his wayward disciple, who sought personal grandeur? He abandoned his foible this time, but he has the itch. He'll try it again. If he imprisoned him in a holographic cell within a world created by his crystal, would that satisfy the dictates of impartial justice? But at what cost to the innocent? Azazel was needed. If Lil admitted his full knowledge of Azazel's meeting with the savage, he wouldn't be able to grant mercy. "At the moment, it's the only way to communicate. We'll fix that eventually, but for now, you must cooperate. You're an important part of this community, and we need to be able to find you. Blessed Zeya, Azazel, I haven't imposed my will upon you. I'm not Ama. I've given you free choice. Recognize your duty. What if your family had been in danger? We're all your family now." Lil's eyes smoldered. Why was he debating? He should dispense punishment and end the matter. He'd promote Kamean to take Azazel's place.

Azazel hung his head and rubbed each finger slowly. Lil had struck a nerve. What if Morgana or Tara had been raped by Petus and he couldn't be found? And for what? His ill-timed venture with Margon? Why would an Alterran meet secretly with envoys of savages? Idiot savages to boot. He thought of little Iskur thanking him. He was loved here, and he should learn contentment. He shouldn't model himself on idyllic, ancient heroes. Those were mere fairy tales. "You're right," he admitted slowly, in a whisper. He slumped into a chair. They sat that way for a long time, the evening shadows deepening. Pride kept Azazel from saying more. Indecision held Lil's tongue.

Even with repentance, Lil wondered if he could trust Azazel. He'd felt his ambition, letting savages turn his head with unctuous flattery. Untamed ambition could rear its ugly head at any time. Lil was an En, born to be the leader, and Azazel was born to be a guardsman, nothing more. As above, so below.

Lil broke the silence, uncomfortably succumbing to the unwelcome role of confessor, his voice neutral. "Learn contentment with the life you create. Heroics may be thrust upon you when you least expect. On your deathbed, with your face wrinkled and your body withering from natural causes, count yourself lucky if you've not been challenged. Go now." *Go now, before I change my mind.* He watched Azazel silently leave. He held the crystal in his palm, concentrating on the fractal patterns within the fine grains. *If I weren't stranded here, I wouldn't tolerate such insolence.*

CHAPTER 21
YOACHIM

Shaman Yoachim, dressed in his long robe and carrying his staff, was a powerful figure. He was in his fiftieth year but retained his vigor and muscular figure. Before the flood, he'd traveled far and wide across Albion, occasionally even venturing onto the mainland. He'd served as Zedah's lover and apprentice. Even though he had only sufficient talent to glimpse the spirit world, she'd taught him to prepare potions and spells. To this was added Yoachim's natural intelligence, excellent memory, and eye for detail. Upon Zedah's death and with Alana's distance, stewardship of Albion fell to him. When Yoachim spoke, the people listened to every word, especially now in the lean, cool years after the flood, when the dwindling population depended on his wise counsel for survival. He'd saved many a life by bringing the starving to the coast to relearn fishing.

This morning, Yoachim relaxed outside his hut, which overlooked a lovely little lake, eating his favorite mixture of nuts and berries. Although such delicacies were thought to be non-existent, grateful villagers had given him their secret stash. His old friend Mota happened by. Surprised that Yoachim could still find tasty berries, and ever hungry, he helped himself. In between mouthfuls, he asked, "Yoachim, have you heard the latest news?"

With an amused twinkle in his eye, Yoachim asked, "What news?" Yoachim knew everything that happened on the peninsula. This land was his.

Mota, between sloppy bites, said, "Do you remember Azazel and the other strangers with Alana at the Summer Meeting a few years ago?"

"Yes, of course," replied Yoachim impatiently, annoyed at being reminded. They didn't participate in the Meetings, and Alana hadn't honored her duties as Earthkeeper. Yoachim had stepped into her shoes. In truth, he enjoyed the position and didn't wish to give it up. "You mean Alana's new village."

"Well," Mota said with authority, "it's too large to be a village, more like a city. Some of the young ones followed them to the place they call Khamlok. They wanted Azazel to train them to be warriors and give them glowing swords, like the one he flashed at the Summer Meeting. One, Petus, just returned. He said that there must be a thousand huts being built. But the leader has thrown the locals out. They hate him."

"A thousand new huts, that's remarkable," said Yoachim with mocking skepticism. "But huts are hardly anything to be concerned about, are they, Mota? These strangers must simply be very industrious."

"But there's more," protested Mota, dismayed at Yoachim's lack of concern, as well as at finishing the last berries. "According to Petus, these men aren't from a faraway land. Semjaza fought Drood with powerful magic and bested him!" He whispered conspiratorially after a pause, "They're actually from the stars."

"That's absurd," scoffed Yoachim.

"That was my first reaction as well," replied Mota, waving his hands. "According to Petus, this Azazel can talk to wolves. Hawks and horses as well. He directs them with his thoughts." Mota tapped his forehead for emphasis. "With all that hunting, they've taken the herds. That's why our people can't find game."

Yoachim raised his eyebrows. His hungry people, the ones he couldn't persuade to move to the coast, were asking for special blessings. He had assumed this was yet another problem from the flood. Perhaps not.

He realized that Mota was still talking, "These people are able to build their huts so quickly because they cut down huge trees using sticks made of nothing more than light." Taking another bite of nuts, Mota grew even more excited. "And here's the best part! These strange men impregnated all the women. The babies were too big. So what did they do? They called their star relatives, who came in a flying ship to deliver the babies through magic." He sat back and awaited Yoachim's reaction, but Yoachim was inscrutable. Reaching closer, he whispered, "I've heard that some of the babies are *abnormal.*"

Yoachim's mind was in turmoil, which he hid from Mota. He needed to investigate his story. He'd been annoyed when the messenger had announced that Alana's city wouldn't attend the Summer Meeting; after the first year, they hadn't even bothered to send a message to decline. He was bewildered why he had had no insight about them. Was it because these people truly were from the stars that his powers didn't work?

"My good friend, I appreciate that you've brought me this news. If you'll excuse me, I have a commitment. I must be traveling this very day. Please understand. We can discuss all of this more when I return." Yoachim stood up and began heading inside.

"Yes, of course, Yoachim." Mota replied with exasperation, pursuing him with his stubby legs. "But what about the strangers?"

"Yes, yes, I'll look into this," Yoachim hastily called after him, "but the strangers will need to wait until my return. I'm afraid that this really can't be helped." With that, he stopped, graciously put his arm around Mota, and said good-bye. This wasn't the first rumor that he'd heard about Azazel.

When Mota was out of sight, Yoachim rummaged through the disorganized items on his worktable, looking for an old drawing on hide from a Future Ceremony that he had found particularly difficult to decipher. "Ah, here it is," he said to his dog, lying beside him. Yoachim remembered the ceremony's occasion well. He'd been at the cave near the hot springs, which was the only place he could use his talent. Ewan and Alana had been present, and he'd even added a drummer to enhance his concentration, permitting him to enter the spirit world. He'd seen a great ball of light travel from a star and come to the Earth, landing nearby in the north. Once here, the ball of light had dimmed, but before going out, it divided into two, a white light and a blue light. For a while the two lights followed the same path, but it appeared that they separated and traveled to distant lands to the east of the inland sea. Yoachim gazed at his lake. At the time of the ceremony, this insight had made no sense to him. Now, he understood part, but not all. He resolved to speak to Alana privately.

He traveled light, since he was readily welcomed at any destination. He carried his staff, a gift from Zedah, which he used to cast spells. Traveling to Alana's city would take weeks.

His prior vision hadn't indicated that the strangers were evil, even if they came from the stars. After all, at least one of them was symbolized by a white light. People from the stars. Why had Alana not told him the truth? He didn't like being lied to, and it troubled him greatly that he didn't sense it himself. She should have trusted him as a fellow shaman. Yoachim mulled over Petus's story of a thousand new huts. He knew Petus, however, and Petus wasn't the sharpest stone in the quarry. He doubted that he could count at all, let alone to one thousand. Still, there must be many huts. Even those with good intentions can run into trouble if they can't control their growth. And with all those little babies, someone must be in charge of their spiritual development as they grew. As the guardian of the peninsula, he wanted all people to have a deep respect for the ancestors and the traditions.

As Yoachim drew near the city, he came across hungry foragers who had been banished, and they angrily confirmed the many new huts and army. The next day in late afternoon, Yoachim approached Khamlok but could not enter; it was surrounded by a reinforced wooden wall that reached the treetops. A well-trodden path led to an opening, which was closed. Yoachim examined the entrance for some way to request admittance but found none. They must not want any visitors, he grumbled. He called out, and a window appeared, revealing only a bearded face.

"I am Yoachim, shaman and guardian of this land," he called out, arms outstretched with his staff in his right hand. "I wish to visit Alana, the Anointed Earthkeeper, daughter of Ewan, mate of Semjaza." The opening grew large enough for him to enter. Yoachim was surprised at the lack of formality in greeting a personage of his stature, but he made allowances since his visit was unexpected. Yoachim passed circled rows of new, well-made huts and racks with hides being processed. People smiled but didn't turn from their work. Recognizing some women, he waved and called to them. They waved energetically but resumed their tasks. He was disappointed that they didn't come to him. They seemed to be in robust health, were well groomed, and may have even put on a little weight, showing their prosperity. Nothing sinister here, even if they were a bit disrespectful.

He strode into the Great House and asked to see Alana. She ran up to him holding little Iskur, delighted to see him. She was richly dressed in a hide dress with beaded trim.

"Life seems to be treating you quite well, my dear." He greeted her with a huge, friendly hug. "And who is this little one?" He hadn't been invited to officiate at any of the naming ceremonies, another instance of disrespect.

"This is my son, Iskur. Look how strong he is already, and he's very smart," Alana boasted.

"He looks just like Ewan, but with your green eyes," he laughed. "May we talk privately, my dear?"

"Yes, of course, Yoachim," she said as she gave Iskur to an older child. "Has something happened?" When they walked outside and were alone, she asked again, "Is something wrong?"

"I hope that *you* answer that question," he replied as they walked together past the abundant fields.

"See our fields?" she said proudly. "We grow grain, and our storage is full."

Yoachim surveyed the wide stretches of field. He knew this land. No sign remained of the lovely trees or the bushes where he'd gathered medicinal plants. Not even a tree stub was in sight where the mighty oaks had graced the sky. His stern look reminded her of Ewan, when she'd borrowed his prized teacup for play.

"There is much activity here. How is life for you, my dear?" Yoachim smiled gently, searching for the old rapport.

"I couldn't be happier," Alana gushed. "Semjaza is a wonderful husband and wise ruler. Everyone has worked tirelessly to build this new city. Surely you're impressed!"

"Yes, my dear. I see." Upset by what he saw, Yoachim couldn't hold back is feelings. The reasons for the Mother's anger had eluded him. As he witnessed Earth's violation, it became clear why his beloved people were suffering. His expression turned grim, and venom dripped from his words. "You've peeled the Mother's skin and exposed her tender flesh. The sun is ashamed and covers her pain, while the winds wail with her pain and her sorrowful tears singe the land. Others are left near starvation."

Alana's eyes widened with shock. "No, it's not that way at all. The skies are cloudy because the dragon damaged the Mother. Zedah knew. The floods happened before Khamlok."

Yoachim spat, "You don't know that the Mother foresees your atrocities?"

Not wanting to be disrespectful, she tried harder to explain. "The Mother provides food. We simply use her gifts and direct the plantings. Our people thrive without wandering. Here, try this bread. We're certainly not taking from others." Rumors casting their good fortune in a negative light couldn't be good omens, she fretted. "Growing our own food gives us more control when the skies are gray. We can teach others, if they will listen."

He reluctantly took a bite. "It's tasty," he admitted.

How could anyone think their plantings hurt the Mother? Dismayed at Yoachim's accusing eyes, she raised her chin in defiance. "People are the Mother's children, and all Mothers want their children to live well. I am Earthkeeper, and this is the way. You're as backward as Drood."

Yoachim angrily tapped his staff into the ground. "And what about that?" He pointed to the deforested mountain. "Is it backward to preserve the ancient trees?"

She scoffed. "How could people live if we're forbidden from accepting the Mother's gifts? Am I violating the Mother if I pluck legumes from the ground and eat them? The Mother made us, too."

"The Mother expects us to take only what we need. What else are you doing?"

"What do you mean?"

"Well," he paused, "I've heard rumors that you are creating an army."

"An army? Why, we have no army," she said, laughing.

"Are you sure there's nothing to it? We've had more than a few young men come here to join Azazel. They're returning very disgruntled, complaining about being ill-treated."

"Azazel isn't creating an army. He's a hunter. If the Danes come, Azazel prepares to defend us, of course. Many who came had bad habits, and they wouldn't follow our rules. They were troublemakers who scared the women, and my husband sent them home."

"Hmm. This city is surrounded by that intimidating, huge wall. Why is that?"

"For our safety! There's nothing suspicious. Walls attack no one." How could anyone complain about these good things?

Seeing his sweet girl's distress, Yoachim relented. For now. Regardless whether it was her fault—he never liked inscrutable

Semjaza or that vain Azazel—retribution was needed to soothe the Mother and alleviate his people's suffering. In coming here, he hadn't intended to be so harsh. Zedah had spoken of her dream of people filling their bellies from plants grown where they pleased, but seeing the expanse of naked land had shocked him. He felt ill. As stewards of the land, people must accept their place within nature's creation. He would rectify the travesty, but he couldn't let Alana suspect his plans. "My child, I know you well. If this is all for the good, I will say no more." As they walked back to the Great House, they were silent. Smelling the aromas from the cookfires, his stomach growled, reminding him that he hadn't eaten that day. "I've been on the road a long time. Could you spare a small meal for an old man?"

"Of course." She gave orders to have stew brought to him, as well as a feast to be prepared that evening in his honor. She would show him the true benefits of Khamlok.

"Thank you, my dear. If you don't mind, I'll just wander around."

"Yes, of course. Please feel free to go anywhere you'd like. You'll overcome your doubts. If you'll excuse me, I need to attend to Iskur." In parting, she permitted herself the bad manners of not hugging or kissing him. How could one whom she'd held in the highest esteem be so narrow-minded? So mean? Did he prefer overgrown weeds over people? If he didn't like her city, let him stay away.

Left alone after eating the stew, which was delicious but contained things he couldn't name, Yoachim strolled parallel to the river and reached a field filled with healthy stalks of wheat and barley. He examined a stalk; it resembled their wild emmer wheat. Although most of the wild grains were brown and shriveled under the heavy cloud cover, these full stalks were thriving. How did they do it? He noticed reflecting devices positioned throughout the field. He continued his walk, coming to the orchard, and he marveled that the trees were so tall with full growth after only a few years. The far edge of the wall became visible in the distance. As he grew closer, he saw a house with windows, where a lone horse hung his head. Next to the building was a roofed pen in which a wolf mother nursed her cubs. She didn't growl as he passed by. Horses and wolves living side by side? He picked up an abandoned wooden sword from the ground. This must be where they practice, he thought. Hunters don't normally use swords, but then again they may need to defend themselves against the Danes, as Alana said, or whatever foe succeeded the Danes. He poked his nose into the structure housing the horse. Hearing hoofbeats, he concealed himself. A hunting party entered the clearing, with Azazel in the lead, the glint of his sword escaping from the scabbard he wore on his back. A floating wagon contained the carcasses of wild pigs and elk. The wolf pack trotted behind them and tamely waited admittance to their pen.

Azazel dismounted. "They need these animals for this evening's feast, for the shaman Alana wants to impress, so take them to the Great House." Yoachim was taken aback; Alana had only made the arrangements a short while ago, how did Azazel know? After handing his horse to an assistant, Azazel ordered, "We have time for one more practice." His assistants brought out boxes that had been hidden in a secret compartment. The men formed a straight row across from targets. Each man took a weapon. In turn, each made a fast circling motion with his arm and released an object, forcefully hitting the target, destroying it. From their skill, they'd been practicing for a while.

When each man had shot, Azazel dismissed them after giving a warning not to drink to excess; he expected everyone at dawn for their usual practice. After he entered the barn near Yoachim's hiding spot, a voice in the shadows remarked, "They're acquiring considerable skill. Soon they'll be able to throw at a full run, and they'll be ready."

Azazel grumbled, "I agreed to *nothing*. I'll have a tray brought to you, Margon, but be gone at first light."

Margon—I know him, thought Yoachim. He's in the service of Queen Hilaba. What's he doing here? I knew these people were up to no good!

With his long, powerful strides, Azazel was soon out of sight. Margon went into the small storage hut and closed the door. Yoachim left his concealment and made his way to the weapons. He examined one, wondering at the supreme sharpness of the pointed stone. This was a great, new weapon for the people of Earth. But surely these strangers had much more sophisticated weapons than this if they came from the stars. "Most curious," he whispered aloud as he returned the weapon to its hiding place. He slipped away through the trees.

At the feast that evening, Alana had many responsibilities requiring her attention, and Lil was busy with Azazel and Rameel. Alana seated Maya beside Yoachim, and she tried her best to engage him in conversation. *She's heaping disrespect on me.* Yoachim was sullen and uncharacteristically silent. Alana's new city was a magnificent accomplishment in so short a time. They had so much food when nearly everyone else faced starvation. What would they do to sustain this population when game could not be found? Is this why they were creating an army?

In the old days, he would have freely discussed his concerns with Alana, but she'd changed. She no longer came to the Meetings, initially saying her people were too busy with their babies. At the time, Yoachim had understood, but now he felt like a fool. These people would have had little problem traveling with infants. He saw that now. No, these people were disrespectful of the ancestors in not following custom, and Alana was remiss in not looking out for her people. Earthkeepers had important responsibilities. These people had shown him, the peninsula's de facto spiritual leader, disrespect. When Yoachim excused himself, saying he would retire early, no one took notice. Not being tired, he gathered his things and left immediately.

CHAPTER 22
RAMEEL AND AZAZEL

"Yanni, would you like to see a bit of the countryside?" Rameel asked one summer day. The fields had been tended, and for once, the day was partially sunny. Despite the cloudiness, he'd grown tan working daily in the fields. Being fastidious, he'd enjoyed a warm bath in the bathhouse and scrubbed the field dirt from his fingernails. His shoulder-length hair was neatly tied at the nape of neck, and his hide shirt, expertly made by Yanni, was spotless.

"I'd love that," she said. "I haven't been outside the wall for a long time. I'll get Maya to watch little Maliki. Where will we go?"

"I don't know," he admitted. "I'll ask Azazel. He's the expert. I'll go to the barn and bring back horses."

When Rameel returned, Azazel, Morgana, and Tara accompanied him on horses. "We've got company," he announced.

"Wonderful," Yanni said, bringing containers of water and a reed basket filled with smoked fish, baked apples, fresh bread, and jam. "I haven't talked with Morgana in a while." She tended the fishnets and supervised the smoking while Morgana busily made clothing. "Hello, Morgana. Hello, Tara."

"Hi, Yanni, I have so much to tell you." Morgana waved, her long, curly locks blowing in the gentle breeze. She wore a necklace carved from an ivory tusk that Azazel had found. Tara, now going on seven years of age, smiled at her. Yanni took the reins, and Rameel helped her to mount, tying the reed basket to his own horse.

They walked casually through the city, happily waving to friends. Outside the wall, Azazel asked, "Where do you want to go?"

"Take us to one of those idyllic spots you talk about," suggested Rameel, feeling relaxed. "I'm confined to the fields. I miss Dalits for these monotonous tasks. I envy your ability to see the countryside."

"You overlook the danger the hunters face," Azazel said, annoyed that everyone thought his job was so easy because of their success. "However, I do know a safe place, at least as safe outside the wall as we can be." After they'd walked for a while and entered the denser woods, Azazel cautiously looked for Drood's shadow warriors.

"Always alert, Azazel?" asked Rameel uncomfortably. "Is there something in particular that worries you?" Peering into the dense foliage, he detected only squirrels and birds. "Is that Drood fellow still stalking you? After the thorough thrashing that Lil gave him, I thought that the shadows hadn't been seen as much."

"They're still out here. As you're riding, you might perceive a shadow where none belongs. At first, you'll think that your eyes are playing tricks or that you've mistaken leaves blowing in the wind. Over time, you improve at turning quickly, catching a glimpse before they disappear. Sometimes you catch the outline of a man."

"Remind me of who they are?"

"A northern tribe named after their leader, Drood, a mystic. Maya says that they're cannibals." Azazel paused. "That's not the only danger. Don't underestimate the beauty of this place. This land is raw wilderness. Snakes could be disguised in overhanging leaves—remember Enuziel. Yesterday, our hunters were charged by a frothing wild boar. Fortunately, Kamean rarely misses. It was the boar's mistake." He laughed. Turning around, they saw that the women had fallen behind, deep in their conversation.

"We shouldn't let our wives fall too far behind," cautioned Rameel. They slowed and waited until they caught up. "Having wives is certainly better than relying on holograms or offering oneself on that abominable circuit."

"I agree. Or the Darian underground."

"Oh?" asked Rameel, his eyebrows raised. "For a guardsman, I'm surprised."

Azazel smirked, diverting attention to the women, who were catching up. *There's more to me than you know.* Walking down a familiar hunting trail, Azazel headed for a river bend. "How are things going for you?"

"Azazel, when we were leaving, I think I had the most doubt of anyone. Yanni is perfect, and I love life at Khamlok. My work has true meaning."

"You were a high executive with the Ministry!" exclaimed Azazel. "You can't prefer working in dirt!"

"Sure, the position ranked high and conferred valuable perks," said Rameel with a chuckle. "But the Ministry had far too many executives, and much of our work wasn't necessary. I used to spend days in meetings endlessly discussing minute points, only to see nothing implemented, nothing achieved. At the time, of course, I thought the work important. After all, the Ministry issued orders governing every product consumed on the planet. My division prepared the catalog of goods permitted for inclusion in the replicators. Other divisions controlled the entire supply side of producing those goods. It took huge numbers of people to identify and obtain the raw materials that were fed into the underground manufacturing plants that supported the replicators, scheduling the Dalits to run those plants, keeping the equipment working, and so on, endlessly. In short, we ran every detail of the economy. We couldn't have performed these tasks, of course, without the quantum computers."

"I thought the House of En was in control," said Azazel, puzzled.

"Oh, they *definitely* were. Nothing escaped their notice. We created a minutely detailed annual plan and submitted it for approval to the supreme leader. When they approved it, we implemented it. Nothing could be modified without the supreme leader's approval. We couldn't, for example, authorize the construction of a new dormitory or the launch of a new consumer product without the supreme leader's express approval. Even undertaking a new theater or musical piece, or a new novel, required the Leader's approval. The artist had to submit a proposal outlining the plot and the ideas, and an En representative always attended the first performance. If displeased by the message, the Ens would forbid the piece, and the hapless artist disappeared—to where, I never knew. The Ens didn't issue guidelines, but everyone knew they favored themes promoting their harmonic philosophy. They once approved an artist's proposal that said she would praise the Alterran spirit. Her play was opening its first performance when the En representative came for a viewing. It told the story of a young female engineer who was unhappy with her destiny certificate and dreamed about becoming a dancer. The author and entire cast were sent for punishment, and the theater was closed." He sighed, remembering that he had been a loyal member of that system.

"I hadn't heard," said Azazel, although he'd always felt that their literature lacked sophisticated ideas.

"I haven't dared to tell anyone that story before, Azazel," he whispered, as if in a conspiracy. His eyes flicked around, conditioned to expect the materialization of an enforcer. *Old habits,* he checked himself. "On Alterra, I would have been in fear that the Net sensors would cull the conversation. Enforcers might materialize within seconds. It's taken all this time to shake free of that fear."

"Yes, we were *well* conditioned," said Azazel with annoyance at the system as well as himself. "There was nowhere to hide." The Net was a utility they could tap into anywhere, but it also permitted the government to monitor every move. No crime was too small. He cringed at the memory of Lil's invasion of his mind. He'd told no one about the incident. Afterward, he'd felt relieved and committed to Lil. He couldn't explain it.

"At the time, I was a true believer. Now I see things so differently," admitted Rameel. "It embarrasses me that I was a part of any system so, so—"

"Evil?" interjected Azazel with a smirk.

"No, that's an exaggeration—so rigid, I'd say. For millennia, they provided for everyone, you know. Some accommodations are justified."

"Nevertheless, we're different now," Azazel observed. "Fortunately, Lil hasn't controlled our thoughts," Azazel said, but he paused. "Not that I'm aware of. He told me, though, that he wants to improve our governance."

"We're growing," reasoned Rameel. "That may not be bad. What does he have in mind?"

"Regular Council meetings and the appointment of an administrator. He asked me to participate."

"That hardly sounds as if you should be concerned," he replied, enjoying the scenery. "That's just good management. He's been good to us, and I trust him. You can't argue with the success of Khamlok, Azazel."

"Maybe. I've grown used to my autonomy," said Azazel. "The hunting and security have gone well, so I don't see why I need a council to direct me."

"Don't view the Council as a threat," counseled Rameel. "Without management, we're more likely to fail as we grow. I think what Lil's doing is brilliant. He's creating an entirely new system, one that rewards individual initiative. That's totally unlike the Alterran philosophy, although don't tell *him* that— he's obsessed with recreating our homeworld."

"Do you think he's intentionally creating something new?" asked Azazel, his eyes narrow with skepticism. "Maybe the ability to exercise control eluded him at first, and now he wants to fix his errors."

"I don't see any sign of that." Rameel dismissed the thought with a wave of his hand. "Although we have no planning body, our resources are allocated smoothly, and things are made and distributed through the actions of many people keeping an eye out for what's needed and trading with one another, setting their own values. I don't have a name for this. I think of it as decentralization. Whatever you call it, it's working extremely well."

"And without punishment protocols," emphasized Azazel.

"Especially without them," agreed Rameel. "Completely unnecessary here. If someone on my work team is lazy and they won't correct it after a warning, I tell the person to find other work, and I recruit someone else. We didn't have this option on Alterra. The Great Awakening guaranteed each person the position described in the destiny certificate. There was no incentive to work. Supervisors were unable to let the person go or even demote them for fear of violating a divine decree. The only recourse was to compel work through punishment. A long time ago, punishment was only administered by the House of En, but slackers became so widespread that the Ens devised protocols delegating it to managers."

"The Ministry of Security had similar protocols."

"I'd heard about that," said Rameel. "When were they used?"

"For many things—accessing unauthorized information, criticizing the supreme leader, straying outside of the city perimeter without a permit—"

"Littering," added Rameel. "An enforcer once materialized after I inadvertently dropped a nourishment bar wrapper. He gave me a low-level shock and cautioned me against environmental contamination."

Azazel laughed as if great waves of mirth were coming from the depths of his being.

"It sounds absurd, I admit," apologized Rameel, "but he threatened me with increased punishment for another infraction of the Alterran Code, and I'm certain he was entirely serious."

"I believe you. I've heard much stranger stories." As a guardsman, Azazel hadn't been assigned to the security details, for which he was glad. "We used to call the Code breakers 'enemies of the people.' Even for accidental violations." He shook his head.

"It's remarkable how we've changed," Rameel admitted. "When Lil first asked us to participate in the hunt, we were so conditioned by the fear of punishment that we agonized for days."

"Honoring a Code is wise," said Azazel, "but the system itself must be rational."

"I used to think the Code made sense. It depends on what your guiding principle is, I suppose."

"Right," said Azazel. "If it does nothing more than perpetuate a dictatorship, it's wrong. But if its underlying premise promotes goodness and honor, then everyone has a moral duty to follow it."

"Moral duty?" questioned Rameel. "The guiding principle of the Great Awakening was supposedly equality for all and the provision of a social net to care for everyone. As Zeya said, we were creating a utopia. Isn't that the highest morality?"

"Those are worthy goals," agreed Azazel. "The implementation went astray."

"How could he have done it differently and yet been successful?"

"The system should permit people to use their talents and to profit from them."

"That's contrary to our very foundation," cautioned Rameel. "Zeya's creed was 'From each according to his ability, to each according to his need.' Under that philosophy, you should be working hard, yet turn over your prized furs to a needy person like Akia, who isn't able—"

"Or chooses not—"

"To function in our city—"

"Or anywhere else," spat Azazel with disdain. "Akia is not stupid, simply lazy, especially when compared to our talented wives."

"All right, Azazel, but the same could be said for those ruffians you tried to train."

"They provided value," Azazel insisted, clicking his tongue at being offended, "when prodded."

"If you say so," Rameel said with a shrug. "As I was saying, in a family group, perhaps even a small cell, the commune philosophy works. But in a larger population, it takes coercion. People don't want to turn over their things to some faceless person who's not working."

"It's theft! The philosophy was fundamentally flawed," scoffed Azazel.

"Mandating equality is a lofty goal, and I feel a bit uncomfortable criticizing it," said Rameel, squirming in his saddle. "But when you're dealing with a population with sometimes vastly different talents and goals, it doesn't work very well, does it? It's easier to suppress the talented than it is to incentivize the slackers."

"Pretty soon, no one works," said Azazel. "I guess one could criticize us for having disparity at Khamlok. My wife and yours make excellent clothing, and they create furnishings that are better made than others."

"Yes, because of their talent and hard work," Rameel agreed. "On Alterra, talent and hard work didn't produce any gain, so people did the minimum that would avoid punishment. That's why Alterra lacked innovation. It was as if we'd reached a pinnacle, and no improvement was desirable. Change was discouraged as wasteful."

"Why was that?" Azazel asked, scanning the trees for the shadows.

"A single innovation required a myriad of minor adjustments in the Ministry's plan. Once, when implementing a simple change order from the supreme leader, the supply chain was disrupted for weeks until we smoothed out all the unforeseen complications."

"The quantum computers couldn't predict that?" said Azazel.

"Too many uncontrollable variables—almost like the randomness of the quantum world itself. Complaints streamed in from throughout the planet. The supreme leader, of course, had to be blameless. He commissioned a special investigation. Everyone, including me, was interrogated. The interrogators publicized the discovery of massive corruption at the Ministry. Planners were publicly humiliated for personal profiteering, and then of course punished."

"I remember that now," said Azazel, ducking to avoid a branch as he turned his horse through a smaller trail leading to the river.

"The evidence was manufactured, of course. A supervisor I reported to, a woman I held in high regard, was shocked so severely that she had to be rejuvenated. So after that episode, no one dared initiate a change. Submission of the annual plan is much easier when it replicates the same plan year after year. That's why my position at the Ministry had become so pointless, and I volunteered for Earth duty the moment it was permitted."

"It must have been a demotion for you," said Azazel.

"More like an escape," Rameel smirked.

"We would never submit to such idiocy now," Azazel asserted.

"You're right."

"This is constantly on my mind," confessed Azazel. "Why *didn't* we have clarity on Alterra? Why did an entire population let itself be controlled by one ruling family?"

"In part, it was the promise of the genteel social safety net, eliminating ugly political debate," Rameel mused, recalling the well-known speeches of Zeya. "A monolithic government promises to take care of everything, cradle to grave, leaving the individual citizen free to pursue loftier matters."

"What loftier matters did you pursue?" Azazel smirked.

"I went to the theater and read books, although the content seemed lacking. I guess, mainly, I entertained myself with the ladies," he laughed, remembering his many trysts. "I was usually content."

"In a way, the House of En shouldered all the burdens for us."

"That's right," Rameel said. "People were taken care of."

"There was no worry about having food or shelter, unlike here," admitted Azazel.

"None whatsoever," Rameel agreed. "Some might think it wise to temper the ambitions of a few to achieve that kind of balance. The system functioned more or less for eons. There were no cyclical ups and downs, no dislocations."

"For you, happiness is merely the absence of pain?" Azazel's eyes glazed over dreamily. *I want more.*

"Is there truly more purpose to life than simply to live?" Rameel scratched his head.

"I feel a true purpose here," confided Azazel. "Even if there is no other point to life, if it weren't for the punishment protocols I might agree. If the Ens had such a great system, they wouldn't have been necessary." After a while, he added, "Why was there no opposition or even mild criticism?"

"The system was pervasive," mused Rameel. "An individual, acting alone, can't effect change. Even in the absence of punishment, there is tremendous peer pressure to conform to the prevailing viewpoint."

"You'd think that there would have been a catalyst to rouse the population," said Azazel. "For example, when the supervisor, your friend, was beaten so badly, why was there no protest? Weren't you disturbed?"

Rameel squirmed. "The Ens were expert at portraying the victims as evil. We thought that there must have been a grain of truth to the story. We imagined her having a secret life."

Azazel looked at him skeptically, his raised eyebrows conveying his question.

"How would we have known any different?" Rameel defended himself, feeling foolish. "They controlled all communications systems. How would protestors have organized? If they tried, the Ministry of Security would have snuffed it out at the first instant. You know their sensors were everywhere. It was easier to rationalize and ignore what was happening." He thought for a moment. "How would we even know a society could function in another form? How would things have been made and distributed? How would you determine who received what? The ancient legends refer to purchasing things with gold, but that system was abandoned long ago. We wouldn't want to degenerate to having the strong take advantage of the weak, would we? So if there's another system that works, I simply don't know what it is. With only the learning taught by the Teacher, we had nothing to compare our system to other than ancient kingdoms that weren't essentially different, simply less efficient."

"Sometimes I think that a different system didn't occur to anyone," Azazel said. "But that doesn't seem right. All those eons of control by the House of En, and I'm the first to think this thought? I'm not that smart."

"You're smart, but I know what you mean," laughed Rameel. "After eons, no thought is unprecedented. Do you suppose something else caused our complacency?"

"You might think this strange, but I've often wondered whether there might have been a physical reason," said Azazel, reaching the river flowing above Khamlok.

Looking at the shimmering water, Rameel scratched his head. "You mean, like something in the water we drink?"

"I can't put my finger on it. Initially, our emotions were tempered on Earth," said Azazel, "and we drank the water and breathed this air."

"Yes, that's true. Nothing changed until we ran low on bars and were forced to supplement our diet," he said, deep in thought. They suddenly looked at each other. "Are you thinking what I am?"

"The nourishment bars," said Azazel, satisfied that he'd finally solved the puzzle.

"That's got to be it!" said Rameel, snapping his fingers. "When we began partially relying on Earth foods, we became more assertive, more independent. How else could we have had the backbone to leave Hawan?"

"Here's the spot," Azazel said as they arrived at a bend in the river with bubbling rapids. He dismounted.

"This is charming," Yanni complimented.

"My Azazel knows all the romantic spots," Morgana agreed happily.

"Darling, I'm glad you like it," said Rameel. "Azazel, I could never go back." He dismounted and helped Yanni.

Helping Morgana down from her horse, Azazel seethed, "Nor could I."

CHAPTER 23

KI

Poring over the latest data, Ki determined that the destructive ash was finally diminishing. Although many monitoring probes had been damaged, those embedded in the northern ice sheets still functioned. In the last week, tremors there had magnified. His scientists concluded that the comet impact had caused cracks in the ice shelf and calculated that a sizable block would fall in about two Earth years, perhaps less. Using holograms to simulate the likely results of the collapse, Laurina feared that a giant wave might strike again. This time though, due to its proximity, the entire peninsula could flood and sink under the water's weight; even a partial collapse would cause widespread flooding. Lil and Khamlok were in danger under all her varied simulations.

Ki prepared a report for the Council recommending that the Ministry commence work on a contingency relocation plan. Immediately after submitting it, he was pleased that Anu requested him to attend the next morning's meeting. He went to the Council chambers early, greeting the members as they arrived, although his father avoided him.

Entering at a brisk stride, Anu promptly called the meeting to order. "Good morning, everyone."

"Good morning, Anu," said Councilwoman Barian, suppressing a yawn. "Why were we brought from stasis ahead of schedule?"

"En.Ki has important news."

"Before he begins," said Barian with a warm smile, "I want to personally thank you, En.Ki, for your tireless efforts. Everyone has noticed, and we are deeply indebted to you."

"Yes, I agree, thank you, Ki," Councilman Pilian added.

With his usual reserve, Ki nodded his appreciation. Inside, he was ecstatic. Producing a holographic image, he displayed the ice sheet's crack and explained the impact of the anticipated wave.

When he finished, Anu, his eyes cold and his voice judgmental, demanded, "En.Ki, there is a high probability that within two years much of the peninsula will be flooded, correct?"

"Yes."

"And is it not true that the traitorous En.Lil and his band of miscreants, who lost faith, stole colony property, and fornicated with Earth women, giving birth to abominations, are living where it will be flooded?" His contorted face was ugly despite the chilling calmness of his voice.

"Answer me, En.Ki," Anu again demanded, increasing the intensity of his stare.

Ki, stunned, stared in disbelief at his father. "If it happens, Lil's city will be destroyed."

"Good! That's as it should be." Anu pounded the table and arose to pace behind the circularly arranged seats. "What we have here is not a mere geological development, but a divine message. Lil and his band think they're like gods by choosing their own path. By disdaining their divine destiny, they have defiled Alterra and thus, all of us. Their evil has brought this destruction." He pointed his finger at Ki, shaking with fury. "En.Ki, I hereby issue an imperial command that you are to refrain from advising En.Lil or his brigands about this so-called geological development, directly, indirectly, through *mencomm,* or any other way at all. Lil is to have no inkling whatsoever. He must suffer for his transgressions through this divine punishment. Do you understand me?"

"I hear you, Divine One," Ki answered formally, making a slight bow. "Does this edict extend to the entire colony? My report recommended that we prepare contingency evacuation plans."

Councilwoman Barian interrupted Anu, "Whatever punishment might be appropriate for En.Lil, the colonists' lives should *not* be forfeit. En.Ki, you are hereby ordered to prepare an alternative facility for evacuation purposes. Please proceed at once."

Ki nodded his head and immediately picked up his materials to leave. "Thank you, Councilwoman Barian. The Ministry will commence at once." With that, he left without glancing at Anu.

Councilwoman Barian coolly asked, "Anu, are you ill? This outburst of yours is not like you at all. I agree that En.Lil is completely wrong in how he dealt with our problems. But Alterrans, as you well know, do *not* go so far as to read divine retribution in natural phenomena. Nor do we condone murder, which this will be if you fail to warn En.Lil. I understand that you two disagreed; you feel disrespected, and you're disappointed. Rightfully so. He lost faith in us. But is his mating the end of the universe? A sign of cataclysmic occurrences? I've read En.Lil's analysis, and it has merit. The Universal Consciousness catalyzed the evolution of both Alterrans and Earthlings, and it intertwined our fortunes through the timewave. Perhaps you haven't interpreted the signs as well as he did. I'll leave that question to our scribes. What we have here is a dispute between father and son. You are the leader of Hawan, and you *must* regain control of yourself. This Council will not become an accomplice to your unwarranted murder of your son. Times are difficult, and we will overlook this deviation if you right yourself. This meeting is adjourned." The Council members disbanded, ignoring Anu.

Stupefied, he slid onto an abandoned chair and numbly stared. It hadn't occurred to him that the Council would fail to support him. The Elders overrode a supreme leader only in the most extreme circumstances. *What did Barian mean that I haven't properly interpreted the signs?*

* * *

Ki returned to the Ministry, slammed his materials on his desk, and ordered a Dalit to bring a flask from his private stores with a drink so strong that it wasn't available in the replicator. His mother overheard and poked her head in. Seeing her unflappable son so distraught, she massaged his shoulders.

"What's Anu done now?"

Ki swiveled to face her. He poured a glass from his flask, handed it to her, and said, "Drink before I tell you."

With a forlorn look at the glass, she grimaced and reluctantly asked, "It's that bad?"

"It's as bad as it gets, Mother." He gave her the report, and she saw there could be flooding throughout the peninsula.

"What are you going to do?" she asked, numb from all the tragedies.

"Yesterday, I sent the report to the Council. I was delighted when they asked me to meet with them, thinking it meant they were finally dealing with our problems." He took a long drink. "After I finished, Father jumped in like a crazy man to rant and rave that the ice crack is divine punishment directed against Lil and the 'abominations.' I was placed under an 'imperial edict' not to tell Lil. Hawan depends on a madman." Ki had the Dalit pour him another drink and motioned that she should tip off his mother's glass.

Uras was speechless. She hadn't thought Anu would go so far as to relish Lil's death. Perhaps he'd had a stroke from his excessive drinking. As chief medical officer, she could demand that he submit to an examination. But there was also the problem of the ice sheet. "How certain are you that it will fall?"

"With the tremors we've monitored to date, it's very likely to occur within maybe two years. On the other hand, if the area experienced another quake, it could be sooner."

"How bad will it be?" After he told her, she asked, "What did the Council say?"

"Fortunately, Councilwoman Barian intervened and countermanded his edicts."

"I'm glad someone in that room was thinking clearly," said Uras, shaking her head.

"When I calm down, I'll direct the scribes to search for a new site with far different geologic features."

"I'll tell Lil so that you're complying with his edict," said Uras with a grimace. Uras returned to her sleeping quarters in the infirmary, relieved that she'd moved. After she focused, Lil soon accepted her probe. "Lil, darling, I'm sorry to interrupt you, but I have some important news."

After absorbing Uras's story, he asked, "The entire peninsula would be flooded? How far inland do we need to go?"

She projected Ki's holographic map. "Lil, are you still there?" said Uras, "I'm not very good at this mind thing, I'm afraid."

"I'm here, just thinking. That flooding would be so widespread that we'd need to transport to safety."

"Although Ki doesn't think it will happen immediately, he's searching for a spot far away from here. Your father forbade anyone to contact you. That's why I'm sending you this instead of Ki. It may be difficult for him to assist you. Somehow, though, one of us will keep you informed. I love you, Lil."

"Thanks, Mother," said Lil fading away.

Every day gets stranger, thought Uras.

CHAPTER 24
363

D espite the deteriorating conditions of Hawan, the Dalits were ignored, forgotten, and unseen by the colonists, who expected them to continue working the same as they expected the water and power to continue running. Dalits were cleaners, janitors, housekeepers, and similar cogs. For many centuries, the Dalits fulfilled their function in the great machinery of the Alterran system. Were they happy and content? They were too busy, and their minds kept too hazy, to think about happiness. The roles of the Dalits assigned to Hawan were, out of necessity, expanded, wherein they learned new skills. At times, they were even enlisted to serve in the infirmary, which was impossible on Alterra. Most importantly, the supply of nourishment bars for Dalits was exhausted, and the Council chose not to share the colonists' dwindling supplies of regular bars. Earth fruits and vegetables raised in the arboretum were prepared for them. In these new roles, with their chemically induced fog lifted, the Dalits discovered that they could learn and function on their own. In the close confines of Hawan, they communicated with one another outside the Net. Interacting with colonists, they learned of the fatal damage to the rejuvenation chambers and the recent deaths. From Anu's Dalit, they became aware that Anu was drinking heavily and acting irrationally. His wife slept in the infirmary.

Fearing for their safety, the Dalits whispered to one another to call a gathering. It had no precise agenda because they weren't skilled in such things. They chose to meet in the abandoned Guard Hall, where they muttered to those beside them about the strange occurrences.

One Dalit slowly rose to speak to them all. "My name is 363. I was the Dalit to Captain En.Lil until he left. I heard many things as his Dalit." She paused, pursing her lips and wringing her hands, feeling uncomfortable at public speaking. "Captain En.Lil is a noble and loyal Alterran. He saw Hawan's food supplies were dwindling, but the Council of Elders failed to act. Seeing that the way back to Alterra was forever closed and that the rejuvenation chambers had failed, he concluded that we must accept things the way they are. There's no way back. To live means to change."

The Dalits noisily talked among themselves until 363 collected her thoughts. "We must plan our futures for the way things are now. Captain En.Lil saw this, and he sought a new life here on Earth. He found a wife so that he could have children, and he took those with him who wanted those same things." She stamped her foot. "Aren't those things that we want too?"

"Yeah, why should we be treated differently?" called a Dalit from the rear of the room.

"That's right!" one at the front yelled.

"They don't even look us in the eyes; they think we're machines!" said another.

Quietly, and with stammering, 363 continued, "I think we should do as Captain En.Lil did. This place holds only death for us. We must escape. I'm not saying that we should walk out the door right now. Captain En.Lil carefully planned for many months. I think we should start planning."

The hall was quiet for a while, but some began questioning her.

"What makes you think we have the skills?"

"I don't know anything but cleaning rooms," said another. "I haven't seen beyond the walls of Hawan. I don't know what to expect."

"There are monsters out there," said another. "We've heard them rumbling."

"What would we eat? Captain En.Lil knew things we don't," worried another.

363 remained standing. "That's true. I'm not brave myself at all. But I've seen what others can do with a plan. Wouldn't it make sense for us to consider developing a plan? What if all of them died and left us alone? Many have died already."

"That's right. I work at the infirmary."

363 bravely continued, "We must keep our eyes open. Perhaps some of us could volunteer to perform a job that's open because of a death, so that we could learn something useful in case we decide to leave."

The Dalit from the infirmary who'd served Ki and Uras tea stood to speak. "That's not all. Honorable En.Ki is worried. Something bad is predicted—a flood. Even Captain En.Lil's new city is at risk. Anu is mad at him. He wishes Captain En.Lil to drown. Ki wants to move." 363 took a deep breath after her long speech, and the hall erupted in emotional chatter.

One shouted, her voice choking with emotion, "If Anu cares so little about his own son, what chance do the likes of us have?"

Over the continuing din, 363 shouted, "We're forever slaves. If something bad happens, they'll think only of themselves. They'll abandon us like their machines. We have no choice. We must escape."

Those in the crowd called out, "That's right!"

"She speaks the truth!"

"They don't care about us."

"We must do something."

363 waved them to be quiet. "This is a serious step, and we must consider it carefully. If we leave, there will be no turning

back. Everyone must agree, and we must all work together in our plan to leave. Think this over, and we shall vote in one month. This is the path followed by Captain En.Lil and the guardsmen. I witnessed these things, and they came to pass. In the meantime, keep your eyes and ears open." Finished, 363 put her head down and left the hall.

CHAPTER 25

KI

The weight of preserving Hawan fell on Ki's shoulders. Anu and the Council continued to make demands as if nothing unusual were happening, isolating themselves in their chambers. Only the rejuvenation research gave Ki hope. After searching the Library, he discovered the original theories underlying its technology. Although refined over the years to boost power, the fundamental principles remained the same. Without new quantum batteries, he needed a new power source. Given Earth's primitive state, he was pessimistic. Being Ki, he didn't give up. He considered an enhancement of Hawan's wave entrapment system, through which the energy of waterfalls was converted into useable energy. Ki had been able to meet Hawan's needs. The mountain granite, with its crystalline coating of nanobots, had been essential to generating energy. His system was at maximum capacity, however, and the rejuvenation chambers required tremendous power.

As dawn approached after another night spent working, an exhausted Ki turned from his work, needing a distraction. Knowing he couldn't sleep, he headed to the deserted observation deck. It was peaceful and quiet, with only the constant hum of the wind outside the protective shield. To the east, the dark edge of the Earth was just beginning to be reborn in a deep rose, which eventually turned pink with the coming rise of the sun. The oppressive clouds broke in a welcome respite. Ki admired the beautiful, swirling clouds catching the first rays. Closing his eyes and emptying his mind, he hoped for inspiration for solving their problems. He began the traditional meditation of emptying his mind and concentrating on the relaxation of each body part. After a while, his meditation was interrupted by the warmth of the sun on his face. Making his tunic transparent, he felt the sun's glow tingling the skin on his muscular chest down to his outstretched fingertips. Slipping on his eyewear, he opened his eyes as the full orb rose over the distant horizon, above the mists covering lower mountain peaks. The first rays were always the most exhilarating. The dynamism and fluidity of universal processes inspired him. Stars were timeless engines of energy, and the blinding sunlight encasing the enclosed observation deck injected noticeable warmth. This is the answer—only the sun could provide the level of energy he needed. On Alterra, they drew power from solar collectors orbiting the planet, which was preserved in quantum batteries conveyed to the surface. Later that morning, after a brief nap, he challenged his assistants to develop a solution.

Mikhale thought aloud, "Sunlight is filtered by the atmosphere."

"I don't want excuses, Mikhale. Find out of it fluctuates over the Earth. Do a study whether there is any location or time of year when there might a window when the rays more directly reach the surface. Or whether there is a location with enhanced electromagnetism."

Weeks went by as they combed data from still-functioning instruments. They believed that on the morning of the summer solstice, the sun's rays would most directly break through the magnetosphere, providing the most concentrated radiant waves. However, the energy could be magnified only in a generator. The only capable substance was ancient granite and sandstone. Rock of the required size would weigh too much to be transported by hovercraft in a single piece. They would need to cut the stone and weld it at the building site. It was too immense a project for their depleted crew. A solution eluding him, Ki was frustrated. He missed the ability to brainstorm with Lil, who frequently had a practical insight. He decided to violate Anu's edict by attempting *mencomm*. He created a bubble blocking the Net, closed his eyes, and thought deeply, probing to reach Lil's mind.

"Lil, this is Ki. I need to talk with you."

The mind probe jolted Lil, and Alana asked what had happened. "It's my brother. Please take Iskur outside."

When she left, he concentrated, "What's wrong? Is the flood imminent?"

"Nothing new on the ice sheet. I'm still working on restoring the rejuvenation chamber. More have died. We want to harness solar energy, but we need your help with constructing a generator."

"More died?"

"There have been accidents and other conditions we can't treat."

"We'll help," Lil said eagerly. *Khamlok's purpose is to save you.* "What do you need?"

"It's still under development," said Ki. "An optimal location for the generator is the plain you described for the Summer Meeting. Our instruments have found unusual electromagnetism there; as if it's a conduit. Earth people must have discovered the special power of that that place, particularly on the morning of the summer solstice."

"Yes, I felt it," Lil agreed. "The Earth people have two concentric, wooden circles there channeling the sunrays at dawn."

"If they achieve an affect with mere wood, surely granite and sandstone would exponentially magnify the power. If I can cut the stone, transport it, and engineer it properly, that's what we'll use."

"The hovercraft could only accommodate fairly small blocks," Lil noted.

"Yes," Ki agreed. "If we cut small ones, we don't have the engineering equipment to fit them together tightly."

"Alana told me of a plant whose juice makes stone light and malleable. When dry, the stone resumes its original consistency."

"That's too good to be true."

"I'll ask her to take us where it grows."

"This could be a major breakthrough. I'll come tomorrow at midday."

Alana found Lil slumped in his chair. "Are you all right?" she asked, gently shaking him. "What's happened now?"

Lil roused himself, but he looked tired. "*Mencomm* exhausts me," he said rubbing his eyes. "Ki needs to build a power generator at the Summer Meeting grounds. Remember that double wooden circle through which the sun rises?"

Alana nodded, sitting down beside him. "Of course."

Lil asked, "Do you know how it got there, who built it?"

"The ancestors. That sacred site is ancient."

"Ki thinks the location wasn't an accident," Lil said. "He can capture the energy he needs there."

"How? Build at the Summer Meeting camp?" She made a face. As Earthkeeper, she didn't like the idea.

"Alana, don't worry. We won't disturb your sacred site. We'll construct nearby. Alterrans incorporate nature's beauty in our structures. Trust me. Your people can use it when we're done."

"What will it look like?"

"We'll use the most durable stone, which is very heavy. You once told me of a plant that allowed birds to build nests in the mountain rock."

"Yes, it's very rare, but I remember where to find it."

"Could you take us there tomorrow?" asked Lil.

"We can't get there in a day, even with the horses."

"Ki will fly us."

The next day, Ki let Lil pilot the craft. Alana eagerly slid into the window seat. Having missed flying, Lil took the long way to see what was happening with the glacier. Ki observed, "Our measurements indicate that the glacier is growing again because of the comet soot and the clouds blocking the sunlight. Hawan is in danger, so we need a new place. To be safe, I've selected a site in the middle latitudes untouched by glacier, where the floodwaters slowly recede. It's close to Eridu."

"Here it is—the glacier is magnificent," he said, circling over top and then flying down the plain. When he'd flown awhile, he asked, "Is it likely the ice sheet will break? Won't the cracks just freeze over?"

"That's possible," said Ki. "But we don't have the manpower to collect the data now that the Guard has left."

Lil grimaced, knowing this was his fault. "Were you able to analyze the data I sent you?"

Ki raised an eyebrow. "From the crystal? About the other dimension?" When Lil nodded, he said, "Our hypothesis is that somehow Drood and Alana connect with another dimension, which could be called another universe, one in which the Quantum Consciousness materializes their thoughts. I don't know if Alana's spirit world is the same as Drood's or yet another one. The multiverse is virtually infinite, you know."

"She usually enters by expanding her senses with psychedelic mushrooms, but also when she's terrified. How might he do it? He takes his warriors along with him."

"He needs a tremendous power source. Perhaps he chanced upon an energy crystal similar to the one I used for your device. I wish we knew his source; we could use it instead of building this generator."

"We haven't discovered an access point on Alterra. Maybe Earth is unique. Its magnetosphere is tremendously stronger than ours."

"It's a possible explanation. Its powerful electromagnetism might be attracting dark energy—on a far lesser scale than a black hole, but strong enough to serve as a brane intersection."

"Hmm," said Lil. "If that hypothesis is true and there is any other intelligent life in the universes, they'll all be attracted to Earth, whether to conquer it or use it."

"We might need a greater commitment here than we envisioned," said Ki.

"Right. We don't want others gaining access to a power this great." Lil flew to the landmark Alana had given him in the mountain range near Hawan. Being unable to land, he hovered and lowered Ki and Alana in harnesses to collect the plants growing from vining trellises hanging on the mountainside. She pointed out the thick tubular stalks with brown, silky threads at the top. When Ki cut the stalk, a liquid, thick like sap, flowed out, which he bagged. Eager to begin analyzing his samples, Ki insisted on returning immediately. Lil flew directly back, not bothering to cloak.

At just that time, Margon was returning from one of his clandestine meetings with Azazel. Hearing a strange whirring sound, he took cover and looked up to see a flying ship pass overhead. He had much to report to the queen.

CHAPTER 26
QUEEN HILABA

"My queen, the strange bird flew above my head, barely above the treetops, I swear to you," reported Margon, standing before Queen Hilaba in her private room. He was faint with hunger, not having stopped to make camp, so eager was he to bring her this news.

"You've never seen one in Khamlok, though?"

"No, my lady. Azazel travels only on horseback."

"Then it's just as Koko told me," Queen Hilaba clapped her hands with excitement. "What's your impression of this Azazel? Could he be our ally?"

"He won't discuss it. We shared drinks. It wasn't mead, but a drink made from grapes they call wine. You would like it. As you know, men frequently speak the truth when drinking. Azazel is the natural leader. He's a great and skilled warrior who works tirelessly for his people. But—"

"There's always a 'but,'" interrupted the queen.

"Yes, my lady. He suspects that Lil, the leader, desires to control him. Through his eyes, the people in his original home were little more than slaves of Lil's family. So he's deeply distrustful. The men he's training look to him for leadership.

That much is clear. When I delivered the sample weapons, I trained his men. Never once did I see Lil come to the practice field or attend the mock battles."

"How strange!" Combat was the only subject of interest to King Azor.

"Yes," Margon agreed. "Also, he said that their defenses are inadequate."

"Inadequate defenses? Hmm."

"If King Azor decides to attack, my queen, you will find many riches there. Stacks of furs, ivory, jewelry, animals, and enough grain and other food to feed all our starving people for years. Is there more that my queen would have me do at the moment?"

"Not right now, Margon. I thank you for your service. I'll see that production begins at once on the war hatchets for Azazel. Now, leave me," she said.

The queen lived and breathed with worry about this new power sprouting up almost unnoticed on their border. An enemy with flying ships would have other magical weapons. With a growing army, they could invade overnight, slaughtering them as they slept. Azor must wake up. History's lesson was that you were either an invader or a victim, and victims were enslaved. Azor, in his prime, had been the strong one. Having a formidable adversary made her squirm. She pictured her fine dwelling torched and herself dragged off as a slave to a new life of emptying chamber pots. Would she be whipped for insolence? Worse, would she lose fingers or an eye for displeasing her mistress with some inadvertent curling of her lips? She shuddered. No, they had to find a weakness that would assure their victory. After days of wracking her brain, the only advantage she could conjure was a surprise attack. From Koko's reports, this sleeping giant of an opponent was concerned with building and raising children. She knew human nature. They wouldn't be content for long. When those children grew to adulthood, they'd be greedy for more land. With their superior numbers, her people wouldn't stand a chance. No, they *had* to strike first. In their weaker state, they needed an ally on the inside. Everything depended upon reaching an alliance with Azazel. Or did it? She wondered what her old friend Yoachim thought about the strangers. Yoachim was the only true leader of the scattered Albion villages. She ordered her one-eyed house slave to find Margon for a special assignment.

She met Margon outside her dwelling, near the muddy flat that had once brimmed with colorful wildflowers; after the stinging, acidic rain, delicate flowers didn't bloom anymore. Her people had been fortunate to discover the underground tubular plants that were now the main staple of their diets. The call to raid the giants' food supplies might rally the starving masses to her cause. She ordered, "Margon, I want you to visit Yoachim in Albion."

"Whatever you command, my lady," he said, having had time to eat and refresh himself, but not having trimmed his long, wispy beard. He wore his long traveling cloak and leggings, which were caked with mud. "Are we no longer enemies?"

She laughed. "You always know what I'm thinking."

"I do my best, my lady," he replied with a weary smile.

"We have a new shared enemy, do we not?" she said, tilting her head and tapping her finger on her pouty lips. She reached down and plucked a dead weed from the mud. "That makes him our new friend."

"I assume you refer to the city of giants, my lady, and you devise a plan in case we cannot make Azazel our ally."

"Exactly so," she said, snapping her finger. There was nothing like intrigue to make one feel young again. "When you spoke to Azazel, he mentioned nothing at all about attending the Summer Meeting or arranging for Yoachim to come to bless the new brood, did he?"

"No, my lady."

"Well, then. Not only are they hoarding food, but they're disregarding ancient customs and not paying proper respect to Yoachim. This Lil acts as if he's the leader. Yoachim can't be too happy about that, can he?"

"Well put, my lady," responded Margon. "What would you have me ask him?"

"Ask him, casually if you can, what he thinks of the giants. My guess is that he hates them more than he dislikes us."

"I imagine so, my lady," said Margon.

"When you have his confidence, point out that we now have a shared enemy that may soon be powerful. Tell him that it's time we formed an alliance. If he agrees, invite him here."

"Very wise, my lady," he said. "Is there more, or shall I leave at once?"

"Go."

"Yes, my lady," he said with a nod, and he turned to leave.

A little more than a month later, Margon entered her village while she was out walking after a frigid rain that had kept her a prisoner indoors.

"Margon, what news?" she asked eagerly, avoiding a puddle in the muddy yard.

"My queen, when I'm more presentable, I'll give you a full account," he said, brushing travel debris from his clothing, his beard now hanging down to his chest. "It was just as you suspected. Yoachim is worried about the giants and their over-hunting. They rudely banished young men, who now aspire to repay them for the insult. They've been trained by Azazel and know the city's layout. He'll arrive in a fortnight."

"Well done, Margon!" she exclaimed with the flush of a young girl. "Go and refresh yourself, and then come to me." Hilaba danced around in delight.

CHAPTER 27

KI

Ki was cautiously optimistic, although his scribes were openly celebrating. The juice derived from Alana's plant, when applied to the granite sample, temporarily made the rock light and malleable. They created a model generating station with interlocking stone pieces that fit so tightly together that, after the stone became dry, nothing fit between them. The scribes calculated that by dismantling damaged buildings at Hawan, they would have sufficient granite for the generator walls. With application of the new juice compound, the pieces could be transported by hovercraft. In testing their models, they applied the excess power to the replicators to replace long-damaged equipment.

To his surprise, Anu announced at a special session of the surviving colonists that he'd received a communication from Alterra. Their scientists had exploded nuclear devices in the planet's inner core, which acted as a catalyst to reinitiate the chain reactions for the core to be self-heating. As the temperature increased, the magnetosphere eventually began to reappear and was gradually screening out harmful rays. Although people wouldn't live above ground anytime soon with the severe surface damage, they now had hope. The supreme leader had authorized use of the terraforming technology that had been developed for alien worlds, which he'd banned centuries before. There was no mention of the intelligent machines, however, and Ki presumed that they were still banned.

The Alterran development caused Ki to change his own plans. With Alterran society having hope for recovery, there was a greater priority for their newfound energy sending Anu back to ascend as supreme leader. If Alterra couldn't activate the portal, then he would activate it from Earth. His calculations showed that he couldn't maintain a high level of power for long, but it would hold long enough for Anu, and perhaps a few others, to return. Uncertain if his plan would work, he kept it a secret from Anu while his testing continued.

Although heavy snow blanketed much of the peninsula, Ki wanted to commence construction so that they'd be ready by the summer solstice. He sent scientists in a cloaked hovercraft to survey a site near the Summer Meeting stakes. Finding no sign of human life in the area, they hovered and cleared an area of snow to mark the location of each stone that would be laid to create the generator walls. They left space between each stone that would be filled with a resonating membrane for the wave energy.

Ki calculated that with the application of the formula produced by the roko juice, which his team synthesized to obtain the necessary quantity, his staff could handle the extraction and loading of the stones at Hawan onto the hovercraft, and Lil's men would unload and erect the stones. Everything was coming together.

CHAPTER 28
ANU

Anu's mood improved significantly now that he was again receiving communications from Alterra, even if sporadic. That Alterran technology was capable of saving their decimated homeworld was a matter of immense pride. But this development also increased his frustration. Since it was his time to ascend, it was urgent that he return. If, in his absence, his father remained as supreme leader beyond his term, it would give the House of Kan a claim that he was no longer the legitimate, divinely appointed leader; they'd claim he was a usurper. Sure that the House of Kan would oppose his father and threaten the peace, and learning that discord was already developing in the densely packed and ill-equipped underground bunkers, Anu obsessed about returning home.

With a mixture of hope and frustration, he groomed himself and resumed making his morning rounds of Hawan. Since Ki had diverted energy to critical areas, the open courtyard was no longer heated, and the once-beautiful gardens were now deep in the freeze of endless winter. Although warmly bundled for the frigid temperatures, Anu felt the chill of the wintry mountain air. He stepped his way through the crusty snow. With Hawan's population now reduced to a fraction of its original size, Dalits filled colonial posts and had little time for grounds maintenance. A pitiful situation, thought Anu. Signs of decline were everywhere. Hovercrafts filled the landing area, since there were few qualified pilots and the energy required to regenerate the fuel cells had been needed for higher priorities.

Varying his routine this morning, he decided to visit the building destroyed in the impact. Nearing it, he wondered why the snow was so trampled. Then he saw that huge portions of the stone walls had been removed. What was this? He scratched his head and searched his memory. The Council had given Ki permission to create an alternative facility. Had Ki begun? The new facility was a continent away. Anu was not an engineer, but there must be an easier way to build it than to remove and transport these heavy stones. He would personally demand an explanation from Ki.

On his way to the Ministry, though, it occurred to Anu that he was overreacting, and he hadn't shown his appreciation to Ki. He was proud of him, working tirelessly to keep everything running smoothly. He considered having the Council pass a proclamation of thanks. Anu found Ki, as usual, at his desk working on a simulation.

Seeing Anu approach, Ki was stunned, quickly hiding his surprise. "Good morning, son," Anu said, his demeanor conveying his old calm self-assurance. "You don't need to rise." After transforming his heavy outer tunic into his pristine silver uniform, he seated himself beside Ki's desk.

"Good morning. You're in excellent spirits." Ki produced hot tea.

Curious after hearing Anu's steady voice, Uras emerged from a nearby room, drying her hair. She'd dyed it her natural brown. Surprised, he asked, "What have you done to your hair?" He fidgeted with a small pyramid on Ki's desk to avoid her eyes peeking at him from under her towel.

"If I'm going to die on this blasted planet, then I want my own hair color."

Anu chuckled. Uras would never lose her spirit. His beautiful wife was aging well. What would it be like to grow old together, as they did in the ancient days? He shook his head and looked away. Surely they would find a solution before it came to that. To break the awkward silence, Ki cleared his throat and said, "Mother has been of immense help in stopping the virus. Through her experiments on survivors' holographic twins, we isolated the strain and created an effective vaccine. Thus far, we've had no new cases."

Desiring to say something tender to reconcile with Uras, but being unable as supreme leader to admit being wrong, he said simply, "That's excellent news, Ki." Looking at Ki, he said, "Which brings me to the reason I came here. I discovered the stone removed from our walls."

"Father, please don't be mad."

Anu put up his hand. "Don't misunderstand me. I'm not here to criticize, but to understand what's going on. You've done tremendously valuable work, and I want you to know how much I appreciate it."

Since his father was rarely complimentary, Ki was speechless. "Thanks," he said simply.

"Without Lil, I need to take charge. I've had a difficult time accepting that we're stranded here. It's a shame that I won't ascend as supreme leader. I would have made a better leader because of my time here. I've gained new insights. If only I'd had the chance." He lightly tapped the pyramid on Ki's desk.

Uras put down her towel. "I'm surprised to hear you admit that."

Making a face, he looked away and put down the pyramid. "Maybe we Alterrans became too complacent, too dependent on the Ministry of Central Planning, and we used the nourishment bar drug too heavily. Our people lost their initiative. I didn't want to admit that our circumstances were going to require us to change. But I guess I just wasn't facing facts. Maybe Lil had a point."

Uras and Ki shared an astonished glance.

"Now, back to the matter of the missing stone. What's going on?"

"Father," said Ki, with a twinkle in eye. "I was waiting to tell you when I was sure this would work. But you're here, so now's the time. Mother, you should sit down to hear this."

Uras was too curious to turn away, and she, rather uncomfortably, slid down beside Anu.

"To get right to it," Ki said, his usually intransigent face beaming with pride, "we're constructing a generator capable of creating high voltage energy. Initially, we created it for the rejuvenation chamber. But with Alterra recovering, we'll use the power to open the portal. We'll send you and the Council back to Alterra."

"What?" screamed Uras, throwing her arms in the air with excitement. Ki grinned at her.

Anu sat incredulous, moving to the edge of his seat. "You can?"

"This isn't a perfect system. Initially, it might work only at one location at one day of the year. But we have improvements under development—"

Anu, confused, put up his hand, "Ki, please, slow down and let me absorb what you just said. You can send me home?"

"Yes," Ki said, grinning as broadly as he ever had.

Anu looked distant. He breathed deeply. Barely audibly, he said, "How sure are you of success?"

Uras jumped up, crying, "Ki, that's absolutely wonderful. You're so brilliant. I knew you'd find a way to save us!" Uras danced over, gave him a big hug, and kissed him on his forehead.

"Please, Uras. Ki, how certain are you?"

Ki explained the process, ending with, "Lil and the Guard are helping us complete the construction. I call the site the Power Circle."

"Oh. Lil is helping you?" said Uras, trying to be casual, not looking at Anu.

Ki replied quickly, "Yes. We don't have the manpower to do this without the Guard."

Anu let out a deep breath as Ki and Uras tensely awaited his reaction. "Uras, you know how angry I am with Lil." He hesitated and drummed his fingers on Ki's desk. "But," he paused, pulling on his ear lobe, "I want to go home more than anything in this universe. If Lil's help is essential to completing the Power Circle, then I'll permit it."

"Anu, that's wise of you," said Uras, putting a hand on his shoulder.

Anu put his hand over hers and smiled. He abhorred reversing a decree, but his ascension was worth any price. "I trust you'll have it ready for this coming solstice?" Mentally, he listed items to accomplish before the ceremonies. The coronation of the ascending supreme leader was a monumental event, even when performed in underground bunkers.

Interrupting his thoughts, Ki said, "That's the plan. We've prepared the construction site and begun transporting the stones. The inner circle is nearly complete. We've performed holographic simulations, and everything's working as we predicted. More tests are required, though. But I suggest you begin your preparations."

"I'll begin this very moment," said Anu, rising and glowing with excitement. "Ah, I can't believe it!"

Ki cautioned, "Keep in mind that this wormhole will be small. In order to send you all back, we won't send possessions."

"Who cares about that?" Uras danced about. "We're going home! I can't wait to see Ninhursag." A twinge of regret entered her mind that she wouldn't see her grandchild Iskur grow up. *Iskur—what's to become of him if Lil returns home?*

"I'll be able to ascend on time!" Anu repeated with a clap of his hands, with renewed energy and a broad smile. "This means more to me than words can say."

"We're going home!" Uras squealed in delight. She ran and kissed a startled Anu, who squeezed her.

"I can't tell you how happy I am, Ki," said Anu, beaming with joy. "Going home. These are words I've longed to say for a long time. I'm going to call an emergency session of the Council this very afternoon. I'd like for you to be there to get the thanks you deserve. You've made me extremely proud." As he was leaving, Anu said quietly, "And tell Lil that I appreciate his help."

CHAPTER 29
QUEEN HILABA

Feeling the time was right, Hilaba went to Azor, whom she rarely saw. Her father had gifted his eldest daughter in exchange for Azor's protection, and Azor had accepted to gain access to land serving as an important buffer against Shylfing. Although Azor left no doubt that he wasn't attracted to his new bride, Hilaba always felt that he respected her mind. She didn't test this belief often. Before leaving her rooms, she'd fixed her freshly washed hair and dressed carefully in the imported cloth from the south mainland. She cherished the cloth, which wasn't available with nearly all the port cities under water. Today she was using all her wiles. When she told the attendant to announce the arrival of the queen, the flustered man asked her to wait while he asked the king's permission. The king was eating breakfast, sitting at the head of his long table with a few key warriors by the roaring fire in his great room. Thinking that her visit might be amusing, Azor permitted her entry.

She strolled in proudly, her back straight and her chin held high. "Good morning, Your Grace. You look well."

Azor replied slyly, "As do you, Hilaba." Smirking, the unkempt warriors kept their heads down as they slurped their gruel from crude wooden bowls.

She pursed her lips, displeased by their disrespect. "I don't wish to waste time. I can see that you're busy with, uh, *important* people." She gave the warriors a knowing look so they wouldn't miss her sarcasm. "So," she said, growing serious, "I'll go straight to the point. I've learned that there is a great dark cloud hovering where the sun sets, and we must act quickly."

"What sort of cloud?" asked Azor with amusement, taking a bite of bread. One of the warriors coughed, choking back laughter.

As Hilaba's story about the blonde giants unfolded, Azor and his warriors quit smirking and listened intently. They quickly grasped the danger as well as the opportunity for plunder. With so many enemies decimated by the floods, there had been no great battles of late. The meager Albion folk had always been too scattered to attract his warriors' attention. Maybe this had changed.

When she paused for breath, Azor interrupted, "Thank you, Hilaba. You needn't trouble yourself further. Togar will see you out."

Seeing Hilaba unwilling to depart, Togar gently tapped her arm and motioned for her to follow. She didn't hide her disappointment at being dismissed prematurely. If they were smart, they'd pose questions and invite a full explanation. She considered kindling their interest by disclosing her strategic sale of the new war hatchets to Azazel as an enticement for him to join their side, but he hadn't committed, which worried her. Since Azor had injured her pride, she held her tongue.

Having an enemy to vanquish turned King Azor into a new man. He ceased his excessive drinking, was too busy for his concubines, and devoted himself into reconditioning his rotund body. The king sent messages to the far-flung lands recalling his surviving warriors and ordered his aides to forge more of the new heat-treated, stone war hatchets.

Although excluded from Azor's war councils, Hilaba continued to hatch her own plans. Without Azazel, her firmest ally was Yoachim, who was now waiting in her antechamber. "Yoachim, my old, dear friend, it's so wonderful to see you," she gushed when entering the room. She held out her hands to him.

"Hilaba, you look as beautiful as always; the years have been most kind," Yoachim said, taking her hand but refusing to call his old enemy "queen." He didn't like her, and after they dealt with Alana's city, he'd terminate this distasteful alliance.

"We both know that isn't true, but I'm glad to hear it." She smiled, studying him, noticing that he'd changed very little over the years. *Does he have potions to prevent aging?* "Let's sit," she said with a grand sweep of her hand. After they became comfortable at a small table, a slave brought brewed tea, and they traded stories of the great flood and their people's struggles. Hilaba soon grew impatient with the small talk. "We have much to discuss. Should we get right to it?"

"That's why I came, you know," he said, amused by her forthrightness.

"I know that your people are afraid of us. They're too primitive to understand why enemies must form an alliance."

Yoachim winced. "Hilaba, let's ignore that for now."

"Yes, let's," she replied, taking a sip of tea. "Have you heard anything new about these creatures?"

"Well, yes, actually. They continue to view the entire peninsula as their personal territory, hunting wherever they please. Now they're even building far beyond their city."

"Building?"

"Yes, at our sacred Meeting grounds," he spat with contempt, his eyes narrowed by fury.

"What are they building?"

"I don't know. Like magic, the snow was cleared, and despite the fact that the ground is frozen solid, a circle was leveled. Yet there's no sign of anyone crossing the snow. Immense new stones have appeared there, stones foreign to that location that are of precise cutting and perfect fit. The pattern mirrors our wooden stakes."

"You're sure it isn't your people or that crazy fellow—Drood, is it?"

Yoachim shook his head. "No, this project is *far* beyond anything that our people could construct."

"That *is* interesting news. You say the stones appeared by magic?" asked Hilaba, feeling humbled by the giants' awesome abilities.

"We heard rumors that Alana's starmen left the main colony. I can only guess that the original colony remains, with all of its magic, and they've learned of the power of our sacred grounds."

As Hilaba analyzed the new information, a huge grin came over her face. "Then you think they'll be busy there on the day of the summer solstice?"

He rubbed his chin and narrowed his eyes. "That's a reasonable guess."

With growing excitement, Hilaba perched on edge, waving her hands. "Alana's starmen may be there as well, don't you think?"

Yoachim shrugged, not seeing her point. "Maybe. It seems likely that anything this big would involve all of their kind."

Hilaba clapped her hands and stamped her feet with delight. "Oh, this is too good to be true." She leaped to her feet and twirled around. "Don't you see? If the group is preoccupied elsewhere, it will be the absolutely perfect time to attack!"

"What?" asked Yoachim, raising his eyebrows. "Attack? Is that why you've brought me here?"

"How else can we eliminate them?"

He furrowed his brows and mused, "The solstice wouldn't give us much time to plan."

"We *must* attack. They'll be distracted with their task at the Summer Meeting grounds. And they'll be spread out."

Yoachim pulled at his long beard, considering her plan. "Can the king have his warriors ready by then? For such a large force to reach the eastern hilltop unseen, we would need to take the long way, coming from the north. Travel might still be difficult at that time of year with this blasted cold."

Hilaba replied, grinning broadly. "I'll see to it that he will. We can count on your full cooperation?"

Yoachim looked out the window, remembering the sting of disrespect. And it was his sacred duty to defend the Meeting grounds for the good of his people. That land belonged to them. The impertinence of these insufferable fools! He nodded his agreement.

"That's wonderful!" Hilaba gushed. "Your gift of foresight and knowledge of the peninsula is precisely what we need, and I trust that you'll gather those unfortunate banished men to our side. After we secure Albion, we'll of course withdraw and leave you as the sole ruler."

"All right, Hilaba," Yoachim nodded. Having made his decision, he was eager to begin. "You can count on me. For foresight, I'll need access to your religious grounds."

After making the necessary arrangements for Yoachim, Hilaba put on her furs and went to Azor, practically skipping in glee across the frozen ground. She found him in the practice yard, despite the coldness of the wintry day. Most of his surviving warriors had returned, and they spent their days honing their fighting skills. A mock battle now raged. A leaner Azor, looking impressive in a bear fur over his muscular shoulders, was annoyed to see Hilaba once again invading his territory. He'd told her he'd take care of this, and he didn't appreciate her meddling.

"You shouldn't be here," he snapped, ignoring her while he directed the larger fighting force against one directed by General Kagan. Aides stood ready to run his orders run into battle.

Hilaba, appearing tiny as she trailed behind Azor's formidable figure, persisted. "I think you'll want to hear what I have to say, Your Grace." Hilaba stood her ground, staring at him until he paused and motioned curtly for her to speak.

Hilaba intoned regally, "Your Grace, I've met with Yoachim, and there is news. May we speak privately?" He studied her.

With irritation, he turned over his task of running the battle to his adjutant. Taking large, quick strides, he went to the edge of the practice field, forcing Hilaba to jog to keep up. Nearly out of breath, she recounted Yoachim's tale. "Your Grace, it's clear. The time to strike is dawn of the summer solstice!" Azor folded his arms and walked a few paces away, thinking. She pursued him, asserting, "They're powerful but isolated, with no inkling of an attack. They won't be prepared."

The king put his hands behind his back and looked at her, considering her arguments. Most of his experienced warriors had arrived, at least those who'd survived the flood, and he needed to keep them occupied. The solstice would be a tight schedule, but possible. A tight schedule would require less food supply. Despite his aides' best prodding, few food stores had been uncovered.

"If you doubt the risks, Your Grace, think of the treasure Margon has seen. Food and furs are plentiful. Your people would be forever grateful if you distribute food to the starving. If the weather deteriorates more, even we might soon be struggling."

Perhaps she was more intelligent than he'd thought, but his men would laugh at him if they heard him discussing war strategy with her. He glanced and confirmed before responding that his men's attention was absorbed with individual combats. "Hilaba, you raise good points, but I'm not comfortable moving so quickly. We don't have sufficient information about the terrain or this enemy. From everything you've said, we have good reason to be cautious. They're not what they seem. You don't understand warfare, and you should stay out of it. Battles must be properly planned."

Stamping her foot, she argued, "I do understand, Your Grace. I understand that the element of surprise is of key importance. It may well be the decisive factor for the, shall we say, weaker opponent."

He winced. Wasn't it presumptuous to assume that they were weaker? He had no first-hand knowledge, only fantastical stories told by that Koko, whose loyalty was always suspected. A worm such as Koko might have been bribed by one of the southern tribes to entice him to attack unnecessarily. The man was known turncoat. There had always been rumors that Koko was a spy for the bloodthirsty Danes.

"I appreciate the need to know the terrain and the enemy, you are very wise and experienced," she continued, exasperated by his reticence. "Yoachim can supply all necessary information about any peninsula location. Not only that, as a shaman, he has the gift of foresight. He'll be your eyes and ears. And there's more. My aide, Margon, has visited their city. He's befriended their chief warrior, a malcontent known as Azazel. He complained that their defenses are inadequate—his very words! This Azazel may even join us if we offer a sufficient incentive. Yoachim can supply warriors trained by Azazel. The leader banished and humiliated them, and they want their revenge. Best of all, they know the city, Your Grace. Only the gods smiling on you could lay such an advantage at your feet."

Azor gazed thoughtfully into the horizon. Good omens were hard to ignore. If he conquered these giants, the storytellers would praise him forever. He'd order that worm, Koko, to compose a new ballad in his honor. "I'll discuss it with my war council this evening. Have Yoachim and Margon attend." He strode back to the war games, immediately giving new strategy orders. As he walked away, Hilaba smiled happily; he was taking her seriously.

That evening, King Azor's war council met at the long table in his Great Hall, warmed by a roaring hearth fire. To avoid distractions from serving slaves, only faithful Togar served their meal, and only water was poured.

"We've not traveled to that wasteland," groused a warrior, sharpening his stone knife. "There isn't enough time to have scouts learn the trails. I wager that the snow is deeper and the air colder."

"Who cares about the peninsula?" asked a seasoned warrior, shaking his head of matted gray hair. "The tale of giants has been exaggerated. Nothing in Albion has ever been worth our time. They're scattered, primitive clans. Even cave dwellers."

"Worse, in the north there are cannibals," cautioned an experienced warrior.

Insulted, Yoachim huffed, "My people are peaceful, not stupid. To the north is a crazy mystic. He's harmless."

"You've offended our guest," King Azor rebuked his men. *Would this alliance unravel before they'd put one foot forward?* "Remember that we're allies."

Yoachim took a deep breath. Although he detested this distasteful alliance, he needed Azor's help to rid his land of the giants. To educate them about the terrain, he spread a thin cloth. "Let me show you the rivers and hills." He placed stones and pebbles to show ridges, roads, and streams, laying out the best travel route for so many. "The giants' city is here." He pointed east of the Summer Meeting grounds, to a place a day's ride from the chalky ridge bordering the lowlands. "At this distance, if some are at the Meeting grounds, they won't be able to rescue the city when we attack."

Margon took a bite of bread and sneered. "He isn't giving you the full story. They have flying ships." He told them what he'd witnessed.

"You lying peninsula scum," a greasy-haired warrior barked at Yoachim.

"We can't fight magic!" exclaimed another. The others agreed.

The king nervously tapped his fingers on the table, the flickering fire highlighting the worried expression on his tortured face. "Flying ships? What magic is this?" Hilaba hadn't told him. *What else did she hide?* "We should abandon this plan. Weapons molded from stone can't begin to fight such weapons, surprise or no surprise." He was vain, but he was no fool.

"I agree with you, sire," said gray-haired General Kagan. He'd seen battles in many places, but no flying ships. No one had knowledge even close to these wonders. "This is foolhardy.

Anyone with flying ships is bound to have other weapons beyond our imagination. We should instead seek an alliance."

The king snorted. "An alliance? What could we offer? They'd only want us to be their slaves!" He emptied his water cup and slammed it on the table, hating the thought of subservience to anyone. Perhaps they were overthinking. For all he knew, his people were unknown to them, and they should keep it that way.

Margon held up his hand, seeking to calm their fears. "It's true, I saw a flying ship. I didn't see one used by the people of Khamlok, however. The story I've heard is that this group abandoned their home, leaving the flying ships with the leader's father. The father's mad at them for leaving, and they cannot return. So they live as we do, except that they have long knives of light. Our new hatchets are sharp and deadly, and our arrows can carry fire to burn a hole in their wall."

Angrily, Azor pointed his finger. "Margon, you speak out of both sides of your mouth. Whether or not they have flying ships is decisive. I don't like the uncertainty. Even if the father is angry, if his son is attacked he'll surely come to their rescue!" He crossed his arms and stared into the fire, envisioning the hopeless battle. Spears and hatchets against flying ships!

"Not from what Azazel told me, Your Grace," said Margon defensively.

"How long has it been since you've heard from this Azazel? Hilaba said he might be turned. Will he stand with us?"

Margon scratched his ear, replying with uncertainty. "Your Grace, it's been a while. I'm not sure. He's a complex man. I thought it unwise to be explicit before our plans were decided."

Azor tapped his fingers even harder on the table. "The time might be right for an invasion. Before I decide, I must know more. Where's Koko?"

Margon shrugged and shook his head. "Koko traveled south for the winter."

Azor scanned the faces of his warriors, seeing uncertainty and fear, and turned back to Margon. "I can't risk the lives of my men if we have no chance. Margon, go to their city. Leave immediately. We must know what this Azazel will do and whether the giants have flying ships or other magical weapons."

"Of course, Your Grace. What would you have me promise Azazel for joining our side?" asked Margon, pursing his lips uncomfortably.

Azor was slow to respond. A man like Azazel would expect to be rewarded with nothing less than the leadership of the peninsula. That was one thing he couldn't give. They were starting this war to eliminate a strong threat on their border. He couldn't simply turn it over to a turncoat; the threat would remain in different clothes. In truth, he had no respect for turncoats. No, he'd need to keep Azazel close, under his watchful eye. Or he would send him to a harmless, inconsequential post. Azor answered, "Promise Azazel that he'll be greeted with great esteem at my court, and we'll find a suitable place for him."

"Yes, Your Grace," Margon said, turning to leave, sharing a knowing glance with General Kagan. Margon inwardly sighed, holding little hope of recruiting Azazel with such a meager proposal. Nevertheless, he dutifully prepared to do the king's bidding. He detested traveling at the height of winter, not because of the cold, but because of his inability to cover his tracks in freshly fallen snow. He gave orders for his usual horse to be ready at dawn.

Margon slowly made his way to Khamlok, being hampered by large snowdrifts. Since the guard recognized him, he was admitted. Staying close to the wall, he reached Azazel's practice fields without encountering a single person. The practice field was empty except for the groomers, who told him that the men were busy elsewhere. Margon was intrigued. In all his prior visits, Azazel and his men had not missed a single practice session. It must mean reconciliation with the leader's father. So they would have flying ships once again.

"How long will they be away?" he asked, hoping it would be through the solstice.

The groom didn't seem to know more.

"Would you take a message to Azazel, without anyone else knowing?" he asked.

The groom raised his eyebrows in suspicion.

"Oh, it's nothing bad," he said, laughing. "I bear a small gift." Although Margon hated to risk compromising Azazel by a direct contact, he couldn't dally at the stables indefinitely, nor could he return to the king empty handed.

The groom replied, "Azazel is busy. I can't promise that I can deliver it."

This was not going well, thought Margon. Either he had to get Azazel to come to him, or he had to go to Azazel. He would wait no more than two days.

He camped near the horses. On previous trips, he hadn't made a fire, not wanting to draw attention. This time was different. No food was sent, and it was too cold to avoid a fire. His feet and hands grew numb. After his fire blazed, he produced some jerky from his pack and chewed slowly to savor the small morsels. Hearing the familiar whirring sound, he searched the sky but saw nothing.

Overhead, Azazel was returning with Lil from the Power Circle. He glimpsed Margon below, although Lil seemed not to notice. Azazel scowled, regretting that he'd complained in Margon's presence. Lil deserved his loyalty. If Ki succeeded in creating the new power source, Anu and the Council would return to Alterra, leaving the hovercraft and the other resources of Hawan to those left behind. With the soot from the impact gradually dissipating, Azazel would be free to once again travel throughout Earth. Even better, under Lil's command they could travel unconstrained by the directive. Eventually, Lil would become the supreme leader of Alterra, which would present new opportunities for him as Lil's primary protector. Under Azazel's influence, the two of them had a rare opportunity to restore liberty to Alterrans. Azazel knew that Margon had been hinting about an alliance with his Queen Hilaba. How could those backward people offer him anything?

He'd amused himself with Margon, nothing more. He didn't want to be bothered.

When the groom delivered Margon's message, Azazel responded that he was busy, but he would have items for trade at his summer visit. Recognizing the rebuff and fearing that he'd be taken prisoner, Margon threw his few possessions into his small pack and snuck away, despite dark skies portending yet another snowstorm. He must advise the king so they would abandon the invasion.

At the end of the cold, snowy winter, animals were starving. When it grew dark, the bitter wind smacked his face with icy droplets of snow, impeding his travel. His hair and feet were snow covered. His teeth chattered uncontrollably. Unable to find the trail, he stopped for the night. Although he tethered his horse, it broke free, frightened by the howling wolves. Fighting the driving wind, Margon gathered wood for a fire. He couldn't produce a spark. Hearing the horse's screams when the wolves sank their teeth into its hide, he desperately slogged through the deepening snow searching for a low-limbed tree. Finding only heavily snow-covered fir trees, he crawled below the weighted branches. The pack waited, its members temporarily sated with horseflesh. In the middle of the night, Margon heard their patter surrounding him. With no fire and his movement constrained, his limbs were impossibly numb. When the pack attacked, he was no match.

CHAPTER 30
THE ANNOUNCEMENT

The Dalits had voted to revolt, but they vacillated. Life on Earth would be harsh. They needed to develop survival skills and gather supplies. As they dithered, they spied to learn the colonists' intentions. They redoubled their efforts to replace deceased colonists at crucial tasks. With their numbers reduced, the colonists were in no position to refuse. Thus, Dalits attained positions of responsibility. 363 even obtained a sensitive job in the Council Chambers. According to their plan, if anyone overheard crucial information, he or she would cause the Alterran anthem to play on the communications monitors, and they would gather at once at Guard Hall.

Speculation escalated when Dalits at the Ministry of Science discovered why Ki's scientists made so many trips carrying huge stones cut from Hawan's walls. Word spread that Anu was again grooming and walking the colony grounds, and that he'd reunited with Uras. When Anu called an emergency Council meeting, 363 snuck into a crevice to learn the truth.

Upon entering, the Council members wondered why they'd been pulled from stasis. "Anu, you look as if you're floating.

Why the huge smile?" asked Councilwoman Barian as she was seated.

"I'll let my son answer that," said Anu, grinning and too excited to be seated.

Ki, standing in the center, projected his hologram of the planned generator. "We've created an energy system that will be sufficiently strong to ignite a small quantity of antimatter extracted from the rejuvenation chamber. Our calculations show that a wormhole will be created that will permit us to activate the Alterran portal. We have only enough power to open it momentarily, but long enough to send a few colonists to Alterra."

At this, the Council members looked at one another in astonishment and joy.

"Ki, I can't believe what I'm hearing. How many colonists could be sent back?" asked Councilman Pilian, sitting on the edge of his seat.

Ki smiled. "No more than thirteen. So we propose to send Anu, Uras, and each of you."

Councilman Pilian gasped, "Ah, this is fantastic news." He jumped up and hugged Councilwoman Barian, who was shocked, but she smiled politely.

"I had thought all was lost. This is wonderful," exclaimed Councilman Djane.

Ki waited for the jubilation to subside before continuing. "We at the Ministry are as delighted as you. A word of caution. We believe that sufficient power can be generated only at dawn on the summer solstice at a place with unusual electromagnetic readings. We've been working feverishly to complete the necessary work at a place we've named the Power Circle. We've been transporting granite from the colony walls and bringing sandstone from the southwest to create the generator walls."

"How is all this work possible with our reduced numbers?" asked Councilwoman Barian.

"Lil discovered a substance that makes the stone temporarily malleable and light," he explained. "We transport small pieces and mold them at the site. Lil and the Guard performed the site work."

"Well, I'm glad they've seen the light," said Councilman Trey. "This doesn't absolve them, but I thank them."

"When will you know for certain that it works?" Councilman Pillian asked

"We will be able to verify it soon," said Ki. "The simulations have been successful."

The meeting was adjourned until Ki could conduct the final test, and in leaving, each member thanked him. "Ki, it's such a nice touch that you're playing the Alterran Anthem," said Barian with a smile and a pinch of his arm. Ki wondered who had programmed it. While gathering his equipment, he noticed the anguished look on 363's face in the shadows.

Within the hour, 363 stood before the Dalits in Guard Hall. "Anu, Uras, and the Council are going back to Alterra," she announced solemnly to their panic-stricken faces.

"What does this mean for us?" a trembling Dalit asked.

363 looked at the floor and stammered, "Ki and others will remain on Earth. At least for now."

A Dalit wearing a white uniform rose. "In the Ministry of Science, it's rumored that scientists learned construction from the Teacher, and Ki has sent them far away. They haven't been seen again."

A Dalit with a maid's insignia stood. "We must act now. They will abandon us, taking all the supplies with them, leaving us here to starve. We must take what we need."

"How do we know that they won't take us with them?" asked the Dalit who maintained the building. "They still need servants wherever it is they're going."

Another housekeeping Dalit wondered, "Maybe. But can we take that chance? This is a matter of life and death for us!"

A Dalit dressed in a white infirmary uniform shouted, "We already voted once. Everyone here voted to revolt. There can be no going back. We *must* act now."

Yet another housekeeper complained, "What plan? I've looked through Anu's portal. We're high on a mountaintop covered with snow. We can't survive outside Hawan in this cold."

Sitting in the rear, a Dalit who distributed nourishment bars argued, "She's right. Do we have any materials to build shelters? Do any of us know how to hunt animals? Yes, we could grab things from the storehouse, but would we have the right things?"

A housekeeping Dalit in the front asked, "And how would we leave? The Guard replacements carry weapons. Do we want to steal weapons and kill people? 363, are you going to kill Anu for us to take over Hawan? For all the fancy talk of revolt, I think it's not going to happen."

The Dalits suddenly stopped their heated arguments. Ki emerged from the shadows and walked across the front. He towered beside the dwarflike 363. No member of the House of En had ever paid attention to them.

Ki cleared his throat and smiled. "I heard your debate." He ran his hand through his hair. "Listen, I can understand why you're upset. I would be too if I stood in your shoes. We've been remiss in not communicating with you. I want to assure you that you are valued members of Hawan and that no one will abandon you. You won't starve." He looked around for their reaction. Seeing astonished faces, he continued. "As you heard from 363—" turning to her, "yes, I know your name—I'm optimistic that we can send a small group back to Alterra in a few weeks. The first to return will be Anu, Uras, and the Council of Elders. Anu will ascend as supreme leader as decreed by divine destiny. As you can see, we've had to dismantle part of the colony for building materials. You've heard rumors about a construction team being gone, and that's because they're constructing a new base in a place we call the Cedar Woods. That's not a permanent name. I'm thinking of calling it Heliopolis. It's in a much warmer climate, since it's growing too cold for us to remain here. I think you'll like it when we *all* make the move."

Relieved at the message, but sensing an opportunity, 363 bravely said, "Sir?"

He raised one eyebrow in surprise, and bent over to scrutinize her.

After furtively glancing around the room seeking courage, 363 stammered, "The Dalits have been serving in colonial positions lately. We've proved that we can do more than menial service. Must we go back to being only lowly servants?"

The Dalits' eyes and mouths were opened wide in amazement, and those in the back jostled one another for a better view.

Ki chuckled. "I've noticed your abilities. I'm working on a plan for having more Earth people be our servants and tend the fields, maybe even the mines. I can't make any promises." Standing straight, he looked around the room. "Now I'll leave you to conclude your debate. But I do hope you'll decide in my favor. I really don't relish the thought of you attacking me." He concluded with a smile, confident that he had persuaded them.

After Ki left, one by one the Dalits, feeling a newfound pride, silently arose and went back to work.

CHAPTER 31
ALANA

Sitting outside the Great House working hides by a small fire, Alana looked up, feeling Lil's presence. Not knowing how he'd appeared so silently, she watched him lean casually against a snowy tree. He looked so handsome and young that she marveled that he was ancient by Earth lives. His lively, blue eyes sparkled with mischief, and his lips hinted at amusement. The man was insatiable. His erotic glance sent a shimmer through her body.

She smirked. "It's a good thing that Iskur is playing with Krishna."

"I knew that," he said, smirking back. "I think it's time to make another."

"Do you now?" she bantered. She'd unintentionally let it slip that that women had been taking herbs to prevent pregnancy. For most, the agony of childbirth was too much to bear ever again. For her though, it was time. Having Lil as her protector, she liked the idea of a large family.

"First, I have something to tell you." He drew her up and held her tight.

Confused, she searched his face. The mirth was gone. "What is it?" she asked, dreading the answer. The men who had been occupied with the Power Circle had resumed preparing for this season's planting. She surmised that the construction was complete, and the question that had been troubling her ever since she'd mated Lil stuck in her throat. *Are you leaving me?* She felt faint.

"My parents are returning to Alterra at the solstice dawn," he whispered, stroking her hair. "Ki's invention works. We hope that we'll be able to resume regular transports."

Alana's mind raced. *I'm going to lose you.* Her lips trembled and she couldn't hold back her sobbing.

Lil frowned with exasperation. "Alana, this is a happy time. Why are you so upset?"

She choked back her tears and lowered her eyes. "What are *your* plans?"

"Oh, you leaped right to that. Don't you trust me?"

How can he sound annoyed? I'm the one who's suffering. "Of course, but you have duties."

With a finger, he lifted her chin and saw her anguish. "Yes, I have. But my father is only now ascending. My reign will not come for many thousands of years. My work here on Earth isn't finished. This planet has become important to us. We're intertwined by the timewave, remember? I'm more convinced of that than ever. I need to pave the way for whatever may come. And I need to study your spirit world. Earth might have the only portal. Thanks to you, I *want* to stay."

She sniffled, and he blotted her face with the edge of his tunic. "How are you paving the way?"

"My plans aren't fully developed. But I'll lead the people here to create a better, more peaceful world."

"Even after the trouble with Petus?"

"We'll need to use other methods, it seems." He held her. He should have known that she'd figure out what was happening. "Hey, I meant this as a happy time. My parents are ecstatic to be returning. What I came to tell you, though, is that we need to move."

"Why?" she asked, disliking the idea. "This place is ideal, except for the cold."

"Yes, it is ideal. But it won't remain so. The weather will grow even colder, making it too difficult to grow crops, even for us. The worst is that there is a crack in the glacial ice, and this place will likely be flooded. It could be worse than the floods of a few years ago."

She pursed her lips. "Where will we go?"

"We're building a new colony far from here, where it's warm. The clouds have broken there, and it's sunny. It will be a big change for you, but everyone will be going."

She smiled ecstatically, her tears drying. "So we'll always be together?"

"You're mine. Of course we'll be together." He put his lips over hers, thrusting his tongue into her eager mouth. He lost himself in her, refusing to acknowledge his family's inevitable objections.

CHAPTER 32

URAS

"Iskur, Grandmother's here!" Alana waived at her approach, while holding the hand of her towheaded child, whose happy grin revealed his baby teeth. She stood outside her private entrance at the Great House, flanked by Maya, Morgana, and Yanni, all of whom wore their best gowns and jewelry. Although Alana's face appeared regally calm, she was nervous.

"Oh, Iskur, you darling child. How you've grown!" exclaimed Uras reservedly. In the years since she'd set foot in Khamlok, she'd been reluctant to return, making excuses to Lil about her pressing medical duties. The truth was that she didn't wish to grow fond of the doomed relationship with the Earth woman or with the hybrid child, whom Anu relentlessly continued to denounce as an abomination. Ama no doubt would as well, if he found out. During her first private talk with Alana, she'd been taken aback by the unspoken question of why Alana wouldn't be welcome at Khamlok. Lil had accurately predicted Anu's furious reaction. Surely this primitive girl didn't expect to parade into their home and take a seat with her honored family. Uras had been glad to help those in need—after all, her life was dedicated to helping the injured and the sick. Nothing, however, required a physician to welcome alien primitives as her immediate family and heirs. Although Uras had supported Lil's efforts to take control of Hawan's problems, her son had gone too far. If they'd stayed forever on Earth, maybe she could have eventually grown accustomed to the idea. Being now homeward bound, she jettisoned any thought of accepting them. Lil's problematic actions couldn't be justified on Alterra, and Anu would need to cover them up. Lil's eventual marriage might be crucial in traversing any fissures that might have opened while living under Ama's authoritarian rule, although she chafed at the hypocrisy. Still, she felt that it would be rude to depart for home without saying good-bye, and she was curious how these hybrid youngsters were developing. So she'd arranged passage on one of the hovercraft that transported workers to the Power Circle. Walking to the Great House that she remembered only vaguely, Uras was surprised that Alana wasn't alone.

Alana welcomed her with a warm smile and embrace, admiring her dark hair. Since summer had finally arrived, or at least the less frigid temperatures that they now knew as summer, Alana had arranged sitting stones outside around a small cook fire, where a fragrant tea was brewing. To make her best tea for Uras, she'd dug into her precious stores of dried flowers, which failed to bloom again under the cool summer temperatures.

"This is delicious, dear," Uras complimented her, anxious to limit the conversation to small talk. "I'm glad that the trees still bear leaves. Ki thinks that you'll have only another few years of this cloudiness. Soon there will be patches of blue sky." She didn't reveal that, for the solstice morning, Ki would clear the clouds to draw the highest amount of electromagnetic energy that they needed so desperately. "He's confident that the Earth will renew itself." Observing Maya gently bouncing brown-haired Krishna on her lap, she asked, "Your children are doing well?"

"Oh, yes," said Maya, with Yanni and Morgana nodding happily. "Nearly all the children are absolutely fine, even if they have extra fingers or toes." She failed to mention Akia's uncontrollable child because the women blamed Akia for bad parenting.

After another drink, Uras smacked her lips. "Alana, this tea is truly delicious!"

"Alana knows all the best ingredients," gushed Maya, believing it her special duty, as Alana's friend-sister, to apprise her mate's mother of her many talents. "She makes medicines, too, from the herbs. She's our Earthkeeper, you know."

"Earthkeeper?" Uras asked.

"Our spiritual guide to the ways of the Mother," Yanni explained while rocking her child. "She has the power to travel in the spirit world and to predict the future. She drew upon her power once to save Lil from Drood's monster."

"She saved my son?" Uras asked, raising her eyebrows. *They certainly embellish.*

"She did!" added Morgana, sensing Uras's skepticism. "Not only him. She and Maya rescued our women and children when they were captured by the Danes. None of us would live if it weren't for their bravery."

"She cures our sick with her herbs," noted Yanni. "She even healed one of our hunters from a poisonous snakebite."

"She's the most revered woman in our land," boasted Maya. "She's from Atlantis, you know. There, she was an acolyte to the high priestess Petrina. And here, Zedah named her an Earthkeeper."

Uras looked impressed, and Alana blushed, pleased that her friends loved her enough to help. They knew how she worried that Lil would return to Alterra, no matter how much he assured her otherwise. "Maya, sweetie, our honored guest wants to learn about her grandson, not me. Iskur, show Grandmother how you can count."

"No! At his age?" asked Uras. It had been millennia since her children were young.

Iskur grinned and precociously counted to ten, proud to show off.

Uras smiled. "So like this father. Lil learned early. We can't expose children to the Teacher until their skulls are hardened, so I taught them the old-fashioned way before then."

"I know about the Teacher," Maya said. "That's how you learn so quickly."

"Yes," said Uras. *How many secrets do these women know?* Uras was distracted by Iskur chasing Krishna around their circle. "Lil used to chase Ki like that," she mused, "until Jahkbar took him for training. I'll never forget the dismayed look in his little blue eyes. I asked Anu why it was necessary to take him so young, but the Ens felt that he was most impressionable as a toddler, and they began his training." She sighed. Sometimes it would be nice to have had an ordinary destiny certificate.

"If you don't mind my asking," said Yanni hesitantly, "Rameel told me that your home city of Daria was beautiful and filled with so many people doing interesting things that it was said the city never slept. What was it like to you?"

"Oh, Daria! Now *that* was a city. So *vibrant*! Every detail treated like divine art, which was meticulously plotted using sacred geometry. It gave you an ethereal thrill to stand at the center. There were beautiful green spaces interspersed among the skyscrapers. Our family enjoyed a suite atop the tallest one, giving us a breathtaking panoramic view. Outside was our own *tri-terran* port, so that we could easily descend to the theater or to simply walk among the crowds without resort to the Net. Physically descending makes me old fashioned, I guess, but Anu enjoyed it, too." She looked wistfully toward the river, unable to dispel the happy Darian memories.

"You must miss Alterra very much," soothed Alana, reaching for her hand and then pulling back, uncertain at her reaction.

"Not a day goes by that I don't miss it," Uras sighed. "The old Alterra, that is. I doubt that life underground is a treat, although Ninhursag told me that it wasn't really so bad. She finds it mystical to live in ancient lava tunnels. The most important thing is that we have our extended family together. The best scientific facilities are housed there. She's thinks it exciting to work on restoring the planet. Oh, here I am, prattling. Tell me more about Iskur."

Alana froze—*The most important thing is that we have our extended family together.* Although dread was creeping through her mind, she attempted a response. "Iskur's memory amazes me." At Alana's request, he stopped chasing Krishna long enough to recite an Alterran epic poem. "We teach him every day." Her voice sounded like a plea. *See what a good mother I am? You'll want Iskur and me to come with Lil, won't you?* Little Krishna stood earnestly by Iskur's side, studying the women with his intelligent brown eyes. When Iskur finished, he poked him, and they resumed their play.

"Why do you bother to teach him?" asked Uras, distractedly watching the children. "He doesn't need literature or Alterran history for forest life." Noticing that the women were sharing scowling glances, she regretted her remark.

Alana looked puzzled. "Lil spends countless hours thinking of ways to teach our children and all our descendants about the gifts of Alterra, the principles of leading a good life, and so many things I can't count them all. Isn't that what your people sent him here to do?"

Morgana frowned and pursed her lips, impatient that they weren't getting to the point. Alana might believe a direct question was rude, but she didn't. "Is Lil returning to Alterra with you?"

Uras's eyes grew large. "What has my son told you?" She didn't want to interfere if Lil planned to distance himself after she left. He had to eventually.

Alana frowned and cast an annoyed glance at Morgana, and then nervously chuckled. "I *know* that he's staying here. He told me."

Uras prolonged her sip during the awkward silence, licked her lips, and set her cup down, all the while loathing the women's stares. "My son, my *other* son, Ki, invented an energy source that will permit our elders and my husband and me to return home. He has insufficient power to send more. Since we're blind to our home conditions, we don't know whether we'll ever open the portal again, and Lil could be permanently stranded here. It is, of course, my husband's expectation that we will be able to resume regular travel in the near future, or at least communications. If the portal is usable, whether Lil will be ordered to return to duty on Alterra is a matter for the supreme leader. I cannot say."

Puzzled, Alana furrowed her brows. "The supreme leader is his father, your husband, is he not?"

"Yes," Uras internally winced, not knowing how much Alana knew. "He will be after the coronation. That doesn't mean that I know what he'll decide. All I know is that Lil isn't leaving with us." Uras wiggled her shoulders to release tension. It would be hours before the hovercraft picked her up. This conversation was unbearable. Surely Lil hadn't told the girl that she and Iskur could live on Alterra in their House.

Listening to Uras's circumspect words, Alana's stomach sank. Her pride prevented her from showing tears. "We have offended you, our guest, and for that I am heartily sorry. My friends mean well. They ask many questions for the sake of their children. As a mother, I'm sure that you can appreciate their worries. As for me, I cannot leave this land. I am the Earthkeeper. So don't worry, I will not embarrass you." Alana straightened her back and lifted her chin to sit as regally as she could force herself.

"I didn't say—"

"You didn't have to," Maya snipped. "That's why we couldn't go to your home."

"Azazel will not return," said Morgana haughtily with full confidence, "so it doesn't matter to me. We worry about Alana. We won't see her hurt." She actually looked forward to setting out with Azazel, on their own. With his powers, it was time for her precious Azazel to find his own kingdom, where he wouldn't have to cower to Lil.

"Nor will Jared return," said Maya, only slightly less sure.

Uras stared at them with narrowed eyes. "You both speak boldly. Your husbands enjoyed an easy life and many luxuries. Alterra is their home. What makes you so sure?"

Morgana heard the hidden meaning, *What do you primitive women offer them?* She couldn't refrain from answering Uras's challenge. "Azazel says that their lives were so controlled by your family that they were little more than slaves." She lifted her chin with the superior air of free people.

"My husband said that you controlled their emotions by adding something dreadful to the food." Yanni hadn't intended to confront Uras, but she was caught up in the mood. Guiltily, she knew that Rameel would strongly disapprove of provoking Uras.

"They told you that? And what did my son tell *you?*" Uras demanded of Alana, her blood pressure rising, afraid to hear the answer.

"Your son works constantly and thinks only of the people's welfare!" Alana answered with desperation. "He says that Alterra was a magnificent place, where everyone was taken care of, living in peace and harmony. He *never* speaks a bad word about his home! He's tried to preserve what he could of your homeworld. Here, though, he hasn't had to make all the decisions for everyone, and he's had time to be happy."

Uras straightened her back and tensed her jaw, perceiving an admonition. "Lil comes from a proud heritage; I'm glad that he hasn't abandoned it, as the others have apparently done." Her eyes burned hatred for Morgana and Yanni. "In every *civilized* society, certain accommodations are made by the populace in order to achieve the superior goal of maintaining a good life for all. Do you think it's easy to maintain a perfectly balanced system? Peace and harmony is the highest form of civilization, and I'm proud to say that my husband's family has conferred a magnificent gift on their people. Even here, you must have rules or else you'd have chaos. You couldn't have achieved this development without discipline. And my son would *not* put up with chaos."

"But your people have no choice in their work—" protested Morgana.

"So what?" huffed Uras, her dislike for Morgana growing with each breath. "It's more important to ensure peace and provide life's basic necessities." She stood, annoyed at herself for arguing with primitives incapable of comprehending delicate principles of governance. With considerable effort, she calmed her emotions. She said evenly, "Alana, if you don't mind, I'd like to take my grandson for a stroll before I leave."

"Yes, of course," said Alana uncertainly, standing as well and giving her Iskur's eager hand. She watched Uras lead him on the well-maintained path toward the river trellis. When Uras was a distance away, Alana demanded, "Why couldn't you hold your tongues? You've ruined everything." She'd squandered her opportunity to become closer to Uras, to make her an advocate, as her own mother had done to influence Petrina to have her admitted as an acolyte.

"We didn't change *anything*, my friend-sister," said Morgana softly, "we merely uncovered the truth."

CHAPTER 33
THE RETURN

After completing one last successful simulation, Ki gave Anu and the Council the good news that his plan worked. The generator was completed in the month before the summer solstice, and the initial readings indicated that the generating capacity was interacting with the electromagnetic anomalies to increase power exponentially. The last link had come when Ki's meteorologist forecasted a patch of clear sky on the morning of the solstice, although Ki still sent hovercrafts aloft to dispel any clouds. At dusk on the solstice eve, Anu, flanked by Uras and the Council of Elders, addressed the colonists assembled in Hawan's courtyard. At the urging of Ki and Uras, Anu had permitted Lil and the guardsmen to be present.

Anu, smiling triumphantly, announced, "I have asked you here to thank you for your faithful service. We've gone through a difficult time. We feared being stranded as the last of our kind. Those fears have proved to be unfounded. Our noble Alterrans are bringing our beloved planet back from disaster." He paused while his people cheered wildly. "Alterra's destiny, now intertwined with that of Earth, brought us heartache.

Thanks to En.Ki, we have turned the corner. As I am leaving you, new facilities will soon be ready. I've been assured that the new colony will be as artfully designed as Hawan. When we are able, we will bring all of you home. I leave you in good hands. My two sons are well prepared. En.Lil has gained special insight into life on this planet. En.Ki has consistently given us invaluable scientific service. Therefore, I decree that En.Lil shall have absolute dominion over all lands and seas to the north of middle Earth, and En.Ki shall have absolute dominion over all lands and seas to south middle Earth. The Cedar Woods of middle Earth shall be a neutral ground. En.Lil and En.Ki, please join me."

They stood beside their father. Lil had not been close to him for a long time, and they smiled hesitantly at each other. Since Ki hadn't been in line for succession, he understood that Lil was being punished by receiving only half. Anu pinned the purple double triangle of command on each of them.

Anu and the Council, accompanied by Ki, his staff, and Lil, entered the ships to fly to the Power Circle. The guardsmen were permitted to take two hovercraft to Khamlok. During the flight, Anu whispered to Lil, "I want to speak privately." Lil led him to the craft's rear. "Son, I want you to know where I stand. The stars decreed that you are the named successor. After your coronation, our entire civilization will rest on your shoulders. Although I can't deny your divine birthright, I've punished you by giving Ki dominion over half this planet."

"Father, at the time, I took the only course of action I could."

"That's an opinion I don't share," he asserted firmly, shaking his head. "A leader doesn't lose faith. How will the people persevere if the leader runs? If our people learn that you defied your destiny and assisted our Guard with desertion, it'll produce a significant crisis. Using you as an example, Alterrans will question their destiny certificates. They'll defy the divine interpretations that our House has so meticulously built as a cornerstone of our society. By not accepting your destiny, you've embarked on that slippery slope that Councilman Trey warned you about. Mark my words—everything is interrelated. One act of defiance will lead to another, and another, until we lose control."

"Zeya never envisioned a totalitarian state with everyone drugged into submission," Lil wanted to say, but instead stared stonily at Anu.

"And your wife and son present a whole set of other problems. Having an Earthling wife might be acceptable here, but you can't bring her home. If it's your desire to remain as named successor, you'll do something about Alana."

"Father, I love her. I don't want to 'do something about Alana,'" he protested. "Before leaving Hawan, I couldn't choose my destiny. I chose Alana to preserve our civilization as well as our family. My meeting Alana was no accident. She accesses another dimension, which we must study. In fact, Earth might be the only place with a pathway to a higher dimension. If you believe that destiny rules the universe, it was ordained that I take Alana as my wife. We join the only two sentient cultures in the universe. It was no accident that the end of the Alterran timewave led us here."

"I know all about interpreting destiny. Don't tell me this is in the stars," Anu said huffily. Another dimension? If he weren't so angry with Lil, he'd be intrigued. He pointed his finger at him. "This isn't about your petty desires. Your life was meant for a higher purpose. Alterra is recovering, and when it does, it will need us to guide the people. Everything rests on us, son. As part of your duties, you must plan. Your reputation *must* be impeccable and your actions beyond reproach. You must lead by example as well as by action, even if it requires personal sacrifice." He paused. "I hope you aren't actually suggesting that your son by this woman will be in line to be the named successor."

Lil put his hand on his father's shoulder. "I'll arrange for the usual succession insemination. Alana's my official spouse, just as Uras is yours. If you'd meet her, you'd understand that she's unique. She's intelligent and capable. She's from the advanced Earth civilization that collapsed into the ocean two decades or so ago."

"She's from that one?" he asked thoughtfully, yet abruptly dismissed the idea with a sharp wave of his hand. "That doesn't matter. She's still an Earthling. Son, you can't give the House of Kan an opening to claim illegitimacy."

"Father, Alana has Alterran qualities," Lil argued. "We've so many similarities, there might have been some Alterran connection in the past, and I'd like to run some genetic testing."

"Oh, we'd have known about that." Anu dismissively waved his hand.

"Maybe it was some rogue mission of the Southern Alliance," protested Lil, grasping at straws. "By our colonization, our planets' timewaves have melded as one. My union with Alana is the start of the new wave. If you'd seen Khamlok's success, you'd know that you don't need punishment to motivate people. Our city progressed because each person worked independently."

Anu emphatically shook his head. "No, no, no. Our society went through that phase once, and it simply didn't work. Harmony requires strict enforcement of rules. Compare it to a gardener who must control all variables to maintain balance, plucking out invasive species to prevent ruination of the entire plan no matter how attractive a new species may be. In the long run, the garden as a whole prospers. The same applies to human society. Progress becomes a mantra that creates instability, leaving too many casualties for the benefit of the few. We shed ourselves of that, and I say good riddance. If we make people adhere to a disciplined way of life, limiting their choices, it's an insignificant price to pay to achieve utopia. You must plan long term for all people's best interests. And by that I mean the *Alterran* people." He paused. "Listen to me carefully. Because of my entrapment here, I surmise that the House of Kan has been launching a campaign challenging the legitimacy of our family's rule. We can't let it claim that our House has no acceptable successor. It's time you ended this foolish self-indulgence. You don't want your grandfathers to learn of this, do you? We're talking about preservation of our dynasty! With Ki's missteps, the Supreme Council won't accept him as named successor. So it must be you." He put his hands on Lil's shoulders and shook him. "For the love of everything your family stands for, come to your senses!"

"I didn't think about the House of Kan," said Lil quietly, consumed with guilt.

"Of course you didn't. You've been off in the wild thinking only of yourself. Maybe I'm partially at fault for not arranging a suitable wife for you. We shouldn't expect you and Ki to be satisfied with holographic women. When I get back, Uras intends to arrange marriages for you both, ones that will ensure our supremacy. If you insist, it might be possible to keep Alana as a concubine while you're on Earth, unless the House of Kan makes too much of an issue about it. I'll feel out Councilman Trikon. We'll need to dress it up some way."

"But—" said Lil.

Since they were landing, Anu abruptly ended the conversation. Returning to his seat, Lil avoided Ki's questioning glance and steadily gazed out the window. His father's logic couldn't be dismissed. How had something that had seemed so right now seem so wrong?

As the craft circled around the Power Circle illuminated with glowglobes, Uras remarked, "Ki, it looks like art, not like a generator."

"Although we try to make everything artistic, it indeed produces the power we require. Mother, you and the others should get some rest. I'll wake you before dawn."

Ki showed Lil how the system performed. "Before leaving Alterra, each person left duplicate atoms in stasis, which are entangled on a quantum level and still vibrating in unison. When the conduit provided by the wormhole opens, the entangled atoms will reunite. We conducted an experiment yesterday with a small wormhole. We sent a message home so they'd prepare. I hope to produce more power than the wormhole requires, which I'll save in these batteries."

"Ki, you always amaze me." Lil understood why his father had rewarded him, reeling from burning pangs of guilt. "Whatever happened to the northern ice shelf?"

"It could drop at any time. When this project is completed, we should take your guardsmen to Hawan until the Cedar Woods has been completed." Neither of them brought up the Earth families.

Ki's countdown clock chimed with a reminder that dawn approached. The travelers took their places before the portal, wearing white translucent robes laced with navigational electrodes. Uras and Anu gave their sons a final goodbye, tears streaming down Uras's face. "I love you both. You'll be with me always!"

As the horizon grew crimson and gold, Anu recited a poem of universal oneness. When the first rays of the solstice sun struck the Power Circle, the amplified energy swirled around them, increasing in intensity and bathing them in blinding white light. When the sun's full corona filled the Circle, it ignited the anti-matter, forming the wormhole in the portal. Councilman Djane led the way, disappearing through the portal's dancing arcs of light, followed by the other Council members. Uras and Anu came last. Ki confirmed that the travelers had rejoined their entangled atoms. When the portal closed, Ki directed the last energy from the anti-matter casing to the makeshift batteries.

"Sir," Ki's aide interrupted. "Look at this."

"Great, one more thing," he mumbled after looking at the instrument readings. "Lil, the ice shelf has partially fallen. Not big enough to flood the entire peninsula, but low-lying points are in danger. Since we can't predict exactly, we must immediately evacuate Khamlok."

CHAPTER 34

AZOR

On a blustery evening in the fifth lunar month, King Azor paced anxiously in the Great Room. "Will this blasted winter never end?" he muttered to Togar as he warmed his hands by the fire. "Margon should have returned by now."

"Yes, indeed, Your Grace. I hope nothing bad has happened," said Togar, bringing a large fur to warm the king's still-muscular shoulders. Gray-haired Togar was a thin man, a southern house slave who'd been given to Azor as tribute. Since Togar had been in his service for many years, Azor trusted his discretion.

"Nothing is going right," Azor snarled.

"Does Your Grace wish to be groomed? That always relaxes you."

The king nodded.

"What troubles you, Your Grace?"

Sitting, Azor let Togar trim his gray-streaked beard. When he started to smooth the tangles in his hair, Azor muttered, "Yoachim, supposedly a shaman, is unable to tell of Margon's whereabouts. What kind of shaman is that? He was supposed to be my eyes and ears on the peninsula. If he can't do this simple thing, how can I trust anything he says?"

"No, Your Grace, he doesn't appear to be a good shaman," replied Togar, moving to the other side of the king's head. "Does he have other value to you?"

Azor pushed him aside, arose, and kicked a log in fury at being misled.

Togar busied himself with cleaning the king's armaments. "He has knowledge of the terrain, doesn't he, Your Grace? I suppose he also knows the local people. Will they be on your side?"

"Yes, but our plan relies too much on the attack being a surprise. Without a shaman's sight, how do we know? I might delay the invasion."

"I understand, Your Grace. I'm sure you're concerned about your warriors, having lost so many in the floods. They've traveled far to prepare for battle; you'll infuriate them. But if you must, you must."

Azor growled at the admonition. "I'll find something else for them to do." Gazing into the fire, he continued to analyze his attack plan. Much had been prepared for this battle. His aides searched for men fit to fight. So much flooding, and the air made others sick. Coughing was perpetually heard throughout the camp. Although Yoachim had recruited Albion men, Azor knew why they'd been banished; they wouldn't follow simple orders. Azor's trainers had had to beat them, and some had died. To obtain needed supplies, his aides had scrounged the countryside, using strong persuasion with the country people to reveal their meager stores. If the giants had as much food as Margon reported, though, he'd be able to feed them. Despite these obstacles, his generals were ready to march. He had to decide.

Azor walked outside, taking comfort in the many campfires breaking night's darkness. He loved walking the grounds, greeting his men before battle. It had been many years since he'd last done so. His bones and joints were less forgiving, but his spirit was alive. In his youth, he'd been fearsome. Taller and more muscular than most, he could outlast any other wielding weapons in battle. Coming from a small northern village, he and his tribesmen had won a few small battles. When word of his triumphs spread, many villages surrendered, desiring protection from the brutal Shylfing. Having amassed an army, he invaded the southern port cities. Although the Danes would plunder and burn what they conquered, Azor left those villages swearing him fealty intact with a pledge of protection. Protection, though, required constant care, with many aides delivering orders. Administration was tedious. He had installed his former generals as stewards in neighboring lands so that they'd be friendly and devoted his time to drinking and wenches. Now, with the prospect of battle, he'd regained his strength, ignoring the discomfort of old wounds.

Azor remained uneasy, his mind devising battle plans only to reject them to start anew with each conjecture about the terrain and his enemy. Always having the decisive advantage in his battles, he loathed proceeding without full scouting and internal spies. He disbelieved Koko's tales that the strangers had traveled from the stars. Koko was a storyteller, and the more fantastic the story, the more demand there was for his services. Clearly, though, by constructing a huge city, they possessed great ability. They might command dark powers to turn the battle in their favor.

He wondered if his men shared his doubts. He decided to assess their mood himself. Strolling the camp's perimeter, he chose the first small sentry fire, where he recognized a hardened warrior, a gray-haired, long-bearded man known to be adept with a spear, a man who had been around long enough that he knew not to have a wagging tongue. "Good evening, Hogar. Nice evening, isn't it?" Azor prided himself on knowing his seasoned fighters' names.

"Yes, Your Grace," replied Hogar, scrambling to his feet and squaring his firm shoulders to stand erect, standing nearly as tall as Azor. Neither his expressionless face nor his steady hands on his spear betrayed his shock at the king's presence. The dancing firelight cast shadows across the man's grizzled face, accentuating deep scars on his forehead and an old gash across his cheek that had healed poorly.

You can tell a man's history by his face, thought Azor. This was a loyal man of few words. "May I borrow your cape for a while?"

"My cape, Your Grace? Oh yes, Your Grace, but it's not much." He shook it to remove debris and offered it, a puzzled expression on his face.

Azor swirled the homespun, patched cape and settled it around his huge shoulders, adequately covering his fine furs and, most importantly, concealing his face. "It's a fine cape, just what I need." As he strolled among the campfires, he heard men joking about their women and complaining about the floods. Mostly though, they grumbled about hunger, a hunger caused by the endless clouds and stinging rain, which ruined plants and left animals too scrawny to provide sufficient meat. Most had joined his army to be fed. Azor scratched his beard and snorted, realizing that the success of his recruitment efforts was due to empty bellies, not loyalty. To probe further, he sat down at a large fire, where three gaunt, long-bearded men sprawled, and asked for water, explaining that he was newly arrived.

"Welcome, friend. You may sit with us tonight and other nights, at least until we reach the starmen," said a dirty, gaunt man with matted hair and a single tooth. He must have been a forager or land tiller, thought Azor. He always assumed that such men were grateful for a bit of adventure and a chance at their share of spoils.

"The starmen?" Azor asked with feigned disinterest. "Who are they? And why only until we get to the city?"

"Hah, you must be from the other side of the world if you haven't heard this story before." The man slapped his leg and roiled with laughter, nearly tipping backward off his log. "That place we're attacking was built by men who came from the stars!" He pointed a dirty finger upward. "Koko's told *everyone* about them. The men are giants, head and shoulder taller than Azor, with gleaming swords that slice through a mastodon with a single stroke."

The toothless man beside him, wearing a patchwork of torn furs connected by hides, chuckled. "And that's not all, friend." Leaning his dirty face closer to Azor, he whispered, "They've got flying ships too—"

"And bands of light that cut a man in half in the blink of an eye," his friend whispered, snapping his fingers.

Azor studied the men. Did they truly believe the stories? Fantastical stories of fire-breathing dragons and changelings were hardly new. Only a child heard such stories as anything more than amusement to pass a dreary night. Azor cleared his throat. "If you believe this nonsense, then why did you agree to fight?"

"Why?" chortled the man with one tooth. "Because I've heard that they have huge huts just to store mountains of food."

"Yeah, that's why I agreed to fight. I'm starving. I need to take food to my family."

The first man put his flask to his lips and paused. "Death by starvation or combat—either way, it's death. We don't stand a chance at all, friend. So drink up. Here, have some of this." The man handed Azor a cup of a thick, dark mead.

When Azor sniffed, the stink swelled through his nostrils. Suppressing a cough, he set it down. "Oh, those are just Koko's fantasies. Stories told so he'll be well paid." Looking at their worried faces, he scoffed, "Why, the tale about light weapons is false." After nervously glancing at one another, the men looked down. The toothless man scratched his scalp, and the one-toothed man threw twigs into the fire. Sensing their fear, he probed for a way to provide solace. "Besides, we have Shaman Yoachim on our side. I've heard that he has magic that will overcome anything these strangers may have."

"I hadn't heard that before," said the toothless man, stroking his chin as he ruminated a moment. "I sure hope his magic is stronger. But," he laughed, changing his tone, "since you just got here and didn't even know about the giants, I don't think you really know." He narrowed his eyes and stared at Azor with suspicion.

"It's what I've heard this evening around these campfires," protested Azor. Thunder, these men were difficult to convince.

"Well, Koko actually visited the giants' city. Many times, I hear tell. And the savages from the peninsula tell the same story." The man paused but continued to stare at Azor. To his ears, the big newcomer spoke with an accent that he didn't like. Too little food was available for his people to be welcoming strangers.

Azor stroked his beard, searching for an encouraging argument. "One thing that might be true, though, and I heard it many times before tonight, is that our enemies enjoy plentiful food even in these difficult times. Far more food than they need, while those around them are starving. Mountains of furs, too. Their hunters found animals that don't suffer in the cold. All that food will be ours for the taking."

"They should share their wealth!" barked the one-toothed man, slamming a bony fist into his hand, his eyes wild with excitement.

The toothless man grinned and held up his flask. "Now, if that's true, it would be treasure worth fighting for!" The third man tapped his flask and nodded his wooly head in hearty agreement. "Well, here's to whatever happens!" His head back, he emptied his flask into his mouth, letting it linger to capture the last drops.

Satisfied at last that he'd discovered from these curmudgeons an argument to incite his army, Azor put his hands on his knees and stood up. Scouts, advisers, and all those others who served him hid facts from him that no doubt everyone else in the land knew. His table had been full, and it hadn't occurred to him that supplies were this scant. "Thank you for the drink. I need to stretch my legs a bit. I'll see you on the battlefield."

"Good luck to you," the single-toothed man replied, patting down his ragged clothing into a pillow.

This conversation deeply worried Azor. The fears of his men exceeded his own doubts. If they perceived anything that confirmed these rumors, they'd run. How would he turn this around? Or was this another reason to abandon his plan? He returned the cape to an astonished Hogar and strode back to the Great Hall.

"Where are Hilaba and Yoachim?" Azor demanded upon entering. The fire of determination in his eyes caused the drowsy servants to spring to life. "Find them and bring them here immediately!"

"Yes, Your Grace," replied an expressionless Togar, always the perfect servant.

Predictably, Togar found Hilaba sitting in the courtyard with Yoachim. Her hair was braided for sleeping, and she wore a coat of stitched rabbit fur against the cool evening breeze. Disgruntled at being commanded to appear so late in the evening, she muttered under her breath as she followed Togar through the passageway, "My husband had better not be losing his nerve." On her way, she smoothed stray hairs, licked her lips, and pinched her cheeks. Upon entering his chamber, she greeted her husband formally. "You wanted us, Your Grace?"

Azor paced before his fireplace and confronted them, his face red with anger. "The men's heads are full of Koko's fantastic stories. They believe we're attacking starmen with magical powers. They're convinced we have no chance. Hilaba, you promised me when all this began that Yoachim would have special sight."

Turning to Yoachim, he demanded, "Shaman, what exactly can you do for me? So far, you've been unable to do a simple thing like locate Margon. I need to know what's happening, and I need to show the men that your magic will protect them."

"I'm a shaman, not a cheap magician," he replied haughtily, tipping his chin upward with indignation and firming his lips. "I need ingredients for a Seeing Ceremony, and it's best done at my special cave."

Turning angrily to Hilaba, Azor said tensely, "Hilaba, you said he'd be our eyes and ears."

Hilaba stared at him icily, folding her hands over her stomach. "Oh, pah! There's no question that Yoachim knows the terrain better than any spy. Why call us here tonight? You should be resting."

"I gave your generals invaluable advice to map the invasion path," said Yoachim condescendingly. "I don't see what more you want."

Azor plopped into his great chair to think, his mind reeling. This plan was so far along, it would be difficult to abort. He'd look like a fool to his men if he didn't proceed. To Yoachim, he said, "You're a religious leader. Can't you at least talk to them and invoke the power of a god or two to watch over them?"

"Our gods are different from yours." Yoachim laid a hand on his shoulder. "Your Grace, why do you worry so? You and your generals have superbly planned every detail. I've given them a path that ends on the low mountain east of Khamlok. In an early morning attack, the rising sun will be in their eyes, if there's a break in the clouds."

Azor rolled his eyes. *We're relying on a break in these blasted clouds?*

"You'll have a well-supplied, seasoned fighting force that is much larger than theirs," Yoachim continued. "Most importantly, they have no idea you're attacking, and they'll be busy with other things. These are good odds. Your warriors are trained to follow orders despite their fear. Attacking Khamlok is no different from any other battle. Now, if you don't mind, an old man needs his rest. I bid you good night."

Azor didn't object as Yoachim left with Hilaba. He wondered if Yoachim was right. Had Azor simply lost his nerve? He decided to make his final decision the next morning. During the night, he tossed and turned from worry, falling asleep only in the pre-dawn hour. When his attendants aroused him in late morning, his generals had broken camp and were ready to march. *It's time to put doubts aside,* he decided.

Finally, the weather was warmer, and the winter's deep snow was melting. The overflowing rivers and the muddy animal trails made for slow progress. At night, he was unable to order the customary camp fortifications on the inhospitable land. His sole consolation was that he saw no sign of opposition, not even scouts. *These giants are too arrogant to take precautions,* he thought. As they marched, he found that Yoachim had indeed directed them along the most easily traveled route. They threaded their way across high ridges and forded low points of swollen rivers. After traveling slowly for over a week, Yoachim informed him that they would reach the low mountain overlooking the city by sundown on the following day. Azor could attack at the summer solstice dawn. The omens predicted a clear sky, so the sun would be blazing over the hilltop, obscuring their advance. Azor finally relaxed. He was going to win.

CHAPTER 35
THE ATTACK

Lil jumped into the closest *tri-terran*. "Great, the fuel cell's nearly empty," he complained aloud, giving the gauge a slap. "It'll have to do." He started the engines and initiated a *mencomm* message. "Jared, the ice sheet has fallen—"

"Lil," Jared exploded by *mencomm,* involuntarily sending him an emotional jolt. "You won't believe this. There's an army of savages, maybe a thousand, amassing atop the mountain. They're yelling and screaming." He watched through binoculars atop the balustrade of the Great House.

"A thousand savages!" fumed Lil, not comprehending.

"It's hard to see. They lined up at sunrise, and the sun is directly behind them. The clouds would have to break at the wrong time. They've painted their bodies. They're jumping up and down, shaking their spears at us." Jared scanned the horizon. "I see archers preparing their bows."

"Don't tell me they're actually going to attack us!" said Lil, ordering the *tri-terran* into top speed, even though the ship would consume the fuel cell quickly.

"Their leaders are rallying them, trying to maintain attack lines," reported Jared.

Floods and savages. What's next? Lil wished that he had his amethyst crystal with him, but he'd had no reason to bring it to Hawan. Through *mencomm,* he projected, "What are you doing to defend?"

"Azazel isn't here. I've sent *mencomm* to the Guard to prepare their weapons. I sent messengers to bring all women and children to the Great House, and we're creating a barricade. They're trickling in. Our wall won't hold back this horde for long."

Lil fought to contain his anger. Where did they come from? Who had the temerity to attack him? He was helping this planet. His people had saved Earth people from the comet, the ungrateful monsters. He sent his thought through *mencomm,* "Get the hovercrafts in the air. Have them fly low. Buzz the enemy. Throw off exhaust. Scare them away. I'll be there shortly." He cut off the *mencomm* to conserve their strengt.

Jared called to Tamiel, who was running toward the Great House. "Man the ships. Use soundguns. If those blasted savages don't scare, use full strength."

Tamiel signaled to the closest guardsmen to follow him and raced to the hovercraft. Jared resumed watching through his binoculars. The sun was higher now, and it was easier to see. The savages' painted leaders ran before them, thrusting their spears and shouting defiantly, exhorting their troops to commence the attack.

Jared called to Rameel, who ran to the Great House with Yanni and her children, "Rameel, we've got to stop them before they breach the wall."

"They aren't actually attacking, are they?" Rameel carried his sword in a scabbard on his back. He kissed Yanni and told her to go inside with little Maliki.

"They wouldn't be there if they weren't. Their leaders are whipping them into a frenzy." Rameel and an aide raced through Khamlok, to hurry the women and children.

Morgana, wearing her scabbard, brought her children to the Great House. "I'll join the fight, Jared. Tara, you stay with the women."

Jared called, "Morgana, you should stay with the women. If the savages get that far, the women will need a last line of defense."

Morgana's face flickered from anger to dismay. "All right, I'll stay here."

Tamiel flew the ship overhead. The savages fell silent, frozen with fear. Tamiel passed so low overhead that he could see terror in their eyes. He blasted his exhaust engine, causing their hair to fly and dust to swirl around them. Cowering on the ground, they spit dust from their mouths and rubbed their eyes. The ships crossed over the men, and a second hovercraft followed behind.

Seeing the trembling savages, Jared called below, "Rameel, it might have worked. For now, they're not advancing."

"What are they doing?"

"Hah. They're lying flat on the ground, too scared to run away," said Jared, laughing.

* * *

King Azor commanded his generals to control their troops. He grumbled to himself, "I was told they couldn't fly like the birds. What other surprises await me?" With his horse nervously jerking about, Azor scolded Yoachim, "It was you who told me not to worry about their fear. So *you* go calm them."

"Why me, Your Grace?" protested Yoachim. "You're their king."

"I fight blood and flesh. You fight spirits and magic. That's why you're here, in case you've forgotten."

"I'm a spiritual leader, not a military commander," he whimpered.

Poking him with his spear, Azor roared, "You try my patience. Shield them with magic!"

Yoachim huffily dismounted, his foot becoming tangled in his long robe. He impatiently shook it lose. Azor snorted with anger at the delay. Refusing to be spurred by his glare, Yoachim took up his staff and straightened his clothing.

Forcing a broad smile, he strode before the lines of cowering men, speaking in the common tongue. "What are you men doing? Get up, get up, all of you! Why do you have such little faith? I, Yoachim, fight with you. There is nothing to fear. The giants are men like you." He lifted up the hair of one of the men lying on the ground and repeated, "They are men just like you."

A warrior called out, "You're not our wizard."

He ignored the remark and continued down the line. "Don't be afraid. You far outnumber them!" A few slowly crawled to their feet. However, most peered through dirty fingers at the ships sweeping low above them.

Yoachim grew angry and spat. "Get up, I say! I will give enchantments only to real men, to those who are brave and standing tall. All cowards who lie on the ground will die."

Azor dismounted, lifted his spear above a prostrate man, and plunged it into the man's back. He hollered, "I can assure you. You'll die if you don't get up."

Yoachim put up his hand. "Wait, great king, these men are rising. They'll fight." To the men, he shouted, "Be not afraid. I have called the great spirits to shield you." He strode regally before the newly formed lines. "The wind spirits will guide your arrows and spears. All true of heart have nothing to fear." With the ship flying overhead, Yoachim thrust his staff skyward, yelling as he circled, "You don't scare us. This is our land. We fight for our land!"

"Our land!" A lone soldier, Petus, took up the cause. "I've lived with them. They're not gods. The leader is a coward."

Azor shouted, "There are storehouses of food inside those walls! Think of your starving families!"

Yoachim cried skyward, "Out of our land!" Encouraging the men to join in, he waved his arms, chanting "our land."

The drummers picked up the beat, with Petus leading the chant, defiantly tapping his spear. "Our land, our land, our land," they chanted, with more joining the chant. The generals nodded their heads in approval and strode before the men, chanting "our land," their clenched fists raised with their spears.

King Azor studied his lines, relieved that the men were responding. His aide handed him his reins. He growled quietly, "Their land, my foot. But if they fight and live, I'll fix that lie later." He mounted his horse and rid behind the lines, thwacking deserters with his spear.

* * *

Jared studied the action atop the mountain. When the troops arose and stood their ground, he pounded his fist on the balustrade, saying aloud, "We can't scare them."

Smelling smoke, Jared saw flames shooting from the wall.

He groaned, "Great. Rameel, the wall is burning!"

Rameel shouted, "They'll break through."

Grimly, Jared gave a general order through *mencomm*, "Prepare for battle inside the wall. Azazel, where are you? Come immediately, no matter what you're doing."

In a short while, Azazel replied, "What's your status?"

"A savage army is attacking. We need your defenders!"

"When we found the tracks, we headed back," he replied. "Nearly there. Azazel out."

Jared shrugged off *mencomm* fatigue. He heard Rameel giving orders to set up barriers around the Great House using whatever was at hand. He saw Alana holding Iskur in her arms as she hurried women and children into the Great House. He shouted, "Alana, do you know who's attacking?"

She called, "Only King Azor from the mainland could command an army."

King Azor, Jared thought. *I've never heard of him.* "There's a bearded old man wearing a long robe, holding a staff, inspiring them. Who's that?"

Alana climbed up a large stone. Squinting, she held her hand over her eyes to shield the sun. "Yoachim! How can that be? He hates Azor. Can't you stop them? Surely their spears are no threat to us. Do you need my help?"

"Don't worry, our ships will stop them. Lil's on his way back, so is Azazel. Where's Maya?"

"She's inside."

"Good," said Jared as he put the binoculars back to his eyes. He muttered aloud, "I can't believe this is happening." They had been prepared to build a civilization, to bring agriculture, orchards, and construction to Earth. Instead, they were about to fight a horde of painted, speared savages. An army this size, however primitive, was deadly.

* * *

The drummers produced a steady beat, and the generals reasserted themselves, getting the last of the frightened troops standing on their feet. With Yoachim's incantations, they ignored the overhead ship and again began shouting and waving their spears. Satisfied that the infantry lines were reformed, Azor signaled the archers. A barrage of arrows swooshed through the air, most bouncing off the hovercrafts but some hitting the deserted huts inside the wall. None reached the Great House. The next wave of arrows carried fire. The archers found their mark, hitting the wall and a hut. Soon more sections of the wall lit up in flames.

The drums quickened, signaling the front line to move forward. They descended slowly, spears pointed at hip level.

* * *

Overhead, Tamiel said to his men, "They won't scare. We won't play nice any more." Communicating with Erjat, who piloted the other craft, he commanded, "We're setting the soundguns to maximum strength. You do the same."

"Will do," said Erjat, signaling his crew.

Tamiel began at the north base of the mountain. He opened the cargo door, and Kamean slid out the sound gun's nose. Tamiel asked, "Are you ready, Kamean?"

"Yeah. They're not going to know what hit 'em," he answered, too enthusiastically.

Tamiel winced. "We fight them. We don't become them. First, give a demonstration. Direct a blast to that tree over there." He pointed. Kamean swiveled and aimed. A high, shrill tone pierced the air. The tree exploded, leaving flames leaping from the stump.

The drums and advancing line stopped. Terror again contorted the troops' faces. Yoachim ran forward, shouting, "Show no fear. They know they cannot hurt you, so they only try to frighten you." Running across the front of the line, he held up his staff, crying, "See, their fence burns, like any other fence. They are only men."

The troops stood frozen.

Yoachim shook his staff at them. "You must fight for our land!"

Petus, looking around and waving for others to join him, picked up the chant, "Our land, our land."

Yoachim stretched out his arm. "Yes, that's right, Petus. You have it. Everyone. Our land. Our land." He ran across the front line, shouting, "Our land." Lifting up both arms, he cried, "The righteous will prevail!" Stopping suddenly, turning his back to the troops, he faced the burning wall. Putting his head back, taking a breath, he screamed a battle cry and began running. To his relief, the troops followed, soon overtaking him. Growing breathless, he stopped running.

Azor rode through the lines with Yoachim's horse. "Well done, Yoachim."

Yoachim scowled, "The Earth spirits will protect them."

He shrugged. Watching the ship getting into position, he said, "Those starmen have only been playing. They're going to get serious. We need to move out of their way."

Yoachim protested, "But we have protection from the earth spirits!"

King Azor snorted, "Don't believe your own nonsense. Get on the horse. We'll be able to skirt down the edges while they're distracted."

Angrily, he mounted, and they rejoined Azor's generals.

Overhead, Tamiel said, "We've tried our best to avoid this. Here they come. We've no choice. Kill as many as you can, Kamean." Tamiel zigzagged his ship slowly to cover the broadest possible distance. Kamean aimed at the lines nearing the base of the mountain, with the soundgun setting less concentrated to cover the maximum range. All the front lines running into the wave path were snapped by an invisible wall of sound. They fell writhing in pain. Blood flowed from their ears; their internal organs bled, and most of their bones were broken. The craft continued up the mountain, with Kamean taking aim at the middle ranks, which ceased their advance, pointing to the carnage below.

King Azor's generals urged the men to advance. Terrified, the warriors refused. They turned their backs and sprinted. "They lied!"

"We aren't protected!"

"Koko was right!"

"We can't fight this magic!"

"They can have this evil land."

The rear commanders speared the first deserters. "Don't be cowards. Stand your ground." When the entire force fled, tripping over one another in panic, the commanders gave up and followed Azor through the trees.

At the burning wall, Azor's force of seasoned warriors assembled to attack. These strong, hardened men didn't flinch at the sight of the hovercraft, focusing only on their battle tasks. They wore boiled leather shirts, breeches, and helmets that were impervious to the poorly made knives of the Albion tribes. In each hand, men carried Azor's new war hatchets, with additional ones in sacks hanging down their backs. A line of men carried long spears, and a band of archers stood in formation, scanning the wall for targets. Three teams hoisted tree trunks found nearby that had been cut for the wall but rejected, and turned them into battering rams. When the flames diminished, they ran at the smoldering timbers, launching the ram, weakening the wall. With repeated thrusts, they caused a wall panel to collapse. A mastodon hide was hastily thrown over the burning ash, permitting the warriors and horsemen to stream through the wall. Their shrill cries sent panic into the people of Khamlok.

Kamean and Tamiel helplessly watched the warriors streaming through the wall. They couldn't direct the soundgun blast with sufficient precision to avoid hitting their own people.

Riding from the mountaintop through the trees, King Azor and Yoachim evaded the soundguns. Triumphant determination lit Azor's face. His strategy was winning. Reaching the wall, they rode through the breach and caught up with the fighters. His men swarmed the huts, which had been so meticulously crafted in precise rows. Most huts were empty of people, and the invaders threw the meager possessions outside in the pathway, planning to retrieve their plunder after the battle. Screaming with triumph, they set the huts aflame. Kranya cowered in a hut, having refused to go the Great House with the other women. She screamed when they entered and begged for mercy. The laughing warriors pulled her by her hair into the pathway, kicked her, and slashed her throat.

A small band of Khamlok archers, dressed in simple hide clothing, stealthily slid among the huts, revealing themselves when launching well-placed arrows. Their numbers were too few. A line of warriors sprinted at the archers, winding their arms to release the deadly war hatchets. Most archers fell, and the survivors sought cover to regroup. Other guardsmen engaged warriors in combat with their swords, bravely keeping the invaders at bay to protect a few straggler women and children who hurried to the fortified Great House. Azazel had trained the swordsmen well, but they were too few, and they were outmatched by Azor's smaller, ferocious fighters.

Azor's men resumed their advance through the concentric rings of huts leading to Khamlok's center. "What's that coming toward us?" a warrior growled with disbelief. A gray wolf knocked him to the ground and tore his throat out in one blurry movement. Wolves attacked other invaders, ripping whatever body part they caught. The warriors launched hatchets at the wolves, but they ran too swiftly. The air filled with whooping. A dozen of Azor's fighters fell, hatchets hitting them. "Arggh!" came Azazel's war cry. He and his fighters galloped to challenge the invaders, who scattered for cover among the burning huts. A hatchet caught a horseman in the chest, and he toppled over. In response, his companion circled his arms and launched a hatchet, splitting the skull of Azor's aide. The king whirled in astonishment that his new, secret weapon was used against him. "That traitor, Hilaba," he spat. "I can't wait to get my hands on her."

Azazel and his fighters jumped from their horses. Azazel, whipping his gleaming sword from its scabbard, confronted his enemy. He stood head and shoulders above the tallest of Azor's warriors, who pointed at him, jostling to be the one to bring down the legendary warrior. Hatchets were launched at Azazel; he pulverized each one with his great sword. Grizzled fighters banded together to rush him. He slashed, cleanly cutting off an invader's head, and spinning with the agility of a slighter man confronted the next one raising a sword against him, and then the next and the next. His opponents' splattered blood covered his simple hide shirt and dotted his face, but he was unscratched. Azazel twirled and beheaded a savage trying to pierce his back. Azazel's trained men formed a line and launched a barrage of hatchets, thinning Azor's ranks.

From the hovercraft, Kamean deftly shot arrows, hitting his targets. Kamean's arrow hit the hut where Azor sought cover, narrowly missing his nose.

Rameel and the twenty guardsmen defending the Great House anxiously watched the battle. "Jared," Rameel called, "Azazel's turning the tide. If he wins, this will be over."

"It's tight," said Jared, still perched on the balustrade. "He needs more men."

"Think we should join him?" asked Rameel. "We shouldn't leave the Great House undefended, but if Azazel doesn't win, we'll be overwhelmed, and it won't matter. We've got the lasers. We could be decisive."

Jared was undecided. It could go either way. "I'll stand guard here. Take your men and help. Watch for any sign that they're rushing the Great House and circle back."

Wielding a laser in each hand, Rameel set out to join the battle. He and his band slashed through the invaders' flanks, dismembering bodies as if slicing through water.

Seeing futility, an ashen-faced Azor ordered his warriors to pull back. Retreat nearly choked him. Azor said to Yoachim, "They've left the center undefended. That must be where they've hidden the women and children." To stragglers, he shouted, "Capture the Great House." To his personal guard, he ordered, "You three, give me protection from those wolves and that man-mountain back there." They dispatched a barrage of war hatchets and lit huts on fire, separating Rameel from the Great House. A hatchet was launched at Jared. The blunt edge hit his head, knocking him unconscious.

Azor shouted, "Break down that barrier!" To Yoachim, he said, "This battle is lost. To reach the mainland alive, we must have hostages. Who should we take?"

With his head lowered, Yoachim replied, "Alana is the leader's wife. You'll know her by her golden hair and her height. Her son is Iskur. For good measure, take Azazel's wife, Morgana, also golden of hair and tall. Beware, she's known as a capable warrior."

When the men breached the doorway, Morgana blocked their path. Her gleaming sword was drawn, and she stood ready to defend. Her eyes blazed with determination. The invaders had heard stories about Azazel's warrior mate. They inched forward warily. An arrow hit one, then another in the throat—Vesta's arrows. Urged on by Azor, warriors kicked aside the fallen ones. A leathery, muscled warrior pounced at Morgana, thrusting his spear in a great downward arc, aiming for her heart. Morgana bent like a reed in the wind, twirling unharmed. Her assailant tumbled to the floor. Morgana thrust her sword through his back and prepared for the next attacker.

Azor dismounted and entered, commanding, "Yoachim, you come with me. Show me Alana." When he entered, Morgana warily backed up to assess him. Hands on hips, he studied her. "I presume that we've already met Morgana."

Haughtily, Azor glared at the frightened women trying to protect their children. He bellowed in the common tongue, "I'm in a hurry. Don't kill this one," he said, pointing at Morgana. "I want her. Now, I need Alana to show herself immediately, or I'll start killing."

Morgana inched forward, readying her sword to attack. Azor produced his own sword, a fine Atlantean sword that he'd plundered from one of the now-destroyed port cities in the southern mainland. Morgana held steady. She could see that Azor relied on the power of his swing rather than the artful skill she'd learned from Azazel. She had no doubt that her sword was superior, but an Atlantean sword was of fine quality. A squad of men took positions surrounding Azor. They pointed spears at Morgana, who remained motionless, awaiting a chance to strike. When Alana did not appear, Azor ordered his aide, "Kill a woman and her child." His men grabbed the nearest woman's long hair and dragged her before Azor. She kicked and screamed, pleading with them for mercy. An aide raised his knife and stabbed the woman and her child. Their blood formed a dark pool of blood, which trickled toward Morgana's booted feet.

Morgana's heart skipped a beat. *I must save my people.* She was outnumbered by merciless cutthroats. Desperately searching for a weakness, she found none. *I must form a twirling circle and plunge into their midst until they strike me down.* A warrior pulled Chigi from Akia's trembling arms. Akia screamed, pleading with desperation for Morgana to give up her sword. *I have let them down.* Morgana slowly lowered her sword and with shame cast her eyes downward. Two heavy warriors rushed her and took her precious sword, treating it as a grand prize. They twisted her arms behind her back and pushed her to General Kagan.

Azor raised his sword to Morgana's throat. He growled, "I'll slit her throat right now unless Alana comes to me. Then I'll set this big hut on fire."

Alana was horrified. She whispered, "Maya, I can't let others suffer for me. I can defend myself. Take Iskur and hide him. If I don't return, promise me you'll raise him as your own."

"Alana, don't do this," Maya pleaded. "The men will regain control. Trust them!"

"No time to argue," Alana said. "Lil will find me."

Alana stepped forward. She put her hands on her hips, glaring at Azor, pointing at Yoachim angrily. "You don't need this traitorous worm to name me. I am Alana, the Earth-keeper, mate of Semjaza, daughter of Ewan, and medicine woman. Who is it who calls my name and attacks my city? What great warrior threatens unarmed women and children?" Azor walked up to her with bemusement, "Another warrior. I'm King Azor. You're coming with me. Where's your son?"

An aide entered, spitting out the words, "Something new is flying in the sky. The battle is over, and the fighters and wolves are moving to surround us. I humbly suggest that you leave now, Your Grace."

Heeding the warning, King Azor abruptly ordered his men to bind the women's arms and legs and to put Alana on his horse and Morgana on General Kagan's horse. He warned the trembling women, "Tell your men not to use their weapons on us. We have your women. We'll set them free when we reach the mainland. If we're pursued, they'll end up the same as them." He pointed to the woman and child on the floor. "Understand?"

The women mutely nodded, tears streaming down their faces.

"Good, let's go. Yoachim, show us the shortest way out of here." To General Kagan, Azor said in a low voice, "It's every man for himself," as he kicked his horse in the side.

Yoachim led Azor and Kagan through Khamlok's pathways toward the gate.

* * *

Coming from the west, Lil landed his *tri-terran* and ran to the Great House. From the air, he'd seen the carnage. Seeing the bloody bodies up close, his heart pounded. "Alana! Iskur! Jared!" he called frantically as he searched for someone alive. Lying in the rubble-strewn path outside the Great House, he found Jared, alive but dazed. He lifted up his shoulders. "Jared, speak to me."

Coming to, he rubbed his head. "They knocked me out. I don't know what happened after that. They were trying to get to the women."

Hearing Lil, the women streamed outside.

"Where are Alana and Iskur?" he demanded.

Maya came with Iskur and Krishna in hand, crying uncontrollably, blurting out, "Azor took Alana and Morgana as hostages. He said to tell you that he'll release them when they reach the mainland, and not to come after them." She knelt down to care for Jared.

"Where's Azazel?" demanded Lil.

Azazel, covered with blood, came running. "We killed many, and those left alive threw down their weapons and ran."

"Good. Jared, are you able to fly?" Lil asked.

"I'll make it," said Jared, being helped to his feet by Maya.

"Where is Morgana?" Azazel asked, searching for her.

"Azazel, they took her and Alana as hostages," cried Maya.

"What?" shouted Azazel. "I'll kill them all!"

To Jared, Lil ordered, "Get everyone into the hovercrafts and take them to Hawan. I'll explain later." Heading toward the *tri-terran*, Lil called to Azazel, "Come with me. The rest of you help the injured, then gather your things and get in the hovercrafts. Go as quickly as possible. A flood's coming."

Reaching the *tri-terran*, Lil and Azazel took off.

"The fuel cell is low," warned Azazel.

"I grabbed the fastest vehicle," explained Lil. "I had expected to go to Khamlok and then right to Hawan." He explained about the impending flood.

"If they don't get stopped by the floodwaters, we're going to need backup." Below, they saw the horsemen reach the first forest ridge.

King Azor watched them overhead, saying to Yoachim, "They must have received our message."

Yoachim replied simply, "Yes," in his discomfort, avoiding Alana's glare.

Azor relaxed a bit and asked, "How fast can we make it back?"

Yoachim replied, "Without the baggage of the full army, and by taking this direct route, we might reach the lowlands as early as late today. Then, a half day beyond that to the mainland. I'm taking you just south of the closest point."

They rode quietly for a few hours. Looking up, Azor said, "That's curious. Where's that flying triangle going?" The ship rose higher in the sky as it disappeared into the clouds to their north. Azor was suspicious, but being on unfamiliar terrain far from his lands, he had no choice but to maintain his course.

Alana pleaded, "If you let us go, I promise you that Lil won't hurt you." She tried using her Earthkeeper powers but was too distraught to enter the spirit world.

"You promise me?" He sneered. "Only your presence will ensure your safety."

Above them, Lil gained altitude to determine the course of the floodwater. In the distance, he saw the waves crashing into the northern shores. As the water cascaded inland, it broke into two raging streams, one flowing into the lowland area where the peninsula met the mainland and the other inundating lowlands near Drood's lands.

"It was a partial break," said Lil. "If the whole shelf had let loose, this entire land would be swallowed."

"Even so, that much water will turn this peninsula into an island," said Azazel.

"They won't reach the mainland, at least not by horse."

"The lowlands will flood well before they get there. That'll stop them."

"Yes, but they might not want hostages," Lil worried. He descended, resuming the trail above the fleeing horsemen.

King Azor looked up. "Oh, the flying triangle has returned." Nudging Alana with his knee, he said, "That mate of yours is being smart. What is he, anyway? Some say he's a starman."

"Some say? What do you think?"

"In the beginning," Azor replied, "I believed he was a mere man, although a giant." He paused. "But now? Now I believe he and his kind are men, but they are indeed from the stars. That's why I had to take you, my dear. For security. Even the weapons of a starman are useless if he has to protect the love of his life. You are the love of his life, aren't you? Or are you just a temporary fling?"

"Lil loves me," Alana retorted. "When he comes for me, you'll be sorry."

"You *are* quite beautiful, but we all must seem as primitive as insects to his kind."

"He loves me," protested Alana, refusing to let doubt enter her mind.

"If you say so. The real mystery is why starmen are living like this," Azor said. "Huts in the forest? Children with Earth women? Now, that's the story I'd like to hear."

Alana angrily demanded, "We were just building a new life, raising our families. If you wanted to trade or to talk to us, you simply could have asked. You didn't need to come with an army. Lil would have been fair to you."

Azor chuckled. "He would have been fair, you say. Fairness is in the eye of the beholder. Considering himself fair, he could make me a slave or permit me the immensely great honor of worshiping him simply because he can fly and I can't."

"Why did you do this to us?" she demanded.

"Why?" Azor smirked. "Because your mate's kind poses a threat to us, or at least they could if they so choose. We couldn't wait to find out. We could only prevail if we acted when you were unsuspecting. You were obviously overhunting. It was just a matter of time before you'd start looking for new land."

"We would have managed our growth in peaceful ways. There is much you could have learned if only you'd sought out our friendship."

"Hah!" he snorted, nearly falling off the saddle with laughter. "You *are* naïve."

"How could Yoachim help you?" she demanded. "He was my friend, and he hated you."

Azor laughed. "Yes, I suppose that he used to hate me, and he'll go back to hating me when this is over. But to your question, what are Yoachim's motives? Basically, this was his peninsula, and you and your new people disrespected him."

"We didn't disrespect him," cried Alana.

"Well, my dear, men are sometimes complicated. You'll need to take up the disrespect with him," replied Azor, having grown bored with talk of Yoachim. He noticed that General Kagan was having a difficult time controlling Morgana, who was thrashing her feet, trying to leap from the horse. "Kagan, if you let your prisoner escape, I'll have your head!" Kagan thwacked Morgana with his riding crop on her buttocks until she stopped kicking.

Alana hated being close to the monster, Azor, and having him touch her while they rode. Her muscles ached, and she was bruised. She ignored her pain, fuming with every thought of Yoachim. She passed her time plotting how she would steal a knife and slash his throat in revenge, hating him more than Azor. She was mad, not afraid, knowing that Lil would rescue her; she grew annoyed that it was taking so long. She needed to get back to Iskur. He was probably crying for her. The wounded required her special care. Only she knew all the herbs. She wanted to draw upon the spirit world, but that step required a clarity that she couldn't muster.

General Kagan came alongside Azor. "Your Grace, do you plan to break? The horses need rest and water."

"We'll rest at the next stream," Azor replied. "We can't risk stopping for long. The starmen no doubt have more weapons that we haven't seen."

Above them, Lil closely observed their progress. "We need to land and convince them that the way will soon be deluged."

"They won't believe you," warned Azazel. "And they might well throw one of those war hatchets and kill you in the process."

Lil smirked. "My clothing will protect me. Since you're not wearing our uniform, you stay behind."

He pressed a communications knob. "Ki, what's your status?"

"I'm finishing up."

"We've had one blasted disaster after another," said Lil.

"The flood?"

"More than that," replied Lil. "We've been attacked by savages. Guardsmen are dead, Khamlok is burning, and Alana and Morgana were taken as hostages. Azazel and I are rescuing them."

"Savages?" exclaimed Ki. "I wish I could help, but I'm at the critical point of harnessing this morning's residual energy."

"Thanks. You stay there; there's nothing you can do," replied Lil. "By the way, the flood waters broke at the top, and they're streaming the lowlands to the west and east."

"We projected that it wouldn't bury the entire peninsula. The travelers made it back safely."

"Excellent."

"Let me know when Alana and Morgana are safe."

"Will do," said Lil, terminating the transmission. From Jared, he learned that the hovercrafts were still evacuating Khamlok.

"When this King Azor sees the floodwaters," said Azazel, "even he won't be so stupid as to attempt a crossing."

"I hope you're right," said Lil. "But he'll be trapped. We need him to react rationally. By the way, how is it you knew his name?"

"There were traders who mentioned another despot gaining power on the mainland," said Azazel slowly. "I surmised that it must be him."

"I see," said Lil. He'd pursue this matter later.

"I've been anticipating another villain to fill the Danes' shoes. That is, after all, why I've been insistent on developing our defenses." Azazel with grim smugness felt that he'd been vindicated. When Lil failed to respond, he asked, "How long will the fuel cell last?"

Checking, Lil said, "Not much longer. We may need to land to preserve power. Jared should be done evacuating Khamlok soon."

Worried about the wolves and the horses, Azazel went into *mencomm*, directing them to safety.

* * *

"Ah, at last," thought Drood, his eyes closed. He had found a way to latch onto Azazel's *mencomm* communication and fix his location. Foreseeing that Azazel's ship would soon land, Drood directed his shadowmen to lie in wait.

* * *

To preserve fuel, Lil flew low, uncloaked, taking comfort that Alana and Morgana appeared to be unharmed. King Azor frequently gazed upward, raising his defiant fist. After proceeding a few hours without change, Lil said, "I'm checking the progress of the flood." He increased his altitude but was surprised that the lowland wasn't flooded. If the horsemen continued at this pace, they might begin their descent. He flew along the cliff edge and discovered that a natural dam had formed, jammed by huge chunks of ice, boulders, and tree trunks. Lil judged that it would breach at any time.

"They might enter before that dam breaks," Lil gasped with horror.

"We've got to stop them!" Azazel huffed, nearly jumping through the window.

"I'll block the path." Lil sped ahead of their horses and landed, concealed by a sharp bend in the trail. He opened the hatch and waited, transforming his uniform into a long, hooded tunic, reinforced to deflect their weapons. If only he had his crystal, he could end the conflict. Azazel, wearing his bloodied shirt of boiled leather, readied his sword, preparing to charge.

When Azor galloped into view, his startled horse reared sharply, nearly dumping Alana. Grabbing her, Azor signaled his riders to stop.

Alana breathed a sigh of relief, thinking her ordeal was over. "Drood" she mumbled, seeing shadowmen appearing throughout the perimeter.

Azor called out, "Starman, you've been smart so far, why be stupid now? I'll kill your lovely mate if you don't leave. I promise you, on my honor, when we reach the mainland, I'll release her. But not a moment sooner."

"A flood invades the lowlands," Lil shouted. "If you descend, you won't make it to the other side alive. All of you will drown."

General Kagan, turning on his rearing horse, shouted, "It's a lie, Your Grace. His weapons are useless. It hasn't snowed or rained in weeks, and there's not a cloud in the sky. There isn't enough water to cause such a flood."

King Azor was unconvinced. He yelled, "Tell me how you know this."

"In the far north, glacier ice fell into the ocean. I saw the flood from my ship. A monster wave will crash at any moment."

"If that's true," General Kagan counseled, "it's even more vital that we cross before this flood arrives, or we'll be trapped. Our horses can swim, and so can we."

"Go to your death if you must," Lil demanded, "but release our wives."

King Azor pointed his spear at Lil and shouted, "Starman, move that thing so we can pass."

Lil's eyes glowed with intensity. "No. Release our women."

Azor glared back. "If you don't move, I'll order my general to slit that one's throat," he pointed at Morgana. He raised Alana's head and put his knife to her neck.

Morgana gasped with surprise, her eyes entreating Azazel to save her. General Kagan raised his knife and slowly cut Morgana's white neck. She skillfully fainted back to avoid the worst of his blade. Distracted and not noticing his miss, the general shoved Morgana from his horse. She lay bleeding, applying pressure to her wound.

"No!" Azazel bellowed and sprinted toward Kagan, wielding his great sword. A step away from him, Azor's warriors struck him three times in the chest and leg with whirring war hatchets. He jerked, still walking, and another hatchet sunk deep into his forehead. He fell, and a pool of blood deepened around him.

"Starman," Azor shouted, "your wife is next!" Lil calculated whether he could cover the distance to Azor before he could cut Alana; it was too close.

"Lil, go!" Alana screamed. "Do as he says!" In desperation, she gambled that the shadowmen, drawing closer, would interfere.

Lil stumbled back into the *tri-terran*. He burned with hatred for Azor, who triumphantly leered at him. He pounded his seat in his fury. He vowed he wouldn't forget that disgusting look no matter how long he lived. Aloud he seethed, "They'll pay for this." He lifted off, not noticing the shadows moving in and covering Azazel's and Morgana's bodies.

"Jared, the savages killed Azazel and Morgana. They still have Alana. Time is running out. Drop everything and get here. Khamlok's not in danger."

"I have your coordinates," Jared replied. "I'm on my way."

Lil resumed flying closely overhead. Azor and his horsemen, continuing to taunt Lil with their clenched fists, reached the chalky rim. Without hesitating, Azor and his men began the steep, difficult descent. "Lil spoke the truth," Alana pleaded. "Can't you hear that roar? Can't you smell the salt water?"

"Then you'd better hope that we travel swiftly, my dear," replied Azor, seeing no alternative. Reaching the bottom, Azor quickened his pace.

Lil, his fuel cell now empty, landed atop the ridge. He paced back and forth in his uniform, watching them race away. He kicked a rock over the edge whenever he pictured the attack. He wasn't accustomed to the death of those close to him. Alana was in mortal danger. Azazel was really gone? He had known life in the wilderness would be difficult, but he hadn't imagined such tragedies. When this was over, he vowed, he would never be put in this position again. He had to rescue Alana as swiftly as possible.

CHAPTER 36
RAMEEL

"Do you think we'll lose Khamlok?" Rameel asked uneasily, seeing the city disappear from sight. Leaving in the last flight to Hawan, he sat nervously in the cockpit with Jared. Maya, holding Krishna, sat behind them, next to Yanni with Little Maliki. Jared needed them to exit swiftly so that he could help Lil.

"I'm worried about Alana," said Maya, tears streaming down her face.

"What's the latest word?" asked Rameel.

"Lil and Azazel are watching overhead," he said. "We're still not sure where the floodwaters will go."

They were silent the rest of the way to Hawan. As they approached the waterfall, Yanni took a deep breath, looking wide-eyed at Maya. As they sped through the waterfall illusion, Maya whispered, "Here is where Alana and I went through the rock wall."

"As many times as I've heard that story," said Yanni, "I didn't truly appreciate how brave you were."

"We're landing," Jared announced. "Everyone, exit as fast as you can."

When he opened the door, those who had come in earlier flights still mingled in the courtyard, having no leader and not knowing where to go.

Rameel jumped and helped others out. Two guardsmen leaped in. "Everyone's out, Jared. Be on your way." Jared immediately took flight, followed by a second ship.

At Hawan, the women gawked at the lovely structures nestled within the forbidding mountain. "This is magnificent," whispered Yanni in awe. "Like art."

"Yes," Rameel said shortly, discomforted by old memories.

Having arrived on an earlier trip, Tamiel greeted Rameel. "This is chaos. You're the senior officer. You take charge."

"Move everyone inside the Ministry," order Rameel. "Scientists will be monitoring the flood."

Little Maliki tugged at Rameel's pant leg. "Hungry." Rameel swung him up and strode toward the sealed Ministry entrance. "I'll get you something soon." To the others, he said loudly, "Everyone, go to the tall building at the point of the triangle." At the hidden entrance, he said his name, but the password failed. While he pondered how to enter, the hatch slid open, and a uniformed scribe began to step out. Startled at seeing Rameel and his people, he drew back, curling his lip with disgust.

Rameel jumped in to prevent the hatch from closing. "We were brought here because of the flood. Do you remember me? I'm Rameel."

The man, hair white and closely cropped, peered at him with a look of mixed distaste and fear. "Entry isn't permitted. No one gave me orders to admit the tr…uh, those who left."

"There wasn't time," said Rameel, holding the door and motioning the others to enter. "Ki arranged for us to come here."

"Commander Ki? No one gave me an order." The scribe worried, fearful of punishment. His languid manner seemed drugged to Rameel, who wondered whether he used to be that timid. "Don't be concerned about punishment," he said, and the fearful man disappeared across the courtyard.

"I'm going up to view the monitors," Rameel told Tamiel. "We need food for the children."

"I'll check Guard Hall for food," said Tamiel, jogging toward it.

Rameel led the group into the lifts and brought them to the control room floor. About fifty scientists monitored the flood on their screens. They stared in disbelief when they saw Rameel's people. On one screen they viewed Ki, Laurina, and Mikhale at the Power Circle. Ki saw Rameel and said, "Rameel, has everyone been evacuated?"

"Yes," he replied.

Tamiel came with bags of nourishment bars. Rameel scowled at the sight of them. Tamiel shrugged. "This is all there was. Just one bar shouldn't hurt them."

Little Maliki began to cry, "Hungry." Yanni picked him up and gently swayed to comfort him.

"Just this once," said Rameel, with his own stomach growling.

"What are you concerned about?" she asked. "Isn't this what you used to live on?"

"Earth food tastes much better."

"We'll get by for today," she said, taking a bar. She put little Maliki on the ground, squatted, and mashed the bar. Tasting it first, she was startled and blinked. "I feel strange. Is there something more than food in this?" Placing the remainder on a table, she said, "I don't want Maliki to eat this."

"Don't go there!" A colonist scolded a child who had wandered too far.

"I wish Jared were here," said Maya, trying to comfort the squirming Krishna and Iskur. Tara stood beside her, holding her fidgeting sister as best she could.

"Where's mommy?" demanded Iskur.

"Mommy will be here soon," Maya comforted him.

Rameel, who had been observing the monitors, returned to Yanni and Maya. "Just a piece of the ice sheet fell. They think it will only flood the lowlands."

"So we'll be able to return to Khamlok?" asked Yanni with relief.

"Not immediately," he said, shaking his head. "There are too many bodies. I don't want the children to see them."

Yamin brought Kosondra, threading their way through the people. Yanni smiled, recognizing her from the birthing. "Kosondra will take you to Guard Hall. It's more comfortable. She'll help you get settled. Dalits will distribute Earth fruits."

Loudly, Rameel ordered, "Listen, everyone. All women and children will go with Kosondra, the woman standing beside me. All guardsmen will stay here. As soon as we confirm that Khamlok won't be flooded, we'll return to bury the dead. Each should obtain a laser for digging."

As Yanni left, she called back, "Please hurry. I want to go home."

CHAPTER 37

LIL

When Jared's ship appeared on the horizon, Lil waved impatiently, and as soon as it landed, he strode up the entry ramp. "The dam is beyond the bend," he said, pointing. "It could break any moment, drowning Alana. We need to snatch her. Get moving."

As they lifted, Lil hurried to the rear. "I'm getting into the rescue harness." Before Jared could respond, Lil stood at the hatch. "Are we near?"

"Ten seconds," Jared replied.

"I'm ready."

"This is too risky," Jared protested. "The water is freezing, and I can't predict its course. Nor can I control the harness with these wind gusts. You might drown or get hypothermia. Remember, you're mortal now. You must think of more than yourself. You're the named successor. You're *not* expendable."

Lil glared at him; mortality wasn't new after all that they'd been through. A thought floated to his consciousness: *This is how it happens at the end for mortals—emotion trumps reason.* "En.Lil. Door open." Jared slowly lowered the harness, which swung wildly as he raced toward Alana.

In the distance, the frothing horses galloped at full speed. Azor and his men glimpsed the mainland cliffs in the distant haze. Lil knew it was too far. Suspended in the harness, he narrowed the gap but heard the dam snap, followed by the roar of the raging waters. Azor and his men froze. Their panicked horses reared as they faced the mountain of ice chunks and water. Azor screamed, "Shaman, if you have any magic, now would be a good time to use it!" Yoachim was frozen.

Azor threw Alana from his horse to lighten his load, and she desperately scrambled to her feet. She watched as Lil's image, tiny in the distance, race toward her. He wouldn't reach her in time. *He's coming for me.* His presence brought her peace and gave her the clarity she needed. *I am the Earthkeeper.* She drew upon the spirit world. The power of the onrushing water was too great for her to hold it back, so she enclosed herself in a cocoon. The rushing water covered her cocoon, and she lost sight of Lil. *He'll believe that I'm dead and quit looking.* Still, she was too terrified of the crashing ice chunks to release it. The inner cocoon glowed with a soft pink light, and she heard Zedah's kind voice. *Child, this cocoon won't save you. You have unfulfilled tasks for your people, but you must first relinquish this body for the next. Do not be afraid.*

Zedah's voice comforted her, but she struggled to believe. *What if I'm hallucinating? I will send my spirit to walk in the spirit world, where I will watch over Lil and my people. Mother, if I die, I trust that mine is a good death. I pray that the ancestors will welcome me.* Feeling content, she closed her eyes and partially released the cocoon, hoping that she could still use it to shield her torso from the ice and cold. Passing as if clearing a path was a friendly oak tree. Through an armhole in the cocoon, she grabbed a limb and felt the tree rising.

By *mencomm*, Lil ordered Jared, "Keep skimming." On his monitor, Jared watched Lil slide over the bar to hang by his knees, holding out his arms. "He hopes that she'll surface," said Jared to his crew, his voice tense. "That's impossible."

He saw a mastodon carcass tangled in the ice chunks below. A massive oak tree sprang from the water and floated atop the debris. His heart leaped when he saw Alana riding a branch. "Lower," he ordered. He hit his foot against something sharp, not noticing the pain. Dangerously, he skimmed across the choppy water, with the harness lurching uncontrollably.

When he neared Alana, she felt his presence. Seeing him reaching for her, she released the last of the cocoon. The tree rolled. Desperately, she stretched her fingertips for Lil's grasping arms. They touched, but he couldn't secure her slippery hands before a wave washed over them. Jared jerked the harness, extracting Lil from the icy water. Lil had been hit by ice, and he grimaced with the pain of a broken shoulder. With his good arm, he waved for Jared to head downstream.

Alana's tree rolled among the waves, and he saw her once again lying on top. Gasping for breath, she shivered, and her lips were blue. He strained to grab her. "Alana, here!" Within inches of her hand, the harness convulsed in the wind. The tree bounced as it bumped an ice chunk. Her arms failing to hold, she slid below the surface, leaving her floating hair barely visible.

"Alana," he yelled with all the breath his lungs held. "Hold on. I'm here." Lil desperately fought the harness. His only chance to reach her was to leave its safety and jump. He hesitated; he was mortal now. If the rejuvenation chamber had been working, without a blink he would have unleashed it. He told himself to wait. He'd grab her when she resurfaced. It would be safer for them both if he were patient. The harness would extract them, and the ship would immediately warm them.

After an eternity, she surfaced, choking. "Alana," he called over the roar of the rushing water, reaching for her. He grew close. In a gust of wind, the harness jerked again. It was impossible unless he took it off. He watched the swirling, rampaging water. Saving her would take a miracle. If he jumped, it was likely they'd both die—permanent death. He loved her deeply, but he was the named successor, responsible for the future of his home world and co-ruler of Earth. His people needed him. He envisioned Anu, Ama, Jahkbar, and Uras exhorting him, *"Lil, it is your divine duty to put the welfare of Alterrans above all else."* Jumping would be suicide. But he loved her, and she trusted him. But Iskur might be an orphan. But wasn't he a strong swimmer? Wasn't there a chance? *I can't live in fear.* His would be a good death.

"Blessed Zeya, no!" Jared gasped. Open mouthed, he watched in horror as Lil released the harness and jumped into the thick current of ice and debris. The tree branch she'd held protruded from the water. With powerful strokes aided by the sweeping current, he reached the tree before it submerged. After pulling himself onto the trunk, he slid along the sides and over the branches, thrusting his hands into the muddy ice water. "Alana, I'm here, fight!" he yelled. Not finding her, he grasped the trunk with his legs and rolled it, slipping under water. Moving from branch to branch, he felt her hair and found her arm. She was still weakly gripping a branch. Hoping that her grip wasn't rigor mortis, he yanked her to the surface. Not breathing, she was blue with cold, and her eyes were glassy. He righted himself and pulled her on top, where he pressed against her chest and blew his warm breath into her mouth. Another tree jammed his. It rolled, and they both fell into the water. He grabbed her once again and tried to keep her limp head above the water. Having no control, he was swept along by the unforgiving current. Debris slammed into him, breaking his other arm despite the defensive settings of his tunic.

Above him, a harnessed crewman was lowered to snatch them, but he failed in the strong wind. Lil clung to Alana's limp body, struggling to keep them both afloat.

By *mencomm* Jared shouted, "Rocks!"

Quickly, a second crewman was lowered. Wildly, the chair twisted uncontrollably in the wind, making it impossible to snatch Lil. Jared pulled up the harness so that the crewman landed atop the boulder as Lil's body crashed into it. A moment later, the first crewman caught Lil's fractured arm, but Alana's lifeless body slipped away from his broken arm, lost in the chaotic water. Lil's limp, broken body was hoisted up.

"Quick, try to clear his lungs," Jared shouted, losing sight of Alana. They applied pressure to his chest and tried to clear his airways.

After several minutes, the crewman said, "Sir, I don't think it's his lungs. His head injury is too severe."

"Keep trying anyway," Jared snapped. After a few more minutes, even Jared admitted that it was futile. Frantically, he shouted, "We can't lose him! We need Ki." Unable after several times to reach him, Jared headed his ship for Hawan.

When he finally reached Ki, he ordered, "Bring him to the Power Circle. I'm still here experimenting with the rejuvenation chamber, and I have a little power preserved from this morning. It's Lil's only chance."

CHAPTER 38

KI

"Laurina," Ki shouted with rare emotion, "prepare the chamber. This is no experiment. Mikhale and Rafale, come. Move the chamber into position." They came running and began shoving the chamber near the control equipment used for the portal.

"What's wrong?" Laurina asked, working the control panel.

"Lil's been injured, mortally," Ki huffed with the exertion of moving the chamber.

"What?" exclaimed Laurina. "Our tests have been so preliminary. I might not have sufficient resources if his injuries are serious. Do you know what to target?"

"I don't know much. Only that he smashed into a boulder trying to save Alana from drowning, unsuccessfully."

"We have little power," grunted Michael, not wanting to be responsible for not saving a named successor.

"We'll see," said Ki, his mind flying through all the possibilities. "The batteries are full from this morning. We'll keep it going as long as we can. Then nature will take its course." Fleetingly, the thought crossed Ki's mind that he could easily let Lil go, say they didn't have the power or that the chamber still wasn't working. His loyal assistants would confirm anything he said. Then Anu would have no choice but to name him as the next successor. No, he thought, dispelling it from his mind. He didn't want to win that way.

"What injuries should I cover in the program?" asked Laurina.

"Head injuries first," directed Ki, while he connected the chamber to the control equipment. "So program for severe cranial trauma and facial bones first. Then cover a variety of possible core injuries. His aura is no doubt low because they headed for Hawan first. We'll need to improvise."

Mikhale attached the battery complex to the chamber while Laurina calibrated the chamber's sensitive equipment. When the hovercraft landed, Mikhale and Rafael retrieved his lifeless body on a mini-hover. Jared trailed close behind.

"Sir, when we get inside, I'll look at your wound," offered Mikhale, looking at Jared's purplish bruise covering most of his forehead. "What happened?"

"Don't worry about me," he ordered. "Focus on Lil. Savages attacked."

When the mini-hover was in place, Ki scanned Lil's body. "His aura's getting dangerously low. Move fast."

Laurina said, "Preliminarily, the results confirm a serious skull injury, fractured cheek bones, broken nose, chipped front teeth, broken arm and dislocated shoulder, broken ribs, knee out of its socket, broken legs, as well as water in his lungs. We'll need high power for a long time to cure this many problems. I wish we had more time to identify each injury."

"We don't have that luxury," Ki said. "Treat the head injuries and clear his lungs. At least we should restore life." Under normal circumstances, a patient's brain activity would have been downloaded for storage in case the rejuvenation process destroyed some or all of the memory. That was one more risk that Ki couldn't control.

Rafael washed the blood from the deep gash on his forehead. After examining his shoulder and knee, he said, "I'll pull his knee straight and reset his shoulder before he feels pain."

Ki ordered, "Put him in the chamber." With Lil's aura diminishing, the window of time was closing. Ki closed the door, and Laurina energized the chamber. Lights blinked as the batteries began supplying power.

Monitoring the readings, Ki said tensely, "So far, so good. Let's hope our luck holds a bit further."

When the chamber was fully energized, Laurina commenced the healing program. Ki went to the window to watch the delicate instruments perform their life-saving miracle. A series of electrical charges infused Lil's electromagnetic aura with chemicals, stimulating his body's immune system to cure his injuries. With time, his aura's glow became steadier and stronger. Ki studied the electrical arcs, which changed to pink if the tissue was healthy.

Jared slumped into a chair and bitterly spat, "I can't believe what those bastards did to us." To Ki, he said, "I don't know the location of Azazel's body, or Morgana's. Alana must be in the ocean by now."

"I'm afraid we couldn't help them even if you found the bodies," said Ki, putting his hand on his shoulder. "We don't have sufficient power to fully rejuvenate Lil."

The clock showed the chamber's sequence progressing. At zero, Ki peered through the chamber door. Although Lil's aura was bright, he didn't move. Ki studied the instruments. "He's breathing again, and he has a heartbeat. Brain activity is too low." Looking worried, he opened the door. Lil, now having the physical appearance of an adolescent boy with his natural chestnut hair, was unconscious.

Losing his characteristic calm, Ki shouted in frustration and hit his fist into his other hand. Breathing deeply, he said tensely, "We've got to figure this out. What alternatives do we have?"

"The most reliable course would be to perform the entire procedure a second time," Laurina said. After checking the battery power, she frowned. "Power is nearly exhausted." Other suggestions were made and dismissed as Ki nervously rechecked Lil's unresponsiveness.

Ki's eyes darted with deep thought. "Shock his brain. Attach electrodes targeting the sensitive points." Laurina prepared the control program while Mikhale attached the electrodes.

Ki closed the door, saying quietly, "Lil, we have sufficient power only if it's your destiny to live." Laurina initiated the procedure, with the batteries sputtering. Two shocks jolted his brain before the batteries were exhausted, and the whirring of the machine ceased. In the eerie silence, Ki waited several moments, afraid to look. Suddenly, he jerked the door and looked in. Lil blinked his eyes.

Excitedly, Laurina called out, "Brain function is returning. It worked!"

"What a relief," Jared sighed with relief, coming to the window.

"Good job," Ki said, releasing a deep breath. He greeted the young Lil, who groggily looked up at him, groaning with pain from his injured legs.

Moving his mouth with his broken teeth to form words, he eventually uttered, barely above a whisper, "What happened?"

Smiling with relief, Ki bent over and gently put his hand on Lil's shoulder. "You've been through a lot, including a partial rejuvenation. You'll need a while to recover completely. We'll talk later." He began to leave.

"Wait," he mumbled, reaching for Ki's arm, but falling back, moaning with pain. "How?"

"How did you die?" Ki finished for him. "You slammed into a boulder while attempting a rescue."

Lil mumbled, his mind hazy. "Don't remember."

"I'm sedating you."

Unable to focus his mind, Lil gave up trying to speak and drifted to sleep.

CHAPTER 39

LIL

"The warm air near the great middle sea will be a tremendous change from these mountains," Ki advised Lil. Lil's bones were finally mending, and he was feeling better, at least physically. "It'll be warm the entire year. We're leaving snow and ice behind."

Laurina had replaced his broken teeth, and Lil felt them to assure him that they were firmly implanted. Not leaving the Hawan infirmary since his accident, he remained upset by his memory loss. He frowned and rolled onto his side. "I wish I could remember the mountains, remember snow." His memories came in blotches, and he didn't have a coherent picture of his life. How would he function as the named successor?

"We've been working on restoring your memories," Ki replied. "You didn't keep a memory book. I suppose that was a precaution to protect government secrets. Your memories are trapped deep inside your brain. We need to tap into them." He worried that Lil's depression would delay his recovery. "We have a plant collected near the equator on Earth's far side. It's similar in effect to Alana's mushrooms. After testing on your holographic twin, we're optimistic that it will unlock your subconscious memories. It won't be a pleasant experience, I'm afraid. The drug is an hallucinogen. It caused the hologram to relive emotional moments with heightened awareness. Delving into the deep subconscious is what brings back retrievable memory."

Lil rolled onto his back. "Can't you transfer the memories from the hologram?"

"They're too unreliable."

"I'll do anything." Lil sighed heavily, so distraught that even Ki felt sympathy for him. "I can't live this way."

Ki and his assistants tested the procedure until it was safe. Coming to Lil's room, Ki announced, "This treatment is unusual, but it's the best we can do. You will relive snapshots of your life. Some will be good, some will cause pain. You will be emotionally vulnerable. Jared will stay with you. To have familiar surroundings, we're administering it in your old suite."

Lil shrugged, his eyes staring vacantly. "I have no choice. How soon can we start?"

"This afternoon."

When Lil entered his old suite, it seemed vaguely familiar, but frustratingly, he couldn't remember where things were. Nor could he remember how long he'd been gone or what he had been doing prior to the accident.

"His recent past will be a shock," Ki cautioned Jared, who wore his silver uniform, with his hair closely clipped in the guard fashion. "His Alterran training is the most ingrained in his psyche, and it's through that lens that he'll view Khamlok and his Earth family."

Jared worried not only for Lil, but also for the former guardsmen who had followed Lil in leaving Hawan. Lil had been different at Khamlok, one of them. The guardsmen's loyalty to him had arisen from respect for his leadership ability, not the fear of punishment. He called upon the stars to give them back the Lil of Khamlok, not the Lil of Alterra. "Lil did what he had to do based on his knowledge at the time. He can't have regrets."

"With the benefit of hindsight when the danger is gone, the view from the front lines gets second guessed," Ki agreed. "History can be an unfair judge."

Taking a deep breath, Jared said, "I'm ready, sir."

Entering the room, Jared greeted Lil. "Peace and harmony, sir." Lil wore his uniform with his commander's double purple insignia.

"Peace and harmony, Jared," Lil greeted him listlessly. "I assume you're here because you became one of my officers. I have few memories of this place."

"We're fixing that," said Ki brightly. "Come, lie down on your bed." Ki gave him a liquid to drink. "Memories will be retrieved roughly in chronological order, although you'll skip your older, embedded ones from before your last rejuvenation. Your recent memories are most vivid. Mundane ones will zoom by. Things evoking a strong emotional response will linger."

Lil soon felt himself entering the twilight between sleep and waking. Images zoomed, beginning with his most recent life on Alterra. These were comforting, and he shared happy family times with Anu and Uras. With excitement, he planned for his Earth venture, and his thoughts lingered at his wonder arriving on Earth through the portal. He zoomed through the early routine of Hawan. When he remembered learning about the geologic disaster on Alterra, he relived the fear of being stranded forever on Earth. He grew agitated.

"What are you remembering now?" asked Ki, examining Lil's eyes.

"Being doomed to life on this primitive planet," he replied glumly. He added, "We can't go home, but I'm grateful that Father and Mother could." Early in his recovery, when he'd wondered why they hadn't visited him, Ki had told him only that they had been able to return home.

Knowing now that the portal had been reactivated, Lil remembered with abject disgust his fateful decision to violate Ama's Non-Interference Directive. He tensed at the hunt and when he met Alana, followed by his confrontation of the

Council. Reliving his sessions in the Library, he felt disloyal. He argued with Alana about rescuing her women, and he again violated the directive. Strangely, he had strong feelings for this Earth woman. He relived the destruction caused by the comet and the deaths that led him to despair for their survival.

When he proposed to Alana and left Hawan, he groaned in agony, "What did I do?"

Jared assured him, "You did what you thought was right, Commander. *Never* forget that. You fought to save our lives."

Lil was offended at Jared's familiar tone, but the intense memory flashes absorbed him. "How could I have abandoned Hawan?" he moaned, his honor offended.

"Sir, your motives were pure. You couldn't foresee that Alterra would recover." Jared was uncomfortable, knowing that the Lil who'd been his friend was gone.

Reliving the mating ceremony and its salacious aftermath, with dread he wondered, *Why isn't she here?* Lil's memories raced on, and he felt waves of overwhelming passion for Alana, remembering his night on the cliff. He had helped Alana give birth. "I had a child? Where is he?" With the distance of time, he was amazed. These were powerful memories of happy times with Earth people, of combining two worlds.

But the memories moved on. Happiness turned to hatred. He remembered Petus sneering at him, and he turned to rage when savages destroyed his handiwork. The rage intensified as the savage king stole Alana and he couldn't rescue her. He raged at the tragic deaths of Azazel and Morgana. He seethed at the savage king's look of triumph when Lil was forced to stand down. With rage consuming his body, he shouted, "Never again!"

He crumpled, reliving Alana's death. Moments later, he thrashed around his room, throwing his life's treasures. "Aggh! Alana!!" Worst of all, he remembered his hesitation at saving her. "Alana, Alana," he moaned, "I failed you." With his memories ending as he crashed into the rock, he fell to his knees and pounded his fists into the floor.

Ki sat with him for a while before prodding gently, "Mother wants you to know how sorry she is that you were hurt and that Alana didn't make it." He paused. "And that goes for me, as well."

"I'm leaving you Yamin's recorder, sir," offered Jared with trepidation, "in case you want to relive our history. Alana is there. Maya wants you to know how heartbroken she is, how all the women are, at her death, as well as Morgana's and Azazel's—" Jared choked, tears in his eyes. "They want you to know how much everyone loved her." He paused, putting his hand on Lil's back. "The women's circle conducted a special ceremony in her honor."

Casting off Jared's hand, Lil spat with fury, "I want to be alone now." His eyes blazed, and his chest heaved. "If only that bastard Azor hadn't died, I'd hunt him down and make him pay for an eternity!"

Jared nodded, keeping his distance. Although most of the guardsman had returned to Khamlok at the first opportunity, ever-loyal Jared had stayed to attend Lil. Nevertheless, he warily watched for signs that the commander would revert to his family's traditions. "I know this is tough for you. We'll have a ceremony to remember them when you're better." Jared said to Ki, "Can you give him a sedative? This is too much for his system. He's still too weak."

With a jab from Ki, Lil slumped, and they helped him into his bed.

"I'll stand guard outside in his room tonight."

"Good," said Ki. "He never loved before. It defied Ama's programming. Call me if you need anything."

CHAPTER 40

KI

Returning to the Ministry, Ki descended to a little-used rear entrance. Mikhale entered, dressed as an Earthling, filthy after weeks in the wild. He walked beside a mini-hover covered with a white cloth, and he removed a wig of matted black hair. "We found a body washed up on shore near the mainland, sir. It's badly decomposed, but we think it's a young female with long hair, originally blonde."

"Let me see." Donning a mask over his nose and mouth, Ki stooped over the body and pulled back the shroud. He opened the eyes. "Green, but grayish green. Not like hers, but the dullness could be the result of the salt water." He examined the battered body and fingered the pouch still clinging to her neck. Wincing from the horror of the decay, he covered her face. "It might be her. We'll run a genetics match from the hologram records. Wait, what's this bulge?" He opened the pocket carefully sewn into the remnants of her tattered furs and found a silver headband, untarnished from the floodwaters. Alana had worn it as she proudly presented her newborn to his mother. "No question. Well done, Mikhale. Laurina, get samples for cloning. Then preserve her for Ninhursag. She might be able to do more."

"I secretly accessed Yamin's recorder and made a special file of all her images and recorded thoughts," said Rafael. "It's not complete, but at least we can preserve that portion of her life."

Laurina asked, beginning to prick the body with a sharp instrument and insert samples into a tube, "Are you going to tell Lil?"

"Not until it's successful. Mikhale, did you find any trace of the bodies of Azazel and his wife?"

"No," he replied. "We found two pools of blood, but no bones or clothing. No sign that they were dragged away. It was as if they evaporated." Examining the site, Mikhale had felt uncomfortable, as if something in the shadows stalked him.

Ki ran his fingers through his hair, deep in thought. "Scavengers would have left some trace. Who would take Azazel's body?"

CHAPTER 41
LIL AND KI

"The area to the east of the Cedar Woods is a large plain," Ki explained to Lil, "which is serviced by four great rivers, which periodically undergo massive flooding."

"Near Eridu, our first outpost," said Lil. "Flooding seems to be the primary feature of this blasted planet."

"Yes. The area is rich in natural resources, with plentiful wild fruits and vegetables. It was extensively flooded after the comet impact, and the population was virtually wiped out. It's still sparsely populated because of the muddy conditions. Where the water is receding, though, is one of the most fertile spots on Earth. I've located an idyllic place for an Alterran-style garden only an hour's flight from our new base."

"The opposite of Hawan," Lil remarked without interest.

"Yes, and not only the terrain. When I selected Hawan's site, I complied with the directive by isolating ourselves. At the Cedar Woods, that won't be possible. All the Earth survivors are going to be congregating in the warmest latitudes. We'll be managing development of Earth people, even working them into our service." Ki sighed. "You don't seem very interested. I have some things to do. I'll be back when I can."

"Wait!" snapped Lil, his eyes narrowed with suspicion.

"What?" asked Ki, running his fingers through his unruly hair.

"If we have the capability of building the Cedar Woods, why didn't you present that option before?" he growled. "I left Hawan because it was deteriorating, and you said that we didn't have the means to repair it."

"That's true. For the intricacies of Hawan, a contingent of master builders was required."

"What about the Cedar Woods?"

"It couldn't be built without Father's cooperation. He couldn't think beyond returning to Alterra, as you know." Ki regarded him calmly. *He's getting uncomfortably close to the truth.* "Stone pillars, no matter how meticulously carved, won't preserve our civilization if we can't rejuvenate. You pursued the means for reproduction, where acceptable women were available. Our views of interacting with the Earth people are evolving."

"I haven't decided yet whether to use them."

Ki smirked. "We must grow grain, and we don't have the manpower without using humans. Your guardsmen won't be content as farmers forever."

"We can repurpose Hawan's Dalits."

"They have more valuable uses. Our base at the Cedar Woods will afford us the opportunity to take measured steps to influence regional developments. If we choose, we can remain sequestered from the rejuvenated Earth population. On the other hand, if we desire to guide their development, we'll be close."

Lil stared at him, wanting to probe his mind, but knowing that Ki had it blocked. *He's always been jealous. He's a master manipulator. I was a fool for thinking things had changed. How much of my fate has been maneuvered by him?*

"I'll be back, brother." Before leaving, Ki gave him an inscrutable smile.

Left alone in his suite, Lil sank back into a dark mood. For the millionth time, he grew enraged when remembering the insolence of Petus and the triumphal glare of Azor. Rapidly pacing the room, he grew more agitated and snarled, "This will not happen again!" His face twisted with rage, he raised his arms in the air and shouted, "On the soul of Zeya, I swear that the Earth savages will fear and obey me!"

* * *

When Ki visited Lil the next day, he brought his *treschet* board. "I thought you might be bored, and I've missed playing. No one else is a challenge." Ki began setting up the game pieces.

"I'm surprised you want to play me, old man, since I always beat you," joked Lil casually, taking a seat across from him.

"Hah, I always win!" Ki protested, a gleam in his eye.

Lil caused his wall panels to display a dimly lit, gray-walled castle from an Alterran legend. They sat near an opening in the turrets. In the distance was Mount Kreshna, the colossal coned volcano that was the dominant feature of their home sector on Alterra. Ki raised his eyebrows, questioning the atmosphere. Lil said curtly, "It goes with the game."

After playing for a while and being comfortably ahead, a calmer Lil asked, "Ki, Father decreed that I should rule the north and you the south. Do you accept the divide? The last thing I want to do is fight you."

"Fight *you*?" Ki laughed, moving a game piece. "I'd win easily. Seriously, I'm fine. I hope you are."

Lil pursed his lips and nodded, moving a piece. "Of course. As Father decreed, the Cedar Woods will be home to us both. We'll maintain the main portal there. The mines will also be under joint dominion."

Ki scratched his head and wrinkled his nose, moving a piece. "The mines? I missed that part of his speech. I recollect that they're in the south, under my dominion."

Lil took his turn, removing one of Ki's captured pieces. "We both need raw materials. There's no point to duplication, especially with our limited number of Dalits."

Ki hesitated, not ready to disclose that he'd promised the Dalits to use Earth people to perform odious tasks. "I'm going to use the technology developed for the Power Circle to build a larger facility."

"Larger?" Lil asked, mildly interested, as he moved a game piece.

"Yes. The whole design will be a symbol of sacred geometry—a main pyramid and two smaller ones," said Ki with enthusiasm, moving a piece. "It will be a deep-Earth wave collection system. Waves from volcanic activity, earthquakes, and earth movements will perpetually fuel our needs. We can beam power across the planet. We simply need to construct receiving obelisks."

"That's ambitious," observed Lil, moving another piece. "Where will you put it?"

"I've selected a site south of the Cedar Woods—thirty degrees by my planetary measurement system. Beside the pyramid will be a unique monument commemorating Father's ascension. No matter what happens, I want people to know that we, the Alterrans, were here."

Lil cocked his head thoughtfully. "I'm impressed."

"Even if we're long forgotten, anyone who discovers this monument will know that only a superior race could construct it."

"I've also been thinking a great deal about the future." Lil rose and walked around the table. Crossing his arms before his chest and leaning against the castle wall, he said, "My time at Khamlok has given me insights. I had been optimistic, but I misjudged. I'll not make the same mistakes again."

Ki wrinkled his forehead with concern. "What exactly do you intend?"

Lil spoke coldly. "In the new cities, I'll control life, but I won't interact directly with the people. I became too close to my men and lost perspective. I'm going to appoint priests who'll serve as a filter. I'll build a temple with dimensions that will awe the ignorant populace. We need the Net so that I can travel to all my new cities. I'll have a portal at my capital, so I can travel easily to Alterra, perhaps even access Alana's dimension, if I can discover its secret."

"You might need to capture Drood to learn his secrets," noted Ki.

"Yes. For now, our portals will do. Father predicted that the House of Kan will cause trouble, and I want to help." He paused and gazed out the turret again. "To guard against surprise attacks, each city will be surrounded by impenetrable, high walls made out of unburnable stone. I'll have a trained, standing army. I won't trust Earth people again. They must be controlled."

"Hmm," he said. From the firm set of Lil's jaw, Ki knew he was serious. Lil might have a good point. He didn't think the marshy shores of the Nile would support the weight of heavy, stone walls. At the Cedar Woods, it was possible, although the Cedar Woods was likely to be more removed from the human population. Perhaps they could create monsters to frighten away stray travelers. A trained army would be wise. After Ki's years of isolation, he too planned greater involvement with Earth people. He would be their god-ruler. "How do you plan to control your minions?" He asked out of curiosity, not disagreement.

"Through ritual, religion, mysticism—the usual. And of course, guards. When necessary, I'll use *mencomm*," he said icily. "I also want you to enhance my tunic."

"Enhance it in what way?" asked Ki, narrowing his eyes.

"With built-in weapons so that I'm not caught off guard without my crystal. I want it to emit electrical charges. Make it appear that lightning bolts are coming from my hands."

Ki cocked his head. "I guess we can do that." He smirked. "Lil, I know that Alana's death has devastated you. I listened to the men. They were incredibly loyal to you, not because they were drugged, and not because they feared punishment, but out of respect! Not everything that happened to you was a mistake, you know. Don't draw the wrong conclusions."

Anger flashed across Lil's face. "Don't question me."

"Hear me out; don't get angry." Ki raised his hands. "I agree that we need to do some things differently, but I don't think the guardsmen are going to go back to Alterran control. They thrived with independence, and they see things differently now." Lil gave him a dark, furious look, but Ki continued. "The problems at Khamlok weren't the fault of independent thinking, you know. You did remarkably well. In fact, you did so incredibly well that you proved exactly what's wrong with our control-and-command economy." Seeing Lil grow incensed, Ki again put up his hand. "Lil, think about this. Khamlok was thriving in the midst of devastation and famine from the abrupt climate change. The so-called problem was that others were jealous of your success."

With derision, Lil spat, "Ki, you've spent too much time in the Library, and you're compromised. Father doesn't recognize it, but I do."

"What?" Pulling back from the game table and knocking over the pieces, Ki lunged for Lil, eyes blazing. He grabbed his shoulders and pushed him. "How dare you say that? I kept this place together when no one else could. I simply applied the innovations of the old thinkers—"

"Whose individualistic methods our society rejected long ago in favor of a more genteel, collectivized life," said Lil coldly. "We don't want to repeat the mistakes of the past."

Exasperated, Ki spun around. "Lil, don't do this. You know as well as I do that our system couldn't deal with the problems we faced. You need a huge bureaucracy to do that level of planning, and it was incapable of innovation. We nearly perished."

"Any level of planning is better than chaos," said Lil firmly. "One must take the long view."

"Are you saying that I shouldn't have saved us? You'd rather die than offend your superior philosophy?"

Lil glared, noticing Ki's familiar mockery.

"You mean it's better to lie down and die?" Ki shouted. "You thought these measures were acceptable at the time. Anu accepted it when my technology sent him home. You wouldn't be alive right now without old knowledge."

Lil thought a moment. He said with forced reserve, "We've lived through some contradictions, it's true. The end of the timewave brought chaos. It's over now, and we should resume the proper path. I sought to preserve our principles of harmony and stability. My error was that I wasn't true to our Alterran philosophy; ultimately, that's what caused my failure. If I had exerted greater control, I could have prevented the likes of that Azor from attacking. All those deaths, including Alana's, are my fault. I should have protected them."

"Just how would you have done that?" Ki laughed coldly. "You're assuming too much guilt. Some things just can't be predicted."

"I let Azazel have too much power." Lil's face contorted as he tried to control his rage but felt the sting of Azazel's betrayal. "He led that savage king to believe that I was vulnerable." He pounded his fist on the table. If Azazel were alive, he'd pay for his disloyalty.

Ki shook his head, bewildered. "I don't know about any of that. But clearly he didn't betray you in the end. From the stories I've heard, he saved Khamlok, and he gave his life trying to save his wife."

"Azazel was a good warrior, but he was a dangerous free-thinker," said Lil. "Zeya was right in killing all of their ilk."

"Azazel was a man of exceptional ability, a natural leader. Our system doesn't provide a place for men like him to excel like—"

"Like in the old days?" Lil snapped. "Natural leaders are nothing but trouble. We don't need their kind. They must be controlled or killed. Eating the Earth food was a mistake. As soon as possible, the guardsmen should be put back solely on nourishment bars."

"I don't think so," cautioned Ki. "They refused to eat the bars, even temporarily, at Hawan. Now that there's no fear of flooding, most have returned to rebuild Khamlok."

"What?"

Ki shrugged. "They were happy there, and they thought you were too. Things were cramped at Hawan, and their wives were unhappy.""You let them go?" He needed to segregate them or find a new way to control them. He hadn't set out to disrupt the social order. It was just as Councilman Trey had said; he had traveled down a slippery slope, one small step at a time. Now that Alterra was recovering, he knew that his actions would be second-guessed. The House of Kan would use his transgressions against his father if they discovered the truth. The deteriorating conditions that had led him to believe that their civilization was doomed would be viewed, in comfortable hindsight, as lack of faith in his people; perhaps even worse, as a betrayal of divine providence. Anu's faith had remained steadfast. Lil had thought him foolish; now, he felt shame for his disbelief. He could try to hide what he'd done, but errors always slipped out. The only way he could do effective penance for his sins would be to enforce his family's principles with renewed vigor. No compromise. He'd stamp out everything else. His father could explain his rehabilitation as a benefit of the rejuvenation. The old En.Lil had been restored. He'd remain on Earth until this ran its course.

Watching Lil's steely face during his inner debate, Ki let out a big breath and threw up his hands. "Lil, how was I to know that you were planning to reverse everything you've done lately?" Ki looked at him in frustration. "Your men thought you were a brilliant ruler. Don't pull back now because of that idiot Azor."

"I've made up my mind," said Lil with a distant, steely look in his eyes. "If that's the way the guardsmen think, they won't be permitted to return to Alterra. They're a virus."

Ki drummed his fingers on the table in agitation. "Look, I agree with you that the Earth people need to be molded—for their own good as well as ours. With our guidance, they can build a decent civilization."

"Hah!"

"Look, they weren't ready for the level of civilization that you brought them."

"You're right. The universal axis synchronizes developments; it wasn't the right time. I violated destiny, and I must fix things. Now let's play this game," said Lil with annoyance, having been goaded into revealing his plans.

"Actually, Father has learned from your experiment at Khamlok. At the Cedar Woods, we can't avoid contact with Earth people. So he plans to persuade the Supreme Council to reverse the Non-Interference Directive." Lil raised his eyebrows. "He agrees that we should use the Earth people. They can be trained to farm. I won't give them technology; I'll keep them busy with just enough rudimentary equipment to take in the harvest."

"Keeping them busy and well-fed is wise," Lil said. *And under my control.*

Book 3 — Resurrection

23391904R00164

Made in the USA
Lexington, KY
08 June 2013